In The Shadow Of The Lighthouse

In The Shadow Of The Lighthouse

The Tanners, Book 1

Pamela Ann Cleverly

This book is a work of fiction. Names, characters, organizations, companies, and incidents are products of the author's imagination or, if real, are used fictitiously. Any resemblance to actual persons, living or dead, or to events, is entirely coincidental.

Copyright © 2016 Pamela Ann Cleverly

All Rights reserved. No part of this book may be reproduced or transmitted in any form or by any means, electronic or mechanical, including photocopying, recording, or by any information storage and retrieval system, without the written permission of the author.

In The Shadow Of The Lighthouse by Pamela Ann Cleverly

CLEVER INK, LLC

ISBN-10: 099705221X
ISBN-13: 9780997052213
Library of Congress Control Number: 2016930344
CLEVER INK, LLC, Mentor, OH

This book is dedicated in memory of my mother

Ann K. Jones

who believed my stories should be shared.

OCTOBER 1984

The saxophone's lilting melody filled the room. Its softness soothed Olivia Bentley's senses. Her life was good now. The horrors of the past finally laid to rest and she was ready to move on—free of the guilt that had haunted her for twenty long years. Olivia had saved the old Captain's house from the wrecking ball and she now felt safe behind its sturdy stone walls. She had friends, lots of friends, and soon she would have the family she so desperately wanted. The roaring fire settled into a hypnotic blend of oranges and reds that danced within the ornate marble fireplace.

Suddenly, the hairs on the back of her neck stood. Her skin crawled, like a snake slithering down her spine. She wrapped her arms tightly around her chest to ward off a chill that came from within. Why? Her mind searched for something . . . a sound perhaps that had invaded her subconscious. A slight movement caught the corner of her eye. But it was just the flick of a feline tail. The kitten, asleep on the top step of the ladder, was obviously dreaming of a chase or perhaps conjuring up new ways of getting in and out of the house. Only the sizzle of still-damp logs mingled with sensuous jazz and she let out a long sigh of relief. She was being silly. She had nothing to fear. It was an old house that rattled and hissed. She would get used to it. Olivia's arm reached toward the mantle for the glass of Bordeaux. The long sigh caught in her throat. The floorboard just outside the parlor door creaked. Olivia's arm froze, and her back stiffened at the unmistakable sound. She was no longer alone.

"Hello, Olivia."

In the few seconds that it took to turn around, her mind raced to figure out how anyone could get inside. The doors and windows were all locked. She was sure of it.

Feelings of relief, confusion and lingering fear all jumbled together at the sight of her intruder. "How did you get in here?" Olivia asked in a voice that she knew must sound uninviting. She hadn't seen her friend in months. She should smile or something.

"Now, where are your manners? Aren't you going to invite me to join you in a glass of wine? The ladder in the middle of the room adds an interesting touch. I never thought of you as the kind to be swinging a hammer. You could hurt yourself."

Olivia took a deep breath, willing her mind to take control of the overwhelming feeling of panic that just wouldn't go away. She glanced over at Spooky, still asleep on the ladder. The black kitten had also mysteriously appeared out of nowhere. Her hand reached up to stroke her throbbing temple. "I don't understand."

"You're thinking about how I got in and not about *why* I'm here. You're worried that you forgot to check a window or door. Every evening with the setting sun you go from window-to-window and door-to-door testing the locks. But never the second floor, only the first. What are you afraid of Olivia? Afraid the past will somehow find its way in. Do you ever think about what you did?"

"How do you know about the windows?" Icy tentacles gripped her heart, her throat tightened, the words came out in a raspy challenge. "How do you know what I do?"

"I've been watching."

Anger simmered, deep in the pit of Olivia's stomach, then clawed its way through the thick wall of fear. "What do you mean, 'You've been watching?' What's this all about? And friend or no-friend, you broke into my house!"

A shake of the head was the only response to Olivia's outburst of anger. Her eyes focused on a hand that had remained hidden behind the black leather jacket. This wasn't really happening. It was just a bad dream and she would wake . . . she wanted to wake now. A log fell in the grate sending a shower of sparks against the screen. This wasn't a dream.

"Dear Olivia, still trying to figure out what's going on? Why I'm here? It's really very simple."

Olivia's breath caught, her heart pounded in her ears. She watched the hand move forward, the gun slowly raised to a point level with her chest.

"This is the night you die."

If death is to be my justice, then what was my crime? Life takes us on a journey down many roads. Some are straight and narrow, others wide with twists and turns and dangerous curves. Mine has been the latter, ever since that fateful week in August of 1964. It was the time when my teenage innocence took the road to adulthood, when raging adolescent hormones blinded good judgment, and adults knew nothing. I will remember that week forever. It is burned in my memory as a permanent reminder of the power of willfulness and jealousy.

CHAPTER 1

August 1964

It was supposed to be just the weekend, the first weekend in August. My grandparents, Leonard and Louise Thompson, had rented the small cottage on the bay side of Marblehead, Ohio, for the first two weeks of August. The Marblehead Peninsula sits halfway between Cleveland and Toledo, dividing the Sandusky Bay from Lake Erie. For the past five years, Gran and Gramps expected us to arrive on Friday of the first week of their vacation, just in time for dinner. We would return home Sunday evening. But that year was different, and by Sunday afternoon, I knew I would do anything, say anything, and use everything that I had learned about manipulation in order to stay for the following week.

Getting there was not easy. The two-hour trip in Mom's station wagon was stressful. It had been hot and humid all day, and the evening was no better. The first hour seemed to fly by for me with the anticipation of seeing my old friends and the prospect of meeting new ones, especially boys. My twin brothers, Bud and Andy, didn't fare as well, and each mile seemed to cause more anxiety until the resulting pushing, hitting, and name-calling caused Dad to pull into a vacant lot, threatening to turn around and return home if the bickering didn't stop. His answer to the ruckus was for me to move to the front seat and relegate each eight-year old to a side window. That left the middle as neutral ground. The new seating arrangement wasn't to my liking but I knew better than to push Dad any further. I had spent the better part of an hour on my hairdo and didn't want to sit in the middle with the fan blowing at me. Mom agreed to let me have the window and after settling over the hump in the floor, she tuned the radio to CKLW in Detroit. And for the next hour, not a peep was heard from the back seat.

Two identical houses, built in the mid 1920s sat at the end of a gravel lane. Ours was the one on the left. It was rather plain looking from the front—just two small windows on either side of the front door, framed by dark green shutters. A simple curved walkway of crushed stone led from the drive to the front door. Two tall pine trees and a maple helped keep the house cool during the August heat. It was too shady for the grass to grow, so the front yard always looked a little scruffy. The only shrubs were two large rhododendrons at the corners, their blooms now long-gone.

The inside, unfortunately, was just as plain. Forty years of damp air and wood smoke from the stone fireplace permeated everything from the walls to the floral covered hide-a-bed positioned in the center of the living room. The only thing dividing the living room from the kitchen was the large dining table. Two bedrooms and a bathroom between them took up the other side of the tiny cottage. The twins would use the smaller of the two. It faced the front of the house and contained bunk beds along one wall with a small nightstand next to it. A funny little lamp that looked like a ship's wheel with a shade perched on top. A small pine dresser with a cracked mirror sat in a corner with an old trunk placed under the front window. The walls were a faded shade of yellow. Only the blue, red, and yellow plaid curtains and matching cotton bedspreads added any pattern or interest to the room.

Mom had spent the last hour sitting between Dad and I with the hot evening air blowing on her from both directions. When we got to the cottage, she was the last one out of the car. She slid across the vinyl seat, then stood looking with dismay at her orange silk Capri pants and top that were now hopelessly wrinkled. Her hair had escaped its pins and hung down around her red and sweaty face, while a streak of black mascara ran down one cheek. She made an attempt to smooth out the wrinkles but the top was stuck to her sweaty back. Looking up at her mother-in-law, she shrugged her shoulders and offered an excuse. "I guess it was hotter than I thought."

Gran patted her hand but did not offer a hug, as she had to the rest of us. "You look fine dear . . . under the circumstances. I'm sure there will be time for you to freshen-up before dinner." Then she turned and walked back into the cottage.

Taking my purse, I followed Gran. I had just entered through the front screen door when I heard Mom's raised voice. "I don't think I will ever be good enough in your mother's eyes. She looked at me like I was something you picked-up along the roadside. Yet, if I had slid out of the car looking like Olivia, she would have thought me self-centered and vain. I just can't win!"

I glanced over my shoulder to make sure Gran wasn't nearby. I watched through the screen as dad looked down at her with a smile. Wrapping his arms around her he bent his head and kissed her with the passion that always seemed ready to explode. "My darling Maureen, haven't you realized in the last sixteen years that I don't give a damn what my mother thinks of you. I love you just the way you are. I love your sexy body. I love the way your black hair tumbles down around your shoulders as you take the pins out of that severe hairdo you insist on wearing. My mother is jealous because I have wanted you since the day we met and I will continue wanting you for all eternity. Now, let's get the rest of this food inside before I decide to take you somewhere else, more private, for the weekend."

What I had heard was not meant for my ears. I quietly backed away from the door and joined Gran in the kitchen.

There was little conversation at the dinner table that evening. Perhaps it was the hot, sticky air that continued to press down on everyone's spirits, or just earlier tensions that refused to let go. Gran was just bringing out the pineapple upside-down cake when Gramps announced he had news. The widow who owned the cottage needed to sell and had offered it to them at a very good price. Dad was concerned about the cost of maintaining it and whether it was a good investment.

"That's so cool! We can come here any time we want, and I can bring my friends! Beach time all summer long!" It seemed like a great plan to me, but dad was still frowning.

Any further serious conversation ended when the boys began jumping up and down and shouting, "Dad, can we get a speedboat for water-skiing? Huh? Can we? You could put it next to the garage and use it every time we come here. Please, Dad, it would be so cool."

"You two are getting far too excited. Why don't we go outside and put some of this energy to good use and unload the car. Livy, how about you help with the dishes?"

Dad and the boys got up from the table and headed for the front door while Gramps looked bewildered. "Well, I guess that's the end of that conversation. I'll go see if my help is needed with the bags."

It was almost nine before everything was put away. Bud and Andy came out to the back porch with the checkerboard to find their grandfather sitting in his favorite rocking chair smoking his pipe and me sitting cross-legged on the daybed with the earpiece in, listening to my pocket transistor radio.

An hour later Gran came through the door dressed for bed. "Well, I don't know about anyone else, but I've had a long day and need to get up early to fix breakfast for the fishermen. Who all's going besides the captain?"

"I am! I am!" The boys shouted while waving their arms. "Livy, are you coming, too?"

Pulling out the earpiece and setting it in my lap, I thought about being crammed in the small boat with my energetic brothers for hours at the crack of dawn. "No, I think I'll sleep in."

Gran's frown caught my attention. Her serious gaze rested on Mom and Dad sitting on the swing under the large oak tree. Mom had her legs pulled up beside her on the seat with her head resting on Dad's shoulder, his head resting on top of hers. "Hey, either of you love birds going fishing in the morning?" Gran stood there while they appeared totally engrossed in the view before them and each other. The moonlight shimmered and danced across the water of the Sandusky Bay. Gran waited a few seconds for a response that didn't come. "I guess not. Neither of them likes fishing anyway." Silently, she turned and went back into the cottage, letting the screen door slam shut behind her.

I continued watching the couple that didn't need words. They just needed each other. There were always the moments when their hands touched, a gentle caress, the looks, even in the midst of daily chores that said they would love each other forever. That was the kind of love I wanted. Wasn't it the kind of love that everyone wanted? Then why did Gran always seem upset by their outward show of love? Why did she never have a kind word or gesture or even try to hide her dislike from Dad? I continued watching as I put the earpiece back and listened to *I Want to Hold Your Hand*.

Birds celebrating the dawn of a new day woke me from a deep sleep. For a moment I wasn't sure where I was. As my vision focused on the inside of the screened porch, I let out a moan, then closed my eyes and went back to sleep. It seemed like only minutes had passed when I was awakened for the second time by the smell of bacon frying and cheerful voices. The clock on the wall read 7:00. "All I want is to sleep in," I moaned, rolling over while tucking the pillow around my ears. I was just dozing off again when the screen door slammed.

"Livy, breakfast's ready. Are you still asleep?"

"Not anymore, I'm not," I said as Bud lifted the corner of the pillow and peered down with a big grin. "Oh well, I give up." Grudgingly, I got out of bed and followed Bud to the kitchen.

After a quick breakfast, I grabbed my pillow off the porch and crawled into the lower bunk in the boy's room. The bed felt good. I fluffed my pillow and curled up on my side as the cool morning breeze caressed my face. Sleep came quickly and peacefully—until the dream started.

I ran along a cliff overlooking the ocean. Someone was chasing me. The deafening sound of waves crashing on the rocks below muffled my screams for help. The person was getting closer. I tried to scream louder, but no matter how much I tried nothing came out. I turned my head to see who was behind me. But I could only see a hand reaching out to push me. Then I was falling. I desperately tried to grab at the side of the cliff as I plummeted to the rocky shore below. I awoke just as I landed.

Mom's voice was soothing as she gently stroked my clammy forehead. "It's okay, Livy. Wake up, honey. You were just having a bad dream." My eyes opened slowly to her loving smile. "Livy, do you want to talk about the dream? I heard you moaning and trying to say something."

It had been so real. The fear of falling, the rush of wind that whipped long hair across my face, then the shooting pain in my back as I landed on the rocks below. It had all been so real. But it wasn't something that I could share. I just wanted to forget the fear. . . the pain.

"No. It was just a bad dream. A shower should wash it all away."

The shower felt wonderful. Perhaps afterwards a walk on the beach would drive away the demons that were still lurking in the back of my mind. Wearing just a towel, I slipped into Gran's bedroom and pulled my new white bikini with black polka dots out of my suitcase along with a pair of flip-flops.

The room was at the rear of the cottage overlooking the backyard and the bay beyond. The walls were painted a soft blue with a pair of blue rag-rugs on the linoleum floor. An old gray metal bed, a simple pine dresser, and a cedar chest were the only pieces of furniture. But white organdy curtains, tied back with bows combined with several floral pictures on the walls, made the room warm and cozy.

I dressed quickly and stood in front of the long mirror attached to the back of the door, smiling at my reflection. Although I looked great in the bikini, which showed off all the new curves that had appeared since last summer, I was still a little self-conscious. I towel-dried my hair and let it fall to my shoulders. Knowing that Gran wouldn't approve of the bikini, I grabbed a pair of white shorts and put them on as well.

It was just after ten when I stepped out onto the back porch to find Mom reading and Gran knitting. "Where's Dad?"

Mom looked up with a smile. "You look great, Livy. Sort of a California surfer look, wet hair and all. Your father went into Port Clinton to talk to an old friend. He should be back around noon. There are some bottles of pop in the refrigerator if you're thirsty."

A tall glass of iced tea sat on the table next to Gran. Seeing that Mom had nothing to drink, I brought a bottle for her as well.

"Thanks, Livy. I was just thinking that a walk on the beach would be nice. Care to join me?"

She put the book down on a nearby table and stood, wearing the black one-piece, strapless swimsuit that showed off her fabulous figure. Her thick black eyelashes framed vivid blue eyes that were set off by large gold hoop earrings, and she appeared very stylish and sexy.

Gran had a strange look on her face as she watched us. I'd once overheard my friend Vanessa's mom saying that I had my mother's natural beauty, the same intense violet-blue eyes and porcelain-like complexion, set off by thick black hair. She went on to say that I hadn't yet developed my mother's sense of style or presence, but that would surely come later. It was almost as if Gran didn't like the fact that I was looking more like mom, but that was silly.

Mom and I walked in silence down to the water's edge. Entering the cool water, we followed the shoreline to the east. It was only about a foot deep unless the wind was from the south. Then the lake could rise several feet or more. The bottom was sandy, and we continued walking in silence past the open field to the beach beyond. The sun was already beginning to feel warm as we passed the Bay Shore Beach Club. The boat dock beyond was deserted and looked like a good resting place.

Out to the end of the dock, we sat down and let our legs hang over the edge, sipping the now warm drinks. It felt good to raise my face to the sun and deeply inhale the fresh morning air. "Mom, why doesn't Gran like you? I know she never says anything, but I can tell. Doesn't it bother you?"

"Livy! That's quite a question, right out of the blue." Mom seemed deep in thought as she stared off to the far shore. "I don't think she really dislikes me as much as I'm not the woman she wanted as a daughter-in-law. I upset the plans she had for the family's future, and she can't forgive me for that."

"I see her watching you sometimes, especially when you're with Dad. She doesn't look mad at you . . . just sort of sad."

Mom looked into my eyes and smiled. "Your father and I were both engaged to other people when we met. It was a party for enlisted men given by a local family in Richmond, Virginia. It was common in those days for wealthy families to host regular social events where they would invite local girls to socialize with the servicemen. It was innocent fun during a period of war and uncertainty. Out of all the men you talked to, danced with and shared a meal with, you could never know who would come back. It helped take their minds off the war and dying, if only for a few hours."

Mom's eyes glazed over as if she was no longer seeing me, she was seeing the past.

"I had attended at least a dozen parties and all the men began to look the same. Not that I was looking. I was engaged to William Morrison, the son of my father's business partner. It had always been assumed that we would marry and join our families together, securing our place in society."

"Wow! Do you mean you were rich? Did you have servants and live in a mansion?"

"Our house wasn't as large as William's, but we did have servants. Not many. Times were hard, and most of the men were off fighting, so we made do with what we had."

"I bet your folks were really mad when you married Dad."

"I assumed they would understand when I told them how much I loved Fred. But all Father could think of was how I had betrayed him and the two families. I had shattered all his plans for the future. He told me that if I married Fred I would be turning my back on the family and would no longer be welcome. He would, in fact, disinherit me. And he did."

"What about your mom? Did she disinherit you too?"

"Mother understood her place and didn't go against Father's wishes. The only time she ever stood up for herself was when she needed more money for the household budget or a shopping trip to New York. Father always gave in. Needing more money was something he understood and accepted. She believed I would marry William and live the same kind of life, only on a grander scale. I disappointed her."

"But you were her only child. Didn't that matter?"

"You're too young to understand society and how it works. Someday, I'll let you read my diaries about my life back then. With wealth comes responsibility and obligations . . . people depend on you. Betrayal is a very strong emotion and one that isn't easily forgiven. I chose love over duty. Although I loved my parents very much, I knew that the love I felt for your father would last forever, into eternity even. So I walked away from commitments, promises, and a way of life. I miss my mother very much, but I understand her position and don't expect forgiveness. The real tragedy is that my parents are missing out on their grandchildren."

"Do they know about us?"

"Yes, I began writing letters to Mother as soon as I arrived in Cedar Hill. Not many because I didn't want Father to find out and censor the mail, but enough to keep her informed."

"Has she ever written back?"

"Not for a long time."

My eyes watched the water lapping against the shore as Mom talked. My ears heard the pain in her voice.

"You still love Dad just as much, don't you?"

"Yes, Livy. Our love is as strong today as the day we married. I pray that one day you will find the same kind of love because it truly is a gift from God."

"How do you find that kind of love? What's it like?"

I absentmindedly looked out over the bay, listening to Mom as she opened up to me in a way she'd never done before. A few motorboats went by, leaving behind a wake that eventually would make its way to shore. One boat made a turn and began heading toward the dock.

"It's magical, Livy. When I first looked up into your father's eyes, it was as if I had known him all my life. Tingles ran up and down my spine, and my heart raced. We even knew what each other was thinking."

Mom had been watching the boat too, and she stood as the small speedboat approached the dock. The two young men in the front seat caught my attention as Mom reached for the line that was tossed to her, and she tied it off. They were really cute and the one had muscles like I had only seen in movies. I wondered if Mom had seen the way they were looking and smiling at me. Grabbing the stern line, I noticed the water skis neatly stowed along the port side as I wrapped the line around the nearest post.

"Livy, I think we should be getting back. It's almost noon," Mom said as she turned away from the boat.

We walked down the dock toward the beach, tossing our pop bottles in a garbage can.

"Thanks for the help," one of the boys shouted. I looked back over my shoulder and smiled.

Mom chuckled. "Polite young men. Kind of cute, too, or didn't you notice?"

"Yes, Mom . . . I noticed."

As we walked past the club, we heard several whistles from the area of the snack bar. Mom and I looked at each other and laughed. A voice came from further down the beach, "Olivia! Olivia! Is that you?"

Mom looked over her shoulder, "Livy, isn't that Meg from next door and her friend, Patsy?"

The girls quickly caught up with us. "Olivia, I was hoping you would come. We're having such a blast this summer! It's the best ever! Oh, hello, Mrs. Thompson." Meg's head turned back-and-forth from one of us to the other, like watching Ping-Pong. "I hope you'll let Olivia hang out with us this afternoon. We're going to go water-skiing."

Mom smiled as she looked at the rather gangly teenager with frizzy, carrot-red hair hanging around her face. Her golden brown eyes, hiding behind black-rimmed glasses, matched the freckles covering her face, as well as the rest of her body. Long legs ended at feet that seemed to be growing faster than the rest of her. The red, one-piece swimsuit didn't do much for her boyish figure, and red wasn't a color she should be wearing. She didn't look fifteen. In fact, both Meg and Patsy looked younger than me, but then I had always looked older than my age. Meg and I had become friends four years before when her family bought the cottage next door.

"Please, Mrs. Thompson, let Olivia stay with us. My mom lets me come here all the time and I hardly ever get to do stuff." Patsy had what Gran would call a good, wholesome, American look. She was wearing a cute two-piece swimsuit with large navy and white vertical stripes, accented with gold braid and stars, giving it a nautical look. At first glance she appeared a rather ordinary, petite girl. Her dark chestnut brown hair was pulled back into a ponytail. But if you took the time to really look at her, you saw bright green eyes in a face with a flawless complexion, high cheekbones and a cute little nose.

"Okay, but you need to come home for lunch first. We don't want to upset your grandmother. You know how she is about everyone being together for meals."

Meg and Patsy turned and ran back down the beach. Mom nodded as if mulling something over while we continued toward the cottage. "I believe Patsy is like a butterfly. One of those girls that no one pays any attention to in school but one day grows up to become a beautiful woman."

"Yeah, but I think she's cute now. I don't think Meg will ever be pretty."

We reached the end of the beach. The vacant lot between our cottage and the club was thick with brush. It was easier, and faster to wade through the shallow water. The cool, wet sand oozed between my toes. "Mom, were you *really* rich, or just kinda rich?"

"Livy, that was a long time ago. The past doesn't matter. What really matters is today."

I wasn't so sure about that. It sounded like it mattered a lot. I had a million questions, but I guessed I would get no answers . . . at least not today.

CHAPTER 2

As we entered the back porch everyone was at the table, laughing and talking at once. Clearly, something important had happened during the short time we were gone.

"You almost missed lunch, Mom, and you'll never guess what Dad did. It's gonna be so cool, and I can't wait to get a boat. Dad, can we go buy a boat after lunch? Huh, please, can we?"

Mom and I looked around the table at each smiling face, then at each other, and shrugged as if everyone had gone mad.

"Okay, Fred darling, it appears that you're the cause of all this jubilation. So what's this about buying a boat?"

"This morning I started thinking about Mom and Dad buying this cottage and whether it was a good investment. So I went into Port Clinton and met with a buddy of mine who is also in the insurance business. He feels very strongly that not only is this area going to be very much in demand in the future, but that real estate prices will go through the roof. If Mom and Dad don't buy the place, he will! So I called Monty Montgomery at the bank and explained the situation. He'll arrange for an appraisal and have the necessary paperwork drawn-up and ready for signatures at the bank in a week or two."

Whether my grandparents bought the cottage or not didn't matter to me. I just wanted to be with my friends, and all I could think about was how much fun it was going to be water-skiing. After a quick lunch, I grabbed my straw beach bag with the essential sunglasses, beach towel, and a new bottle of Coppertone.

"Hey Livy, are you going to take us swimming now?" asked Bud as I passed the table.

"No, I'm going water-skiing."

"But you always push us on the raft and inner-tube!" exclaimed Bud.

"Yeah, we want to go swimming." Andy said in a whiney voice.

"Not today. I'll be with my friends." I glanced at the clock and let out a sigh. "I have to go."

Mom pushed her chair back. "I'll take you swimming."

"But Livy takes us far!"

"Hey boys! How about we take my boat and head over to Johnson's Island?"

Andy wrinkled his nose. "Ohhhh noooo! Livy took us there once and we saw a snake in the water!"

"We'll be in the boat, and I'll pull it up on shore. We can explore the island and find the site of the old Confederate prison and the cemetery." Gramps waited for their response.

Bud nodded his head in agreement. "Okay. Are there lots of snakes on the island?"

Gramps chuckled. "If we come across any, we'll just chase them away. They're afraid of us and we'll act real mean."

"Yeah! This is more fun than swimming!" Bud exclaimed. "Bye Livy! We don't need you."

It didn't take long to find Meg and Patsy lying amongst the many sunbathers. They were the only ones under a colorful umbrella. Meg and I had become friends right from the start. We both had younger brothers to take care of and spent most of our time playing water games with the boys or listening to the radio in the shade of the large maple trees that dotted the shoreline. Meg's fair Irish skin burned easily, and she preferred to stay out of the sun, leaving me the task of pushing the boys up and down the coast on inflatable rafts or inner tubes. We met Patsy at one of the dances the year before and decided it was nice to have a local girl to hang-out with.

Spreading my beach towel next to Patsy, and away from the offending umbrella, I sat down. Within minutes I had donned sunglasses and was sufficiently oiled to soak up the hot rays of the afternoon.

Meg sat up and slathered more sunscreen on her arms. "It's too bad you're only here for the weekend. This is the best summer of my entire life. Back in June, we met David and Ricky Morgan who are spending the summer at *Stone Cottage*. They're cousins and have their own speedboat. The four of us go water-skiing almost every day, and Patsy's in love with Ricky." Almost as an afterthought, she said, "They think we're seventeen."

Patsy rolled over on to her stomach. "Yeah, and Meg is thinking up all sorts of sneaky schemes to get David's attention."

"I am not. He likes me."

"You should see how she gets him to spend hours in the water with her while he tries teaching her to water-ski."

Meg had been skiing since she was old enough to hold the tow-rope. I thought he must be the most stupid guy around if he hadn't caught on to her schemes by now. And neither of them looked seventeen.

Suddenly Patsy squealed with excitement. "Here they are now!"

It was the boys from the speedboat whom Mom and I had helped that morning. Meg made the introductions while Patsy jumped up and grabbed one boy by the hand. "Olivia, this is David and that's Ricky. They have the boat I was telling you about. Olivia is staying with her grandparents in the cottage next to mine. She's just here for the weekend."

David stood about six feet tall with thick sandy-blond hair and brown eyes. Ricky was quite the opposite with dark brown hair, and eyes that were a lighter shade of brown, not like the deep, chocolate brown of David's.

Feeling self-conscious, I watched both boys staring at me and my black and white polka dots. I felt the urge to wrap the towel around myself, but that wouldn't be cool. Instead, I straightened my back and looked into David's eyes with a haughty challenge that I didn't feel.

Ricky snickered, but David didn't seem amused. He reached down for my hand and pulled me to my feet. He was not only cute, but also strong.

"Know how to water-ski, Blue Eyes?"

Learning to water-ski was just one of many new experiences all crammed into the afternoon. It was much harder than David made it look, and I failed miserably. My usual good coordination abandoned me and I just couldn't get my butt out of the water. David tried his best to help, but his every touch on my exposed skin sent me into a whirlwind of emotions. I couldn't concentrate on anything except the new feelings racing through my body, and it was obvious, by that sly smile, that he knew exactly what he was doing to me. The glaring looks Meg sent my way shouted that she also knew. And was furious. I was ruining all her carefully laid plans for conquering David.

Patsy spent most of the afternoon shoulder-to-shoulder with Ricky, like Siamese twins, while he drove the boat. Meg spent the afternoon throwing insults and sarcastic remarks at me. Her childish behavior just made her appear like a spoiled little girl. By the end of the afternoon my arms were sore, my leg bruised, and my ego in shreds.

It was late afternoon when I walked back to the cottage and saw Mom sitting alone on the swing. She seemed to enjoy my animated rendition of the afternoon's events, although I left out the parts about my body going into hysterics every time David touched me. Thoughts of him filled my head for the next two hours as I showered and dressed for the dance we were planning to attend later that evening. Was it only the bikini and being in the water with his nearly naked body that allowed his touch to send electrical shocks through me? No boy had ever caused these uncontrollable reactions before, and I wondered if it would feel the same when we both had clothes on. Did he make Meg feel this way too? It was clear to me now why she pretended she didn't know how to ski. How many hours had she spent in the water with David's arms around her?

Now, however, the person looking back at me in the mirror could only be described as fabulous, sexy, and much older than my fifteen years. The lime-green sheath, that I had convinced mom to let me borrow, stopped just above my knees and hugged every curve. Thin spaghetti straps held up a low, scooped neckline with just a hint of firm breasts peaking over the top. I looked as good as Annette Funicello in the movie *Beach Party*. David was going to be my Frankie Avalon and would definitely approve, but I wasn't so sure about my family.

"Wow, Livy!" The twins shouted in unison as I approached the kitchen table.

"I see." said mom with a smile.

Dad tilted his head toward Mom. "Isn't that your dress, dear?"

"Yes, and I have to say it looks much better on Livy. I think you just may need to put a padlock on our closet! I can see a raid on my wardrobe in the near future."

"You're gonna knock'm dead," Gramps said with a chuckle.

Gran's scowl didn't need words to express her disapproval. Any comment that could have forced its way through her pursed lips was stopped by Meg's appearance at the front door. "I'm sorry about this." She was breathless as she pushed open the screen door, "But my little brother is throwing up all over the kitchen floor. My mom asked if I could ride with you?"

Dad got up from the table and pulled the car keys from his pants pocket. "It would be a real pleasure to drive two such lovely ladies to the dance."

"Can we please stop and pick up Patsy? It isn't far." Meg stood meekly with her hands behind her back, swishing her full skirt back and forth. Her white halter-top dress with large red polka dots hung from narrow shoulders with little else to hold it up. A red sash, with a large bow at the back, set off the full skirt. She'd tried to pull her curly red hair into a sleek French twist with a long red bow at the edge, but it was already beginning to escape its pins, and the red pointed-toe pumps only made her feet appear larger.

Meg followed Dad out the front door, and I overheard Mom talking to Gran. "Poor Megan. She tries so hard to fit in with the crowd, but I'm afraid she'll always take the backseat. Olivia looks so much older."

"Maureen, you spoil that child. It's not right, her looking older than her years. You'd better keep a tight rein on her or she's liable to run wild."

"I'm sorry you feel that way, Louise, she really is a good girl. She's almost sixteen and will be driving in a couple months. She's not a little girl anymore."

"It's not right. I smell trouble ahead. Mark my words."

CHAPTER 3

Vehicles of all descriptions were crammed in the small parking lot of the Bay Shore Beach Club and I noticed one particular flashy red hot rod blocking part of the drive.

"You lovely ladies have a good time. I'm going home and beat two small boys at Chutes and Ladders." Dad slipped me a folded $5 bill as I opened the car door. "Just in case you need it."

"Thanks, Dad, you're the greatest." Being the last to get out of the car, I turned to wave as Dad maneuvered the white station wagon back down the drive. The sun was still hot in a clear blue sky and a gentle breeze was blowing in off the bay.

The large room was filled with more teens than I could count. Even though all the windows were open and the ceiling fans whirled at top speed, it was still oppressively hot inside. It was just as we were passing the hall leading to the restrooms, when Meg shoved me to the side against the wall.

She leaned against me with her head blocking the view from the others. "Listen real good. You're here 'cause Patsy invited you. These dances are what we do every week, and you're just a visitor. Stop trying to steal David. He belongs to me!"

That was okay with me, he wasn't worth losing a friend over and there was a whole roomful of guys for me to conquer. I gave her a hard shove sending her backwards. "Sure. Whatever you say."

"What was that all about?" David asked when Meg and I caught up with them.

"Just girl talk. Meg asked me if her red petticoat was showing." We followed David to a corner table where Ricky was waiting. The approving looks of dozens of interesting faces gave me the confidence I needed and promised an evening of fun.

We had just taken our first sips of the cold drinks before us when the music started. Patsy and Ricky headed for the dance floor while Meg pulled David to his feet. He must have felt my eyes burning through his shirt because he turned his head to look back at me. Quickly, I shifted my gaze to the crowd of faces before me and stopped at a cute boy. He was obviously of Italian descent, with dark wavy hair dipping low over one eye and slicked back on the sides. My smile was all the encouragement he needed to walk toward me with a swagger. His name was Tony Marelli, and he certainly didn't lack in dancing skills . . . or flattery.

He knew all the latest dances and was the most popular boy in the room. He was sixteen, lived across the bay in Sandusky and had his own car. By the end of the evening he had invited me to go with him to all the local tourist attractions, including Cedar Point Amusement Park. Unfortunately, I had to explain that I would be leaving the next day. But maybe next year I would come for the summer and we could get together. I wasn't sure about that, but Tony seemed to like it and we exchanged phone numbers.

All evening Meg kept David busy and away from me. It was during her trip to the bathroom that gave him the opportunity to approach me for a slow dance. Once again his touch sent tingles racing through my body. Breathing became difficult when he pulled me to him and the pungent aroma of his aftershave sent my senses in a whirl. I lost myself in his arms as he guided us across the dance floor. But when the music stopped, one of Tony's friends stood before me for the next dance.

There were no more tingles or flutters, just hands resting on my waist whenever the dance allowed.

The last dance had just been announced when a rather studious boy with thick glasses approached Meg. I briefly wondered if David had encouraged him to do so, as he took my hand and guided me to the far side of the room. This time I was ready, and eagerly settled into David's arms allowing all the sensuous feelings to wash over me, pressing my body closer. Once again, the music ended all too quickly. I was left breathless. David steered us close to the bar and ordered two soft drinks to take outside.

"Meg's going to be really mad if she see's us out here. I'd better get back to the table."

"She's occupied for awhile. I wanted to have a few minutes alone to tell you how beautiful you look tonight."

"What about how you feel about Meg? She practically thinks you're going steady or something."

David shook his head in denial. "She has a crush on me. She's a nice girl, but definitely not my type! Really! And what's with her and red? She needs a major wardrobe overhaul."

I took a deep breath wondering what to say. What would Annette say in a situation like this?

"*You're* my type, Olivia."

We sat on the picnic table, under a blanket of stars. The lights from across the bay twinkled as the moon cast a rippling glow across the water. It was a magical night, and David cast a spell on me that I couldn't deny.

I noticed Mom sitting alone on the swing when I arrived at the cottage.

She moved to one side making room for me. "You look happy. Must have had a good time."

"Oh, Mom, I had a great time! I met some really cool kids. Most of them live close by, or in Sandusky and Port Clinton."

It was nice sitting alone with her. We were both quiet for a few minutes engrossed in our own thoughts, just watching the moonlight dancing across the water.

"Mom, how did you know that Dad was the right one? You had to be really sure since you were walking away from your family forever."

"Wow, Livy, you are full of deep questions today." She was quiet for so long that I thought she wasn't going to answer. "It's hard to explain because it's about overwhelming feelings that suddenly flood your heart and soul. The first time I looked into his eyes it was as if I had known him all my life, our souls had known each other through eternity."

Mom gave her foot a push and the swing rocked back. "I was nervous, tongue-tied and felt like a blubbering fool, but when he took me in his arms and guided me across the dance floor, it was as if I had come home. We were two people gliding as one across the clouds and through the universe, only our hearts speaking to each other through our eyes. My nerves tingled every time he touched me or I felt his breath caress my skin. Without him I was lost and could not find my way in the world . . . nor did I want to try. Someday, Livy, you're going to find the same love and then you will understand."

"I hope so Mom. I really hope so."

The sound of a boat motor woke me from a sound sleep at dawn. Sitting up, I could see Meg's father heading out into the bay for a day of fishing. There were more motors off in the distance and birds singing and the leaves rustling in the big old oak tree. Thoughts of David lulled me back to sleep until kitchen noises and the smell of fresh coffee woke me again. There wasn't a cloud in the sky, and it was already getting hot. It would be a perfect day for another try at water-skiing. Smiling to myself, I entered the kitchen.

The conversation over breakfast quickly turned to what kind of boat Dad would buy.

"It needs to be fast and big enough to hold all of us for skiing and going to Kellys Island and Put-in-Bay. Tony say's there are a lot of places to go around here," I added.

"Will you take us swimming today, Livy?" Bud asked with enthusiasm.

"No, I'm going with my friends again today. I just know I can figure out how to water-ski with a little more practice. We have next year. You'll be older and we can do more stuff together. I promise!"

Thoughts of David filled me with excitement. I couldn't waste any more time discussing Dad's boat purchase or how the boy's would spend their day. I excused myself from the table and headed for the shower.

The wet towel slowly slid to the floor. It was as if I saw my body for the first time. Hesitantly, I ran my hands over full breasts and my tiny waist, then down over narrow firm hips. This was the body that David would see and I remembered the fire that raced through my blood when he touched me. A droplet of water fell to my shoulder as I hooked the top of my bikini. It was the other new one. The turquoise brought out the color of my eyes and fit perfectly. After running a comb through damp hair, I pulled it back with a rubber band and put on a matching turquoise, oversized shirt and slipped on a pair of flip-flops. Standing for a moment before the full-length mirror, I gave a smile of approval to the person staring back at me who looked older and more confident than she felt. Yep, just like Annette Funicello.

Ricky had found a pair of shorter skis in their boathouse for me, and they made all the difference. It didn't take long before I was skiing with confidence but my legs and arms were tired and I needed to take a break.

Meg wanted to ski next and although David didn't think we had time for another beginner, Meg insisted that she could do it this time. She cinched the ski belt as David tossed the longer skis into the water.

"David, I need your help to get started. These skis are too hard for me to put on by myself." Meg was looking rather helpless, but David wasn't buying into it.

"You'll be fine, just remember what Olivia did. We've practiced for weeks, you don't need my help." David motioned for me to sit on the rear seat next to him as he told Ricky to ease forward. Then when Meg gave a nod that she was ready, Ricky gave it the gas and the boat sped forward. Meg got up with no trouble and we headed back down the bay. We all watched in silence until Meg motioned that she was heading to the side. She easily took the wake and was at our side seeming to fly over the water.

"Imagine that, already skiing like a pro and two days ago she couldn't get her ass out of the water!" David turned toward me and smiled, "Olivia, do you *have* to leave tonight? Is there any way your folks would let you stay for the week? I really like you and we've had a great time together. I know we'll have fun next week, and besides Ricky and I are having a party next Saturday at our house. I would love it if you could be there."

"I don't know. It's pretty short notice."

David's smile was enough to melt my heart as he took my hand in his. "Please try. The party is all day and we have a pool and tennis court, and Ricky and I are grilling burgers and hot dogs and Mom is a great cook. You would really like her. Please, Olivia. Please say you'll try."

As we got close to the cottage I saw that everyone was in the yard or sitting on the dock.

"Okay, I'll try if you let me ski one more time past our cottage. Everyone will be able to see me." David motioned to Meg that we were going to stop. Ricky pulled back on the throttle, then swung the boat back around and came to a stop next to Meg.

"Well Meg, you're a real surprise. First time up and you're skiing like you've been doing it all your life. Hand me the skis . . . Olivia is gonna ski past her cottage."

Meg climbed back into the boat and took off the ski belt and threw it at me. I knew she believed that I had told David about how she had learned to ski four years ago. But I hadn't said a word about her.

Leaning over, she whispered in my ear, "Thanks a lot for telling him I could ski . . . *friend*! I'll remember this and be sure to pay you back." As I looked around at the others it didn't appear that anyone else had heard her.

Meg sat down on the rear seat in a huff. I jumped into the water and put the short skis on with no trouble, then got into position and nodded.

The boat moved forward. *Please, God, help me do this right so I can make them proud of me.* I rose out of the water with the ease of a seanymph shifting my weight to feel more stable and in control. David motioned that they were going closer to shore and I saw the cottage ahead. Everyone looked up to see the boat that was approaching fast and close to shore. I carefully took my left hand off the bar and felt the added force on my right arm, but I was still okay. Hesitantly, I raised my arm over my head and waved. It only took a few seconds for everyone to recognize me. I could see the twins jumping up and down on the dock next to Gramps who was waving both arms. Mom and Dad ran hand-in-hand, wading in to their knees and shouting encouragements. Even Gran was waving.

Ricky turned the boat back out into the bay. I saw the wake coming at me fast, and all I could think to do was put both hands on the towrope and relax. "I can do this, just keep the tips up and bend my knees," I said out loud, then before I had time to worry, I was over the wake and still up. "I did it! I really did it!" I screamed and a wave of happiness washed over me. I could hear more cheering behind me and knew everyone had watched my triumph. Ricky slowed the boat and I let go and collected the skis, while waiting for them to come alongside.

Ricky and David were still talking about how far I'd come in only one day when we pulled up alongside the dock.

Ricky jumped out with the bowline and tied it off. "I take full credit for Olivia's success today since I'm the one who thought of the short skis!"

"You mean kid's skis, and I think I did just as good. Better even, and I don't see anyone paying any attention to me and telling me how great I am."

David got out and wrapped the stern line around a post. He reached down for Meg's hand and helped her out of the boat. "We know, Meg. We all saw how great you were, but I don't like being made a fool of. Just how many wasted hours have I spent in the water with you this summer? You can ski better than me!"

I followed Meg who was stomping down the dock in a huff. "Meg, I didn't tell him anything, I promise. You can ask Patsy!"

"Yeah!"

I gave up trying to explain because she wasn't ready to listen and just watched as she walked toward the snack bar. Patsy and Ricky soon came along holding hands.

"Don't let her get to you," Patsy said with a chuckle. "She sees you as competition and you must admit you look a lot different than you did last summer. Besides, you're going home today and won't see her again until next summer. Maybe by then she'll get some boobs and a new hairdo."

These conflicted thoughts were still in my head as I half-listened to the lively conversation over dinner. Meg had been my friend for four years and I didn't want to hurt her feelings. I may never see David again, but these new and exciting feelings made my heart pound and my skin tingle. Dad looked at his watch and said we would have to leave soon if we were to be home by eight. It was at that moment that I knew I couldn't leave. I couldn't leave David . . . not yet.

It took all my manipulative skills, and for a moment it appeared I might not succeed. I had, before coming to the cottage arranged for my best friends, CeCe and Vanessa, to spend a day with me at the Cedar Hill Country Club and then sleep over tomorrow night. Mom thought it was important to honor my prior commitment to my friends and extremely rude of me to ditch them for casual friends who I wouldn't see again until next year. But finally, everyone who mattered gave in, and I moved my bags to the boy's room.

As the last suitcases were being loaded into the station wagon, Mom motioned for me to follow her outside to the swing. "Now, Livy, we're letting you stay because your grandparents can use some help, not just so you can have fun. However, I do remember what is was like to be your age and how important friends are. You really were great at water-skiing, considering it was your first try. I was very proud of you." She paused and turned to look at me. "You seemed so grown-up this weekend. So have fun this week, but remember, you're not a little girl anymore. You're a woman and with that comes responsibility."

"Oh, Mom . . . you don't. "

"I'm serious, Livy, and so are adolescent hormones. I can tell by the way boys look at you and you look at them. Your body is getting all caught up in the feelings of the moment. It's called passion and lust. It's an incredibly strong feeling in which your whole being is swept away on a tide of emotions, and you feel helpless to pull away.

But you must always listen to your heart, not your body. And think before you react, because only your mind can read both." She took me in her arms for one of her bear-hugs and kissed my forehead. "I'm only a phone call away if you need to talk. Remember Livy, I'll always love you."

"Thanks, mom, you're the greatest. I really mean it!"

Later, I stood on the front stoop with Gran and Gramps waving as the white station wagon drove down the lane. A sense of exhilaration filled me, knowing that I had won. I was free to continue having fun with my friends, and to see where my relationship with David would take me.

I would remember those feelings of winning, of getting my way, and of manipulation. I would remember them every day for the next twenty years.

CHAPTER 4

I awoke the next morning to the songs from what sounded like a hundred birds. The sun's rays streamed in through the open window. The room was cool, and I snuggled into the lightweight covers. That's when I noticed that my radio was on the nightstand. Gran must have checked on me during the night, removing the radio and gently pulling the sheet and blanket over me.

After breakfast, the three of us headed for Port Clinton. Gramps dropped Gran and I off in front of the A&P before heading to the hardware store. The ferry dock wasn't far, so I walked over to a bench and sat while Gran shopped. The various types of people who got on and off the huge boat fascinated me. Some had bags for shopping. Some had cameras around their necks. There were even people with bicycles and baby buggies. I easily passed an hour fantasizing about life on the tiny island and the busy port of Put-in-Bay. It seemed like I had been sitting only a few minutes when Gramp's familiar dark blue Buick pulled into the parking lot. I would have to leave my thoughts of the island for another day.

 We returned to the cottage, and after a quick lunch, I changed into my bikini with the black polka dots and again stood before the long mirror. The tan I'd been working on all summer made me look older, old enough for David to be seriously interested in me. He'd convinced me, while we sat on the picnic table after the dance that he wasn't interested in Meg. Now my only concern was how to handle her jealousy.

That evening, as we finished dinner, Gramps suggested that we go for ice cream. We drove to the quaint town of Marblehead, on the other side of the peninsula, to the Dairy Dock. The small ice cream stand sat along the main road, near the ferry dock. From there we drove the short distance to the lighthouse. We walked out to the huge rocks at its base, finishing our cones as the setting sun splashed the sky with vibrant shades of pink and orange. We sat there, taking turns telling what best or worst thing happened that day.

"You know, Princess, I think it's been three years since we've come here. I believe the best time for me today is right now, sitting here on a beautiful night with my two best gals," Gramps said then quickly licked at a runaway drip.

I'd been watching the few small fishing boats bobbing up and down with the waves and several sailboats making their way to shore. One boat in particular had caught my attention. Not just because it was bigger than all the rest, but because it was slowly making its way through the water with ease. "I think right now is the best time for me, too, Gramps. I was gonna say water-skiing with my friends was the best, but I changed my mind. This is so peaceful and quiet, and that boat over there is so pretty."

He looked over toward Kelleys Island. "Yep, she's a real beaut, nothing prettier than a Chris. To my way of thinking, there's no boat on these waters better than a Chris-Craft. But I'll never be able to afford a boat as fine as that one."

"One day, Gramps, I'll marry a very rich man and buy you a boat just like that. Maybe, I'll just buy you that one!"

Gramps laughed and continued to watch the Chris as she cruised along the shoreline. "What do you say, Louise? Would you like to have a boat like that and drift through life without a care in the world?"

Gran shook her head, a stern look on her face. "You're both talking nonsense! The most we're ever going to be able to afford is what we have right now. You shouldn't be putting foolish ideas into Olivia's head! Olivia needs to be the good little girl she is and think about working hard in school. That way she can get a good job and meet a nice young man to marry and have children."

"Dreaming never hurt anyone, Louise. As a matter of fact, this country was built on dreams." He looked at her with a smile that crinkled the corners of his eyes and continued. "As I recall, *you* even had some when you were Olivia's age."

We fell into a routine over the next few days. Gramps and I usually took his small boat out in the early mornings, and on the days when the fish weren't biting he would give me driving and docking lessons. By the end of the week he told me I could take the boat out anytime I wanted. That was the greatest compliment he could have given me. We seemed to grow closer with each passing day. Gran was another story.

Meg's sarcastic remarks bounced off my skin that was now growing thicker, and we all enjoyed an afternoon of water-skiing. Every day brought new adventures and not all of them included Meg. Her brother broke his arm, and Meg had to baby-sit while her mother took the little guy to the hospital in Port Clinton. That was the day we took the boat to Cedar Point and anchored off the beach near the Arcade. Ricky won Patsy a big blue bear, and David presented me with a darling white French poodle with pink bows at each ear, along with his first kiss. Without Meg in tow, I felt comfortable holding David's hand or snuggling closer when he put his arm around my waist. His kisses were given quickly, and often with laughter, at the top of the Ferris wheel, in front of the wavy mirror in the fun house and at the crest of the roller coaster just before the plunge that took my breath away. They were public kisses, not the ones I knew were waiting. By the end of the afternoon, our relationship had taken a turn in a new direction . . . to where, I didn't know.

Friday morning, just as Gramps and I walked up to the cottage from the dock, Patsy came around the corner. She and her mom had stopped by the O'Brien's cottage to pick up Meg for a day on Kelleys Island and asked if I would like to join them. It only took a minute for me to get ready, and we were waiting in the car when Meg came out of the house. She didn't look all that happy to see me, but once we were on the ferry the tension between us seemed to be carried away on the wind. The three of us stood at the rail watching the bow waves turn to a million diamonds in the morning sun. It was my first time on a ferry, and I just knew it was taking me to a wonderful adventure on the island.

Mrs. Paterson's sister worked in the island's general store that had been in her husband's family for generations. A bicycle rental rack stood outside, and each of us was given a bike to ride for the day along with a bag containing our lunch.

It was a family kind of island, interwoven with a history that went back to the ice age. The quaint Victorian town on the south side facing Marblehead was small, just a few commercial buildings and streets to label it downtown. Patsy took us to Inscription Rock where we ran our fingers over the large limestone boulder covered with ancient art made by the Indian tribes that once inhabited the island. We then rode along Lakeshore Drive, past interesting old homes dating from the 1800s, then headed north past the small airport. During the winter months it would be the residents' only way on and off the island. That is, unless the lake was frozen solid and some brave souls would drive their cars across the ice to Marblehead.

Meg and I rode side-by-side behind our self-appointed tour guide. Only an occasional vehicle passed, more often a golf cart than a car. Each waved at Patsy.

I pedaled up next to her. "Do you know everyone on the island or is everyone just friendly?" I asked with a chuckle.

She laughed. "Both". Then she raised up off the seat and peddled faster. "Come on!"

It took a minute to catch up. "What's going on? Why are we speeding up?"

"Don't you hear that?" She motioned with her head toward the right. "I think I hear my cousins!"

Meg caught up red-faced and wheezing as we veered to the right. "Dozens of what? Can we stop? I need to rest for a minute."

Turning toward Meg, I shouted. "Cousins! Patsy thinks she hears her cousins."

"So?" Meg gave a sweeping motion with her left arm. "I thought the town was that way. We need to stay on the main road."

I continued following Patsy toward the sounds of laughter, shouting and water splashing. Meg continued to fall further behind.

Patsy stopped at a rise overlooking a narrow beach filled with kids of all ages. "Come on!" she shouted as she grabbed her lunch bag out of the bike's basket. "This is gonna be so much fun!"

We lost track of time somewhere between lunch and searching the shallow water for beach glass and a pick-up game of volleyball. It wasn't until Meg complained about being in the sun too long that I noticed she was working on a good case of sunburn.

After saying our goodbyes to Patsy's cousins and their friends, we headed up the sandy rise to our bikes. We all complained of screaming calf muscles as we set off riding past the remains of once flourishing vineyards. Patsy made another stop when we came to a sign identifying the glacial grooves. Patsy excitedly told how they were made some 30,000 years ago and were probably the largest in the world. It appeared as though a giant claw had made the grooves, which were about fifteen feet deep and thirty-five feet wide. There had been other grooves on the island, but the extensive quarrying that had been going on since the mid 1800's had destroyed them. I think I would have found them more interesting if I hadn't been so tired from the highly competitive games of volleyball.

"This is all great, but we need to get back to the store. We weren't supposed to be gone this long," complained Meg.

Taking Titus Road west, it connected with W. Lakeshore and Patsy stopped at the large ore docks, where ships came in to be loaded with the limestone from the quarry just across the road. The huge steel and cement docks appeared out-of-place on the small enchanting island. Kelleys Island wasn't the large tourist destination that Put-in-Bay was, just a few miles to the west on South Bass Island. Gazing across the narrow body of water, I compared the graceful stone Ionic column that was Perry's Monument at Put-in-Bay to the huge cement blocks of the dock covered with rust here on Kelleys. Suddenly, a cold chill ran its icy fingers down the back of my neck. A cloak of danger put my senses on high alert. It was as if the ghosts and demons of the past were upon me, or perhaps a premonition of the future. Whatever it was, I had never felt this way before. It was just plain creepy. Just like that horrible nightmare.

"Come on, Olivia! We're going to be in trouble if we don't leave now!" Meg shouted as she got back on her bide and peddled on down the road toward town.

It was late afternoon when we returned the bikes to the stand and found Mrs. Paterson and her sister sitting on the front porch of their house, just a short walk from the store. We said our goodbyes, then headed toward the ferry dock. The big boat glided smoothly into the slip, with the horn blasting to announce its arrival to the town. We waited in line with everyone else who needed to get to the mainland. It was just like I had seen at the Put-in-Bay ferry dock in Port Clinton, only this time I was standing in line with them—the ones with bicycles and baby carriages and bags of all sizes, and, of course, the cars and motorbikes. To everyone around me it must have seemed ordinary, nothing special. No smiles or laughter. It was almost as if they were riding a bus instead of this great monster of a boat that cut through the waves so effortlessly. Patsy, Meg and I ran to the rail for the four-mile trip. We watched fishing boats bobbing up and down while sea gulls flew all around us with their raucous cry.

"Patsy, you are so lucky to live here! I wish I lived here instead of Cedar Hill."

"You wouldn't think that in the winter when the lake is frozen and the island people have to fly back and forth. And you don't have many friends because all the summer people leave after Labor Day."

Listening to the deep drone of the engines and feeling the deck vibrate beneath my feet with its great power was both comforting and exhilarating. I closed my eyes and let the warm moist air caress my face. Yes, it would be worth the winter hardships just to have the rest of the year on the water. I couldn't wait to tell mom.

My excitement couldn't be contained as I told Mom about each day's activities. "It's so wonderful here! I think I wanna be the captain of a ferry boat or a big ship when I grow up."

Mom laughed, "You get your love of the water and boats naturally. You're a McLeod after all."

I had gone with Gran and Gramps to the payphone outside Mutach's Food Market to call Mom and Dad as promised.

Gramps motioned for me to give him the phone. "This is long distance, Princess, I need to talk to your dad and you'll have plenty of time to recount all your experiences when they get here."

I gathered from the conversation that Dad had a surprise for them and would arrive around noon on Saturday, but we would have to leave that evening by six. Gramps was relaying the message to Gran and I as he listened to his son.

"NO!" I shouted, grabbing the phone. "No, Daddy, you can't! David and Ricky's party is all day Saturday. They have a boathouse and swimming pool and tennis court, and they're having fireworks after dark. Please, Dad! Mom knows all about it and said I could go. Please, Daddy, I'll just *die* if I can't go! You're gonna ruin everything!"

After a brief wait while he conferred with Mom, Dad came back on the line and said they would arrive on Sunday around noon.

We did our nightly stop at the Dairy Dock then drove on to the lighthouse. There was a family having a picnic on the far side and a few teenagers climbing over the larger rocks on the point. Gran plopped down on the first flat stone we came to. She started in on me before I'd even gotten settled.

"Olivia, I'm ashamed of you! You don't care about anyone but yourself! Your parents had plans of their own, but you don't care about them, it's just what you want! You whined, and pleaded and would just *die* if you couldn't stay for the party! Well, mark my words, young lady. You're heading down Trouble Lane and one day you'll pay for your behavior. You're not the hot-shot you think you are. You're just a spoiled brat!"

Gran tossed the remainder of her cone in the water then got up and quickly walked to the car. Gramps and I followed behind at a safe distance. I didn't understand why she was picking on me all of a sudden. Was it because I was looking more like mom and doing stuff with my friends? I felt horrible that I had made Gran so angry.

I glanced over at Gramps hoping to see a look that said this wasn't really so bad. I didn't want Gran mad at me for the rest of my visit.

"Don't fret, Princess. Her world just isn't going as she planned. You're growing up fast. She'll get over it."

That would be the last time the three of us would sit together at the lighthouse, reflecting on the day's events. It would also be the end of my childhood innocence.

CHAPTER 5

We made the drive back to the cottage in silence. I didn't feel like playing cards or reading and went to my room. I couldn't ignore the aching feeling that Gran's comments had caused. Was I really such a bad and selfish person who always had to have my way? Gramps never complained, nor did Mom and Dad. Sleep finally came with tears still wet on my cheeks.

The dream came again that night. It was dark with an angry black sky and billowing gray clouds that kept the moon hidden. The ocean was just another shade of black, the waves crashing on the rocks below. I ran along the cliff, screaming for help. The same dark shadowy figure was behind me. I turned my head and looked over my shoulder to see a hand reaching toward me, ready to push . . . then I was falling. I screamed. The air rushed past my face. And horrible pain as I landed on the rocks below.

"Olivia, honey, wake up. It's only a bad dream, you're okay, honey." Opening my eyes I looked into Gran's face and saw the concern in her eyes. "What's wrong with your back? Why are you arching it like that?"

"I'm okay, Gran, it was just a bad dream."

Gran bent down and kissed my cheek, then turned on a nightlight as she left the room.

Saturday morning, and once again I woke to boat motors and birds signing at dawn. I wondered if every day began this way? The air was cool and I snuggled further under the blanket, thinking about David and what it had felt like when he kissed me. They were wonderful memories, but doubts were starting to set in. I wondered about the party. Would he pay special attention to me even with Meg there? I wondered if he had kissed Meg the same way he had kissed me. He'd said that he didn't care about Meg, but was that just something that all guys say? I didn't know what to think, but I was aware of a knot in the pit of my stomach just thinking about Meg in his arms.

After breakfast I went with Gran and Gramps to Mutach's Market for a few grocery items. We were standing in front of the meat counter when I heard a voice behind me. David and Ricky walked toward us. David's smile had my heart doing cartwheels. I introduced them to Gran and Gramps just as a woman walked up behind the boys. David introduced his mother to us. Except for her sleek blond hair, which was pulled to one side, she was a female version of David, with the same large velvet brown eyes.

"Hello, Olivia, I'm glad to finally meet you. David has told me so much about you and how much fun you've had. I hope you're coming to the party later. We're here to pick-up our meat order for the barbecue." She smiled at her son, then turned back to me, "I think David is planning to feed an army!"

"Well, we only have one grill so I figure I'm gonna be at it for hours!"

Gramps nodded with a smile. "Hey son, we have one we won't be using. You're welcome to use it."

Later, Gramps helped David put the grill in the back seat of his bright red hot rod.

David reached out his hand to shake Gramps'. "Thank you, Mr. Thompson. This is very generous of you. I'll bring it back tomorrow."

The top was down, and Gramps admired the custom paint job. "Boy, I remember when these cars were new. I have to say they didn't look this good." I watched Gramps slap the rear fender as David drove off. Then we walked arm-in-arm back to the house.

"Nice fella." Gramps said and I just grinned.

It was just after noon when Patsy knocked on the door. Meg had caught something from her brother and was sick in bed. She wouldn't be going to the party. Patsy and I giggled as we walked out to the car. My day was already looking better!

A few minutes later, Mrs. Paterson turned into the drive leading to a quaint old house with a plaque over the front steps, identifying it as *Stone Cottage*. Mrs. Morgan greeted us in the driveway and explained how the large bungalow had been built in 1920 out of local stones, washed smooth by the waves. After walking through the massive oak door, she showed us to a bedroom and bath where we could put our beach bags. She then took us through the kitchen to the back door where the party was just beginning. David was playing croquet with Ricky and a couple of boys that I didn't recognize.

Holding the screen door open I took a sweeping glance around the yard. Every head turned toward the newcomers. This was a crowd of older kids and for just a moment my insecurities shouted for me to turn and run back to safety. But this was just where I wanted to be. I had to fight my family to win this day. Thanks to an hour spent in the bathroom, my makeup and hair were perfect, just like I had seen in the latest magazines. My white short shorts made my legs look longer, and the short midriff top with rows of white eyelet ruffles trimmed with black velvet ribbon set-off my waist. My long hair was pulled back with a matching black velvet ribbon, tied in a bow at the front. I hoped that I could act as old as I looked.

It made me happy to see the appreciative grin before David whistled his approval. All the other boys watched with a look of envy, which was just what my self-esteem needed. He handed his mallet to Patsy and suggested that he show me around. Taking my hand, he introduced me to each of his friends while walking past the pool and on down to the boathouse.

After entering the small garage-like building, David closed the door behind us and turned to me. "Isn't this place the greatest? I'm so glad we got to stay here this summer. I'm even happier that I met you. You're so beautiful, and I love being with you."

David's arms wrapped around me as I tilted my head back and gazed into smoldering depths of brown.

This was the moment of my fantasies—being alone in David's arms. This was what I had been waiting for. "Kiss me." I said with an intensity that surprised me.

His kiss left me breathless. My fingers took pleasure in the soft waves of his hair. Every nerve in my body screamed for more until a loud banging on the door and laughter beyond reminded us that we were not entirely alone.

"Hey, what are you two doing? It's awfully quiet in there!"

The moment was shattered, and David pushed me away. "Come on, let's get out of here, I wanna show you the tennis court." There was no one outside when we left the boathouse. No one lurking in the vicinity with guilty grins, so we headed toward the court.

"Do you play tennis? If not, I can teach you. I'm pretty good."

"Yeah, I play. I'm sure I'm not as good as you, but my mom and I play at the club during the summer."

"Club?"

"The Cedar Hill Country Club. I don't live in Hicksville, you know. We actually have schools and stores and banks and even a movie theater. Now, where are the rackets?"

After a couple heated games of tennis . . . I won. And a few laps in the pool . . . I let David win, it was off to the grills. We had a fun time flipping burgers and dogs and I helped David's mom carry massive amounts of food out to the long table set up under a tree. She talked to me about her family, about the summer and asked questions about my family. We laughed about silly things and I liked the way she made me feel. Like I was important and not like some problem child. It was obvious that she thought I was older than fifteen, and a twinge of guilt picked at my conscience. But the deceit was well under way and had been initiated by Meg and Patsy long before I arrived on the scene. Besides, seventeen felt far too good to go back now.

After everyone filled their plates and found a place to sit, David and I found our way to the lounge chairs beside the pool. Watching him eat, I thought about how comfortable it felt being with him and how nice his mom was. I pictured us married with our kids running around. They'd have his blond hair and my blue eyes. I wondered if Mom had felt this way about Dad at those parties when she first met him. David took our empty plates and said he would come back with another soda. I watched as he strode away. Muscles rippled across his broad shoulders. Closing my eyes, I fantasized about how it would feel to be alone in his arms. Would I go giddy and swoon like in a Doris Day movie or be consumed with passion like in *Goldfinger*.

He returned with two cold bottles of pop. "Let's go for a walk. There's a special place that I want you to see." Taking my hand, he guided me down past the boathouse and along the shoreline. At first it was pretty rough going, and he had to help me over some of the rocks as the waves gently rolled in. We walked in the water for quite some time before we rounded a bend. And there it was before me . . . the lighthouse. We climbed over a shelf of flat stone and into a small sandy area protected on three sides by trees and dense underbrush. Surrounded by a few huge boulders, a circle of rocks had been used as a fire pit. Beer and pop bottles littered the area. It was obvious that this was the favorite hangout of the local kids.

I threw my arms out wide with excitement. "I love this place! Well, not right here. I've never been on this side, but my favorite place in all the world to sit and think is on the far side of the lighthouse on the big rocks."

David turned to face me, his hands slowly moving down my arms, stopping when they reached my hips. "Then I'm glad I brought you here because you're my favorite person in all the world."

His kiss was gentle with soft lips that explored mine then moved to my neck. I felt his tongue explore the hollow and slowly move down to my shoulder. It tickled and gave me goose bumps. I didn't want to laugh and maybe hurt his feelings.

"David, kiss me again."

His kiss moved to my mouth. I pressed my body against his. My arms wrapped around his neck pulling him closer, just like I had seen in movies. I was breathless when David, without warning, scooped me up against his chest and carried me toward the circle of rocks. This was unexpected and I worried that he would drop me.

"David, put me down. I'm too heavy. You're going to get hurt."

"Don't talk, and you're not heavy at all. Stop squirming."

David gently lowered me to the sand. He stood looking down at me with smoldering eyes and a question that I was yet to understand. This was all new to me and I didn't know what do or say. All I knew was that I wanted to feel his lips on mine. I wanted him to kiss me so I reached up for him. "Come here." I whispered.

David slowly lowered his body next to me and rested on one elbow, looking down at me. His eyes held mine in a gripping spell. His fingers caressed their way across my stomach, hesitating just a moment before reaching for my breast. He leaned over and gave me a kiss that was soft and gentle. I kissed him back until a warm sensation drifted through my body, and our kisses deepened.

David's hand moved to my back, fumbling with the hook of my bikini top. Our kisses became more passionate and demanding as he pulled my top away. He turned his head to kiss each nipple. The heat that had settled between my legs turned to a raging inferno when his teeth teased and nibbled. My hands explored his hard, rippling muscles. Moans escaped from deep within my throat while his mouth did magical things with nipples that sent new feelings of desire racing through my body. His hand moved from caressing my stomach to between my legs.

No one had ever touched me there and I was a little embarrassed. I wasn't sure if I was ready for what would happen next. My body seemed to have a will of its own, and my mind fought for control. I felt the last piece of my bikini being pushed down and I kicked it free. An intense need for something more pushed me forward.

"David, I love you. I've never felt like this before. I don't want you to stop. I want this feeling to go on forever."

"Oh, God, Livy, you're so beautiful . . . I love you too." His kisses became more demanding as our hands explored. Yes, this was how love felt and I was going to marry David. He pressed his long hard body to mine and gathered me in his arms, kissing me with a passion that was new and exciting. The inferno threatened to consume me when he lifted his body above mine and looked deep into my eyes. "Livy, are you sure about this? We can stop if you want."

My eyes drifted down, and I saw his thing. How did it get so big? I had only seen my brothers penis when they were learning to pee in the toilet. I had seen drawings in health class and knew where it was supposed to go but his was huge. That was just what my mind needed to take control—or at least toss some water on the flames of desire. I'd never gone beyond petting before and I didn't know what to do next. Suddenly there was a flood of questions racing through my mind. Would he show me what to do? Would it hurt? Would I get pregnant? Would he still love me if we didn't do it? What would Mom say if she found out?

Sensing my hesitation, David pulled back. "Livy, what's wrong?"

"I'm sorry, I just don't know what to do next. I've never done this before," I said, my words echoing my thoughts.

David gasped, then flung himself onto his back, throwing his arm over his eyes.

"Olivia, why didn't you tell me? It never occurred to me! How can you have so much passion and still be a virgin? Just how old are you anyway?"

He might as well have thrown a bucket of cold water over me, and he wasn't calling me Livy anymore. "It doesn't matter. Everyone has to have a first time."

"How old are you?" he repeated.

"I'll be sixteen in two months."

He groaned. "Fifteen. How could you be just fifteen? I thought you were seventeen or eighteen."

David stood shaking his head as he pulled on his blue trunks. He then walked across the sand and into the water. He looked down the shore in both directions while splashing the cool water over his body. "It's okay, nobody's around. Put your suit on, then come here."

I was hooking my top as I reached him, and we waded further into the water. David bent down and washed the sand off my body. It was a very sweet and intimate moment. I reached out and ran my fingers through his hair. "I'm sorry, David, I didn't think my age would matter."

He jerked his head out of my reach then stood. "Maybe not to other guys, but it does to me." He turned and took a step back. "What about Meg and Patsy? Are they only fifteen?"

I didn't want to continue the lies, but I couldn't rat on Meg and Patsy either. I was leaving and they had the rest of the summer. I just couldn't spoil that for them. Besides, if I did, they would never speak to me again.

"I've always looked older, and you didn't ask. I guess Meg and Patsy just look younger than they are." That at least was the truth.

He began walking in the direction of the cottage. My heart shattered at the sight of his strong back moving away from me. He stopped and looked over his shoulder just as I brushed the first tears from my cheek.

He reached out with one arm. "Come on Livy. We're going to swim back after we make the turn ahead. I don't want anyone thinking that your red eyes and wet cheeks are from crying."

"No one but my parents and brothers have ever called me Livy."
"Do you mind?"
"No, I kind of like the way you say it."

Patsy's mom stopped by just before dusk and the two of them left shortly after the fireworks. David offered to drive me home, and I offered to help with the cleanup. Heavy clouds were moving in, along with a cool wind when David said we'd better leave. He'd left the top down on his hot rod, and before getting in he pulled a blanket from the trunk and wrapped it around me.

"I'm glad we had the party today. I'm afraid some nasty weather is coming our way."

Possessive feelings of love enveloped me like a warm cloak and I reached over to hold his hand as it rested on the gearshift. "I'm glad the weather was good, otherwise we wouldn't have gone on our walk. I know that I disappointed you, but age shouldn't matter."

"I've never felt like this before. I love you, Livy, but I really don't know how to handle this. I'll be away at college, and I guess you have high school to finish. And there's our parents, I know they won't approve."

"I'll be sixteen in October. And Cleveland is less than a two-hour drive from Cedar Hill. And although my parents won't be happy, my mom will understand how I feel."

"I know my mother already likes you and all that my father cares about is that I get good enough grades to get into med school. We can see each other whenever I come home for breaks."

I knew my friend, Vanessa had lost her virginity when she was fifteen and that didn't seem to make a difference to anyone. Besides, it was just like Mom had said it would be. David was the man I wanted to spend the rest of my life with, so having sex with him shouldn't matter. I would find the time to tell him tomorrow.

He turned down the lane to the cottage, and I leaned over and kissed him. "I love you, David Morgan."

"And I love *you*, Olivia Thompson."

He parked the car and came around to open my door, then walked me to the cottage. He wove his fingers through my hair tilting my head back. His kiss was no longer gentle, but firm with the promise of a new beginning. For just a second, as he raised his head, I thought I saw the curtains move in the window of the cottage next door.

CHAPTER 6

The sound of distant thunder woke me at seven. I sniffed. The smell of coffee and bacon told me it was time for breakfast. I changed into white pants and a blue and green plaid shirt and headed toward the kitchen. My hair hung loose around my shoulders.

Sitting down to a mound of scrambled eggs, I wondered whether Gran and Gramps could see the difference in me. Yesterday, I sat at this table, a girl looking for fun and attention. Today, I was a woman in love, one who almost experienced the mysteries of sex.

Gramps put down his fork. "It looks like our luck has run out with the weather, Princess. It said on the radio that we could be in for quite a storm. I'm going to need your help putting the tarp over the boat. Since we're buying this place, I'm leaving the boat next to the garage until I can get back here in a couple of weeks."

"You can count on me, Gramps, and I'll come back with you to help."

The thought of being with David over the Labor Day weekend filled me with excitement. I couldn't wait to tell him. I was helping secure the tarp when I heard the familiar rumble of David's car coming up the lane, and walked over as he stopped in front of the garage.

"I thought I'd better get this back to you before it starts raining. It looks like it might get nasty." Olivia watched as David got out of the car wearing khaki colored shorts and a plaid short-sleeved shirt.

His tan legs stretched as he leaned over the side of the car and pulled the grill out, placing it in front of Gramps. "Would you like me to put this in the garage, Mr. Thompson?"

"That would be great, son. And then could you help me with the last of the lines on this tarp and move the trailer closer to the garage?"

"Sure thing!"

David and Gramps discussed the best small boat for Lake Erie, while putting the top up on the car. They had just finished when there was a loud clap of thunder.

"I'm sorry to rush out on you, Mr. Thompson, but this wind is already picking up steam and the rain won't be far behind. Thanks for helping me with the top." David got in his hot rod and leaned out the window and waved. "Bye, Livy."

Gramps chuckled. "You let him call you Livy? I thought only family was allowed to call you that."

"I guess I just like the way he says it."

"I like David, although I believe he must be around eighteen or nineteen, and too old for you. Then again, we all have summer flings."

The rain had been coming down hard for hours. Loud thunder put me on edge as I arranged the last items in the suitcase. It was noon when I entered the kitchen to see that Gran had set out cold cuts and leftovers for lunch. Another loud clap of thunder shook the cottage.

Gran stood with her hands balled on her hips. "Fred should have been here by now, I hope they didn't have car trouble. This is no kind of weather to be changing a tire. I wish we had a phone!"

Gran nearly shouted to be heard over the pounding rain on the metal roof. She was making me nervous and I dropped the bag of sugar on the counter. I swallowed back tears of frustration as I reached for the washrag to wipe up the mess.

Gramps set their suitcases next to the front door. "Relax Louise. I'm sure they're fine. They probably got a late start."

I finished packing the kitchen supplies and wiped out the cabinets while Gran watched out the front window. "I don't like this. They should have been here by now. We need a phone!"

The round, yellow plastic clock on the kitchen wall showed one o'clock when Gramps suggested that we go ahead and eat. "Maybe they stopped somewhere along the way for lunch until the storm passed."

I was just finishing the last of the ice cream when I heard tires crunching on the gravel driveway. "They're here!" Jumping up from the table, I ran to the front door.

But it wasn't them. Feelings of panic and terror kept me frozen in silence as I watched the black and white car with the red light on the roof slowly come to a stop.

"Gramps. It's a police car."

I stood watching the police officer get out of the car holding an envelope. A chill ran through my body. My heart pounded in my chest. He slid the envelope inside his rain-slicker and with his head lowered he made a dash through the rain to the front door. I could only nod when the officer asked if Louise or Leonard Thompson were there. I watched my hand shake as I pushed open the door to let him in. Gran held her hand to her mouth as she and Gramps rushed to the officer's side.

"Mr. and Mrs. Thompson?" he said as he took his hat off.

Gran and Gramps both nodded, but said nothing.

"There's been an automobile accident in Sandusky involving a family named Thompson."

I went to Gran's side. "No! No, it's a mistake! It's not them! It can't be!"

The officer gave Gramps the envelope. "This was found in the car and contains the loan documents for a cottage at this address. I assumed that the family was on their way here. I wanted to give you the news in person." The three of us sat huddled together while he continued. "It was raining hard and visibility would have been extremely poor. A semi was passing several cars that had pulled over. The driver said he never saw the oncoming car in the downpour until it was too late. He did everything he could to swerve out of the way." He took a deep breath. "I believe they were killed instantly"

Whatever else he said, I didn't hear. I just couldn't control the sobbing, the shaking, or the waves of chilling cold that seemed to consume me.

It was still raining when we packed-up the Buick, locked the cottage and drove across the Bay Bridge to the police station in Sandusky. Mom's mangled white station wagon was still suspended behind a tow truck in the parking lot. The police station was sterile and cold and I just wanted to go home. But I didn't know where home was now that my family was gone. Everything had changed and it was my fault.

I couldn't stop crying as we walked back to the waiting Buick. The rain had stopped and I looked up to see the sun shining through the clouds. Gran put her arm around me as we sat next to gramps in the front seat. I rested my head on her shoulder. "It's my fault they died."

"No dear, it's God's will."

"But if it wasn't for me wanting to go to David's party, we'd have left yesterday, and they wouldn't have died."

"You don't know that. You may have all been killed if that was God's plan. It wasn't your time. God has other plans for you."

"Do you mean that God wanted them to die? Why? Bud and Andy were only eight years old. What did they do that was so bad?"

"We don't question The Almighty, Olivia."

"But it's not fair! They were good . . . they were all good."

Suddenly Gramps pointed at the sky. "Look, Princess, a rainbow! God is giving you a sign. He's telling you it's not the end of your world. There will be a pot of gold at the end. You just have to have faith."

CHAPTER 7

No one in town could ever remember four members of the same family dying at the same time. Both rooms of Cedar Hill's largest funeral home had to be used. I still felt totally responsible for their deaths and wanted to help with the arrangements. I was adamant that my brothers' caskets were to be placed next to each other and touching. Since the twins were inseparable in life, I wanted them together in death. Mom and Dad were to be in the adjacent room, the brown accordion-type plastic wall pushed back to make it into one huge room.

Friday evening, I walked into the room holding the hands of Gran and Gramps. The closed caskets were surrounded by flowers of every color. Blankets of flowers in the pattern of a patchwork quilt draped over the twins. Red roses cascaded down over my parents to signify the undying love they had for each other. It looked as though everyone in town had sent flowers. I walked over to a large and very elegant arrangement next to Mom and read the card from the Morgan family of Cleveland.

I had just sat down in front of Andy and Bud when a darling blue wicker basket with two small teddy bears surrounded by white rosebuds caught my attention. My heart ached as I read the card.

For the brothers I never knew.
They will now romp in heaven's playground
and live forever in the hearts of those who loved them.
David Morgan

Putting the card in my pocket, I took the basket off its stand and centered it on top of the boy's blankets so they could share it.

The sickly sweet scent of fresh flowers filled the air. I had all but tuned-out the organ music in the background along with the drone of the window air conditioners. I tried to accept the many condolences with the grace and manners that Mom would have wanted, but by the end of the day I couldn't remember a single face. Except for my best friends, Vanessa and CeCe, who had stayed at my side.

When it came time to be seated for the funeral service, Gran and Gramps both put their arms around me then guided me to the front row seats. I'm sure the Minister's words were meant to comfort and bring hope to the living, but my young heart was too angry to hear. The many eulogies brought fresh tears to my eyes and a lump to my throat. I realized how much my parents were loved and respected. That's when I first noticed a stunning older woman dressed in black with a long black veil over her face. She sat in the last row and a man wearing a grey uniform stood beside her.

At the conclusion of the service everyone was asked to leave the front two rooms. The doors were closed so the caskets could be made ready for transport. I was nearly to the front door when I remembered the basket and ran back.

I slid open the door just as two of the men were taking off the floral blanket.

"Wait! I have to do something first."

The men stepped back. I found the blue basket and walked to Bud's casket holding one of the teddy bears to my chest. I rested my free hand on the shiny, dark brown lid and leaned in close so only Bud could hear what was in my heart. "It seems funny to hear you called Angus because no one calls you that. I'm so sorry Bud. I know that I wasn't very nice to you sometimes, and you got on my nerves a lot, and I didn't like you picking on Andy, but all that's okay." I wiped my tears and took a deep breath. "I know that I never told you, but I love you Bud, and I always will."

One of the men sensed what I needed to do and lifted the heavy lid of the casket. He opened it enough so I could get my arm inside. The white satin felt like a pillow. I laid the bear in the soft folds. Then I walked over to Andy. "My little Andy, you were always the good one. Looking to me to end your battles and pick you up and brush you off. I will miss your laughter and your smiling face and both will remain in my heart, and I will love you forever." With a trembling hand, I tucked the little teddy bear inside next to Andy and looked up at the two men through a sea of tears.

All eyes were on me as I parted the doors. I hesitated, choking back the sobs that so desperately wanted out. I had never felt so sad, so angry, and so helpless and I was afraid that once I allowed the tears to fall, I wouldn't be able to stop them. Taking a deep breath, I walked back into the wide front hallway.

People were already making their way outside. Friends and neighbors, Dad's business associates and clients along with members of the Cedar Hill Country Club made up the bulk of the mourners. Olivia was surprised to see that nearly every member of the powerful Montgomery family seemed to be to be there. The Montgomery wives, Victoria and Jacqueline, were both looking elegant in beautifully cut suits and matching hats and each was wearing a single string of pearls. The only other woman in town who could outshine the Montgomery women . . . was Mom.

It took nearly every strong male in attendance to be pallbearers for the four caskets that would be taken to the four waiting hearses. I stood at the front door trying to collect myself for the next step in this nightmare. Wearing one of the new outfits that we bought earlier in the week, I looked very grown up in the black sheath, which stopped just above my knees. My hair was pulled up in curls on top of my head and a large black velvet bow held a small black veil.

As my gaze panned the waiting crowd, it stopped at the woman standing beside another limo parked away from the others. She stood straight with the aid of a cane and looked regal in her black dress and long veil. Our eyes met and she smiled with a slight nod of her head. It was a sad smile. Maybe she had lost her family as well. There was something so familiar about her.

The ride to the cemetery, on the edge of town, seemed to take hours. Our lengthy procession must have included nearly everyone in town. The four coffins were carried to the family plot where Thompsons had been laid to rest for more than a hundred years. A sense of panic washed over me. I would now have to leave them. With a feeling of desperation, I looked up into the eyes of the mysterious woman standing at the gate to the Thompson plot. I forced a smile, and began walking across the uneven ground toward her. But my new patent leather heels kept getting stuck in the soft ground. When I finally reached the gate and looked up, the woman was gone.

I waited at the gate until everyone had paid their respects and filed out. "Gran, who was that woman in the long veil that was standing here? I think that's her in the limo that's pulling away."

Gran turned toward the road. "I believe she was Millicent Montgomery. Winston, Lionel and Monty's mother. It's a real honor that she came. Only a Montgomery would be rich enough to have her own limousine."

Friends and neighbors brought food to the senior Thompson's house for a reception after the funeral. I just couldn't endure anyone else saying "I'm sorry," so Vanessa and CeCe came to my room with me.

Celeste Cellini had lived next door until my family moved to the Heights. We'd been best friends since we were toddlers. Back then I couldn't pronounce her name and I'd shortened it to CeCe. We were about the same size, but her pale blond hair and big brown eyes were in sharp contrast to mine. She and I met Vanessa Martin when we were in the first grade.

Vanessa was two years older than we were, but we still had fun. It was like having a big sister. Vanessa's mom owned Flo's Beauty Shop, which was located on the first floor of an old Victorian house on Main Street. The family lived in the top two floors. CeCe and I thought it was the coolest house we had ever seen. We would sit on the swing, which hung from the ceiling on the big front porch, and wait for Vanessa. I think she liked the idea that she watched out for us, chasing away any of the bullies who tried anything. She was tall for her age, and her hazel eyes seemed to change with her moods. Her hair was a soft chestnut color that glistened with gold in the sun, until she heard that blondes have more fun. From then on, her flaxen locks would range from platinum to strawberry. Her dad owned Martin's Garage, which was only a block away from the house. Sometimes in the winter we stopped there to get warm or to see some neat car he was working on.

The pressures of the past week had finally taken their toll. In the privacy of my room, I broke down and let the tears come. "My family is gone, and it's all my fault."

CeCe wrapped her arm around my shoulder. "It's not your fault. It was an accident. You had nothing to do with it."

I grabbed a tissue from the box sitting next to me on the bed. I thought about what she had said while I wiped the tears. "Yes, it was. If I hadn't fallen in love with David we would have come home on Saturday."

Vanessa let out a dramatic sigh and shook her head. "Look, I've been in love with lots of guys. So will you. So you can't blame everything bad that happens to you on love."

"This is different. I'm going to marry David. It happened just like Mom said it would." I punched my pillow in anger. "Because of me, she won't help me pick out my wedding dress. My family won't be at my wedding."

CeCe stood and motioned with her hand for Vanessa to join her. "I think you should try and sleep. We'll be your family, now and forever."

I cried myself to sleep, but an hour later I was awakened by troubled dreams of my last hours with Mom. We would never again have those mother and daughter conversations. I wouldn't be able to tell her that I had found her kind of love, or tell her about how wonderful David made me feel. Did Mom know that I loved her? I couldn't remember ever telling her.

CHAPTER 8

The sparkling blue water of the swimming pool reflected back through the tall living room windows. I could almost see Mom lying on a chaise lounge reading the latest novel.

We hadn't always lived here. When Mom and Dad first got married, they rented an apartment in an old Victorian house on Main Street. Lionel Montgomery had been Dad's buddy since childhood. He'd suggested that Dad get into the insurance business since all the servicemen coming home and starting families would need insurance. Dad ended up getting a job with the largest agency in Cedar Hill and was soon making enough to buy one of the new bungalows that were springing up on the edge of town. They moved in just before it was time for Mom to give birth to me, and she named me after her mother.

Gran and Gramps had brought me to my parent's house to get the rest of my things, now that I would be living with them.

Gran and Gramps had been childhood sweethearts, living on neighboring farms in Cedar Hill, Ohio. She was the oldest of six children, and spent most of her time taking care of her younger brothers and sisters and helping her mother with the housework. Gramps, on the other hand, was the youngest of four brothers. He'd never liked farm life. His best friend's father worked for the newspaper in nearby Mansfield and arranged for both boys to apprentice as typesetters at the paper after they finished high school. Gramps never left the newspaper and worked his way up to a supervisor in the department.

Gran and Gramps were married the year after graduation, and the young couple lived with Gramps' family until they could afford an apartment of their own. I wondered what had drawn them together, since they had opposite personalities. Gramps, looked at each day as a new adventure and talked easily to everyone he met. His eyes sparkled in his rather round face with its bushy eyebrows that seemed to grow in all directions, and his mouth was always ready to smile. Gran, on-the-other-hand, seemed to view life with a scowl and kept to herself most of the time. Her features were strong and angular, with thin lips that gave her a stern look. Yet when she was happy, her whole face would light up with joy.

The three of us met with the attorney earlier that morning to review the contents of the wills. I was the sole heir. Since I was still a minor, the proceeds from the sale of the house and its contents, plus the considerable insurance money I would be receiving, was to be put in a trust fund and the monies invested by the executor of the estate, Lionel Montgomery. He was my Godfather, and I had always referred to him as Uncle Lionel. My grandparents would receive a generous monthly stipend for my care and expenses. I, too, would receive a monthly allowance. The attorney suggested putting the house on the market as soon as possible. It was at its most beautiful then, in early fall, when the view out over the golf course and the hills beyond was ablaze with color.

Banging sounds coming from my parent's bedroom brought me back to the present. Gran emptied the contents of Mom's dresser drawers onto the bed just as I entered the room.

I ran toward the bed. "What are you doing? These are my mother's things!" I screeched.

"Yes, dear, but they have to be packed up for the poor. The sooner we get them out of here the better."

"Why did you start with her? Why not Dad's things?" Every unkind gesture and snide remark that she had made toward Mom flashed through my mind. "You hated her and can't wait to get rid of everything that was hers! Well you can't throw it out! It's all mine, the lawyer said so!" I threw myself on the bed and put my arms around Mom's things.

Gramps came in from his sorting in the garage. "Hey, what's all this shouting about? Louise, what's going on here? Olivia's hysterical!"

"Gramps, please! Don't let Gran throw away Mom's clothes!"

Gramps looked from me to Gran. "Louise, why don't you start in the kitchen and let Olivia sort through Maureen's clothes? We're not in that much of a hurry."

Gran shoved the last drawer back in place and stormed out of the room. Gramps sat down on the bed next to me and put a comforting arm around my shoulder. "Have some patience, Princess, this is hard on her too. She's lost her only son and doesn't know how to handle her grief. She's trying to keep it inside because she wants to be strong for you. She loves you very much. She just has a hard time showing it."

Over the next few weeks, Vanessa and CeCe went to the house with me after school and on weekends. Packing was easier with them there. We gave the few tools that were in the garage to Vanessa's dad. I kept some of the boys' favorite toys, books, and stuffed animals and gave the rest of the toys and clothes to the children's home on the edge of town. I always thought it was strange that a town as small as ours would have an orphanage, but I guess people in the city thought the kids needed the cleaner air of the country.

Sorting and packing was made easier as we talked about our latest boyfriends. Or in Vanessa's case, her current boyfriend, and all the boys she wanted to date. Especially Winston Montgomery III who had been driving around town in his bright yellow hot rod. He had said "Hello" to Vanessa at the funeral. I bragged about David's car being nicer, since it was a convertible and Winston's was a coupe. My memories of David were kept alive by talking about him. But eventually they both told me that they didn't want to hear anymore until I had something new to say.

Mom and Dad had a big walk-in closet, very unusual for those times. Dad got only one wall for all of his clothes, while Mom had used the other three sides for her extensive wardrobe. Her lime-green sundress wasn't hanging neatly with the others. It was now in my closet and my mind wandered back to the last time I stood here.

"Mom, have you seen my transistor radio?"

"No, but you might ask your brothers. Have you finished packing? I'm going to need you to help me load the car."

"I'm almost finished. Can I take your lime-green sundress with the spaghetti straps? And your peasant blouse? It will look great with my yellow Capri pants. Have you seen the bag with my new bikini and shorts?"

Mom put down the shirt she was folding. "Olivia, we're only going to be gone for the weekend. I don't see any reason that you should need to borrow my clothes when you have more than any fifteen-year-old I know. But you might look on the floor of your closet. That's where everything ends up."

"I'll go look." I shouted as I headed toward my room.

It wasn't long before I was back at my parent's room. I saw that the suitcase was open on the bed and she was packing for both herself and Dad. She was still beautiful at thirty-six. Her long black hair was usually pulled sleekly back in a French twist, which showed off her intense violet-blue eyes, long thick black eyelashes and a flawless complexion. She used little makeup other than mascara, rouge and lipstick unless she and Dad were going out. Then her makeup made her look like a movie star. Her clothes, however, were not as conservative as her makeup. She instinctively knew the styles that showed off her perfect figure, and the latest fashions were new and exciting. Each year she looked forward to this carefree weekend when Dad's parents would keep us kids occupied, leaving her to swim and lie in the sun and read. Most of the time she would wear a strapless black one-piece swimsuit and flip-flops, but she was also taking her new leopard print bikini that Dad liked, along with a pair of shorts and a couple of tops. She'd already packed Dad's things, easily fitting their clothes into one suitcase and was adding the new Ian Fleming book, *You Only Live Twice*.

"Mom, you were right. I found the bag with my new clothes on the floor of my closet. My radio was there too. *Please*, can I borrow your dress and top? I really need them. There may be a dance at the beach club, and I don't have anything of my own to wear. *Please Mom!*"

Mom slammed the top of the suitcase in place and snapped the locks. "All right! I don't have time to argue."

Just before Dad arrived home from the office, Mom put the two smaller suitcases, along with her train case, in the back of the station wagon. She turned and reached for mine. "Olivia! What's in this? You must have enough clothes in here to last for a month! We're only going to be gone for two days!"

"Yeah, but I have to have enough clothes and everything else that I need to be absolutely *gorgeous!*"

The sound of coat hangers rubbing together brought me back to the present as Vanessa pushed past me.

"Wow, Olivia! I've never seen anyone with so many beautiful gowns. It's like your mom was a movie star or something!"

Mom had a beautiful figure. Dad liked showing her off at the country club and various social events, wearing her fabulous clothes. Vanessa, CeCe and I spent the next two hours trying on clothes. At least for a short time I was able to forget why we were there.

Vanessa stood before the floor-length mirror wearing a short red silk cocktail dress with a sleeveless, low cut scooped bodice, and a skirt with row after row of organdy ruffles. "I just love this. I'm so jealous. All these beautiful clothes are yours now." She danced the Monkey to imaginary music, with masses of red ruffles fluttering up and down.

It looked so good on her that I gave it to her, along with the matching red high-heeled sandals and handbag.

CeCe modeled a short yellow sheath, with a matching jacket and hat. "Wow, that is so nice of you. Can I have this dress? And the hat too?"

"Sure." It felt good to make my best friends so happy. I almost forgot about the horror that brought us to Mom's closet.

I kept a few of Dad's shirts, the ones I liked to wear around the house or out by the pool. In the end, I couldn't bear to part with anything of Mom's. I talked Gramps into making an area of their attic into a cedar closet for all her clothes.

Mom and Dad had purchased the model home completely furnished, including artwork. It only seemed right that I should try to sell it that way. The only exception was the portrait of Mom, which hung on the wall in their bedroom. It had been painted in July of

1945 and showed her sitting sideways on a gilded bench, wearing a beautiful ivory silk ball gown with a low-cut bodice and narrow little straps. One strap had fallen off her shoulder, and she looked out from the painting with a smoldering, seductive look. Yards and yards of a full silk skirt billowed out around her, and in the back, at her tiny waist, were huge matching cabbage roses that cascaded down. Her hair was pulled back and piled high on her head with ringlets hanging down the back. Her only piece of jewelry was a magnificent choker of pearls.

"Wow, I've only seen paintings like that in museums. It looks like a wedding dress," said CeCe.

"I wish it were. Mom left that dress behind when she married Dad. She said she didn't know what happened to it, but thought her father probably had it burned."

"Too bad! It would look just fab on me!"

We used Dad's black Pontiac convertible to make several trips to my grandparent's house. Boxes of clothes filled the trunk. We laid Mom's gowns, still in individual zippered bags, across the back seat. The portrait was carefully wrapped and laid on top. By Friday afternoon we were finished.

CHAPTER 9

The cottage now belonged to Gran and Gramps, but it held no joy for me. The day was overcast and cool, and so were my spirits. David and Ricky had driven over to say how sorry they were. Ricky said he couldn't imagine the pain I must be feeling at losing my whole family at once, leaving only my grandparents to care for me.

David took my hand. "The last time I saw you, you were a carefree fifteen year old. Now, just three weeks later, you look older. The smile on your face doesn't reach your eyes, and the sparkle that I loved so much is gone."

It was all I could do to hold myself together. Being with David was what I had dreamed about. But now that he was standing in front of me, all I could do was smile and fight to hold back the tears.

"The boat is already on the trailer and we're leaving first thing in the morning," David said. "Mom wants to avoid the heavy traffic on Labor Day. This afternoon, Ricky and I are going next door to the beach club for lunch and to play a few games of pool. I know you're probably not in the mood, but I sure would like it if you came by. If you shoot pool like you play tennis, it'll be a real competition."

I fought with the overwhelming grief that rested in the pit of my stomach. "I'll try," I said, then ran for the bedroom, leaving David and Ricky to say goodbye to my grandparents.

An hour later I joined Gran and Gramps at the kitchen table. With a body that was numb, I focused on trying to eat a tuna sandwich that my stomach didn't want.

Gramps pushed his now empty plate to the side. "Princess, it breaks my heart to see you this way. It's as if the very energy that had fueled your enthusiasm for life is gone, used up, leaving behind someone who is only half alive. It's as if your soul had climbed into that coffin with your mother, and I'm wondering how long it's going to be before you take it back, and begin to live again."

Gran smiled in agreement. "Olivia, honey, why don't you go meet up with your friends? We can manage here, and it might be just what you need to brighten your day."

The pain in Gran's eyes made my decision. I nodded, and excusing myself from the table, I went out the back door and headed across the field to the Bay Shore Beach Club. The jeans and long-sleeved, blue plaid shirt protected me from the thorny weeds that grew across the path. This route was a lot shorter than going around in the water, and it didn't take more than a few minutes to reach the other side. I still blamed my relationship with David for the accident that killed my family. If I hadn't been so selfish they would still be alive. But after seeing him again this morning, feelings I'd thought were dead suddenly sprang back to life. As I reached the edge of the field, my heart reminded me that our love was truly special. I just couldn't bear losing him, too.

With that realization, I ran across the sand, breathless and happy for the first time in three weeks. Smiling from ear-to-ear, I reached the back door of the club. I stopped just outside the open door to catch my breath before entering. And then I heard Meg laughing. My heart stopped as I saw David with his arm around her waist. He was bending down, saying something into her ear that made Meg lean into him even more. She looked up into his eyes and laughed again . . . and then she was kissing him. Quietly, I backed away from the door before anyone could see me, and leaned against the wall for support. No! No! This couldn't be happening! Suddenly, the tears were back. They did that often, and I felt like I'd been kicked in the stomach. Feelings of anger and betrayal rushed through me. What I had seen shattered my heart into a million pieces. I couldn't think clearly, so I ran back across the field to the safety of the cottage.

Over and over, I kept asking myself why. Why Meg? David had told me he wasn't interested in her. Why couldn't he be happy with just me? He said he'd never met anyone before that made him feel like I did. Why did he lie about being in love with me? Was sex all he wanted, after all? Had he turned to Meg because we didn't make love on the beach? Had he had sex with Meg while I was away burying my family? Why did he have to do this now, when he knew I was coming to the club to see him? He'd asked me to come. Tears rolled down my cheeks. I sobbed into my pillow for yet another death. The death of my love for David—the love I had thought was strong enough to last forever.

Gran's knock on my door woke me. She poked her head into the room. "Olivia, honey, there's someone here to see you." The clock on the nightstand showed 4:00. Apparently I had slept for several hours.

I walked through the front door to find David standing next to his car. "Aren't you at the wrong house? Meg lives next door."

David looked confused. "What are you talking about? I've been waiting all afternoon for you. I thought you were coming to the club," his voice rose with agitation.

"I did."

He shook his head in denial. "But, I didn't see you."

"No, you didn't . . . but I saw you." It was all I could do to keep my voice calm and controlled—much calmer than I felt.

He moved a few steps forward with outstretched arms. "Livy, please, what is this about?"

I raised my hand. "Stop right there. Don't call me that. Only my family called me Livy, and they're all dead!"

"Livy . . . Olivia, please get in the car and we'll go somewhere and talk about this."

The anger building deep within me couldn't be controlled any longer. "No . . . you go . . . and I never want to see you again!"

I ran back into the house, closing the door behind me, sealing out any further words from David. I watched through the curtains as the red hot rod drove down the lane and was soon out of sight.

Once again, I had no appetite at dinner. Later that evening Gramps found me on the swing under the oak tree. "I couldn't help but notice something's wrong between you and David. Anything you want to talk about, Princess?"

"No, I don't wanna talk about anything."

"I've got a hankering for an ice cream cone, and I happen to know a place that makes the best chocolate around. Want to come?"

As we drove by *Stone Cottage*, my gaze in that direction didn't go unnoticed by Gramps.

"Want to stop? I see David's car in the drive," he said.

"No. I want ice cream."

After stopping at the Dairy Dock, we found our way to the lighthouse and our favorite rocks. We had finished our cones in silence.

Gramps took a deep breath then let it out slowly. "My favorite time today is right now. The sky is blue with those big puffy clouds, and the lake is calm, and I feel at peace for the first time in weeks."

"Gramps, why do guys lie? Why are they such jerks?"

"Well, Princess, you're not the first woman to ask that question. I believe Eve was probably the first. But unless you can be more specific, I don't think I have an answer."

"Why can't they be honest about how they feel and not just tell you what they think you wanna hear?"

Gramps shifted his position on the rock. "I don't know Princess, but if you're talking about David, he seems like a pretty straight shooter to me. Seems like the kind of well-mannered fella that you could depend on."

Was that statement supposed to make me feel better, or make me open up and tell him what was wrong? Keeping my thoughts to myself, I just sat and stared at the woods on the far side of the lighthouse, remembering the magical place it had been.

The next morning, Gramps asked for my help cleaning out the garage to make room for his small boat and trailer. I heard a car coming down the lane, and looked up to see a black Cadillac pulling up to the house. It looked like Mrs. Morgan's car, and I panicked. "Gramps, please, I'm not here!" Before he could argue, I ran around behind the garage.

"Didn't mean to startle you, Mr. Thompson. I borrowed my mom's car since mine already has the boat and trailer hitched to it. Is Olivia here?"

"Ah . . . well . . . no she isn't at the moment, David, but I sure could use a hand if you have the time."

I heard them shifting things around in the garage and then pushing the boat and trailer inside.

"I don't mean to be nosey or anything. But, I like you, son, and Olivia seems heartbroken over something, and it has to do with you, and what happened at the beach club yesterday."

"Damn, Gramps, what are you doing? Let him leave!" I whispered.

"I know, but I didn't see her yesterday, although I waited until late in the afternoon."

"All I know is when she left here she was happier than I've seen her since your party, but she came back a short time later in tears.

You know, she's been through more in the last few weeks than anyone should endure, let alone a fifteen year old. She's a bundle of nerves, and you need to give her time."

"I know that, sir. Do you happen to remember about what time she left for the club?"

"Yeah. It was just after noon. She got up from the table and ran out the door. It couldn't have taken her more than five minutes to get there."

"Thanks. That helps. And once again, I'm real sorry about your loss. I have to leave. We're all packed and ready to go, but I wanted to say goodbye to Olivia first. Please tell her I'll call her next week."

I listened as David backed out of the drive. Feeling sure that he was already heading down the drive, I poked my head around the corner of the garage. But he was pulling up to the O'Brien's cottage.

Gramps startled me as he came around the other corner. "Just what was all that about? I thought you liked David. Had a lovers quarrel, did you? Well, it's only the first of many, and besides, from what I saw, he's ready to make up!"

Before leaving Marblehead for the season, we inspected every inch of the cottage and made notes of what needed to be done next spring.

"The first thing I do next year is have a phone put in!"

Gran was right, but it was this year that we'd needed a phone.

Grabbing my suitcase from my room, I noticed the poodle David had won for me at Cedar Point. It sat on the coverlet, eyes vacant and uncaring. I tossed the offending animal up onto the top shelf of the closet and closed the door.

CHAPTER 10

School started the following week. It actually felt good to have something normal and familiar going on in my life. David called every night for two weeks but I wouldn't take his calls. Finally he got the message that I didn't want to talk to him. Then he started writing letters. I returned them all and soon those stopped as well. I had gained a new strength and hard shell. I wasn't going to let some self-centered, over-sexed guy make a fool of me . . . a second time.

October 31st had always been my favorite day of the year, not just because Mom always had a party and we all spent many hours planning our costumes. It also happens to be my birthday. Since I was turning sixteen, Gran was determined to go ahead and have a party even though my heart wasn't in it. To keep it simple, we decided on a "Sock Hop" theme, and Gran helped me with my costume—pink poodle skirt and all.

This year the 31st fell on a Saturday. Gramps and Gran took me to the license bureau to get my temporary drivers license. Then, on the way home, Gramps said they had a surprise for me and we pulled into the local Ford dealership. We walked into the showroom, and there it was—a red Mustang convertible with a big pink bow on the hood. All the employees yelled "Happy Birthday!" The owner of the dealership explained that Dad had ordered the car back in July. After the funeral, Gramps decided not to cancel the order since the car was paid for. He knew how happy Fred would have been to give his daughter such a wonderful gift for her sixteenth birthday.

With a lump in my throat, I drove the car out of the lot with Gramps at my side. Gran followed behind in the Buick, then veered off in the direction of home. Vanessa had already taught both CeCe and me how to drive and Gramps said that I took to driving like a duck to water.

After driving around town and stopping to show CeCe and Vanessa my wonderful present, we went home. I remembered the small box that I had found hidden under a hat on the top shelf of Mom's closet. I knew it could only be my birthday present from Mom. But, I also knew that Vanessa and CeCe would hound me until I opened it, so I hid it from them. With new excitement, I ran upstairs to my room. The box was wrapped in pink with a lovely pink silk bow and I opened it to find a diary, complete with lock and key. Inside she had written:

> *My darling Livy,*
> *I give you this diary just as my mother gave me my first journal when I turned sixteen.*
> *This is a very special year for you and deserves a place for you to write down your most private thoughts and feelings. I still write in mine, but not as often.*
> *Life slows down as one gets older, and so did my writings.*
> *Love Always,*
> *Mom*

The party was a great success with twenty or more kids twisting through the house. Everyone brought their favorite records and Gramps played the part of a DJ. Gran kept the food coming and actually seemed to be enjoying herself. Vanessa and CeCe both brought their current boyfriends and were seen dancing through Gran's rose garden. Later that night I wrote in my diary . . . beginning with David's party.

The realtor was right about the house looking its best in the fall. We had one of the best seasons ever, with warm days and crisp cool nights, and a glorious show of colors that enveloped the house in a blaze of fall splendor. The house sold immediately to a doctor and his family who bought it along with all the furnishings.

Back in the late 1950s, Monty Montgomery took some of the family's land on a ridge overlooking the Cedar Hill Country Club, which the Montgomerys also had built, and started a development of modern homes similar to those that were popular in California. Cedar Heights was born with homes of the future. He built a model home on the best lot at the end of a cul-de-sac, advertising it as "The Modern Woman's Dream Home." It had state-of-the-art appliances and even drapes that opened and closed with the push of a button. The ranch style house was designed with an open floor plan for entertaining and large floor-to-ceiling windows overlooking a kidney-shaped pool, which was set into a stone patio. Monty took us on a tour during a special V.I.P. open house and Mom fell in love with it, saying that it certainly was her dream house, furniture and all. I still remember her excitement when, two years later, on their wedding anniversary, Dad pulled into the driveway. We all walked up to the front door, and Dad gave her the keys to the house.

Adjusting to life at my grandparent's house didn't take that long. It had always been a second home to me. A large gracious colonial, it was built in 1917 in what was generally called Cedar Hill's Garden

District. Gran took great pride in her rose garden. She tried not to be too critical, and having my own car helped give me the freedom that had been just beyond my reach in the past.

School was boring, and the guys that asked me out all seemed like boys after David. There was a part of me that wanted to give in and call him, but he was away at college. I needed his number, but I didn't want to talk to his mom. She had been so nice to me. I just knew she would ask me a lot of questions that I didn't want to answer.

I loved my car and all the attention I got, but I didn't like driving in the winter on icy roads. Thunderstorms terrified me and reminded me of death. Because I didn't like driving in them I became pretty much of a fair-weather driver. CeCe and I rode to school in Vanessa's car on bad-weather days and I drove on the good ones. It all worked out perfectly.

Vanessa seemed to tire of boyfriends quickly, and she passed them on to CeCe and me, so we were never without dates. I guess that's just what best friends do.

That winter was difficult for me, especially the holidays. There were only three of us at the dining room table for Thanksgiving, and I didn't have much to be thankful for. Then Christmas came too quickly. The twin's laughter and excitement had always been so much a part of the merriment. After all the presents were opened, I would spend hours playing board games and helping them assemble model airplanes and battle ships. Now, the twinkling, colored lights of the tree blurred through my tear-filled eyes. I wished there was some way to turn back time. I would give anything, make any promise to God, if only he would give me my family back.

The New Year came in quietly. I missed watching Mom get dressed for the New Year's Eve Ball at the Cedar Hill Country Club. She'd look like a movie star and Dad was so handsome in his tuxedo.

The church service the following Sunday was about correcting the wrongs done to others and paying for the sins of the previous year. We were to go forth in the new year with the fear of God in our hearts. I sat listening with anger in my heart. I couldn't accept that a God who let my family die was good. Someone I should obey and make sacrifices for, and yet both love and fear.

I glanced back over my shoulder. Did anyone else have a problem with the sermon? A few dozed with bent heads. A man directly behind me began to snore. Maybe no one actually listened. But I did.

None of the church services had made any sense to me since the accident, and I just couldn't endure anymore. Quietly, I got up and walked down the aisle and out the front door.

It was one of those beautiful winter mornings when the sky is a brilliant sapphire blue. The air was still and crisp, and the tree branches and rooftops were covered in a thick blanket of fresh snow. It looked like a fairyland. The town was quiet, with everyone either in church or at home with their families.

My hands burned from the cold. I'd left my gloves in the car. My breath billowed from my mouth like an angry dragon. Shoving my hands deep into my coat pockets, I thought about how unfair life was. I was angry with myself because I had caused my family to die. I was angry with David because he had lied to me. I ached inside because I would never see him again and that meant that my family had died for nothing. It was all because of David. I kicked the fire hydrant as I passed by.

I was still mad an hour later when I heard the car in the driveway. Then, the side door slammed.

Gran was furious. "What is wrong with you, Olivia? Are you sick? Why didn't you tell us what you were doing? We looked everywhere for you, and so did The Reverend!"

"I can't do this anymore, Gran! I can't sit in church like I believe what Reverend Mills is preaching! Trying to make me believe God is good! Well, He's not! He killed my family. I hate Him!"

"Olivia, stop this blasphemy right now! You don't know what you're saying!"

"I hate Him! I hate Him." Gramps walked in just as Gran slapped me across the face.

"What the hell is going on in here?" Gramps shouted.

"You're right." Gran said, breathing hard. "And that's just where Olivia is going! To hell!"

My head jerked back. No one had ever slapped me, and my hand immediately went to my cheek. I was horrified. I didn't think that my life could get any worse—but it had.

I turned to leave the room, but Gran grabbed my arm and jerked me back.

"I'm not through with you yet, Miss. You're not the only one hurting here! I know you lost your father and your mother and your two brothers. And that's a tragedy! But I lost my only son, my daughter-in-law, and my two grandsons. I'm mad too! But I have to keep myself together. For you! And you had better thank the good Lord that he has seen fit to let your grandfather and me stay awhile longer on this Earth to take care of you—or you and that fancy car of yours would be living in the orphan's home!"

Gran's face was red and she trembled. Gramps stood before us, tears in his eyes, shaking his head sorrowfully.

I didn't want the situation to get worse, and it would if I stayed. Yanking my arm out of Gran's clutch, I grabbed my coat and purse and stomped out the door.

Looking at the front of Vanessa's house, I couldn't remember anything after backing out of our driveway, or the drive here. Anger still consumed me, although part of me was ashamed for losing control. My nerves were raw and ready to explode without notice, and it was comforting to see Dad's convertible sitting in the driveway.

For the two weeks while we cleaned out the house, Vanessa had loved driving Dad's Pontiac. Her own car was old and always breaking down, although her dad tried his best to keep it running. When it came time to sell Dad's car, Mr. Martin asked if he could buy it for Vanessa. He offered some cash, and an agreement to take care of all the service and repairs to my Mustang for as long as I owned the car.

I climbed the front stairs to the Martin's second floor apartment. When I went inside, Vanessa was in her room listening to records. I told her every detail of what had happened since entering the church that morning. "I don't ever wanna go back there again! Do you think your parents would let me live here? You have a big room, and I could help with the chores!"

"I don't think running away is the answer to your problems, but maybe getting a new look will help. Come on. Let's go downstairs to the shop. I need practice for my cutting class, and if I mess up too badly, my mom will fix it!"

Turning on the radio, we sat on the floor of the beauty shop with stacks of hairstyle and beauty magazines. Finally, Vanessa decided on a very short and sleek style that was becoming popular with the British invasion and the *Mod Look*. I was completely comfortable with my bouffant, shoulder-length styles and wasn't sure whether I had the courage to show up at school with something so radically different. But Vanessa convinced me that this was just what I needed to get me out of the doldrums and start the New Year with a new look and new attitude. She kept my back to the mirror, and when she finally finished and turned me around, I could only gasp at the person looking back. My long black hair was now chin length and very straight and smooth with a side part. She had brushed it to one side, and it swept down along one eye and hugged my chin almost meeting my mouth, with the other side tucked behind my ear. Now, all I needed were bell-bottoms. Vanessa's mom gave her an A+ for the very difficult cut, and only touched up the back, to give it some movement.

I have to admit it worked. I went back home that evening with a new look and a new attitude. I even apologized for my bad behavior as Gran looked at me with a rather doubtful expression. It was as if the three of us pretended the morning never happened.

Gran assured me that my hair would grow back.

CHAPTER 11

Winter dragged on, and I continued to let Vanessa do most of the driving. Finally, the daffodils began poking their heads up through the snow, and spring was just around the corner. I hadn't been back to church since that dreadful day when I pushed Gran to the breaking point. I always had an excuse, like a headache, a stomachache, my period, or studying for an exam. After a couple of months, Gran stopped asking me to go. We seemed to be skating on thin ice, both going out of our way not to say or do anything that would cause the other to slip and fall.

Once in a while, I would try to do something I knew would please her. So, the first warm weekend in May, Vanessa and CeCe and I drove to the cottage to clean and get it ready for the summer season. There was no sign of anyone next door at the O'Brien's, and that made me happy. We washed windows and floors and took the bedding to the Laundromat. My heart ached as we passed *Stone Cottage*.

Not wanting to dirty the kitchen, we ate our meals next door at the Bay Shore Beach Club. It had lost its magic over the winter. Now it was just a place to eat. The only place that hadn't changed for me was the lighthouse. It didn't seem to have the same aura of enchantment for Vanessa and CeCe as it did for me. By the end of the weekend, they both said they were impressed by my new summer playground and assured me that I would meet someone else that summer. Someone better than David Morgan. I wasn't so sure. I still had a desire, deep within me, to call him and tell him that he was forgiven. But my stubborn Scottish pride wouldn't let me. Despite my conflicting thoughts about David, life was beginning to feel good again. Now I could have fun without feeling guilty for being alive. I didn't want to open any old wounds, or fall back into that awful pit of darkness.

We went to the cottage again for a week in June after school was out. The O'Briens were already there, but I never saw Meg. Gran told me Mrs. O'Brien had said Meg had enough to keep her busy at home . . . whatever that meant. Each day, Gramps and I would go to the marine supply store at Gem Beach. We looked at used boats and fantasized about them. One afternoon on the way home, we took a different way and cut across the peninsula, and there—sitting in front of an old farmhouse—was just the boat we'd been looking for. And it was for sale.

"Gramps, do you see that? It's a Lyman. You said it's the best boat for Lake Erie, and it's on a trailer!"

Later, we pulled in the drive with the boat and trailer hitched to the back of the Buick. Gran stood in the doorway with her hands on her hips as we got out of the car and walked toward her.

"Hi, Gran! Would you believe that it just followed us home?"

She didn't say a word. Just stood there shaking her head until she turned around and walked back inside. Gramps and I looked at each other, grinning. The fact that we didn't get a lecture meant it was okay.

He loved that boat and spent every available moment working on it. It was his fishing boat and my ski boat, designed to take the unpredictable Lake Erie waves. Gramps was happy with my handling of his new toy and felt comfortable letting me take it out alone.

We went to the cottage often that summer, and I was allowed to take either CeCe or Vanessa. I guess Gran thought it would make up for the loss of my brothers. It didn't, but it did help pass the time. That year Vanessa was dating Danny Capelli, whose father owned Capelli's Grocery Store, so she wasn't always available. Most often, CeCe ended up going. That made Gran happy because she liked CeCe's quiet, easy-going personality. CeCe and I looked forward to the dances at the Bay Shore Beach Club where I often saw Tony Marelli and his friends. Although I enjoyed dancing with him, dating was out of the question. Gran was convinced that all Italian males were not to be trusted. I still missed David Morgan and watched with great expectation each time the door opened, hoping that he would walk in. But he never did.

The summer went by all too quickly. By October, it was time to put the cottage to bed for the winter. Gramps and I took the Lyman out for one last trip around the bay. What a difference a month makes in a resort community. Most of the cottages were tightly shuttered or their windows boarded up against the fierce winter storms yet to come. Floating docks were pulled onto shore, and boats sat securely on their trailers. It was all rather sad . . . the end of a season that had been filled with much activity and laughter. The bay was quiet. There was a nip in the air, and the wind picked up as we returned to the dock. Back in the cottage, Gran had made a pot of hot chocolate. Tossing my jacket on a chair, I flopped down on the sofa. As hard as I tried, I just couldn't shake my melancholy mood.

The closing of the cottage became an annual ritual. Weather permitting, I would find my way back to the lighthouse to spend some quiet time on the rocks. Oftentimes the wind was cold and strong from the north. I would stand, huddled against the massive base for protection while the waves crashed on the rocks below. My eyes lingered on the old stone mansion at the end of the peninsula, and I wondered about the family that found comfort behind its thick walls. If I turned to look in the opposite direction toward the woods, I couldn't help but remember my magical time with David Morgan. It still hurt. So I continued to focus on the house or on the ferry that continued to carry passengers to Kelleys Island until the lake became thick with ice.

School started for CeCe and me, and life fell into a routine of classes, sports, and boys . . . mostly boys. Vanessa and her boyfriend, Danny, had graduated in June. Danny had enrolled in a Community College in a neighboring town, majoring in marketing and merchandising. He'd worked in his dad's store since he was old enough to put cereal boxes on the shelves. It was understood that someday he would take over his dad's business. Vanessa graduated from beauty school and worked in her mom's shop, but she still had time to hang out with us on the weekends.

Gran called Vanessa a hussy and a flirt with a wandering eye. Perhaps she was right. Vanessa never could stay interested in one guy for very long. Sure enough, by Christmas, she'd found someone older and better looking and had broken up with Danny.

Knowing what it was like to be dumped by the person of your dreams, my heart ached for him. It only seemed natural to invite him to basketball games and dances. It wasn't dating, just helping a friend recover from heartache. But adolescent hormones took over. By the Junior Prom, I had his class ring wrapped in pink angora. Gran was furious. I'm not sure what upset her more . . . that I was going steady or that Danny was Italian. She hadn't liked Tony Marelli either, the few times he'd stopped by the cottage. Gran claimed that Italian men were fast with the ladies. I should find a nice English fella, like David Morgan—if she only knew.

Our senior year went by in a flurry of parties. Uncle Lionel insisted that I attend college, even though I just wanted to marry Danny and have babies. The funds from the sale of my parent's house had been set aside for college, and Uncle Lionel said that I could go to any school in the country. But I wanted to stay close to Danny, so I enrolled in The Ohio State University.

CHAPTER 12

The top was down on my Mustang, and the only thing visible in the rearview mirror was my long turquoise scarf fluttering in the wind. I was embarking on a new adventure. The road south to OSU seemed straight and narrow and without any foreseeable obstacles. I needed this time away from Cedar Hill. Gran had wanted to load all my things in their car so she could get me settled-in and organized, but this was something I needed to do for myself. This was a new beginning, and it felt good. The powerful little car raced ahead, taking me to a new life and new challenges, and I was ready.

Being on my own and living in a dorm was a new experience. I was surprised to find I was an even better student than I'd been in high school. My relationship with Danny continued. Even Gran had come around and admitted he was a good catch, saying that everyone had to eat, and Capelli's was the only grocery in town. Being a couple was comfortable. Neither of us made demands on the other, and since Danny had rented an apartment in one of the old Victorian houses in town, it was also convenient.

Mom wouldn't have approved. After all it wasn't the exciting, passionate love she and Dad had known. But I'd already experienced that kind of love with David Morgan, and that raging bonfire had blown itself out with the first strong wind. Comfort and security was definitely better, and Danny and I planned our future together.

I was surprised to see Winston Montgomery III in one of my business classes. I hadn't seen him since the funeral, and Uncle Lionel seldom talked about his nephew. He'd been thrown out of every east coast Ivy League school he attended, and this was his last chance or his father was cutting him off. He probably wouldn't have, but the threat was enough to sober-up Winston. With my help he was getting through his classes, though not without a struggle. He had his own apartment off-campus, and I finally had the opportunity to introduce him to Vanessa on one of her visits. She'd been using me as a way of getting in with the college crowd without actually going to college. They had a thing going on for a while, and she would often spend the weekend with him. It couldn't have been called a relationship—at least not in Winston's eyes. She wasn't someone he could take home to Mummy. But it was the time of sex, drugs, rock and roll, and they had fun while it lasted. Then Winston grew bored and moved on to someone else. We had several classes together, and I spent many hours at his apartment studying. One of our friends started calling him Win, and it stuck. I thought the name suited his fun-loving personality better than the stuffy Winston.

Our senior year came too quickly, at least for me. I had loved school and was planning to go on for my Masters in Business Administration. Win would graduate as well, with my help, and in the process we had become great friends.

Finally, Spring break of 1971 was upon us. There were six of us who hung-out together. We wanted to go somewhere more exciting than Florida. Steven convinced Win that Las Vegas would be a lot more exciting, and it would give him a chance to test some of his mathematical theories. Win was the only one of us with any cash, so he got rooms in a motel along The Strip. When we weren't in one of the many casinos, we could be found hanging-out around the pool, drinking and smoking pot.

Win pulled the flask out of the cooler sitting between our lounge chairs and took a swig. "I can't believe graduation is just a few months away."

"Why, you hate school with a passion?"

"My mother's planned a summer vacation for us. We're visiting a few of her friends along the east coast. One month alone will be spent on Cape Cod at the estate of her best friend from school. She's determined to snare a Vassar girl for me. All the Montgomery men have married Vassar girls. Believe me, our money will buy the best of the lot."

"Well, what if you don't like her?"

Win took a long swallow from the flask. "I don't have to like her—I just have to marry her."

"That's barbaric."

"What about you and Danny? I don't see you running home to the man of your dreams every weekend."

"That's different. We're in love."

Win raised his flask in a salute. "Is it?"

I grabbed the flask and took a sip, then a mouthful and swallowed. I leaned back and thought about his words.

I too, dreaded graduation. It meant the end of my freedom and moving back home until my marriage to Danny. Even the thought of the wedding didn't seem to make me happy. I always had an excuse when Danny suggested that we go shopping for an engagement ring.

"Maybe you're right. Marrying Danny is safe. He'll make a good husband."

Win got up and headed toward the pool. He turned just before jumping in. "What we both need is to take control of our lives."

The freedom of Las Vegas was exciting, but Win and I seemed to be in a drunken stupor most of the time. I don't know exactly how it happened, but by the end of the week we had walked down the aisle of one of those cute little wedding chapels, nestled under the boughs of huge old trees in an oasis of casinos. I left Las Vegas as Mrs. Winston Montgomery III . . . and Mummy wasn't going to be happy!

CHAPTER 13

To say no one was happy was putting it mildly. Gran was furious. I had given up a nice, stable young man like Danny for the town playboy. Vanessa was mad, too. Apparently she'd had hopes of getting Win back. But Win's mother, Victoria, was the angriest of all. She yelled and screamed and cried and wanted the marriage annulled. But we hadn't told anyone until after graduation. By then we'd been living as man and wife for several months. We'd been reveling in our feelings of independence. Win's father's reaction was more practical. He stated that Win had made his bed and would now have to lie in it. Everyone else would just have to deal with the situation. And by 'everyone else,' Win's father meant Victoria, known by some as Muffy. I always thought that her old school nickname was somewhat of a contradiction. Muffy sounded cute and soft and cuddly—and Victoria was none of those things.

Later that week, Win and his father sat at the far end of the drawing room with their after dinner cocktails and cigars, leaving me alone with Victoria. She was always impeccably dressed, makeup perfect, and not a hair out of place. I never knew what her real color was, since the bleached blond was obviously not her own. I sat on some kind of French style chair, too ornate to be comfortable. Victoria stood in front of me in a black silk suit, with her hands clasped in front of her. She looked down on me with a superior air. "Olivia, dear, had we been made your guardians, I would have sent you to a proper finishing school as soon as possible after the unfortunate demise of your family. There, you would have learned the essential qualities needed to become a lady, and thus make a suitable marriage into a fine family."

Her implication was that my upbringing and education had been less than acceptable, and I couldn't let that go unchallenged. Holding my head up, I looked her straight in the eyes and very calmly said, "Victoria, I may not have had the privilege of attending a finishing school or been taught the finer points of being a lady, but I believe that I still managed to make a good marriage, in a fine family."

She glared at me with one of her "Don't mess with me" looks. Then with a huff, she turned to leave, hesitating at the door. "I will see you here, tomorrow morning at ten o'clock . . . sharp!"

She left the room, and I could hear the clack of her heels echoing across the marble foyer. Her husband stood with his elbow resting on the corner of the fireplace mantle. He'd been observing without a word. I looked at him apprehensively. But he only smiled and winked. Perhaps I had a friend in the enemy camp.

Victoria must have taken her husband literally because she dealt with me as a general dealt with his troops. The privilege of choosing a Vassar daughter-in-law had been denied her, so she was determined to create her own. She set up her own boot camp, although it was in the disguise of a stately stone Georgian mansion. Our drills consisted of how to set a proper table, which silverware to use with which dish, how to handle the servants, and how to mingle without offending anyone. I had instruction in etiquette and proper posture, deportment and diction, and most important of all . . . which length of pearls to wear.

I had loved my hip-hugging bellbottoms, hot pants, mini-skirts, and see-through blouses. I thought they made me look taller and set-off my tiny waist and large breasts. I also loved the attention I got from every male who set eyes on me. My lingerie came from Fredericks of Hollywood, and I felt terribly sexy and feminine. However, Victoria didn't approve of any of it. It wasn't the proper attire of a Montgomery wife. So, I gave in to her demands, and adopted the fashions of an older generation.

She was relentless. My only chance to be myself was when I went home to the lodge.

During the 1890s, the first Montgomery had bought several thousand acres of hilly, wooded land on the edge of Cedar Hill, about halfway between Cleveland and Columbus, Ohio. He built a large hunting lodge of stone and logs, with a wide front porch overlooking one of several lakes. It was a bastion of male camaraderie. Weeks at a time were spent hunting and fishing, smoking cigars and telling stories in the billiard room or the grand hall. The lodge remained a haven of testosterone until the early 1920s, when the town began to grow and the Montgomery land and money were available for expansion. The family took up permanent residency in the palatial stone mansion, leaving the old hunting lodge for occasional guests. I guess we were considered to be in exile, but Win and I made the lodge our home, and I loved the somewhat shabby décor . . . such a welcome difference from the formal elegance of the main house.

We enjoyed horseback riding through the hills and skinny-dipping in the spring-fed lake. We were pretty evenly matched tennis players, and I loved Win's world of money and privilege.

Victoria, feeling cheated out of a huge lavish wedding for her only son, insisted on a formal reception at the country club, to be held the third Saturday in July. A whirlwind of activity ensued as the General planned her campaign. She insisted that I be a part of the whole operation. Not because she valued or wanted my opinion, but because it was another venue for her tutelage. I received constant reminders that my upbringing had been lax.

"Olivia! Stand up straight, be proud—you're a Montgomery now. Olivia! Do not slouch—your mother never slouched. She should have been stricter with you. Olivia! Hold your head up—you're short enough, as it is." To remind me of how a lady should carry herself, she made me spend the days walking around with a book on my head. But I never knew anyone who walked around looking like they were wearing a back brace. I just didn't feel natural. I soon felt like a puppet . . . and Victoria was very good at pulling my strings.

And then there was also the discussion of what I would wear to our reception. Victoria planned a shopping trip to her favorite stores in Chicago. Here, I put my foot down, and insisted that I would choose my own dress, and that it would be appropriate. I remembered Mom's beautiful gowns and how I'd carefully hung the zippered bags in Gran's attic all those years ago, wondering if I would ever have the chance to wear any of them. Because the hippie movement was in full swing and there wasn't much structure to clothing, much less evening gowns, Victoria was beside herself with anxiety. Maybe she thought I would appear in some peasant dress with flowers in my hair.

Gran and I headed to her attic to search through the closet containing Mom's clothes. Finding a gown that would do nicely, Gran offered to bring it to the house on the day of the big event. She cradled it against her chest as she stared off, looking at the attic rafters and seeing a different world beyond. Her soft words were more for herself than me. "It shouldn't have been such a shock since Fred followed the war news daily and watched the progress of General

Eisenhower and General McArthur. The week before he left for Norfolk, Virginia, he talked about getting engaged to his longtime girlfriend, Sally, and would we help him pick out a ring. Leonard and I couldn't have been happier. We had gone through school together with Sally's parents and years later watched our children play together, attend the same schools and then to our delight ... date. It had always been our dream that they would marry and have children of their own, and we would all live as one big happy family. Fred presented Sally with the ring at his going away dinner, held at our home the evening before he left. For the next few years we worked with Sally and her parents planning the wedding. Sally already seemed like the daughter we never had and she was included in all of our celebrations."

Gran paused and walked over to the dormer window, as if she could see into the past. "I don't know why it never occurred to me that Fred didn't seem to care about the details or talk about the plans he had for the two of them. I realized later that Fred's references to Sally made her seem more like a sister than his future wife. Six months before he was due to be discharged the letters stopped. He said it was hard to find the time to write and would see us soon."

"I'm sorry, Gran, you must have been worried."

"I'll never forget that day. He'd called early that morning to say his train would be arriving around three in the afternoon and could we pick him up. He asked that Leonard and I come alone because he had a surprise for us. I was so excited. My son was coming home. I cleaned his room, put fresh linen on the bed, made his favorite cherry pie. I put a pot roast in the oven before we left for the station. The train was just pulling in as we began to make our way to the center of the platform. We both looked back and forth along each car at the disembarking passengers, but Fred wasn't among them. Then, just as we were about to give up, he appeared in a doorway at the rear of the train. He waved as he descended the steps, then stopped and turned back to help someone behind him. What a gentleman, I thought to myself as we walked toward him. The woman stepping onto the platform was lovely. No wonder Fred wanted to help her. She was wearing a very fashionable—and obviously expensive—tailored suit of periwinkle blue with a matching hat set at a jaunty angle. Her pumps and handbag were as black as her hair, which had been pulled-up in a roll under her hat. As we got closer I could see that her eyes were the same shade of blue as her suit. She wasn't just attractive . . . she was beautiful. Perhaps the most beautiful woman I had ever seen."

Suddenly, Gran turned toward me with a look of anger that I hadn't seen on her face in a very long time. It was as if she saw someone else standing before her. "Fred smiled and took her hand and began walking toward us. 'Hello, Mother. Father, it's wonderful to see you.' He dropped her hand and put his arms around me. Then turned and shook his father's hand. 'Mom, Dad, I would like you to meet Maureen. My wife.' At that moment I died inside . . . and I could never forgive her."

CHAPTER 14

Our big day arrived with a clear blue sky, and it was already hot when we pulled up to the clubhouse amongst a dozen trucks and vans. An army of workers were unloading boxes of flowers, and the band members struggled with their instruments. General Washington himself couldn't have done a better job than Victoria's command of the preparations.

At one o'clock Victoria and I arrived at Flo's Beauty Salon where we were able to relax and be pampered under the skillful hands of Flo and Vanessa. Victoria's medium length blond hair was piled on top of her head in an elegant mass of curls, while Vanessa pulled my long, straight, shiny black hair back from my face and created long ringlets that hung gracefully down my back. Vanessa had graciously offered to come to the house an hour early to do my makeup and help me dress, and it reminded me of old times when we were little girls and loved to play dress-up in her mother's bedroom.

When our hair was deemed perfect, Vanessa followed Victoria and me back to the Montgomery home. Victoria had given us the use of one of the many guestrooms. Vanessa soon had the beautiful floral-papered room looking like a Hollywood star's dressing room, with clothes and cosmetics laid out for us. The adjoining marble bathroom was ready for my makeup application.

An hour later Victoria appeared in the doorway for a progress check, wearing a simple but elegant beige silk gown with a beaded halter neckline and beautiful diamond and ruby earrings. She walked in as Vanessa was lowering my gown carefully over my head. The silver lame' fell in shimmering folds, as soft and iridescent as butterfly wings.

Victoria let out an audible gasp as she took in the scene. "Where did you get such a exquisite creation?"

I guess that meant she approved. "It was my mother's."

Victoria hurried across the room and pushed Vanessa out of the way. "Here let me zip it. You must not snare the fabric." I could feel Victoria looking for the label. The name Mainbocher didn't mean anything to me, but apparently it did to Victoria as she let out a very unladylike snort and replied. "Where did your mother find this? Some second-hand shop, no doubt."

Years later, I would learn that Mainbocher was the first successful American couturier in 1930s Paris. He had been a favorite of the Duchess of Windsor and had designed a very similar gown for Her Highness. He achieved worldwide fame in 1937, when he designed her wedding gown. In 1940, he left Paris for New York to open a salon next door to Tiffany. My grandmother had purchased the gown as part of my mother's trousseau.

The image reflected in the mirror was that of a Greek goddess. The soft draping of the gown fell to the floor with a little train at the back. The narrow straps held a deep v-neckline, and the plunging open back ended in soft folds at my waist. Vanessa helped me with silver high-heeled sandals that made me taller.

Victoria stood back, smiling her approval. "All it needs is my pearls . . . I'll be right back."

"Don't bother, Victoria. I've brought my own."

She followed me to the dressing table and a beautiful leather case. Turning the small key in the lock, I pressed a tiny button, releasing the top of the box to reveal a magnificent pearl dog-collar. Intricate bars of gold and diamonds held the ten rows of pearls in place on each side, while the back bars and clasp were even more ornate. The bottom of the box contained a drawer, where a long strand of larger pearls lay protected in the satin lining.

"I won't be wearing that one, it will only detract from the beauty of the dress. Don't you agree?"

She only nodded as she watched me carefully remove the choker from its holder, then I handed it to her to put around my neck. Adjusting the rows of pearls before the mirror, I glanced up to watch Victoria. She'd picked up the box and was looking at the small gold plate on the front. I saw her bewildered expression as she read the name . . . Cartier.

She came back to my side and gazed at me in the mirror. "I admired that necklace on the one occasion I saw your mother wearing it. She had a wonderfully long neck that could carry it. You look like her."

That was the greatest compliment Victoria could ever give me, and I almost kissed her . . . but I didn't. Leaving Vanessa to get dressed, we went downstairs for the pictures that were to be taken before we left for the club.

Victoria rushed ahead to get the photographer in place. She wanted a staircase shot.

Hesitating, for just a moment at the top of the stairs, I looked down at my husband standing in the hall below. Win was so handsome in his tuxedo. He watched me glide down the stairs, with the small train floating behind me. His smile told me he approved, and he got down on one knee, taking my hand. "My beautiful lady. Will you do me the honor of accepting this ring, as my token of love and the great privilege of having you as my wife, for the rest of our lives?" He slipped a ring on my finger. I gazed down at the biggest diamond I had ever seen.

"I hope my finger is strong enough to hold this thing up!" Everyone laughed, but I felt suddenly nervous, and wished I had said something romantic.

I felt like Cinderella, and my prince was charming and attentive the whole evening. My carriage was the Montgomery's long black limousine, and my gown shimmered in the light as I was helped out of the car. Win looked proud. He took my arm and guided me into the packed clubhouse. It appeared that all of Cedar Hill was in attendance. The applause was deafening as we entered the room.

The food was beautifully prepared, but I was too nervous to eat. Later, after the dinner, Win took my hand and guided me to the dance floor. Skillfully leading me around the room, he bent down and whispered in my ear. "Are you wearing anything under this dress?"

"No."

"You little minx! I will have to take care of you later!"

Win's father danced with me next, and then Uncle Lionel cut in. "Your father would be proud. Close your eyes, Olivia. Imagine that you're being held by your father, and he is telling you what a wonderful young woman you have become." As he guided me around the dance floor, I felt that Dad was with me. I loved Uncle Lionel for giving me that moment.

Gran and Gramps seemed to be having a good time at a table with their friends. But every time I looked, Gran kept wiping her eyes with the lace handkerchief she always had ready, tucked in the sleeve of her dress.

It was a beautiful, wonderful evening with candles and fragrant flowers everywhere. There were even islands of flowers and candles floating in the pool. We danced on the patio under a million stars in the warm summer sky.

I fell in love that night. Up until then it was a marriage of convenience. It was a way for me to officially put David Morgan in my past, and a way to walk away from Danny Capelli. I was happy and looked forward to all the wonderful years ahead with Win at my side. Even Victoria's comments to anyone who would listen, about how she had created me, couldn't mar the magic. At the evening's end, before my carriage turned back into a pumpkin, I found my way to an isolated corner of the patio and looked up into that glorious night sky. I felt my mother smiling down on me. I whispered, "Thank you, Mom, for being my Fairy Godmother and giving me this wonderful gown to wear. I wish you could be here. I love you." Walking back through the open French doors, I hesitated and turned, looking back at the fairytale patio. It really was magic. With tears in my eyes and a lump in my throat, I turned and walked back into the room.

It was time for my prince and me to leave. I sought out Vanessa to thank her for all her help. Then I gave her and CeCe a hug and told them that I would see them soon. Uncle Lionel, the only one who had been truly happy about our marriage, had given us a three-week trip to Hawaii as a wedding gift.

I had three fabulous weeks with Win, making love in our luxurious suite with the ocean view. When we weren't having sex, we played at being tourists. He knew how to have fun and we enjoyed everything the Big Island had to offer. We snorkeled with Manta Rays, toured coffee plantations and marveled at the majestic waterfalls along the Hamakua Coast. I was surprised one day when Win rented a sailboat. Knowing how to sail was something I hadn't known about him. We had a wonderful time sailing along the Kona Coast and we fantasized about one day buying a boat and sailing around the world.

We walked on black sand beaches and explored Kilauea. Each night there was a luau and exotic foods to sample.

Win made friends easily and was the life of every party. If there was one thing I would learn from Win, it was how to have fun. The Montgomery money was free-flowing and I realized that it could buy happiness after all.

Our trip to paradise ended all too quickly, and we returned home to reality. Two weeks after our return, Win's father called him to his office for a father and son discussion. Now that Win had the responsibility of a wife and hopefully a family soon, he needed to settle down and enter the real world. That meant a job, and he was to report the following Monday to the Vice President of Operations at the hospital. I knew what he really wanted was to keep an eye on his son. It would be Win's first job. I don't think he really took his father's implied threats seriously. Secretly, I agreed that Win needed to grow up, settle down, and not see the world as his playground. The hospital was probably the best place to start.

Win's grandfather had been a doctor. Years ago, he'd taken some of the Montgomery land on the edge of town and built the Montgomery Hospital. He continued with his large medical practice and hired a cousin, Morris, to manage the administrative aspects of the hospital. Things went along pretty well until old Morris began spending more time in affairs with the nurses, instead of the affairs of the hospital. Cousin Morris got the boot when Winston II graduated from Harvard. Win's father ran a pretty tight ship, and the hospital prospered—although everyone knew that Winston II had also drifted from his homeport with the occasional alluring and agreeable nurse.

With Win gone during the day, I had a lot of free time on my hands. Victoria insisted I accompany her to Garden Club meetings, the local Woman's Club, and all her various charities. It was supposed to be part of my education in being the proper Montgomery wife. Although I found the meetings interesting, I couldn't see myself making a career out of the Montgomery social obligations.

When I poured out my frustrations to my father-in-law after Christmas dinner, he smiled at me and nodded his head in understanding. "I've expected this, Olivia. You're far too intelligent to be happy with a gaggle of old women. Besides, it's a waste of your education. I have an idea, but I need some time to work out the details."

CHAPTER 15

Two weeks later Winston stopped by the lodge in the middle of the afternoon. His assistant of twenty years had, for some time, been talking about retiring, and Winston had made him an offer that was too good to refuse. I was more than qualified for the position, and he thought it was just the challenge I was looking for. Although I didn't realize it at the time, accepting the job would take my life down many new roads . . . not all of them smooth.

The month I worked with my predecessor before he moved to Florida went by quickly. By his last day, I felt confident I could handle the job. Being able to have lunch with my husband at the hospital was an added bonus.

We found that driving separately was easier. I had to leave for work earlier in the morning and often got home late. Win had bought a new red Corvette convertible. I was still driving my Mustang.

That is, until Victoria cornered me after one of our Sunday dinners. "Olivia, dear, you have got to stop driving that old Ford. It doesn't fit the Montgomery image."

The very thought that she would attack my Mustang was unthinkable, and of course, I rebelled. "Then how come Win gets to drive a Corvette?"

"That is different! He is a man. Besides, it's new, and it suits him!"

"My father gave me my Mustang. I won't give it up!"

"Then put it in the garage! You got it when you were sixteen, Olivia. It's time to grow up!"

"What do you suggest I drive?"

"I'll take you to the Cadillac dealership and let you pick out anything you want."

"A Cadillac? That's an old person's car!"

"Just do it, Olivia!"

The following Saturday, I left to search for my car before dear Muffy was up and about. I didn't want her tagging along telling me which car fit my new image. The owner of the dealership said Victoria had called to say she would be bringing me by. I explained I was on my own—Mrs. Montgomery had other plans. After looking at every car in the showroom and on the back lot, I slumped down in a chair feeling defeated. That's when I noticed a truck parked across the street. The car carrier was being unloaded. The last car to come off the truck was a yellow convertible.

Running over to the window, I pointed to the truck. "What's that?"

"That's an Eldorado. I ordered it for my wife. There's also a nice white one that was just unloaded."

"I want the yellow one!"

Win had dropped me off to pick up my new car at the dealership after work on a day when we knew that his parents would be at home. I was used to the dexterity of my high-spirited little Mustang. In comparison, driving the Caddy was like maneuvering a boat through the city streets. I honked the horn several times as I drove up the long driveway. I stopped just as Win ushered his parents through the front door. Dear Muffy had a horrified expression, with one hand resting over her heart, as she descended the steps. "Olivia! What have you done? It looks like a huge yellow canary!"

The top was down, and I felt exuberant having one-upped my mother-in-law. I threw my arms out to emphasize the car's enormous length. "It's a Cadillac, Victoria!"

Her face turned a very unladylike shade of crimson. "This isn't what I had in mind!"

"You said I could pick out anything on the lot," I said in my most innocent voice.

Winston doubled over in laughter, as he turned to his wife. "She's got you, Muffy. This round goes to Olivia!"

After that life fell into a routine. I rarely saw Gran and Gramps except for holidays or special occasions, although I continued the yearly ritual of opening the cottage in the spring and putting it to bed in the fall.

CeCe and Danny Capelli became engaged at Christmas. They set their wedding date to be the last week in July. Vanessa and I were asked to be in the wedding party. For the next six months, the three of us girls spent as much time as we could on the arrangements. It felt just like old times.

Vanessa had been dating one of Win's cousins on-and-off since our reception. Knowing what the Montgomery women thought about marrying the 'right' girls, I knew the relationship wouldn't last. Vanessa still worked at her mom's beauty shop, but she wasn't very happy with the amount of money she was making. I suggested she consider enrolling in a nearby secretarial school. Perhaps I could get her a job at the hospital when she finished.

And then another Christmas was upon us. The lodge nestled under a blanket of snow, and we enjoyed cross-country skiing and ice-skating on the frozen lake. On a cold snowy Sunday, Win and I went out to search the countryside for the perfect Christmas tree. After Win cut it down, we gently laid it on the sleigh that had been taking the family trees back to the main house for generations. I felt so alive listening to the sleigh bells as the horse pulled Win and I through the pine forest. Giant flakes of snow fell from the sky. I laughed as they drifted onto my eyelashes and tickled my nose. Our breath billowed before us in the cold afternoon air. The horse nodded his head and sighed, seeming to enjoy the outing as well while he followed the well-worn trail back to the lodge.

CeCe was pregnant with twins, and I had loaned Vanessa the money for secretarial school. Gran and Gramps didn't seem to mind that I wasn't around much. I think they both knew that my life was perfect. And it nearly was. The only thing that would have made my life complete would have been if I, too, were pregnant. I loved my job and it had become my child. I focused all my energy on the day-to-day operation of the hospital.

Winston had delegated more and more responsibility to me. This gave him more time for his beloved golf and various medical conferences around the world. Win hadn't been happy with his initial job, so his father kept moving him from one department to another, hoping that something would interest him. But, I knew it was work itself that Win found so distasteful. Despite that, his father and I tried to keep him busy with whatever job we could find for the moment.

At the end of April, CeCe gave birth to twin boys, and I became a godmother. How I loved holding those tiny little boys. I couldn't help but think about Mom and what she must have felt holding her own twins. As time passed, I longed even more for a child of my own.

May was the time to open the cottage after its long winter nap, and I once again enjoyed springtime on Marblehead. Gran seemed to be mellowing over the years—or perhaps it was just that her criticism waned in comparison to Victoria's acid tongue. We actually had conversations. For the first time, I felt comfortable opening my heart and allowing her to see who I was, including how much I wanted a family of my own. Gran assured me that when God was ready, he would give me a child. Perhaps it would happen sooner if I went to church.

That didn't make much sense to me. What I needed was for Win and me to have sex more often. The fact was I was spending too much time at the hospital. And after buying a Thoroughbred, Win was spending too much time with his friends at the racetrack. I enjoyed riding my father-in-law's horses through the hundreds of acres of rolling hills we called home, but I didn't enjoy the atmosphere at the track. And I certainly didn't like Win's new friends.

The winter of 1973 was upon us, and once the snow began to fall, it seemed to continue with only short periods between storms. The only good thing was that Win and I were forced to spend more time at the lodge before a roaring fire in the huge stone fireplace. The frequent storms took out power lines, and we were sometimes left in the dark. The main house had its own generator for such occasions, but the lodge had never been deemed worthy of such an extravagance. We kept warm with the aid of the fireplace and a huge old wood-burning stove that still maintained its place in the kitchen. We slept under a pile of warm comforters and began to rekindle the old passion that had nearly been forgotten. I thought it a wonderful time, and on Christmas morning, I gave Win what I thought was the most wonderful gift of all . . . I might be pregnant.

Win didn't seem very excited, but it didn't matter because I was happy enough for the both of us. The months flew by in a flurry of activity and excitement. Winston made arrangements for me to take a month off after the baby was born. He even tried to have patience with Win since his son was finally giving him a grandchild.

After painting the nursery a sunny yellow and having new carpeting installed, I looked forward to shopping for baby furniture.

Victoria, however, had other plans. Once more, she took over, leaving me no say in the matter. I returned home from work one day to find Victoria and Win admiring their work . . . the room was done. There were even little socks and undershirts in the dresser drawers. Neither of them could understand why I lost my temper and stormed out of the room. After all, they were only trying to help and to save me all the aggravation of having to find the time in my busy schedule for shopping. I didn't believe Win enjoyed the shopping trips, but only went along to please his mother. As long as he kept in his mother's good graces, he could maintain his lifestyle and his hobbies. And at the moment he wanted another Thoroughbred.

Although I was upset that the planning for the baby's room had been taken away from me, I found solace in keeping to my busy schedule knowing the baby was always with me. I'd begun to feel little flutters, which soon turned to kicks and jabs. This was something the co-conspirators couldn't take away from me, and I reveled in the knowledge that the baby was all mine . . . at least for a few more months.

Victoria was soon absorbed in interviewing nannies and planning for her grandson's enrollment in private schools. She was convinced that there would be another Winston running around the house. Privately, I was hoping for a girl . . . just so I wouldn't have to deal with another Win.

The carefree, fun-loving Win I fell in love with now appeared irresponsible to me. He had wanted to take control of his life, yet he continued to let his mother run it. I wondered if he would ever grow up. What about our son, or would it just be his son?

One Saturday in May, CeCe came by to announce she was pregnant again. We talked about how wonderful it was that we were experiencing this together. Usually, I was too tired after work to do anything, but CeCe often came to the lodge if she could get her mother-in-law to baby-sit the twins. She taught me to crochet, and we spent many happy hours making little blankets and hats.

My doctor occasionally stopped by my office while on his hospital rounds and said my body was made for babies. I was fit-as-a-fiddle and could probably have the little tyke out in the fields and be back working in the afternoon. I didn't feel quite that ambitious, but I was putting in full days and didn't think I would need to take the entire month off Winston had suggested.

I didn't see much of Win. He was searching the country for another horse. Vanessa had graduated from secretarial school, and, as promised, I got her a job in the hospital secretarial pool. She would make more money, with full benefits, and there would be opportunities for advancement. She and I had lunch together as much as possible. Helping her gave me great pleasure.

It was a wonderful time in my life, with my best friends close by, a job that I loved, and a beautiful place to raise our children. Win was rarely home. But when he was, he was happy—which was all that I needed. The only thing missing was that my family wasn't here to share this with me.

CHAPTER 16

By the beginning of June, I was huge and rarely comfortable. I could barely get into or out of a chair without help. I was being kicked and jabbed and was beginning to believe that Victoria might be right. I was having a boy, and he would grow up to be a boxer.

My patience and sense of humor had deserted me, and even CeCe and Vanessa were keeping their distance. Win's happy disposition seemed to be the result of him always having a drink in his hand. It became a great annoyance to me, but then everything seemed to bother me. Then the dream began. It had been almost ten years since that horrible dream plagued me. It came several times a week. Each evening, I dreaded going to bed, in fear that the horrible figure in black would, once again, push me over the cliff, and I would awaken as I hit the rocks below.

The third Saturday was yet another of the countless fundraisers. Win and I were expected to attend and show family support, and of course I was still in training. Victoria never missed a chance to correct me. One would think that being pregnant with her grandchild would allow her to lighten up a little, but it didn't. I never seemed to live up to her expectations. The temperature had been in the 90s all week. I felt like a wilted flower as I dressed in a cool lavender silk gown. It had a low, scooped neckline, an empire waist, and ruching on the bodice that made my already large breasts appear even larger. My ankles were swollen, so I chose a pair of flat silver slippers decorated with pastel colored jewels. The air conditioner in the window wasn't keeping up with the heat in the large room. I was feeling too hot to even think about putting something around my neck, even though I had pulled my long straight hair back in a chignon. I settled for a pair of large silver chandelier earrings and stood before the long mirror, imagining that I looked much as my mother would have looked when she was pregnant with me.

The air-conditioned dining room at the country club was cool and comfortable. I had no appetite and just picked at my meal. Victoria sat on the other side of Win and pushed a glass of white wine toward me. "Here, drink this. You're as restless and fidgety as a mother cat, and I want you calm for mingling later." She was in another one of her moods. I didn't know whether it was due to my being inattentive or Win's excessive drinking. The baby had been kicking all evening. I shifted my position, hoping to make us both more comfortable. I knew it irritated Victoria, but I didn't know what else to do except excuse myself and retire to the Ladies Lounge, which would have been unacceptable.

Win followed his father to the bar for an after-dinner cigar. That was Victoria's cue to begin mingling, and I put on my public smile and joined her. She looked stunning in a simple, but elegant, long white gown that shouted designer and expensive, and her aristocratic bearing caused heads to turn. She did her job well. After an hour or so of following her around the room, I excused myself and went back to the table. I hadn't been there for more than a minute or two when Winston came over, asking for the whereabouts of Win.

"I don't know. The last time I saw him was when he left with you. Is something wrong?"

He seemed puzzled by my remark. "We had one drink and a cigar in the bar. Then he said he was going to check on you. Are you sure you haven't seen him?"

A sick feeling crept into my stomach. It must have shown on my face as I shook my head at Winston. He looked down at me with sympathetic eyes. "I'm sorry, Olivia, you deserve better than this. But I can't say it's going to get any easier."

His words echoed in my head as he walked back to the bar. I had no idea what he meant, but I needed to find Win. Walking over to the French doors, I looked out onto the patio and didn't see anyone, but decided to take a closer look. As the door opened a wall of oppressive hot, humid night air blocked my way. I just knew Win wouldn't be out in that heat. Closing the door, I turned and headed toward the smaller dining room that was used on a daily basis, and was now closed for the night. A frown crinkled my brow. I was being silly. Winston's words shouldn't have caused me alarm. But they had and that sick feeling was still in the pit of my stomach. The door eased open silently, and I peered into the darkened room. Light from the outside patio cast a soft glow over Win and a tall blonde woman. She was wearing a short white chiffon cocktail dress, and her hair fell to her shoulders in a mass of large curls. They seemed to be arguing.

I must have made a sound. She saw me first, then Win turned and exclaimed, "Olivia, what are you doing here? I thought you were working the room with Mother."

The woman whispered something to Win before turning and walking toward me. Her large brown eyes reminded me of a doe, with a haunted look about them. She was beautiful. For some reason I felt sorry for her as she glided past me and out the door without a word, leaving behind a soft floral scent of expensive perfume.

Win's behavior had worried his father and now it worried me. And thrown into the mix was anger, but Victoria's lessons demanded that I remain in control. "I'm tired. The baby is trying to beat its way out. And your father is looking for you."

Win came to my side, but the sick feeling was still with me. "Who is she, Win? What is this about?"

"She's a nurse, and she's in trouble. She was asking for my help. That's all there is to it."

"I don't understand."

"She had an affair with a doctor. She's pregnant, and she doesn't know what to do. She already has a two-year-old son, and the doc is married."

No wonder she had a haunted look. "What about the boy's father?"

"He didn't want anything to do with her after she told him she was pregnant. He's out of the picture."

I could almost feel sorry for her. Except that I knew there was more to it, and Win was hiding something. My mind raced for possible answers. "Do you know the doctor's name?"

He put his arm around me, guiding me out of the room and back toward the bar. "No, I don't." The smell of alcohol was strong on his breath, and I wondered how much he'd had to drink.

Winston was sitting at the bar talking with a few friends. He stood as we approached. "Would you excuse us, Olivia? I need to talk to Win . . . alone."

"Sure, I'll just go look for Victoria."

Entering the dining room, I saw Victoria talking to several of her friends from the Garden Club. I was too tired for more idle conversation, so I found my way to the lounge and a comfortable chair to wait out the remainder of the evening. The baby seemed to relax as well and gave me a few precious minutes of comfort.

It was about ten o'clock when Win came up to me with teeth clenched and red-faced. He was obviously angry about something.

He took the last swallow of his drink and set the glass down on a side table with enough force to turn heads. Then he pulled me up roughly from the chair. "Come on, we're going home!"

That was fine with me. I was tired and had been ready to go home for the past hour. Between tossing and turning every night trying to find a comfortable position—and the nightmares—I hadn't been getting much sleep. Win had long since moved into one of the guestrooms, claiming my restlessness disturbed him.

The valet brought the shiny red convertible to the front entrance. I walked around to the driver's side, startled when Win grabbed my arm. "Where do you think you're going? This is my car, and I'm driving it!"

"No! Win, you're drunk! Please, let me drive!"

He continued to push me away. The valet was still holding the door open and began in a sheepish voice. "Perhaps, she's right, Mr. Montgomery. You ought to let her drive this time."

This only made Win angrier. "Shut up! Or you'll be looking for a new job!"

He pulled me around the car and opened the passenger door. "Get in, Olivia!"

"I'll ride with your parents, but I won't go with you!"

Win's face turned red. He raised his hand to slap me then stopped. "You're my wife . . . and you will go with me!" With that he shoved me into the car and slammed the door closed.

I'd never seen him like this. His driving wasn't bad in town, but he became reckless as we reached the back roads. He hadn't spoken since we left, but all of a sudden he began to laugh. At first it was more of a chuckle, but then it turned into a sinister, seemingly uncontrollable laugh. He turned the wheel from side to side and forced the powerful car from one side of the empty road to the other. I guessed that he was trying to scare me. Fear for the safety of our baby consumed me, and I begged him to slow down. But that only added fuel to his fire. My stomach was too huge for the seatbelt, and I was being tossed back and forth against the seat. The top was down, and I tried desperately to hang on to the side of the car. We were going so fast, we seemed to fly around the next bend. I screamed to Win to slow down for the bridge ahead—but he only laughed.

CHAPTER 17

Familiar voices, far off in the distance, and a terrible pain in my head brought me back from the darkness. I tried to focus, but there were only shadows behind a foggy curtain.

"She opened her eyes. Look, her eyes are open. Get the nurse!"

It was Gran's voice. Then I felt a squeeze of my hand. Turning my head, I saw her through the fog, then Gramps standing behind her.

I could see them more clearly now and I tried to talk, but there was a tube down my throat.

Gran pulled the handkerchief out of her sleeve, dabbing at her eyes. "You're going to be okay, honey. The good Lord has spared you."

I saw that my left arm and leg were in casts hanging from some sort of apparatus.

Remembering the horrible drive home with Win, I looked up at Gramps with a question in my eyes. He, too, had tears in his eyes as he spoke. "It was a terrible accident, but you survived. We've been with you these past two days, praying that you would recover. It's mighty good to see those beautiful blue eyes again."

He had said accident, but I didn't remember an accident. I remembered being tossed around in the car and afraid for my baby. I moved my hand from Gran's and touched my flat stomach.

"They tried real hard, Honey . . . but they couldn't save her."

Her. A girl. Win and I had a daughter. Through the pain in my head I remembered Gran's words. 'They couldn't save her.'

No, it wasn't true. My baby was alive. But one glance at Gran and Gramps told me more than words ever could. I felt the tears streaming down my cheeks. My heart already knew I would never hold my baby.

Gran reached over with her lace edged handkerchief and wiped the tears from my cheeks.

Dr. Stevenson walked into the room and asked my grandparents to wait outside for a few moments. He was our most skilled surgeon, and the Chief of Staff. He was usually a jovial man, but now he was serious with an uncharacteristic frown. I knew then that I must be in pretty bad shape.

"You've given us all a pretty good scare, Olivia. Winston has been beside himself . . . he was afraid he would have to train a new assistant."

All I could mange to get out was a faint groan.

"I'm sorry, Olivia. I should have known you aren't ready for my jokes, but Winston is going to have to do without you for quite some time. Nearly every part of your body was affected. You were thrown from the car and landed in the rocky riverbed. It's a miracle you survived."

I tried to talk to him with my eyes, but I wasn't getting through. I wanted to know about Win and thought the worst, since no one had mentioned him. Dr. Stevenson looked at me with sad eyes and spoke, "I know you have a hundred questions. I'll be happy to answer any of the medical ones in a day or two, when I feel we can safely remove the tube. The personal questions will have to wait until Win stops by, which I'm sure he'll do once he hears you're awake at last."

So, he was alive, but I couldn't dredge up any joy in the fact.

I spent the next two weeks in the ICU. Once the tube was taken out, I could begin to talk and ask questions, and deal with the answers. Winston stopped by twice a day to check on me. On one of those occasions, he told me it was the valet who, fearing for my safety, found him and explained the situation. Winston immediately found Victoria. They left minutes later and came upon the wreck as they reached the bridge. They could see that the car had hit the guardrail and flipped over landing front-end down in the river. Winston sent Victoria ahead to call for help, while he slid down the embankment to get to the car. It was resting in a vertical position against the bridge. Win was still strapped in his seat, and pinned against the steering wheel with a nasty gash across his forehead and cheek, but he was still alive. I had been ejected out of the car. With the light of the full moon, Winston found me unconscious in shallow water at the river's edge. He stayed with me, holding my head above the water and watched the river turn red with my blood until the ambulance arrived. Win was pulled from the car. He regained consciousness in the ambulance on the way to the hospital. Besides the large gash, he also sustained broken ribs and a dislocated shoulder. He was released after spending the night in the hospital.

Win came by the next day with his arm in a sling, a large bandage running from the left side of his forehead down to his left cheek. He was badly bruised and looked terrible, but he was walking. I couldn't find it in my heart to feel sorry for him.

He leaned against the window ledge and winced with pain. He looked me in eyes then focused on something on the floor. He stayed quiet for several minutes and I wondered just why he had come. Then he straightened, putting his good hand into the pocket of his trousers.

"Olivia, I'm so sorry. It's my fault. I killed our baby. I was angry and drunk. Please forgive me. I'll stop drinking, and I promise to be a better husband. I'll treat you like a princess, if only you can find it in your heart to forgive me." He took a step toward me. "Please, Olivia, I love you. I'll always love you."

I asked him to leave.

Moving to a private room meant I was finally on the road to recovery, but it also meant a steady stream of visitors. Gran and Gramps came every day, in the morning and again in the afternoon. CeCe stopped by every other day. Victoria sent flowers. Winston came by every day and kept me informed of the hospital business and family activities. Vanessa stopped by most days and had her lunch with me, while she filled me in on all the hospital gossip and what was happening around town. She told me she was dating a young doctor and thought he might be the one to get serious about. Win stopped by once a day for a few minutes. He always brought flowers and professed his love. My room was quickly beginning to look like a floral shop, or a funeral home, so I started sending bouquets to the various nursing stations and waiting rooms.

One evening, after all my visitors had gone home to be with their families, Uncle Lionel came by with a small arrangement of miniature pink roses in a ceramic baby shoe. We talked about the baby. The doctor said she had black hair. Uncle Lionel was sure she would have looked just like me. It actually felt good to talk about her. Everyone else avoided the subject. He let me cry as we talked. I told him how much I missed her movements, and how I would sometimes wake in the night with muscle spasms and feel my stomach, thinking she was still there. He called her my little angel and said she would always be with me.

Then, I told him about the recurring dream I'd been having, the one in which I was flying through the air. In the dream, I would turn my head and see him standing at the window in the ICU next to an old woman dressed in black, with a black veil covering her face. She looked like the same woman I had seen years ago at the funeral, the one Gran thought was his mother, Millicent Montgomery.

Uncle Lionel told me he was sorry if the dreams were disturbing, but he had no idea what they could mean, and his mother hadn't gone to the funeral. He stayed for another hour or so. After he left I was consumed by feelings of loneliness. He had been Dad's best friend. Somehow when he was with me, it felt like Dad was looking over his shoulder.

Life didn't seem to mean much anymore. I was alive, but there didn't seem to be anything to live for. I mourned the death of my baby, the hospital was running just fine without me—and Win. My insides boiled every time he walked into my room. I just couldn't forgive him for killing our daughter. My body healed . . . but not my soul. After almost two months in the hospital with what seemed like constant activity, Dr. Stevenson came into my room while Gran and Gramps were with me. He did the usual reading of my chart, and asked how I felt. Then he sat on the edge of the bed and looked at me with a fatherly expression.

"Olivia, I'm happy with your medical progress. You're actually way ahead of what I expected. Truth is, I don't believe this is a healthy place for you anymore. In fact, I don't think your life in Cedar Hill is what you need right now."

I thought I was doing great and said so.

"Olivia, I'm talking about your mental well-being. You just lost the baby that meant the world to you. Those scars are going to take a lot longer to heal. I know what your home life is like, and you don't need that now. What you need is to get far away from Cedar Hill for a month or two." He looked at all three of us, as we sat there with our mouths open. "Is there someone you can stay with? Perhaps, a family member in another city?"

I shook my head. "No. Dr. Stevenson. Thank you for your concern, but my grandparents are all the family I have left, and they live here in town."

Gran whispered something in Gramps's ear, and he nodded. She looked at Dr. Stevenson and smiled. "Well, it's true that we live here, but we have a cottage on the Marblehead peninsula. I'd be happy to take Olivia there for as long as she needs."

We decided Gran would drive me to the cottage in their Buick. Gramps would use my car and come on the weekends. Win thought it was a great idea, but Victoria protested, saying it didn't look good for the family for me to suddenly leave town after my hospital stay. She said it pointed a finger of blame and would arouse questions as to why I couldn't recuperate with my husband. It was Winston who finally laid down the law. He said I'd be better off away, on my own, where the air was cleaner. I got the feeling there was a deeper meaning to his statement.

By this time my casts had been removed. I could move around rather slowly with the aid of a cane. On the day I was released from the hospital, Dr. Stevenson took me up in his plane. I let the wind take my baby's ashes. They drifted over the home she would never know, over the pastures where she would never keep her pony and the woods and hills where we would never ride together. She would never hear the sleigh bells as we bring home the Christmas tree, or delight in the winter snow. The wonderland we called home would never hear her laughter, for now she plays with the angels until that time when I will join her.

CHAPTER 18

It felt good to be back at the cottage, even though an excursion on the boat was out of the question, at least until my body healed. I enjoyed sitting on the dock and walking in the shallow water, and before long I was strong enough to walk over to the Bay Shore Beach Club for lunch. My cane was always at my side, and my slow, stiff movements attracted a lot of attention. There was always someone close by to help carry my food to the best table . . . the one under the large old maple tree. It was the same table, under the same tree, that I had sat with David Morgan. Our initials were still faintly visible in the old wood.

Gran kept insisting the death of my baby was God's will, but I couldn't accept that. Win had killed our daughter with his reckless behavior—only thinking about himself—and I was still angry with him. Because of me, my family died. As a fifteen year-old, I was self-centered and always had to have my way. And I was still angry with myself.

Meanwhile the lighthouse called to me. I drove across Alexander Pike Road, through the massive quarry. I couldn't pass up the opportunity to swing into the parking lot of the Dairy Dock and order my favorite chocolate cone. With the use of my cane, I made the long walk out to the familiar rocks. It was slow going and I had to stop several times to rest and lick at the dripping chocolate. The gentle sounds of waves washing over stone soothed my senses and heightened the memories of the past. My gaze followed the shoreline to the north, past the old stone mansion and across the white-capped lake to Kelleys Island. My head filled with thoughts of my lost family and the memories of another time when I sat on this very spot with the innocence of a fifteen-year-old.

A speedboat came in close to shore and brought me back to the present and the reason for me sitting here in the protective shadow of the lighthouse. This was my healing place. As I sat on those giant rocks, I wondered if my anger over losing the baby was due to my great love for this child of Win's, or because I was trying to replace my family and failed. Once again, my family had been taken from me . . . but this time it wasn't my fault. The gentle waves washed over the lower rocky slabs at my feet. The seagulls called to me, as they swooped down and soared back up into the sky. I began to feel cleansed, and calm, and at peace.

We had been at the cottage for a month, and I sat on the swing reading. It was now a favorite pastime of mine, just like it had been for Mom. The sound of children's voices and laughter pulled me from the pages of the novel. Looking over toward the O'Brien cottage, I saw an attractive blonde woman walking down to the water's edge, accompanied by three children of varying ages. Many minutes passed while I watched, enjoying the children's antics. Turning, the woman looked up and waved in my direction.

"I hope the children aren't bothering you. They can be little monsters." she shouted.

Her voice seemed vaguely familiar, but I couldn't remember ever meeting her. I placed her somewhere around my age. Thinking it might be nice to have someone to talk to, I picked up my cane and walked over to introduce myself. "No, the children are fine. Their laughter is probably just what the doctor ordered."

The words 'little monsters' triggered memories of long ago summers. Meg had referred to her little brothers as monsters.

"Meg, is that you?"

The woman pulled off her sunglasses and moved closer. "Olivia!"

"Wow, Meg, you look wonderful!"

"Thanks, but it's only an illusion. The real Meg is still under this dyed hair and pancake makeup. Contact lenses got rid of the glasses!"

This was the first time our paths had crossed since that fateful summer nine years ago. Mrs. O'Brien had told Gran that Meg had become pregnant when she was fifteen and had to get married. The struggling young family had lived in an apartment in her parents' basement.

Meg brought out glasses of iced tea and we sat on faded, green Adirondack chairs facing the bay. Tears filled Meg's eyes as I told her about the accident and losing the baby and how the doctor had recommended some quiet time in the fresh air.

"I'm so sorry, Olivia. You've had so much tragedy in your life. First, your family and now this." Meg tried to wipe the tears, but made a mess of her makeup, with black mascara smudged on her cheeks. "I'm so sorry . . . I'm so very, very sorry. Now I feel even worse about being so mean to you that summer."

"Don't worry about it, Meg. That summer was a lifetime ago, and we were both young. There's nothing for you to be sorry about."

"Olivia, I'm so ashamed, but I was so jealous of you. All you had to do was walk into a room and every male who saw you, wanted you. No one ever looked at me. I was just your weird friend."

"Meg, that was ancient history, it's not important."

"I know you saw David and I kiss that day at the club. And I have to explain."

She wiped her eyes then blew her nose again. "It was that day over the Labor Day weekend. I was having a sandwich at the snack bar over at the beach club when Ricky and David walked in. They sat down with me and ordered, and we talked about how terrible it was that you lost your whole family like that. All through lunch, all David could talk about was you, and how much he loved you."

Suddenly, chills ran through my body. A pain in the pit of my stomach told me something dreadful was coming.

"Even his mother liked you. He told me she was gonna invite you to visit over the holidays. Then I watched as they played pool. David kept walking over to the door to look for you. That's when I told him I would watch and let him know when you arrived. Olivia, I hope you can understand. I was so jealous . . . I hated you! When I saw you running across the sand with that big smile . . . well, I went a little crazy. I walked up behind David. He was about to shoot, so when he pulled the cue stick back, he hit me in the stomach. I yelled and doubled-over, pretending to be hurt. He put his arm around me to help me stand. I saw you at the door, but he didn't, so I smiled up at him and laughed. And then I kissed him. I knew how it would look to you. Please forgive me, Olivia, . . . please."

My body went numb, my heart pounding in my chest.

"David figured it out after talking to your grandfather. He came over and confronted me. He was so mad, I thought he would kill me."

I choked back a sob. I could hardly breathe. Shaking my head, I pried myself out of the chair and walked back to the cottage.

Meg came rushing to my side. "Olivia, please. I was just a kid."

I pushed her aside with my free arm and continued to the back door of our cottage.

Dizziness washed over me. Holding onto the railing to steady myself, I climbed the few steps to the porch. The slamming of the screen door behind me was the last thing I remembered. Then the darkness claimed me.

"Oh my God, Olivia! Please, God, let her be all right." She was calling for an ambulance as I began to feel my limbs again. I had spent far too much time in hospital rooms lately, and didn't want some doctor asking a lot of questions, and poking at my still sore body.

"Gran, I'm alright. Really, I am. It was just a little accident."

"Oh, yes," she said to the person on the other end. "We're okay. No need to send anyone."

Gran helped me to my room and settled me in bed. After she left the room, I remembered the white poodle David had won for me, so many years before. In a fit of anger, I had tossed it up on the top shelf of my closet. I pulled the chair over and carefully climbed up, and found the dog shoved in the back corner.

Later, when Gran peeked in to see how I was doing, she found me sitting on the bed, rocking back and forth caressing the white poodle. "I'm so sorry, Olivia, but you'll have another baby one day." Then she closed the door.

Gran thought I was still mourning the death of my baby . . . but this time I wasn't. I was mourning the death of my first love . . . a love that had been killed by Meg's jealousy.

The next morning, I sat down for breakfast with red, puffy eyes. "Let's go home, Gran. I've had about as much fresh air as I can take."

CHAPTER 19

I was glad to see the Eldorado in the drive when Gran and I arrived back in Cedar Hill around three o'clock on Saturday. Gramps was happy to see us, but I wasn't so sure how Win would feel. He'd called every Sunday evening to ask how I was coming along. The calls didn't last long and he assured me he was fine and to take all the time I needed. Gran had the kettle on the stove and was placing tea bags in the pot. I decided to call the lodge to let Win know I was back. Then I'd relax in Gramp's recliner with a cup of tea.

After the tenth ring I was ready to hang-up when the sound of heavy breathing stopped me. "Win, is that you? Are you okay?"

"Huh? Who's . . .?"

"Win, I tried calling all morning to let you know I was coming home today, but there was no answer."

He sounded confused. "This morning? Oh, yeah, I was out riding. Ah, later I went for a swim." He hesitated for a moment. "So . . . Olivia . . . you're back! Are you sure you're not rushing this? I didn't expect you for another month."

That wasn't the response I was hoping for, and I was losing my patience. "I'll have Gramps transfer the bags to my car, and be home within the hour."

Win was silent.

"Is there a problem with me coming home?"

"The place is a mess. Why don't you stay put for tonight, and come home in the morning? You don't want to overexert yourself."

"What happened to Maria? She does an excellent job of keeping the place clean."

"Well, I told her she didn't need to come by since it was only me here."

There was that ache in the pit of my stomach. Something was very wrong. "Win, I'll be there in an hour!"

Everything looked normal from the outside. But then I walked through the front door. The living room appeared as though a battle had been fought within its four walls. What had gone on here? Win came racing down the stairs as I walked toward the kitchen. "It looks to me like you *did* need Maria!"

Win rushed past me and stopped, blocking my way into the kitchen.

I used my cane to swat at his leg and moved past him. "Win, what have you been doing?" I stopped at the sink. There were several wine glasses in warm sudsy water. "Since when do you drink wine? Has Cedar Hill run out of Scotch?"

He spun me around and took me in his arms and gently kissed me. "I had some friends over . . . it ended up being an all-nighter. I'll bring in your bags."

Watching his back as he left the room, I wondered what else I was going to find. I found it upstairs. It was obvious the bed had been hastily made. Clothes were strewn across the floor, and two damp towels lay on the chair. My eyes fell on the lampshade that was tilted to the side.

"I changed the bed for you, darling. I guess I'm not very neat when Maria isn't here."

He took me in his arms and nibbled my neck. My body was already beginning to betray me with a major shudder. He'd worn his long chestnut brown hair brushed back from his face, showing off his boyish good looks. Now, because of the bright pink scar, he was parting it down the center and letting it fall across his cheek, giving him a rakish, sexy look. The old feelings were taking control, and although my mind was still angry, waves of sensual desire were flooding me with a hunger that needed to be sated. I turned toward the bed and noticed something out of the corner of my eye. A pink bra hung from the curtain rod . . . pink wasn't my color.

"What the hell is that?" I shouted, pointing to the offending object. He at least had the decency to look embarrassed.

"Never mind, I know *what* it is. To *whom* does it belong to?"

He moved toward me, but I put up a hand to stop him. "It isn't what you think. I said I had a party here last night. One of the couples came up here."

The pain in the pit of my stomach was nothing compared to the pain in my chest. My heart ached knowing Win was lying to me. "Get out of here. Just leave me alone."

"Olivia, you have to believe me. I didn't do anything wrong. I love you."

"Go." I shouted and used my cane to point the way out of the bedroom.

He stopped just outside the door. "I'll move my things into the guestroom," he said without turning to look at me.

He left and went downstairs, leaving me standing there in the middle of the mess. I wanted to throw myself on the bed for a good cry, but I walked to the nursery instead. I needed to be near my little angel. I needed to touch her clothes and feel the soft yellow blanket I had so lovingly crocheted. Slowly I pushed the door open.

And I walked into an empty yellow room.

"Win!" I screamed and listened to his footsteps on the stairs. He seemed to take his time. When he reached my side, I continued. "How could you do this? How dare you? She was my baby!"

"I'm sorry, Olivia. I did it for you. Mother said it was the best thing to do. You really shouldn't live with that constant reminder of her."

He left the room and I slowly lowered myself to the floor and sat alone with my thoughts.

I wanted to believe him. We had a wonderful life up until the accident. Well, maybe it was wonderful before I got pregnant. I thought back over the past year. Our life had been happy as long as Win was happy . . . and I couldn't quite remember when the last time was that I saw him happy. I felt so alone, just floating on a sea of uncertainty. Could Win and I put the pieces of our life back together? I knew there would always be a part of me that hated him for killing our daughter . . . for nearly killing me.

Once again, Victoria had taken control of my life, and I was angry. Getting mad at her would just demonstrate bad manners, and give her another reason to criticize me. So I held my feelings inside, and called Winston.

The following Monday, I walked, with the aid of my cane, into my office. Thankfully, it was just as I had left it. For the first time since the accident, I felt comfortable. Winston and I shared a secretary, and she'd left a stack of folders on the desk for my review.

It wasn't long before Winston arrived holding two mugs of steaming coffee. "It sure is good to have you back, Olivia. If the Board of Trustees ever realize who really runs this place, I'll be out of a job."

I chuckled as he handed me the mug. "The weekend didn't go very well. It took Maria all day yesterday to clean and get everything back in order."

Maria had been with the Montgomerys for the past twenty years. Coming from a family of migrant workers who worked the area farms in the summer months, Maria, from the age of fifteen, cleaned for Victoria to make additional money for her family. The maid stayed behind at the end of the season when the pickers moved on to warmer climates. Victoria made sure the girl received an education, and Maria became a permanent member of the Montgomery staff.

"Victoria had everything in the nursery packed up and put in the attic, and Win made a shambles of the lodge. I feel I've completely lost control of my life."

Winston looked like a man who had the weight of the world upon his shoulders. "I'm sorry, Olivia. I wish there was something I could do to make this easier for you. You've had to endure more than anyone should have to deal with. To be frank, I'm afraid it's not going to get better. Over the years, I've tried to instill a sense of duty and responsibility in Win, but his mother is overindulgent and can always justify his behavior. He can do no wrong in her eyes."

His remarks didn't make me feel any better.

"You are the best thing that ever happened to Win. I hope you'll always stand by him." Winston got up and walked toward the door, then turned. "Don't overdo it, Olivia. I need you here." His choice of words were puzzling, and somewhere in the back of my mind I heard a warning.

CHAPTER 20

Fall came with a brilliant show of color. Although I couldn't ride the horses yet, I took great pleasure in long walks along the trails with the leaves gently falling around me. The air was cool and crisp with the scent of pine, and that wonderful woodsy, pungent smell of rotting leaves and apples mixed with wood smoke that only happens in the fall. I seemed to appreciate my surroundings more than I did before the accident. Life had given me a second chance, and I was going to enjoy each day to the fullest.

Winter soon followed, and the lodge was, once again, nestled under a lush blanket of snow. An evening in front of a roaring fire with a glass of wine and a good book was the perfect finish to a usually stressful day at the hospital. I was lulled into thinking this was how I would spend the rest of my years. But all too quickly, my world came crashing down upon me . . . again.

It was the day before Christmas. The sky was a brilliant blue, and the snow crunched beneath my feet. I had driven to Mansfield, looking for those last minute gifts that are never on my list but suddenly seem so important. I had just come out of my favorite boutique—with my one free arm loaded with bags and was heading for my car—when I saw them.

Win and the blonde nurse I had seen him with the night of the accident.

She wore a black mini skirt, knee-high black high-heel boots, and a Silver Fox jacket . . . the same kind that Win had given me the Christmas before. Their backs were to me. Win had his arm around her, while she held the hand of a small child. They walked to the parking lot behind the stores and approached a dark blue, rather sporty car and stopped beside it. She turned into him, and he took her in his arms for a long kiss. When she finally pulled away, I saw she was very pregnant. The little boy watched them, then turned his head and looked at me.

I saw Win's face in miniature.

Stepping back around the corner of the building, I leaned against the wall for support. My heart pounded and the gut-wrenching pain in my stomach had me gasping for breath. The hand holding the cane shook. I couldn't seem to stop it. The starting of the car's engine and the crunching of the snow told me that they had left.

Several people stopped to ask me if I was all right. I could only nod that I was. Not wanting to draw any more attention to myself and take a chance someone would recognize me I slowly walked to the car. I just sat there completely numb, my whole body shuddering. Was this what Winston tried to warn me about? Does he know about this? Is the baby Win's? What about the little boy? Was it only a coincidence that he looked like Win?

Win didn't come home for dinner. When he finally arrived around eleven o'clock, he said he had been helping some friends put up their Christmas tree and lost track of the time. I was stunned at how easily and convincingly he could lie. If I hadn't seen him with my own eyes I would have believed him. How many other lies has he told me over the years?

Win leaned down for a kiss. I pushed him away. My skin crawled. How could he think about kissing me when he'd been with another woman? He was disgusting. This man, who I had known since we were children, was a total stranger.

Anger and my pride wanted to confront him, but there was this persistent little nagging in the back of my brain that wanted me to wait. Taking my book, I took a deep breath and calmly wished him a good night, and went up to my room. There, I sat in the middle of the bed with my knees drawn up under my chin. The moonlight cast eerie shadows around the room. As I let my mind wander, more questions surfaced. The little boy appeared to be about two years old . . . just about the time that Win bought his first racehorse, and began spending less time at home. Was all that time really spent at the track? Was she the reason Win had kept Maria away from the lodge while I was gone? Had she been here? Had she been sleeping in my home . . . in my bed? Did the pink bra I had picked off the curtain rod belong to her? I'd been a fool to trust him. Men couldn't be trusted—I should have learned that lesson long ago.

Christmas was always a lavish production in the Montgomery household. The servants had their celebration on Christmas Eve while Winston and Victoria were at the club with their friends. The next day the servants were happy and jovial as they served us a traditional Christmas meal. The food must have been delicious—Victoria wouldn't have allowed anything less—but I don't remember eating. Afterwards, we adjourned to the large drawing room where a magnificent tree stood between the French doors. A fire cast a warm glow . . . warmth that couldn't reach my chilled heart. Elaborately wrapped gifts had been carefully placed beneath the tree, and Victoria approached me with a large box wrapped in gold.

"I hope you like this, Olivia. I spent a great deal of time picking it out for you. I must say you look dreadful. I hope you don't have the flu or something and give it to us all."

She never took a day off of criticizing me, not even for Christmas, but she was no longer my main problem. "Thank you. And no, I'm not sick. At least not physically."

The box contained a beautiful violet-blue cashmere sweater and matching slacks. Winston gave me a very expensive leather briefcase with an even more expensive and elegant gold fountain pen inside.

Win waited until all the other gifts had been opened before he presented me with a small, elegantly wrapped box. "The best gifts come in the smallest boxes . . . just like my little Olivia."

His complements no longer had an effect on me. It was just an act for his parent's sake. The beautiful diamond heart on a silver chain was exquisite, but I didn't take it out of the box. I sat looking at him with hatred in my heart . . . and contempt in my voice. "Did you get *her* one too? Just like you got us matching Silver Fox jackets last year!"

I had taken him off guard. He stood for a moment with his mouth open. I could almost hear the wheels in his head grinding away, searching for the right words. "Olivia, I don't know what you're talking about. What woman? I love you! You're my wife!"

I couldn't be nice any longer, and I couldn't control my anger. "The woman I saw you with at the club the night of the accident. The same woman I saw you with yesterday. She was wearing a Silver Fox jacket exactly like mine. And she was holding the hand of a little boy that looks exactly like you!"

He ran his fingers through his long hair, and his face turned red. He glanced over to his mother with a pleading expression, then back to me. "Olivia, I don't know what you're talking about. You must be mistaken. I love you. How can you think this of me?"

I looked over at Winston. His forearms rested on his knees, his head bent . . . he knew. Calmly, I collected my gifts, except for the necklace, thanked Victoria for her hospitality, and left the house. It would be the last time I saw the inside of that monument to wealth and good breeding.

Win had the good sense to stay out of my sight that night, but Victoria came by the lodge the next morning while I was having coffee. The fact that Victoria arrived before noon made this a very important visit. She accepted a cup of coffee, and we sat facing each other before the fireplace, like two warriors about to go into battle.

"Olivia, I am very sorry that this dreadful situation has to come to light at this time. But men will be men. You shouldn't let this bother you so. Infidelity has existed since the beginning of time. We learn to turn our heads and graciously accept our men's offerings and gifts when they have overindulged. You are being so bourgeoisie about this."

I couldn't believe she was telling me to forgive Win. "Somehow, Victoria, I can't see you putting up with this behavior from Winston!"

She actually appeared to feel sorry for me. And speaking in a voice meant to calm my raw nerves, said "You're wrong, Olivia. Winston has strayed over the years, but it never lasts. Montgomery men have always had an eye for a pretty girl, but they look to us to maintain the stability of the family. These little flings are never serious. I am sure the child you saw is not Win's. But if it turns out that it is . . . well, Winston will take care of it."

Win hadn't had an innocent fling. No casual romance . . . Win had a *family*. It was obvious I was going to get no help from this quarter.

I stood and took a few steps in the direction of the front door. "I realize the great imposition coming here at this hour was to you. You have made your feelings clear in this matter. Now I must ask you to leave."

"Don't be stupid, Olivia. Look how far you've come. You have a duty to this family and an obligation to me."

"Thank you for reminding me, Victoria. Now please leave."

* * *

Divorce is never easy, but I was not only divorcing my husband, I was divorcing the Montgomerys and the Montgomery lifestyle. I was divorcing a job I loved and the town I grew up in. The Montgomery family pretty much controlled the town. If I was going to begin a new life, it would have to be somewhere else . . . far away.

Winston was the only Montgomery I was going to miss. Except for Uncle Lionel, but my relationship with him went a lot deeper than marriage and divorce.

Winston stopped by my office and closed the door. He took his time getting comfortable in the chair opposite me. He cleared his throat before speaking. "I need to come-clean about what happened."

He didn't need to tell what that was. I just waited for him to continue.

"I received an anonymous letter the day before the accident. It had been left on my desk. I won't go into the details but it was about Win's long-standing affair with a nurse. I confronted Win at the club the night of the accident. I demanded he cut off all ties to that woman or I would cut *him* off."

Winston took a deep breath. "I feel totally responsible for Win's behavior that night and for the accident."

"No. You did what you felt best at the time. There was no way you could ever imagine what would happen next. Win was like a madman. I know he was drunk, but it was almost as if he were trying to kill us both. No sane person drives a car the way he did that night without a death-wish."

"I saw your lifeless body in the river and prayed to God that you were still alive. I sat there, holding your head above water, praying for His help. I made you a promise that I would make it right. I just haven't known how."

He stood and reaching over the desk, took my hand. "I'll find a way, Olivia. I promise."

A few days later Winston called me to his office, Uncle Lionel was there. Winston handed me a check. "This is the best I can do, Olivia. I wish I could do more, but nothing can ever make up for what has been done to you. The money is from Win's trust fund."

Feeling he was trying to buy me off, I refused the money. It was Uncle Lionel who stepped in and convinced me it was money that was owed me. Win had to start paying for his mistakes. I signed over the check to Uncle Lionel without looking at the amount and told him to invest it as he saw fit. I never wanted anything to do with Win or the Montgomerys again. I quickly changed my name back to Thompson.

There was still the matter of where I would go. Overwhelming feelings of panic, mixed with depression, kept me from taking any positive steps forward. It was Winston who finally came to my rescue. He had made some calls to hospitals in the Cleveland area. East Side General was looking for a Vice President who would be in charge of marketing, fundraising, and physician and patient relations. It was a tall order, but Winston convinced the President to take a look at me. Three months later, I was living in a furnished penthouse apartment overlooking the sparkling waters of Lake Erie.

CHAPTER 21

My life with the Montgomerys would be just a memory. I drove out of town with tears in my eyes and anger in my heart. I had taken only my personal possessions, and those easily fit in the trunk of the Cadillac. I traded in the yellow Eldorado for a white one. White is pure, the absence of all color. My life had enough color in it. It didn't need any more.

Once again, I found myself taking a new road in my life. The others had all been those with many dangerous curves. I hoped this one would be of the straight-and-narrow variety. But I knew history has a way of repeating itself. Although I hoped for an easier route, I would accept what life threw at me—and deal with it, as I always had.

The job at East Side General was demanding, but without family and friends, I had all the time in the world to adjust. My new boss was the president of the hospital. Hilda Morganstern was a tall blonde woman of German descent. She was somewhere in her forties, with a habitual frown and thin, firm lips that rarely remembered to smile. She'd graduated from Radcliffe and Harvard Law School. Although she had an impressive education, she had no real experience in running a hospital. She made it clear she wanted me to make all the right decisions, the ones that would make her look good and make money for the hospital. And that was okay with me. She ran a tight ship and took a heavy hand with the physicians, which I knew from experience was a train ride to disaster. A Cold War existed between the physicians and administration. Each day I walked a tightrope, creating the illusion that both sides were in control. A beautifully decorated office, and Joann, a newly-hired secretary who seemed shy but competent, also came with the job.

During my second week, I had an unpleasant surprise. Donation reports for the past five years had kept my attention all morning, when Joann interrupted to say an old friend would like to see me. The door opened, and Meg walked in.

"Hello, Olivia, surprised to see me?" she said with a chuckle.

Her betrayal, lies, scheming and jealousy came to me in a tidal wave of miserable feelings.

"I couldn't believe my eyes when I read the memo announcing Olivia Thompson as the new Vice President. I knew it was you, since it mentioned you had come from Montgomery Hospital in Cedar Hill. I hope we can forget the past and be friends, because I don't want a vice president mad at me."

Bad luck seemed to follow me everywhere. With all the hospitals in the whole Cleveland area, I ended up at the one where Meg worked. I took a moment to compose myself. "Meg, I'm surprised to see you. I didn't know you were a nurse."

"I'm not. I came here about three years ago. I work in the accounting department. I sure hope you're not still mad at me. We can be friends, right?"

"You think we can be friends? After what you did to me?"

"Well, yeah. We were kids, we're adults now."

"I've learned to move on with life and not dwell on the tragedies. But I can never forgive you for what you did. Your treatment of me was vicious."

"But, Olivia . . ."

"Enough, Meg. We're both here, and I'll deal with that. Just stay out of my way."

Joann buzzed me on the intercom to say I had an important call. Meg had the good sense to leave without another word.

Living in a big city was a new experience for me. I loved all the fine restaurants and stores, the hustle and bustle, and all the ethnic cultures. My days were long, often with a cocktail party or formal event in the evening, requiring me to keep several changes of clothes in my office closet and toiletries in my private bathroom. A steady stream of fundraisers, dinners, and community affairs had not been listed as one of my many duties, but I was adjusting. Not having any friends of my own was helpful.

It was during one of these events, about six months after I arrived in Cleveland, that I met Brian Bentley.

That evening I refreshed my makeup, brushed my hair until it fell in soft shining waves, and clipped on large rhinestone earrings. Feeling I needed a softer look, I had recently cut my long hair to shoulder length, creating a mane of curls and waves. The long, low cut, fitted black dress with spaghetti straps needed no other adornment, and after slipping into black silk pumps, I was ready to leave for the most glamorous hotel in town. Hilda had explained it was a benefit sponsored by our accounting firm, and she assured me it didn't matter if I knew anyone or not.

The ballroom shimmered in the soft lighting from the huge crystal chandeliers. Hundreds of candles danced with the air, while the deep red and gold carpet made the room look like something out of a European palace. The women were wearing everything from dressy suits and cocktail dresses to ball gowns. I was glad I had chosen something in between. Searching the room for a familiar face ended in disappointment. Feeling self-conscious about being alone, I went to the bar in the adjoining room.

I'd draped a long black chiffon stole around my shoulders before leaving the office. I took a moment to secure the ends over my arms to help keep it in place. A Chardonnay seemed the perfect drink for a lady alone as I surveyed the room from the protection of a corner. That's when I first saw him. He was leaning against the end of the bar and was the most handsome man I had ever seen. Tall with thick black wavy hair and strong, expressive eyebrows and a touch of a five o'clock shadow that gave him a slightly foreign look. I watched as he talked easily to his companion. When he laughed his blue-green eyes twinkled and creased at the corners. He was slim and looked like a movie star in his tuxedo.

Suddenly, the man he was talking with began waving at me, and motioned for me to join them.

"Hello, I'm Richard Brewster." Shaking his hand, I tried to place this man in his early sixties. "Aren't you Olivia Thompson? Hilda said she was sending you in her place tonight. I recognize you from the hospital, although I have to say you look different tonight. We're with the hospital's accounting firm. I handle the hospital account."

"Oh, yes. You're sponsoring this event," I said, embarrassed that I hadn't known who he was. I remembered seeing him with Hilda, but now my eyes went to his friend.

"I'm sorry, where are my manners? Olivia, this is Brian Bentley, one of the other partners of the firm."

My stole fell around my waist. His hand reached for mine and raised it to his lips. "A beautiful name for a beautiful woman. I'm very pleased to meet you, Olivia."

His deep velvety voice sent waves of excitement through me. I had an urge to kiss that cute little dimple in the middle of his chin. Surely, all Victoria's training should have prepared me for moments like this, but I was totally at a loss for words. I merely took a sip of wine and smiled.

Someone motioned to us from the doorway, and Brian took my arm. "We need to be seated and you are at my table. Allow me to play the gentleman and escort you to dinner."

He was tall, about 6'2", but he moved with the grace of a dancer and the assurance of royalty. I was awed by his presence.

The conversation over dinner was lively. Everyone included me in the topics, and I began to relax and feel comfortable with this merry band of men and their wives. Brian was the only member of the firm who wasn't married. He took much kidding about his single status, although he made it quite clear that he enjoyed his bachelorhood. A discussion of Cajun and Creole food began during dessert. Brian couldn't believe that I had never experienced the true taste pleasure of the Louisiana Creole cuisine. He promised to remedy that in the near future.

The following week, I found my thoughts wandering to Brian and how extraordinary he seemed to be in every way. Each day brought disappointment at not hearing from him, although my mind tried to convince me it didn't matter. Then, on Thursday, he phoned my office.

"Hello, Olivia, this is Brian Bentley. I was wondering if you might be free for dinner this Saturday?"

"Yes, I'm free. I'd like to have dinner with you."

"I have a client who loves authentic Creole food. He and his wife want to take us to their favorite restaurant. There are some great clubs in the area."

"Sounds wonderful. How should I dress?"

"A cocktail dress would be appropriate."

Saturday afternoon, I dressed with extra care. The reflection of the woman looking back at me from the long mirror was elegant in a very short black beaded silk dress with a halter-top. Strings of faceted black beads hung from it's high waist and gave the dress a movement of its own. I'd pulled my hair back in a chignon, put on Mom's pearl and diamond earrings, and slipped on strappy high-heeled shoes. The woman I saw had an air of confidence about her, as if she knew who she was and felt good about it . . . but that wasn't entirely true.

Brian arrived promptly at four o'clock and within minutes we were sitting in his luxurious black Mercedes heading downtown. He turned into the entrance to Burke Lakefront Airport and parked the car.

Mystified, I asked, "Are you going to tell me where we're going?"

With a twinkle in his eyes and a smile that melted my heart, he answered casually, "We're going for the best Creole food money can buy."

"And just where might that be?" I asked with playfulness in my voice.

"New Orleans."

CHAPTER 22

That was the most magical night of my life. I thought Victoria had taught me everything about money and what it could buy. But nothing had prepared me for the luxury of that Lear jet. Stewart and Marjorie Royal were already onboard when we arrived.

After introductions were made, Marjorie patted the seat next to hers. "Sit here, Olivia, Stewart and Brian have some business to take care of. They'll be in the back at the table. We'll be taking off soon."

I sat down and buckled up. "Brian told me your husband is a client of his."

"The Royal Paint Company is. Stewart's grandfather founded the company. Actually, Brian handles our personal finances as well."

I wasn't expecting that bit of news. The whole world used Royal paint. Now was the time to put everything I had learned from Victoria into play.

Marjorie turned her head toward me and smiled. "Don't let it worry you for even a minute." She reached over and squeezed my hand. "We're just normal people." She then nodded her head in the direction of the cockpit. "This is just one of the perks."

I smiled back at this woman who I instantly liked. She was so easy to talk to and before I knew it, the pilot announced that we were approaching New Orleans.

There was a limo waiting for us at the airport. Brian was a total gentleman, always a step ahead of me to open doors, take my hand to help me up from a seat or step off a curb. Win seldom thought about anyone but himself, and I found myself having to consciously let Brian take the lead.

For the first time, I realized what it means to be a celebrity or super rich. Strangers seem to recognize money without being told you have it, and we were given the royal treatment wherever we went. Galatoire's on Bourbon Street introduced me to the true flavors of Creole dining. The scents and sounds of the city were a new experience, as were the many colorful characters we met along the way. We tasted the delights of the many bars and clubs in the French Quarter, and I found myself in a new and very different world, enveloped in the sweet scent of jasmine. I couldn't help but stop and peek into the many charming courtyards with fountains splashing and gaslights bathing everything in a sensuous glow.

Marjorie suggested we stop at one of her favorite clubs before we headed back to the airport. We sat at a table in the courtyard, and listened to the lilting sounds of the saxophone. She looked at me with a warm smile one might bestow on an old friend. "I've loved watching you this evening. I'm seeing the city through your eyes . . . fresh and alive and exciting." She glanced over at Brian and winked. I wasn't sure what that meant, but he smiled back at her.

We lifted off the ground as the sun came up, bathing the city in gold, and I promised to return to this enchanting Mecca of the bizarre and my newfound love called jazz.

I couldn't help but compare Win to Brian. Win had to be the center of attention, always gathering a crowd around him like the Pied Piper. I found it amusing at first, but as the years wore on it became annoying. Brian had an aristocratic air about him that turned heads without drawing undue attention. He treated me with respect, always making sure I was having a good time. Win was all about Win having a good time . . . I was just along for the ride. Brian was almost too good to be true. My heart kept reminding me that men couldn't be trusted.

The following week we enjoyed a romantic dinner overlooking the lake in my penthouse apartment. The sunset was spectacular that night.

Just like in New Orleans, we found ourselves finishing each other's sentences, saying the same thing at the same time, and liking the same things. We couldn't stop touching each other with gentle caresses. It seemed the most natural thing in the world, when I found myself guiding him toward the bedroom with the Champagne bottle and our glasses. We made wild and passionate love until we both collapsed into sleep, exhausted, and then awoke to make love again with the first rays of the rising sun. Later, we drank Mimosas with a breakfast of omelets and toast as the sunlight put down a blanket of shimmering diamonds over the lake.

Our weekday schedules were demanding, and I didn't see him again until the following Saturday. He'd said we would spend the day around his pool, and later he would prepare dinner. He suggested I might want to bring a change of clothes for the evening.

Knowing he lived in Shaker Heights, I expected him to have a nice home, but nothing prepared me for his magnificent English Tudor mansion. As he turned into the drive, all I could say was, "Wow!"

His broad smile told me he was pleased with my response. "I guess that means you like it. The house is a bit larger than I need, but it's the only home I've ever known."

"It's a great neighborhood. My Uncle Lionel lives less than a mile from here on South Park Boulevard."

He appeared surprised. "I didn't think you had any family in Cleveland. What's your uncle's name? Perhaps I know him."

I grinned knowing he would recognize the name. "Lionel Montgomery."

"I wasn't expecting that. He's only one of the wealthiest and most influential men in the state! You are just full of surprises, but I must say it explains a lot. You're so self-assured. You show good breeding and have an aristocratic bearing about you. You scream old money."

"I hate to disappoint you, but he's not really my uncle. He was my father's best friend. Although I *was* married to his nephew." And my mother-in-law gave me a crash course in the art of being a lady. But I didn't want to go there, and kept my thoughts to myself.

Brian had parked the Mercedes on the large circular drive in front of the dramatic carved stone entrance. I waited while he came around to my side and opened the door. My hand slid easily into his causing an instant stirring deep within me. He guided me down a well-worn brick walk to the massive, ornately carved oak door. "You're a fascinating woman, and, like a rare diamond, I look forward to viewing all your facets and watching you sparkle."

The house was filled with fabulous antiques and art that his parents had brought back from their many European trips, yet it felt welcoming and comfortable. After giving me a brief tour of the main rooms, he took me upstairs to one of the guest bedrooms and put my tote bag on the bed. "You can use this room to change into your bathing suit. I thought we could have lunch on the patio. I'll meet you outside."

The room was beautifully furnished in the gracious period of the 1920s with a large floral print paper in pinks and greens. The pink tufted headboard was covered in the same silk fabric as the bedspread, and delicate crystal lamps with pink-fringed shades sat on bedside tables. I hung the dress I planned to wear for dinner in the closet in the adjoining dressing room. The pink marble bathroom beyond it reminded me of an old Hollywood movie. Even Victoria would have been impressed.

After putting on a black bikini and a matching long cover-up, I slipped into sandals and found my way out to the patio. Brian's housekeeper, Consuelo, served us a delicious lunch consisting of an exotic flavored chicken salad with grapes and pecans, accompanied by fresh fruit.

I studied the rear façade of the house, with its castellated stone tower and mullioned windows. This wasn't the glass-and-chrome setting I had pictured Brian in, and my curiosity was too much to contain. "What did you mean when you said this was the only home you've known?"

"This was my parent's house. They bought it shortly after I was born. I inherited it after they were both killed in an automobile accident when a drunk driver hit their car."

Feelings of remembered horror suddenly washed over me, and sympathetic tears filled my eyes. "I understand how difficult a time that was for you."

My tears must have confused him because he changed the subject. "My father had been a prominent Cleveland attorney. He was extremely disappointed when I chose accounting over law as a profession. But I knew I could never have reached his level of greatness and didn't want the competition. So, I chose accounting. He lived long enough to see me become a partner and was very proud of my success."

I suddenly felt an emotional connection to this man who I'd only seen as charming and seductive.

The afternoon flew by as we played tennis and swam in the pool. Brian had given Consuelo the night off. He grilled steaks while I prepared baked potatoes and a tossed salad. We ate on the patio under the stars, and he served an excellent bottle of Bordeaux from his wine cellar. Before dinner, I had showered and changed into a black silk, ankle-length, sheath and pulled my hair back in a sleek chignon. I left off any underwear and shoes . . . just because I knew it would drive him crazy.

We had so much in common and felt so comfortable together. We shared our dreams and our fears. We shared the experience of losing our families to automobile accidents. We both felt the need to have children, and although I loved my career, I would have gladly given it up to be a full-time mother.

That night, we made love in the pool house, under a million stars, while being serenaded by a symphony of night sounds.

We became an item, as they say, and accompanied each other to our many social events. Gran and Gramps invited us to Cedar Hill for Thanksgiving. Gran quickly fell under the spell of his charm. He was, after all, of Irish and English descent . . . not the forbidden Italian, like Tony Marelli and Danny Capelli.

Brian invited me to accompany him to Paris for Christmas. It had become a tradition with him to go abroad, since he had no family. He claimed that Paris is at her best at Christmas time. We went shopping and he bought me a black full-length mink coat, "Just to keep the chill off." One evening, while we were in the Eiffel Tower, as the city's lights sparkled before us, he asked me to marry him.

I didn't hesitate. "Yes. I will marry you."

The following June, we were married at the Royal's estate in the rolling hills of Lake County. Marjorie and I were as giddy as a couple of debutantes planning the wedding. We laughed, drank wine, planned the menu, drank more wine, and picked out my wedding dress over another glass of wine. It was a fun time and ended with a beautiful day surrounded by three hundred of our closest friends. Gran and Gramps had front row seats next to Stewart and Marjorie.

My life with Brian could only be described as enchanting—a fairytale. The only dragon in our story was his gambling. I didn't realize his occasional trip to Vegas with his buddies was much more . . . it was an addiction. One I didn't see until after he'd slipped the very expensive Cartier designed wedding band onto my finger—but I was so much in love, that it probably wouldn't have made a difference.

Everyone loved Brian. He had charisma and charm and impeccable taste. Gran and Gramps had their favorite suite of rooms they used whenever they came for a visit, and their visits became more frequent and lasted longer.

CeCe visited us whenever she could get away from the kids, which wasn't very often. Vanessa loved the house and occasionally came on weekends. It was during one of these visits that she pulled me into the pool house. We needed to talk—alone.

"I've got a problem. And it's not my fault. I promise."

It was never good when Vanessa said she had a problem. That always meant she wanted me to fix whatever the current catastrophe might be.

"Tell me." I said motioning toward the rattan chairs.

"I lost my job. Because of Win."

This couldn't be good. "Just tell me what he did."

"Did you know he got married a month after your divorce?"

"No. And I don't care."

"Well, I cared. What he did to you was horrible. Cheating on you. Getting that bitch pregnant. I just had to tell him what I thought."

"And? That shouldn't get you fired."

"I tried to make his life miserable. I wanted to make him pay. I guess, I went a little too far and he went to his father."

"What did you do?"

"It doesn't matter. It got me fired and now I don't have a job. Please, you have to help me."

Her actions on my behalf seemed extreme and just plain foolish. But, once again, I felt compelled to help her.

CHAPTER 23

The months turned into years, and Brian's extravagant lifestyle became normal to me. Friends were always around for impromptu gatherings, lavish parties were given several times a year, and we always left for Paris the day after our annual black tie Holiday Party. Brian was more than generous, showering me with wonderful gifts. The morning of our wedding a big black Mercedes sat in the driveway with a huge white bow on top. There were little boxes from Cartier's and Tiffany's after trips to New York and big boxes from his favorite couture houses of Europe.

Both of us worked at demanding jobs. I was at the hospital each morning by seven o'clock. All too often I was still there at ten in the evening if there was a Medical Staff Meeting, or at one of the many committee meetings requiring my presence. Brian had clients to entertain, board meetings and trips to various parts of the country, often to California. I began to wonder how many of those trips were necessary, and how many were a reason to stop in Vegas on his way home.

I would occasionally join Brian and our friends for an afternoon at Thistledown Racetrack. Sitting with a large group in the dinning room was fun. Everyone laughed at me for picking the pretty grey horses or those with funny names, but it was often my horse that crossed the finish line first. I always scanned the room before entering for any sign of Win, but he was never there. Brian asked a couple times a year if I would like to join him on a trip to Vegas, and he even asked if I would rather go to Monaco. My answer was always no, although Monaco was tempting. If gambling was his only fault, then I could live with that. It certainly couldn't be called a disease with Brian—more like a bad habit. I never complained. Life was too good to rock the boat.

The boat! That was another generous thing he did for me. Brian had listened for hours as I reminisced about the cottage, the lighthouse, and the old boat that I had promised to buy for Gramps someday when I married a rich man. Brian and Gramps met with a Mr. T, the owner of Port Clinton Yacht Sales, and, with Gramps's help, he identified the boat that had cruised the Lake Erie islands for many years. The *Lovely Lady* was found on a cradle in the back lot of a graveyard for old boats. Brian was able to have it restored enough for her to become a respectable member of the Portage River Yacht Club. He surprised me with the keys on our wedding anniversary. We spent many happy weekends cleaning and polishing until the old girl cruised the islands with dignity, once again.

Brian never really loved her the way that I did. To him she was just a smelly old boat, but for me, she represented the resurrection of my childhood. I'll never forget the feelings of pride and unbelievable happiness the first time I steered the *Lovely Lady*, with Gramps at my side, around the Eastern side of Kelleys Island, and the Marblehead lighthouse came into view.

Vanessa fit right in. She quickly moved from one department secretary position to another, until she'd gained enough experience to be promoted to a desk in Administration. Her outgoing personality enabled her to get along with everyone from the person emptying the wastebaskets on up to Hilda. Vanessa was very supportive and encouraging of my new pet project.

I believed, with a passion, that what the community needed was a pediatric care unit. Not a fancy, high society type of care with all the frills and designer décor, but a basic, down-to-earth unit that would provide the best possible care for all children, regardless of their family's ability to pay. Children died every day in the neighborhoods, from gunshots, abuse and run-of-the-mill diseases that barely slowed down children in the suburbs. I wanted to give every child a chance at a healthy life.

Hilda wasn't convinced the Board would approve such a huge project that would mean a drain on the future budget, when other, more profitable, venues could be pursued. But if I could obtain the necessary funding, then she would consider going forward with the plans.

Vanessa and Joann helped me organize the hospital's annual fundraiser, the event I would use to help launch my project—the Andrew and Angus Thompson Memorial Children's Unit.

Vanessa was able to book Cleveland's largest and most elegant ballroom for the event. It was the same one where I first met Brian. The guests mingled around the silent auction items, exclaiming over the wonderful selection of trips to condos in warmer climates and fabulous jewelry. I was happy to see the couple walking toward me. "Olivia, you're the most beautiful woman here tonight. Well, except for Jacqueline!" Uncle Lionel turned toward his wife, then back to me. "You look so much like your mother."

"Uncle Lionel, you old flirt. You're going to make me blush! But now that I have you here and you're so overcome with my beauty, I want to ask you to dip into that generous charitable fund of yours and donate to the new pediatric care wing I'm trying to convince Hilda we need."

Uncle Lionel laughed and rubbed his chin. "How can I contribute to something that doesn't exist?"

"If I get enough commitments, the Board will have to take the project seriously."

I had always liked Uncle Lionel's wife. She didn't take herself too seriously and had tried to come to my defense whenever Victoria went on a rampage against me. I considered her a good friend. She smiled at me now. "Olivia, I know how much you want to help children. I think it's a wonderful project, and so does Lionel." She touched her husband's arm. "What do you say dear?"

"Okay, I can see I have no say in this . . . a hundred thousand dollars if you get this off the ground, and I'll even throw in some equipment."

Across the room, Hilda looked regal in a royal blue satin gown with her hair cascading down around her shoulders in glorious waves of shimmering gold. But she was watching us with a questioning eye, and I knew that frown meant trouble.

"Thank you, Uncle Lionel, that is most generous of you. But if you give me a million or two, I'll name it the Lionel Montgomery Pediatric Care Unit."

Uncle Lionel burst out laughing and slapped his leg. "Olivia, you little horse trader! I thought your father was the best wheeler-dealer that I ever knew, but I see you've got him beat! He'd be real proud of you!"

Hilda was heading our way with a scowl. "Mr. Montgomery? Is everything all right?"

"All right for you, but not all right for me! This little lady just took a million dollars out of my pocket to help sick kids!"

"Thank you. That's very generous." She gave them her warmest, big donor smile. "I hope you both enjoy the evening."

Hilda bent down and whispered in my ear. "We will discuss this in my office Monday morning."

Yes, I was in trouble . . . *again*. I watched her stiff, straight back, as she walked away.

The theme of the evening was "Island Magic." Vanessa had surpassed anything I could have imagined. Dinner was served in the main ballroom, which featured a grand curved staircase leading to an upper balcony surrounding the room. Palm trees and torches brought to mind a Hawaiian luau, and the bar was turned into a Tiki Hut.

The last of the guests had been seated. I hurried up to the balcony where Vanessa and CeCe were seated at a table along the rail. Vanessa assured me everything was going as planned, and I needed to get back downstairs to my table to watch the opening show with my husband.

The large crystal chandeliers went out just as I reached the staircase. Hawaiian drums began to beat. I hesitated to give my eyes a moment to adjust to the dim light given off by the torches. I began my descent just as a dozen waiters dressed as Hawaiian warriors came through a door on the far side of the room holding large silver trays above their heads. Each tray contained a large chocolate cake in the shape of a volcano, spewing red flames and smoke. The warriors circled the room, kicking off the rest of the evening's festivities. But I barely gave them a glance, intent as I was on making it down the stairs without catching my heel in the hem of my gown, and falling at the feet of a warrior.

My gown was one that Brian had brought back from London. Creamy, white silk, it's silver bugle beads created long stems starting at the hem and climbing up to form palm fronds that held my breasts. I knew the figure-hugging, backless style showed off my body to perfection. As I slowly descended the staircase, thousands of beads glittered in the torchlight. Reaching the bottom step just before the first circling warrior, I saw Brian standing beside my chair.

I hurried across the path of the flaming cake toward the first row of tables. Bending down with a smile, he whispered. "Well, my darling, you certainly know how to make an entrance. There isn't a man in this room that could tell you what those warriors were holding, as you glided down the stairs. You appeared to be totally naked under those silver leaves caressing your breasts."

After we were both settled in our seats, I leaned over and whispered, "I am."

The jungle drums drowned out his response.

The evening, complete with hula dancers and a Hawaiian-inspired menu, was a great success. I danced and mingled until midnight. Vanessa told Brian that he could take CeCe and I home. She would stay until everything was finished and the last guest departed. CeCe and I each took one of Brian's arms as he led us out to the lobby door, where our car was waiting. Once again, I felt like Cinderella.

But Monday morning, my world would turn into a pumpkin and mice.

Nothing could have prepared me for the verbal attack awaiting me on Monday. Hilda sat behind her large mahogany desk. Her hair was pulled back and secured tightly in a bun. Her dark blue suit was the armor she always wore when going into battle. She began firing before I had a chance to sit down.

"Olivia, I hired you because you came highly recommended. I was under the impression that you were competent enough to run a hospital. Obviously, it was a two-bit institution in a one-horse town!

That circus you put on last night was a disgrace to our reputation. And you looked like a cheap whore flirting with the very men we rely on to keep these doors open!"

I knew for a fact, from the flood of calls Joann was receiving this morning, that last night had been a huge success. But I had a feeling this wasn't the time to argue.

"You're to have no further contact with Lionel Montgomery. There are to be no more lavish productions at the hospital's expense. We were there to make money, not spend it! Do I make myself clear, Olivia?"

"But, he's my . . . "

"Is . . that . . clear?"

"Yes, it is."

Her accusations were uncalled for and untrue. I wanted to defend myself. Feelings of anger toward this woman I had respected consumed me. I wanted to tell her of my connection to Uncle Lionel and about all of the complementary phone calls I had received of a job-well-done. But, I didn't. She, obviously, wasn't ready to listen. I pulled my shoulders back and walked off her battleground with dignity.

Hilda kept her distance for the next few weeks, which was a blessing. Meanwhile, I handled the flood of contributions coming in on a daily basis. I wanted to offer Vanessa a job as my assistant, but we both knew Hilda would never approve it. So Vanessa helped me on the side, and we both hoped Hilda wouldn't find out.

Vanessa also became my lifeline, as the waters at home became turbulent. Brian was in town, but seemed troubled about something that he refused to discuss with me. He didn't have an appetite and began drinking more than the occasional glass of wine at home.

His preferred beverages were now scotch and bourbon. There were phone calls late at night that he took in the library, often followed by yelling and swearing. He stopped inviting friends over and declined dinner invitations. All he would say was it didn't involve me, and he would handle it. He continually told me how much he loved me. Our nights in bed certainly proved that, as his lovemaking became more aggressive. I feared he was suffering from a terminal illness and afraid to tell me. But nothing could have prepared me for the event that would change my life . . . again.

CHAPTER 24

Early April in Cleveland can only be described as dreary. Winter has not yet given up its hold and there is just a hint of spring on the horizon. Depressing days, when the sky is gray with a misty rain that just won't let up. A gray blanket of doom seemed to follow me to work that day. My budget reports still hadn't come down from Accounting. Hilda was out of the hospital until late afternoon, and Meg wasn't anywhere to be found. Vanessa had called in sick, and everyone I met seemed to be in a foul mood. Filling my briefcase with the remaining letters that needed answering, I left my office early, telling Joann that there would be plenty of dictation ready for her to type in the morning.

Brian's Mercedes and Porsche, along with the vintage Aston Martin he had shipped home after a recent trip to London, were in the garage, but it seemed strange there were no lights on in the house on such a gloomy day. Putting my briefcase down on the kitchen table, I called out that I was home. No answer. The door to the library was ajar. I walked in.

It appeared that Brian had fallen asleep at his desk. I tiptoed over to his side to gently wake him. That's when I saw the blood covering the desk, spilling over onto the floor . . . and the gun in his limp hand.

The police found the note on the corner of the desk. It was in his bold, but somewhat shaky, handwriting.

> *My Darling Olivia,*
> *I'm so sorry to have to do this to you after all that you have suffered in the past. I know that I am one more man in your life who has left you, but I see no other way out. You must always remember that I love you with all my heart and soul. But gambling has always been a demon, which I thought I could control. It has gained the strength to rule over my judgment, my convictions, and even my career. It has become my greatest weakness. I know that I could ask for your help, and you would give it gladly. But how long would it be before those demons raised their ugly heads and took control again?*
>
> *I have failed you, Olivia. In a weak moment, I destroyed all that is good in my life. I cannot stand the thought of watching your love die and turn to hate, and your undying trust shatter before my eyes. Forgive me, my love, for leaving you with the pain and shame, but I cannot bear the alternative. Hold your head high, Olivia. Follow your heart and dreams, they will never fail you.*
>
> *I do this unforgivable thing knowing that your love will carry me into eternity. I will always be at your side.*
> *Your Brian*

Consuelo arrived home just as they were putting Brian's body into the ambulance. The officer in charge took a full statement from her. I managed to hold myself together until the last police officer had left, but as soon as the door closed behind them my world crashed. My head tingled, followed by numbness that continued down to my toes. I needed to get upstairs to the safety of our bedroom. I grabbed the banister. My chest felt ready to explode. I needed to breathe. I took a deep breath and pulled myself up the stairs. Dizziness waited at top step and I fell to my knees. I crawled in a fog of pain to the bedroom, then holding onto the door, I tried to stand. Then there was only blackness.

"Olivia! Olivia! Are you okay? Answer me! I can't open the door! Olivia, please answer me!"

Something kept hitting me in the back, then a voice yelling at me through the fog. I crawled away and my head began to clear. Consuelo rushed into the room.

She got down on the floor and wrapped her arms around me. "Oh, thank the Lord. You're alive! I was so worried when I couldn't open the door. I was afraid you had joined our Brian. My heart is too weak to deal with another death."

She helped me into bed, then promised to come back with tea.

No, this couldn't be happening to me. Why does everyone I love have to die? How could he do this to me? He loved me. I felt betrayed and angry, and I hated him for leaving me like this. An accident, I could accept, but not taking his life. What could have been so terrible, that it drove him to kill himself?

The library was cleaned of all traces of the "unfortunate situation," as it was being called. I had to deal with the endless phone calls from reporters and lawyers while I grieved for my lost mate. Death was not, after all, new to me . . . just unexpected.

CeCe came as soon as she heard the news and proved, once more, that she was the sister I'd never had. I thought it would be easier since neither Brian nor myself had any family—but it wasn't. I really don't know how I would have handled everything without the help of Brian's secretary.

The day of the funeral, I pulled my hair back in a chignon and slipped on the black Chanel suit that Brian was so fond of. As an afterthought I added my mother's pearl earrings. The ones with the large teardrop pearls that hung from diamond bows. They were his favorite, and I had worn them on our first trip to New Orleans. The only other jewelry that I wore that day was my elaborately carved diamond wedding band. The ring had been designed for Brian at Cartier's. Nothing but the best was ever good enough for him, and he paid the ultimate price in the end.

CeCe draped my black mink coat around my shoulders before we joined Vanessa who was already in the long, black limousine waiting at my front door.

The procession to Lake View Cemetery was long. I stood at the gravesite for nearly half an hour waiting for the last car to arrive and park. I had time before the ceremony began to look around at the many huge monuments and old stone mausoleums. Brian would be at peace here, in the company of the various leaders of industry and social greats, including President Garfield and John D. Rockefeller.

It broke my heart to say goodbye to my darling Brian, and our fairy-tale life together. Unlike most fairy-tales, this one hadn't had a happy ending.

The state of Brian's finances was as unexpected as his death had been. His attorney stopped by the house with the news. He looked as grim as an undertaker.

He glanced around the foyer. "Is anyone else here? I would prefer to speak in private"

"We can use the living room. Consuelo is out for the afternoon."

"I think the dining room may be better."

He set his briefcase on the table before him and removed several documents.

"This isn't good, Olivia."

I shook my head. "I don't think it can get much worse."

"This all has to go."

"All of what, exactly?"

He waved his arm in the direction of the ceiling. "The house and everything in it."

A chill swept through me. "I don't understand. There has to be a mistake."

"I'm sorry but there is no other way to cover Brian's gambling debts."

"What about insurance? He had several policies."

"He cashed them in two months ago."

"I don't understand. Where's the money?"

He pushed the paperwork toward me.

"There's no insurance money."

I got up and walked over to the large mullioned window overlooking the backyard. "His indebtedness is large enough that everything must be sold?"

"Much of this artwork and furniture belongs in museums."

"We know. I've enlisted a New York auction house."

I slumped into the chair next to the window. "How could I have not known he was in this much trouble?"

"This large gambling debt just happened a few months ago. It could have gotten ugly."

"He never said a word to me."

"Olivia, I've know Brian for many years. I wasn't aware of this either. Everyone knew he liked to gamble. But it was all small stuff. Nothing he couldn't easily handle. I'm as surprised by this as you are."

I took a deep breath. "I'll find an apartment."

"The estate includes the house, it's contents and the cars. You can, of course, keep your personal property."

The details and extent of Brian's gambling and indebtedness spread throughout the newspapers and television. Considering he was a partner in one of the city's most prestigious accounting firms it remained the leading story for days. So, when it came, I considered Hilda's phone call asking me to meet with her a welcome diversion from the nightmare I was living.

Entering Hilda's office, I noticed she was, once again, wearing her navy blue suit. Her long blond hair was pulled back in a bun, and she had on her no-nonsense face.

"Good afternoon, Olivia. Thank you for coming in at what I know is a difficult time. Before we start, I want to say how sorry I am for all your personal problems. I don't know that I could handle all the pressures of dealing with the funeral, the press, and the prospect of losing everything you own. I truly am sorry for the death of your husband."

Taking a deep breath, I blinked away the tears, which always seemed to be just below the surface. I was getting that horrible feeling in the pit of my stomach. I knew Hilda hadn't called me to her office just to say she was sorry. She could have stopped by the house to do that.

Hilda straightened the stack of reports that sat in front of her.

"Olivia, we're having some problems. The finance department can't find all of the funds listed in your budget reports. The numbers don't match those from reports showing the deposits made from the charitable donations. The Hospital is short money claimed as coming in from the various fundraisers, as well as private donations over the past two years."

A wave of confusion sent my mind into a whirl. "I don't understand. All of the contributions have come in as promised. To my knowledge they were all accounted for. My monthly reports to the finance department are complete and accurate. I would stake my reputation on it. Just how much money are we talking about?"

"As close as we can determine at this time, two hundred and fifty thousand dollars. Olivia, we can't find a quarter of a million dollars that you claim we have."

My heart pounded in my chest. Taking a deep breath, I shook my head, "No, that just isn't possible. There has to be a mistake."

"You've put the Vice President of Finance's job on the line as well. You couldn't have gotten away with this for two years without help. I'm having a full investigation done on him too."

"I'm telling you, Hilda, your information is wrong. Where did this come from?"

"There's no mistake. I'm sorry, Olivia, but I have no choice but to terminate your employment."

My chest felt ready to explode. "Hilda, I assure you that I had nothing to do with this. I can't believe what you are accusing me of could even happen here. Our accounting practices are solid."

"It did happen, and all fingers point to you. Brian's suicide put a big black mark against the hospital. After all, he was a partner in our accounting firm. The press is having a field day with this!"

"Don't drag Brian into this. He had nothing to do with this hospital. East Side General was not one of his clients."

She pushed the stack of reports toward me. "These don't lie."

"Hilda, I couldn't do this. I'm here to improve the reputation of the hospital. You know how important fundraising is to me. I have a wonderful relationship with our benefactors. As much as I complain about some of their eccentricities, I would never do anything to jeopardize our affiliation with any one of them. As far as the money is concerned . . . I don't need it!"

"Olivia, I've always considered you a friend and I know you're financially ruined. It's been all over the news for days. Brian disgraced all of us, but . . ."

"But nothing! I didn't know Brian was going to kill himself! Besides, from what you've just told me, whoever did this has been at it for at least two years. For the past two years, I thought Brian and I were worth over three million dollars. Why should I risk embezzling for only two hundred and fifty thousand? It doesn't make sense! I didn't do it!"

"I'm sorry, Olivia. I don't like having to fire you and add to your humiliation. The Board will decide what charges are to be filed and when."

I scooted to the edge of my chair. "Excuse me, Hilda, but do I understand you correctly? The Board is going to have me arrested for embezzlement?"

"I'm afraid so, Olivia."

"So you're telling me, the only people I need to plead my case to are on the Board of Trustees?"

"Yes, but they already have all the facts."

"Fine. Then put me on the agenda for the meeting."

"The agenda has already been mailed out to the members."

"Then I'm an add-on, Hilda. But, be assured, I will be there!" My eyes never left hers as I stood and walked toward the door, hoping that my legs wouldn't give out. "I'll be in my office packing my personal belongings. As my good *friend*, I'm sure you won't find it necessary to have security walk me out to my car."

Joann was typing as I walked past her into my office, closing the door behind me. Sitting behind my desk, I looked around the room, full of my personal touches and framed photos that meant so much. The picture of my family that I had taken with my new camera, in front of our house . . . the year my world fell apart. Next to it was a picture of Gran and Gramps sitting together on the swing in the backyard of the cottage. They had died the year before in a plane crash . . . and it was my fault. I had wanted to give them a vacation they would never forget, and now they rested in the sea. The third picture was of Brian and I at our wedding . . . we were so happy. I looked at the pictures . . . they were all dead. Everyone in my life was gone, and now my reputation was about to die as well . . . destroyed by something I didn't do.

The buzzing of the intercom brought me back to the present. "Mrs. Bentley? I just made a fresh pot of coffee. I thought you could use it."

Joann came into the office a few minutes later and set two mugs on the desk. She looked worried as she sat down in one of the Queen Anne high-backed chairs.

"Joann, I don't know how much you already know, but . . ."

"Hilda called me into her office this morning and said you were going to be fired. She said I would continue to work for Vanessa until your replacement could be found."

"Hilda told me there were inaccuracies in my financial reports. I just don't know how that could be. You sent everything to finance immediately after I signed-off on them. And I know, without a doubt, those reports were correct."

Joann looked rather nervous as she held her mug with both hands to stop the shaking. "Mrs. Bentley, you can't think that I had anything to do with this! You are the best boss I ever had. You always treated me real nice and made me feel important. Not like other people around here."

"I'm sorry, Joann. You misunderstand me. I don't suspect you. But have you heard about any irregularities? Noticed things that didn't seem right at the time? I need to make some sense out of all this."

"No, I don't know what happened, but it's a real shame. You're a real fine lady and the docs are really gonna miss you."

"Thank you. You've been an excellent secretary, and I want you to know how much I appreciate all your help and dedication."

"I'm sorry. I'm sorry. I'm real sorry!" She wiped tears as she got up and left the room.

Joann seemed to be overreacting. Why the tears? And why would I ever think she could be part of this? Joann was good at her job, but she didn't have the brains to be part of an operation of this magnitude. I thought the whole scene appeared a bit melodramatic. An hour later, I stood looking around the room. It felt cold and sterile. The happy memories had already left. In their place, lies and betrayal.

CHAPTER 25

Wearing my most conservative navy blue suit and plain white blouse, I paced back-and-forth outside the Boardroom door. Everyone was already inside, and the meeting would begin after cocktails and appetizers. At precisely five o'clock the secretary opened the door. She ushered me to an empty chair at the head of the table and a glass of ice water set before me.

The Chairman began. "Members of the Board, Olivia Bentley has requested the honor of addressing this Board in order to give her side of the allegations made against her. In consideration of the magnitude of the charges and the effect they will have on her future, I felt it only fair to give her time at today's meeting."

My heart raced and my stomach churned. These people held my future in their hands. I needed to be convincing. I prayed my voice wouldn't give away my fear.

I took a deep breath. "Thank you, Mr. Chairman, and members of the Board. First, I would like to say what a privilege and honor it has been to work with all of you these past ten years. Hilda has given me the facts concerning the embezzlement. I want to address these concerns before they become formal charges against me."

Looking around the room, I saw a few smiles, a few questioning frowns, and Hilda, her lips pursed holding her water glass in a death grip. Gathering my courage, I turned to Chairman Richards, who smiled and nodded his head.

"Hilda has told me inaccurate financial reports have led you to believe I am the person responsible for missing funds. I've spent the past several days trying to figure out how this misappropriation of funds could have been done without my knowledge, since I alone was responsible for all of the charitable events. I have no explanation. From what Hilda has told me, financial need is my sole motive for embezzling approximately two hundred and fifty thousand dollars. That I somehow knew, two years ago, that my husband was going to gamble away our savings, as well as lose his entire net worth of over three million dollars! Am I correct in the assumption that you believe I'm the one who risked my career, and my reputation to steal two hundred and fifty thousand dollars, when I was already worth over three million?" Pausing, I looked around the table for any sign that I was getting through to these people who held my future in their hands. Taking another deep breath, I continued. "You all knew my husband. You've been to our home many times. Did any of you ever think we might be having financial difficulties?"

There was whispering around the room as I waited for an answer. I wasn't surprised to hear Hilda speak.

"Olivia, we all know that you and Brian lived very well. In fact, that is part of the problem. Now you've lost everything. The house and its contents are to be sold. It's all over the news and besides, I have the details from a reliable source. You're ruined, Olivia. Under the circumstances, you have to be desperate for money."

"Hilda is right," came a voice from the end of the table. "A quarter of a million dollars could give you a new life somewhere."

I couldn't believe my ears... they just didn't get it. "Do you mean that you are willing to have me arrested on charges of embezzlement simply because you believe I'm destitute? *That* is supposed to be my motive?"

Heads began to nod in agreement. Chairman Richards's eyes slowly circled the table, stopping at each member. "Olivia, I'm sorry. I knew your husband well. I considered him a good friend. And you have made a tremendous difference here at East Side General. You've single-handedly ended the cold war that existed between the doctors and administration. Not to mention the plans for the pediatric care unit, which was entirely your project. But the facts speak for themselves."

I placed both hands on the table and leaned forward. "Mr. Chairman, if I can prove to you that I don't need the money, not now, or in the past, would you consider holding off filing charges against me until a full investigation can be made?"

"Olivia, how long will obtaining this proof take?"

"Would you allow me to make a phone call?" I heard a few mumbles around the table about it getting late. "Please, my future is at stake."

The secretary got up and brought the phone from a side table. Taking a business card from my handbag, I handed it to Chairman Richards.

"Are you serious? You want to call Lionel Montgomery?"

"No, I want *you* to call him. That number will ring to the private line in his office." Suddenly the whispers stopped, and everyone was paying attention. "I'm sure none of you in this room know of my life before I married Brian. I don't like to talk about my past. Brian was my second husband . . . Winston Montgomery III was my first."

A buzz of whispering filled the room until Chairman Richards called for quiet. "Please continue."

"I was given a rather large settlement at the time of our divorce, which Winston's Uncle Lionel invested for me, along with a trust fund that I've had since 1964, when my parents and brothers were killed in an automobile accident. I think this call may help with your decision."

The room was silent as Chairman Richards made the call and Lionel came on the line. He then handed the phone to me. "Here, he would like to speak with you."

"Hello, Uncle Lionel, as I mentioned earlier, I'm in a rather desperate situation here. You can clear up a few important concerns the Board has with me by telling Mr. Richards how much I'm worth. Ballpark will do, it doesn't need to be exact." I handed the phone back to the Chairman.

All eyes were on him as he listened.

His head turned toward me with an expression that went from interest to disbelief. His left eyebrow raised, his eyes grew larger. He took a deep breath then turned to face Hilda with a look of contempt. "I do appreciate this information Mr. Montgomery, and yes, I agree that this should not be made public knowledge. I see no reason for anyone else to know of Olivia's personal finances. Thank you for your help. This information makes a big difference." He put the receiver gently on the cradle.

Turning back toward me, he took a deep breath. "First of all, let me formally apologize to you, Olivia, for the grievous errors that have brought you here. If Hilda values her position with this institution, she'll find out how this travesty happened and who is responsible. An audit will be done to determine if the money was actually taken or were the reports altered in a way that makes Mrs. Bentley appear guilty of embezzling. You will find out who is behind this. Won't you, Hilda?"

Hilda's face turned a brilliant shade of red. She swallowed. "Yes, sir."

"Secondly, if we press charges, I've been assured this institution will never see a dime of Montgomery money again. While, that would be financially devastating, it wouldn't be the end to Olivia's project, because she could fund the pediatric care unit *herself*!" Talking amongst the members around the table broke out and Chairman Richards had to use the gavel to gain control. "Olivia, there will be no charges filed against you, and since this whole travesty got out of control because of your wish for privacy, everyone in this room will honor that. No one at this table will ever divulge what has occurred tonight, relative to your personal life. Past or present." He pointedly looked at Hilda before he continued, "Does *everyone* agree?"

"Yes" was the unanimous answer.

I had won this battle. But a nagging feeling warned me the war wasn't over yet.

CHAPTER 26

Vanessa called each day to see how I was doing and give me the latest hospital gossip. Although Consuelo had been with Brian since he inherited the house from his parents, I saw no need to keep her on. What I needed was to be alone to put my life back together and find my new direction. I gave her a generous severance and letter of recommendation, knowing it wouldn't be long before she had a new job.

With everyone gone, the house was quiet and lonely. I had far too much time on my hands and memories kept flooding back with a suddenness that took my breath away. Every room I entered reminded me of a wonderful moment alone with Brian. Of lavish parties with music and laughter. My heels tapped across the marble floor, and I remembered our first Christmas together. We had gone shopping for the largest tree we could find. After getting the monster tree through the front door, we didn't know how we would be able to get it into the living room—much less decorate it. Brian got the bright idea to leave it where it was . . . in the two-story entrance hall, nestled in the graceful curve of the staircase. It was a lot easier to decorate as we leaned over the banister!

The following week was one of trepidation and turmoil for me. An appraiser and his assistant arrived from the auction house and literally turned the house inside out. He was a short little man with dark beady eyes and slicked-back, black hair. Each day, he wore the same gray pinstriped polyester suit, but with a different colored shirt, opened at the neck. His assistant was a carbon copy only taller. I thought they looked like a couple of vaudeville entertainers, dancing around the house to their own music.

We had the "Battle Of The Attic", which lasted almost one full day. Eventually I was able to prove, through old family photos, that the furniture was my grandparent's and the various other items including my mother's clothes, were all I had left of my family. The appraisers also tried to get their hands on my mother's portrait, which hung in the bedroom over the fireplace. Apparently, it was painted by a famous artist of the day and was quite valuable. Fortunately, I looked enough like my mother that had I been wearing the dress the painting could have been of me. Luckily, I'd had the foresight to hide my jewelry from their beady little eyes by placing it in the bottom of the box containing my brother's train set in the attic or they would have tried to take that too.

CeCe came back and helped me pack the items I wouldn't need in the next few months. Vanessa came over each night after work, and all three of us focused on cleaning out the library. I still had questions surrounding the circumstances of Brian's death and my gut told me the answers I needed were in the desk. I concentrated on that while CeCe and Vanessa went through the file cabinets.

Vanessa found the folders with data on the trips Brian and I had taken to Europe. She read aloud the names of all the hotels we stayed in and how much they cost, along with all the gifts he purchased for me, including the mink coat on our first trip to Paris.

Vanessa waved the folder in the air. "This just isn't fair! How do you get all the rich guys and the only rich ones I find are married?"

"Maybe because I've married for love and not money. Men can smell a gold-digger a mile away."

"I'm not like that. I just deserve the same as you. You didn't love Win. No one could *really* love Win. He just used people. He used you."

I let my mind wander back to my marriage with Win and the turbulent years. "I did love him . . . in the beginning."

CeCe put down the stack of folders she had been going through. "I agree with Vanessa, Win's a real asshole. I still have to live in the same town as him."

"Well, the gossip flying around my mom's beauty shop is the new Mrs. Montgomery isn't finding life with Win all that great either. She refers to Olivia and Victoria as the two bitches."

"Winston must be keeping a tight hold on Win's purse-strings because his wife is buying everything at Capelli's on credit," said CeCe.

Vanessa chuckled. "Yeah, word on the street is that Win had to pay-off Olivia with half of his trust fund."

"That's a lie. Win was quite capable of throwing away his money without my help."

"Yeah, but the Montgomery's still blame you for all their problems. I'm sure they always will." CeCe picked up another folder. "You can sure tell Brian was an accountant. Everything he ever bought is listed with the name of the store, the date and how much it cost. That black Chanel suit you wore to the funeral cost five thousand dollars."

I scanned the stacks of folders. Everything was itemized and each trip had its own folder. I decided this was information that should not fall into the hands of the Beady Eyed Brothers, so we boxed everything personal and took it to the attic. Brian's check books, financial statements and the suicide note were carefully placed in my briefcase to review when life slowed down.

Finally, the cataloging was completed and the date for the auction was set. I was given two weeks to have my personal possessions removed from the house. I arranged for a storage company to collect everything in the attic the following week, along with a few garment boxes in my room. CeCe went back home. Everything was tagged for the auction, and I no longer felt at home in my own house. I was ready to move on.

The following Monday I got a call from Dan Richards asking if he could stop by.

"Are you asking as my friend or the Chairman of East Side General?"

He chuckled. "I guess I deserved that. A little of both, this is really important."

"Okay, I'll be home all day."

Twenty minutes later the doorbell rang.

Dan entered the foyer and glanced around the room. "It's lost a bit of its charm."

"Yeah, well, I've gone with a new look called Auction House Chic."

They both walked toward the living room. "Please sit anywhere, and don't worry about the price tags. It's a bit like living in a warehouse."

He chose the small, seating area in front of the fireplace. It was now sterile and clear of any remains of the once warm embers.

"I'm so sorry. I'll always remember the happy times and your gracious hospitality." Dan set his briefcase on the floor next to his chair.

"There were many wonderful times, and I'm learning to deal with the rest. I take it you're here to discuss Hilda."

"The audit has been completed. There's no missing money. Someone altered your reports and your old reports to make you look guilty. We don't know who that person is, but considering the evidence it looks like someone in the finance department."

"I'm glad it wasn't a case of embezzlement. I can't imagine who would do this or why."

"The Board is going to ask for Hilda's resignation."

Olivia stood with her back to the fireplace. "Surely you don't think Hilda is behind this? What could possibly be her motive?"

"She's merely been a figurehead since you came onboard. It's you the doctors respect, and the Board knows the important role you've played. I suspect she's jealous of your popularity and what you've been able to achieve. I'm sure that played a role in her condemning you so quickly."

"When I met with her, she had a stack of my reports in front of her. She said that the reports didn't lie."

"She approached me with the same reports. She assured me the Vice President of Finance was the one who blew-the-whistle. He noticed a discrepancy on your last report then did a review of your reports for the last three years. He found that money was being diverted over the last two years."

"She was a difficult woman to work for, but I honestly believe she only wanted the best for the hospital. I don't know why she was so convinced I was guilty."

"She obviously trusted the finance department. She condemned you before getting the facts. I blame myself for letting this go so far. I believed her. I should have demanded an audit right from the beginning."

Olivia sat down. "I've thought a lot about who could have wanted to destroy my reputation. I just don't have a clue who that might be." Meg's name kept rattling around in my head, but I didn't want to share that with Dan. "Losing her job is going to destroy her career."

"Speaking of jobs, we now come to the reason for my visit." Dan's smile and easygoing manner was back. "After reviewing all the facts and new information, the Board is officially offering you the position of President of East Side General Hospital."

"Does Hilda know? This isn't going to put me at the top of her favorite person list."

"I'm sure she's expecting it."

The offer was tempting. A part of me wanted to go back and redeem myself. There was also the pediatric wing that I wanted so badly and could now see becoming a reality if I were at the helm. But it was my ego that wanted the job, not my heart. The walls of the elegant room closed in on me with tags hanging like cobwebs on all the things I had grown to love . . . the trappings of a bygone world.

"Under the circumstances, it's a real honor to be offered the highest position in the hospital. But, I believe it's time for me to brush the cobwebs aside and walk alone, down a new path, and leave these dark shadows behind."

Dan nodded his head slowly. "You're an amazing woman, Olivia. Most people would have taken the job just for spite, if nothing else. What are you going to do?"

"I don't know."

I was ready to scream a few days later with the phone ringing with well-meaning friends who gave their advice on what I should do next. I was overwhelmed with the possibilities. That night, I tossed and turned and listened to the clock in the hall chime the hours. My world had fallen apart, there was nothing left, and all I wanted to do was run.

It was five o'clock in the morning as I sat in the dimly lit kitchen with a cup of coffee, staring at the pile of mail and magazines. Feelings of despair had a tight hold on my heart, when my brain finally registered that my eyes were looking at the Yacht Club letterhead. Pulling the envelope from the stack I slit it open. The *Lovely Lady* was back in the water and everything checked out. The auction house was not interested in a thirty year old, wooden boat that was surely infested with dry rot. Everyone but me had all but forgotten it.

Then, in an instant, I knew. It was all clear . . . like a message from Brian.

CHAPTER 27

Once I made the decision to leave, I ran upstairs and packed the few clothes that still remained in the closet and dresser. Everything else was already in storage. I had been using Brian's favorite coffee mug, the one from Caesar's Palace, and I grabbed it off the kitchen counter on my way to the garage.

The bags and boxes containing everything I needed to start a new life were crammed in the back seat and trunk, as the powerful car ate up the miles along Route 2, heading west toward Port Clinton. The radio was tuned to an oldies station with the volume turned up. It was my fourth Mercedes and still had that new car smell. Brian had surprised me with the gift just a few months before. He'd put the car in my name, saying, "No one can take this away from you." It had seemed a strange comment to make at the time . . . but now I understood.

I crossed the Bay Bridge to the Marblehead peninsula. A warm southerly breeze kicked up the choppy seas below me. The morning sun danced off the whitecaps, offering a stunning contrast to the clear blue sky. Cheerful yellow daffodils waved their sturdy heads, promising that warmer days would follow to bring forth the green canopy of summer. I stopped at the Cheesehaven for a few items, including cold cuts, fresh bread, and of course, cheese. The store had been a landmark since 1949, and had always been one of Gran's favorites.

After setting the bags on the floor of the front seat, I turned left out of the parking lot then headed into the quaint town of Port Clinton.

It only took a few minutes to reach the yacht club. The *Lovely Lady* rested at her dock. Opening the cabin door, I was assailed with the damp, musty odor of stale air that had been trapped inside all winter. Brian had called her a smelly old boat, and she certainly was that now. I opened all the windows and doors to let in the warm spring air, then went back out to unload the car.

The sun was just setting and I had everything stowed away. I'd taken down and washed the Venetian blinds and then attacked the windows until they glistened in the afternoon sun. Cleaning all of the mahogany paneled walls, doors, and built-in cabinets would remove any surface mold and have the old girl smelling better, but that project, I decided, could wait for a new day.

I went across the drive to the clubhouse for a long hot shower. I brushed my hair until it fell in soft waves on tired shoulders. Slipping on black slacks and a black cashmere sweater, I treated myself to a lovely dinner at the Island House Inn.

By the end of the first day of my new life, I felt good about myself and my decision to leave the city of Cleveland behind. Brian and I had stayed at the inn during the restoration of the *Lovely Lady*, until she became what Brian called "fit to live aboard," which took several months. The elegant old inn had been built in 1886. We'd been on a first name basis with most of the staff who told us wonderful stories of the times when Clark Gable, Spencer Tracy, Lauren Bacall and Humphrey Bogart were also guests while having their Mathews yachts commissioned.

The hostess escorted me to my favorite table. "Will Mr. Bentley be joining you this evening?"

I would have to get used to these questions. "No. Brian passed away recently."

"I'm so sorry to hear that. What a tragedy. We were all very fond of you and your husband. He had a wonderful sense of humor. We'll miss him."

Sitting back in my chair after finishing a delicious meal and sipping a full-bodied Cabernet Sauvignon, I wondered how long it would be before my days could be lived without thinking about Brian. I may have left Cleveland behind, but I'd brought Brian with me. I remembered how his deep rich voice would fill this room with laughter, and how the waitresses had all fallen under his magical spell. His ghost would remain here for a long time.

The *Lovely Lady* welcomed me home with soft lights illuminating her cabins. That night after I slipped between the covers, she rocked me to sleep. For the first time in over a month, I slept soundly. I didn't wake in a panic after nightmares, or reach for a strong body that was no longer there. I just slept until the morning sun washed the cabin in bright new light, along with promises for the future.

I spent the next couple of weeks cleaning and polishing until the *Lovely Lady* was once again the pride of the club. One day toward the end of May, I decided to visit the old haunts of my childhood. I hadn't been back to Marblehead since I'd taken Brian the day he presented me with the keys to the *Lovely Lady*. I'd wanted to show him where it all started.

Because it was now lined with travel trailers of various sizes, I almost missed the lane to the cottage. The field next door was a mobile home park. I drove over to see the Bay Shore Beach Club, but all that was left of it was a concrete slab. An elderly gentleman walking his dog told me it had burned down several years before, and there were no plans to rebuild.

My mood turned melancholy as I turned right onto Bay Shore Drive, passing the golf course and condos at the entrance to Bay Point. I followed the road around the curve heading toward the lighthouse, my eyes searching for *Stone Cottage*. Surely a home as lovely and sturdy as that would still be there, but it wasn't. In its place stood a row of contemporary looking condos. Shaking my head, I thought back to Dad's belief that one day this land would be valuable. He'd been right. But I couldn't help feeling the price was too high, and now the charm was gone forever. I drove on past the park that edged the quarry. And, suddenly, the familiar lighthouse stood proud and tall. I turned onto the drive, then parked and stepped out onto familiar ground. I picked my way over the rocks to find my favorite rock at the base of the lighthouse, the one where I'd sat as a young girl. As I'd done then, I looked out over the calm water toward Kelleys Island.

My attention settled on the windows in the old stone mansion glistening in the afternoon sun. I remembered the times when Gramps and I would sit here pondering the events of the day, or just life in general. I was thankful the mansion was still standing. At least that little piece of my past was still alive.

I watched the cool, clear water wash up over the stone ledges and then recede, carrying with it my sadness. Closing my eyes, I turned my head up to meet the warm sun, letting the cool air caress my face while I listened to the gentle breeze rustle the new young leaves in the trees. I belonged here. This was where I felt whole and at peace, and I sat there just soaking in everything that Mother Nature presented, until a chill brought me back to reality, and it was time to leave.

As I approached the bend in the road that would take me into the small town of Marblehead, I looked down the gravel lane leading to the old stone mansion and noticed a FOR SALE sign. Without thinking twice, I turned down the gravel road and stopped. The once-beautiful wrought iron gates were hanging off their hinges. Before me stood the house that sat in the shadow of the lighthouse . . . now no more than a run-down relic of the past. The ornate Victorian gingerbread was broken and missing in places, as was the railing on the front and side porches. It was obvious no one was living there. I pitied the person who would take on this monster of a bygone era. I hoped they had deep pockets.

CHAPTER 28

The dreaded Memorial Day celebration at the club was upon me. I needed to prove to myself that I could live a normal life without Brian.

The yearly picnic was underway with the threat of rain. My strategy was to arrive early and get seated in order to avoid making an entrance. I had my bratwurst, loaded with grilled onions and green peppers, along with various salads, and chose a small table off to the side. Children screamed with glee as they played various outdoor games. I reflected back to previous years when Brian could be found in the middle of the ruckus. Looking up, with a mouthful of potato salad, I watched in horror as the Commodore's wife walked over and sat down in the seat opposite me.

"I hope you don't mind, but I felt so sorry for you sitting here all alone. I noticed you were watching the children . . . such a pity you don't have any of your own to comfort you. I know how much Brian wanted children."

Her words might have been intended to comfort, but her tone did quite the opposite. "I wanted children also . . . it just didn't happen."

"Of course you did. I admire your courage, Olivia. I don't know of another woman who would continue in a prestigious club like this on her own, without a husband. But then . . . you seem to be doing all right with ours."

I couldn't take anymore of her sweet-as-honey voice when it had become very clear that she was nothing more than a viper. Standing before her, and using my best sweet-as-pie voice I said, "I feel just terrible about ending this delightful conversation, but it looks like rain, and silly old me left my windows open." Her mouth fell open. After tossing the offending food in the trashcan, I walked back to the boat and closed the windows. I knew it wouldn't be easy without Brian, but I was still the same person as the year before, when they considered me a favorite member of the inner circle. Now they were treating me like a whore after their husbands!

An hour later I sat beneath the protection of the Marblehead Lighthouse. A storm brewed out over the lake. I didn't remember making the decision to come, or most of the seven-mile drive ... it just happened. All I knew was I'd needed to get away. I hated the feeling that I'd become a prisoner trapped in a life without Brian.

Being a holiday weekend, there were quite a few tourists milling around. Kids of all ages were laughing and screaming as they ran across the grass and climbed over the rocks. It was better here, and I was enjoying the people, not like back at the club where the laughter hurt. The waves crashed at my feet, finally forcing me to move to higher ground. Leaning with my back against the cool white wall of the lighthouse, I felt its strength. The scene before me was tranquil with the old stone mansion bathed in a ray of sunshine against the dark purple storm clouds. Taking a deep breath, I felt a sense of calm wash over me.

The wind picked up. The sea gulls left their foraging for another day and headed inland. I decided it was time for me to leave as well. As I approached the bend in the road, the FOR SALE sign caught my eye, and once again, I found myself in front of the tall gates. Rain came down with a sudden force, blowing debris across the lattice beneath the battered porch. I watched from my warm, dry car and said out loud, "Poor old house, you look like I feel—no one to love us."

The wipers couldn't keep up with the horizontal sheets of rain as I passed through the town of Marblehead, on my way back to Port Clinton. Strong wind threatened to lift the big Mercedes. Just then I noticed a new marina and restaurant on my right. I decided the Marina DelRay looked like a good place to wait out the storm, so I turned in.

After slipping on the parka from the backseat, I made a dash for the wide porch that ran along the front of the building. I proceeded to the hostess station where a young woman with a big, warm smile greeted me. The place was nearly full, and she took me to a small table in the corner near the window. It was a good vantage point to see the dining room as well as the marina. The room was filled with every type of customer, from local workers to families and older well-dressed couples. Deep blues and reds set the theme for the nautical décor. Heavy, rugged furniture sat on a carpet of royal blue with a red and gold pattern. Large maritime prints in heavy gold frames covered the walls and added to the ambience.

My meal was delicious. Several times my eyes met those of a good-looking man sitting at a table near the door. He seemed to know everyone and had a warm smile and easy laugh. I was enjoying a second glass of wine and watching the storm rage beyond the window when I heard a sound at my side. I looked up into blue-green eyes, not unlike Brian's. "Hello, I'm sorry if I appeared to be watching you, but aren't you Olivia Bentley?"

I was surprised that he knew my name since I couldn't remember ever meeting him. He was clean-shaven with thick, wavy, sandy-blond hair and appeared to be about my age or perhaps a little older.

He was well groomed, which was in sharp contrast to his dirty and greasy work clothes.

"Yes, I'm Olivia Bentley. But I'm afraid if we've met, I don't remember."

He reached out his hand. His grip was firm.

"I'm Travis Tanner, and no, we haven't met. But I know you own the *Lovely Lady*. You and your husband did a beautiful job restoring her. My family owns Tanner Marine Service, and I love to work on old boats. That's what I was doing today . . . working on an old Lyman."

"That's nice. I'll have to remember that, should I find myself in need of a mechanic."

He asked if he could sit down. I surprised myself by saying yes.

"How come you're not at the Portage River Yacht Club's Memorial Day celebration?"

"I was there earlier, but it was too much family and politics." I began to feel uneasy. "How do you know so much about me?"

"Not you particularly, just the *Lovely Lady*. Most of us grew-up watching her cruise these waters." Those twinkling eyes, looking deep into mine disturbed me. "Have you thought about moving her?" I shook my head no. "This is a great new marina. It's well run, and there may still be open docks that will take her length. We're a lot friendlier than those folks in the big city!"

His easy smile and dimples conveyed a sense of humor, and I laughed at the thought of Port Clinton being called a big city. "I'll give it some thought."

We both noticed that the storm was letting up as the sun was going down. "Well, Mrs. Bentley, this has been a pleasure. Remember me if you ever need any work done." He reached out to shake my hand. "Just call the service center and ask for my . . ."

"Travis Tanner. Yes, I remember, and I won't forget."

He casually walked between the tables and acknowledged several people, saying goodbye to the hostess on his way out.

The waitress came with my check. She was one of those he'd said goodbye to. "Travis seems like a nice guy."

"The best. He's a real gentleman and part of our local color."

I wasn't exactly sure what that meant as I paid the bill and put my parka on before walking out into the rain.

That night I fell asleep listening to the gentle sounds of rain hitting the canvas, and this time it was a different pair of blue eyes invading my thoughts.

The sounds of waves lapping against the hull woke me, but there was no morning sun to brighten the day. After putting on a sweatshirt and jeans, I walked over to the clubhouse for breakfast. I was heading to a small table in the corner when I heard my name. "Olivia, over here! Please join us." I turned to see a couple that Brian and I had often socialized with. He was a doctor in Toledo, and she the very spoiled daughter of a doctor whose only occupation was spending her husband's money. It made me happy to sit with someone who actually wanted to be with me. I sat down with a smile . . . but the smile quickly faded.

"Olivia, dear, we're so sorry about your loss. I just don't know how you can hold your head up. Brian had no right to disgrace you the way he did. Worst of all, he left you with nothing but that old boat! I just don't know how you face each morning!"

"I really appreciate your concern, but I'm not feeling well. You know, one of those female things." Slowly getting to my feet, I walked out into the gray gloom and headed back to the *Lovely Lady*. I spent the rest of the weekend on the boat reading and sipping wine while listening to soft jazz. Finally, all the upstanding members of the club went back home to their perfect lives, and left me alone with my fears and heartache.

After breakfast, the next morning, I slipped on jeans and a black turtleneck, and then unlocked the car and slid in behind the wheel. The scrap of paper on the visor caught my eye as I put the key into the ignition. It was the name and phone number of a realtor. I must have written it down the day before, although I didn't remember doing so. Getting out of the car, I walked across the road to the clubhouse and made the phone call that would change my life . . . again.

CHAPTER 29

With the phone call made, I jumped in the car and headed toward Marblehead. The day was sunny, with big puffy cotton ball-like clouds in a bright blue sky creating a lovely background for the big old mansion. Up close, the house was in far worse shape than I'd imagined. I shook my head and considered getting in the car and driving back to safety. As luck would have it, before I could act, a car pulled in and stopped behind mine. A short, rather round woman got out and walked toward me. My eyes were drawn to unruly, curly red hair containing a fair amount of gray. Cheeks that were perhaps a little too rosy glowed in a round face. Her golden-brown eyes ended in laugh lines . . . a clear indication of the bubbly personality within. She was probably somewhere in her fifties. I laughed to myself, wondering if her name was Mrs. Claus.

"Hello, Mrs. Bentley. I'm Emily Elfin, and I'm so happy to meet you."

Well, I was close! She extended her hand, and it was soft and warm. I took an instant liking to this storybook figure before me. "I'm glad to meet you as well. I have to tell you that this house has intrigued me since I was a kid when I would spend time at my grandparent's cottage. I used to believe it was haunted."

Her whole body seemed to jiggle as she laughed. "It may be! Still want to see it?"

"I think I can handle it."

"It's a grand old house and deserves to be saved."

We turned to look at what had once been a beautiful example of an Italianate Victorian mansion. "The house was built in 1867, the same year the Kelley Mansion was completed on Kelleys Island. It was designed by the same architect. The Captain was a good friend of the Clemons family, who owned most of the land at this end of the peninsula, and was able to purchase this parcel. It allowed him to keep an eye on his ships coming and going from the dock nearby. The house was a wedding gift to his second wife, and has remained in the family until now. Its currently owned by two elderly sisters. They've been moved to a nursing home in Port Clinton, which is why the place is in this condition." She pulled one of those old fashioned skeleton keys from her pocket as she guided me around to the side steps. "The front steps aren't safe. We only use the side door."

As she put the key into the lock, I couldn't help wondering why I was standing here. This had to be the dumbest thing I'd ever done, although it didn't hurt to look.

Emily lifted the heavy door slightly as she turned the knob. "I think the house or the porch settled, so there's a trick to getting this door open. But it's worth it when we get inside." We walked into a narrow hall paneled in golden oak with a bench on one side. I peeked into a small room on the opposite side, with coat hooks lining three walls and another row closer to the floor. "The Captain had fourteen children. Their names and heights at different ages are still visible next to the door . . . this room was the family coat closet."

We then walked into the large entrance hall, also paneled in golden oak before entering a large room to the left of the front door. "This was the parlor, which nowadays would be considered the living room." It had two large windows, which faced the front, and on the porch side were windows on either side of an ornate fireplace.

Crossing the large entrance hall we entered a library paneled in rich mahogany with floor to ceiling bookcases, and a ladder that ran along a brass rail. A large desk with ornate carvings sat in the center of the room, and on the end wall was a fireplace with a lovely black marble mantle and French doors leading to the wrap-around porch. "This was the Captain's escape from the family, and is pretty much as it would have been back then." I felt warm and safe in this room and could imagine him sitting in a comfortable chair in front of a fire, smoking a pipe.

The next room contained a hospital-type bed and a small dresser, as well as, a beautiful old Chickering square grand piano. "This was the music room. I understand there was also a harp, which the sisters donated to one of the local churches."

Emily pushed open two large pocket doors, and we entered a room at the back of the house. A large picture window with a window seat gave an unobstructed view of Lake Erie. Another set of French doors led to the porch. An ornately carved, built-in buffet graced one wall. A similar design was used around the fireplace just to the left of the French doors. A beautiful brass and cut-glass chandelier hung in the center of the room, but was pulled up against the ceiling over an enormous bed. It was the biggest bed I had ever seen. The headboard had to be seven feet tall. A carved face in the center looked down over the bed. The tall footboard was equally ornate, with wide sideboards and huge carved feet.

I must have had an amazed look on my face because Emily laughed as she said, "Yes, this is the dining room," She moved to the foot of the bed. "The youngest of the sisters had the bed brought downstairs so she could be close to her sister who was a semi-invalid. The matching furniture is upstairs in the room the Captain shared with his wife. He had this set made for the house and it contains many examples of rare woods."

"I now understand how all those kids came to be," I said with a chuckle.

I followed Emily through a swinging door and found myself in a large butler's pantry. Along one wall was a metal counter with a sink and above it a window. Every inch seemed to be filled with cabinets, and the upper ones all had glass doors.

Emily stood in the middle of the room. "Do you see how the door into the dining room is offset from the one into the kitchen? That's so guests sitting at the table, would never have to look at the mess in the kitchen, when the door opens."

"This whole house is amazing and I could easily get lost, but now I want to see the kitchen."

Emily pushed open another swinging door, and I followed her into a rather small room, compared to the size of the others. The kitchen was considered the heart of modern day homes, but it definitely was not the heart of this house. There were few cabinets. A large porcelain sink and counter with graceful legs was tucked under the window. An old rounded-top refrigerator sat on the opposite wall, with a large worktable in the middle of the room. Next to the sink was a monster of a stove, right out of the Addams Family, with several ovens and a giant hood over many gas burners and warming compartments.

Emily laughed. "And it works!"

At the far end of the room, two large windows looked out onto the side porch. An old wooden table and two chairs, neither of which appeared safe to sit on, stood underneath. An open door showed a small octagonal room at the end of the porch that was flooded with light and had a magnificent view of the lighthouse and the lake. Emily gazed toward the lake as she spoke. "This was the morning room. It faces east and would have had a wonderful panoramic view until the addition was put on in the 1920s."

The back door opened onto a breezeway with a rickety door beyond leading to the addition. I told her I didn't need to go there, so she showed me the back servant's stairs that went from the basement to the attic. I didn't feel any strong urge to see that either, so we headed back through the hall to the front of the house. The staircase was massive with a large, carved newel post. At the top of the landing, a huge window surrounded by a wide band of stained glass—giving the illusion of a picture frame beckoned. I found myself drawn up the wide graceful stairs to gaze at the vista beyond. It was magnificent. I had found the heart of the house.

After seeing six large bedrooms and a couple of bathrooms on the second floor, we followed the main staircase all the way to the top. That ornate cupola, or "crown" as I had always called it, was a small round room with many windows. You could see everything from there—the lake, the islands, the lighthouse, and the tiny town.

"The Captain's wife spent many hours up here, reading to the children and watching for her husband to return to the dock."

Imagined scenes of how beautiful it would be with snow falling or during a thunderstorm danced through my head. The third floor contained the servant's rooms and storage, which didn't interest me either, so we headed back down. The stair height had been carefully calculated so a lady wouldn't have to struggle up or down with long skirts, but glide gracefully.

Slowly descending to the landing, I looked out over the lawn to the lake. "I had no idea it would be so wonderful. It's as though once you pass through the door, you step back in time. The feelings and scents and aura of the ages are still all locked-up here."

Emily sighed. "It's a shame this could all end."

"I don't understand what you mean. Someone with a large family would surely love to have this house. The price doesn't seem unreasonable."

Emily turned and headed down the steps. "There's a developer in Toledo who has been after the sisters for years to sell, so he can build lakefront condos and make a fortune. The sisters are fighting to hold on to it with the hope of finding a buyer who will restore and maintain the house, and not tear it down."

I thought about The Bay Shore Beach Club and *Stone Cottage*, both long-gone. "I noticed that similar developments have been built throughout the area, it's not the same charming place anymore."

"And it's only going to get worse as land becomes more valuable. The quarry covers almost the entire interior of the peninsula, which means that our available land is limited and anything on the lake is prime real estate."

I stopped in the large foyer admiring the paneled walls. My gaze went back up the stairs to the landing and the magnificent window. "How much time do the sisters have?"

Emily struggled with the side door. "Nursing homes are expensive, and the sisters' money is running out. That's why this place is in the condition it is. The sisters need help . . . soon."

"I wish I could be the one to save it, but it's a huge undertaking."

"Do you want to show it to your husband? I could arrange for you to pick up the key and look at your leisure."

"I don't have a husband."

"But, I thought, Mrs. . ."

"My husband passed away recently. I'm staying at the Portage River Yacht Club on my boat, the *Lovely Lady*."

"Not the old Chris-Craft that somebody purchased about seven years ago?"

"Yes."

"What a small world! That boat had been in my family since the day she was built!"

Emily suggested that we continue our discussion over lunch at the local diner. She introduced me to her friend Mavis, who owned the restaurant. Emily and I sat in a booth for hours talking like a couple of old friends who hadn't seen each other in years.

Years ago, Emily had been engaged to her childhood sweetheart. She'd been planning a beautiful wedding for the week after his return from the Army . . . but he never returned. No man had interested her since. She was the youngest of six children, and still lived with her mother in the house she grew up in. She was completely dedicated to her job and the community.

We were just getting ready to leave when Travis Tanner walked in and sat down at the counter. "Hello, Emily, nice to see you again." He had a smile that came easily. "Hello, Olivia. Have you thought any more about moving the boat? In fact, do you know that Emily's family owned her before you?"

"Yes, she told me, and, no, I haven't looked into moving it yet. But I'll stop by the marina and check it out."

Emily and I both went our separate ways. On my way back to the boat I found myself turning into the parking lot of the Marina DelRay. The small store and office smelled new. I looked around, a man in his 40s asked if he could help.

"Yes, I think so. Travis Tanner thought you might still have some available docks."

"You're a friend of Travis?"

"Sort of. The dock's for a forty-five footer that is currently at the Portage River Yacht Club."

His eyebrows went up as he stroked a rather full, dark brown beard. "Why would you wanna leave? You must be paid up for the season, you're gonna lose a lot of money."

Coming here was foolish, and I turned to leave. "I thought I needed a change of atmosphere. But maybe this wasn't such a good idea."

He ignored my movement toward the door. "Forty-five feet? Yeah, I have a couple spots left. Why don't you give me some information, and I can hold one for a few days to give you time to think about it." He nodded toward a chair and pulled a form from a file cabinet before sitting at his desk. "By the way, my name's Gus. Now I need the information about the boat, Mrs . . ."

"Olivia Bentley. It's a forty-five foot Chris-Craft, Double Cabin with a Flying Bridge."

"Year?"

"1954."

He looked at me with a quizzical look. "You mean 1974, right?"

"No, I mean 1954."

His voice carried more than a little sarcasm, "Does this boat have a name?"

"*Lovely Lady*."

He started to jot down the name, then his mouth fell open, and he looked up with a start. He dropped his pen, then slapped the desk, a big grin appearing on his face. "Well, you don't say. For a minute, I thought Travis sent you in here to play a practical joke on me! If you're really serious about moving her, I have a great dock that would be perfect for you, and it would be an honor to have her here. Why, the *Lovely Lady* is literally an institution around these parts. And Travis is the best man to keep her running."

Shaking his big, rough hand, I said I would like to think about it for a few days.

"Tell your husband that we'll take real good care of him. Just ask for Gus."

"Yeah."

I felt Gus's eyes burning through my back as I opened the door of the Mercedes, and I waved without turning around. Feelings of confusion and dismay filled my head as I drove back to the boat.

I had felt so alive and good about myself after leaving Emily that afternoon. But then, all too quickly, my confidence got shot down again—this time by a scruffy man with a beard. Why couldn't I be taken seriously, just for myself? Why must women always be seen as just another appendage of a man?

The *Lovely Lady* sat patiently before me. Brian and I had saved her and brought her back to life. My life felt so empty and meaningless . . . perhaps I needed to save another ugly duckling.

CHAPTER 30

The next morning, I made a phone call from the clubhouse. "Hello, Uncle Lionel, it's Olivia."

"Olivia, where are you? Several people have been calling me, asking where you are. I've been worried. Are you all right?" I heard the concern in his voice.

"I've needed some time alone to get my head straight and my life back into perspective. Uncle Lionel, do I have enough money to buy a piece of history and preserve it for future generations?"

"Sure, unless you're thinking about buying the Statue of Liberty."

"Hmm, more like Monticello."

"If that's what you really want, I'll transfer the money."

"It is. It really is. Thanks, Uncle Lionel."

The next call was to Emily. "Emily, it's Olivia . . . I think I need to see the basement."

Emily and I sat in the same booth at the diner. She pulled out a pair of small reading glasses that she perched on the tip of her nose. I laughed to myself because she really did look like Mrs. Claus. I signed papers saying I would restore the house and property and not resell for future development. I offered the asking price, providing that the furniture and fixtures remain.

Feelings of panic rushed through me as I shook Emily's hand.

"Don't worry, I'm sure the sisters will accept this offer, and I should have an answer tomorrow afternoon."

The next afternoon, I called Uncle Lionel from Emily's office and told him where I was, and about the house and how much money I would need. He was very encouraging, giving me the name of a former employee who was now the manager of a bank in Port Clinton. Emily knew the bank manager, and she called him to say I was on my way.

The ornate stone and brick building with intricate grillwork identified it as Victorian, probably of the 1890's vintage. The manager explained that Lionel Montgomery had already called. After reviewing the documents that Emily had given me, he said everything appeared to be in order and he would call Emily when the transaction was completed.

"I see you list your current address as the Portage River Yacht Club."

"Yes, I'm living on my boat, the *Lovely Lady*."

"Emily mentioned that you own her grandparent's old boat. I'm so glad to see her cruising these waters again."

"Everyone I meet seems to know that boat. She sure gets a lot of attention."

"What are you going to do with a house that big?"

"I haven't a clue. I just know that I have to save it."

He slipped the paperwork into a file folder. "You might consider turning it into a Bed and Breakfast. Knowing the sisters the way I do, I'm sure they would approve."

"Bed and Breakfast? I've heard of them, but never stayed in one. It sounds intriguing."

By the end of the week, I was back in Emily's office. The funds had been transferred into the sisters' account, and I had my new savings and checking accounts. I'd made a good salary at East Side General, and Brian insisted that he be the sole provider of the household. So there would be enough money to keep me going until the Bed and Breakfast became a thriving business. I just had to figure out what all that entailed.

Emily had the keys in her hand and smiled, shaking her head at me. "You certainly have friends in high places. If you had told me you planned to pay cash, I probably could have arranged a better deal."

"I'm happy with the deal." Her words sparked concern. "Emily, I would appreciate it if you didn't tell people that I paid cash for the house. I really am just an ordinary person who's had some bad luck. Perhaps one day I'll tell you about it, but right now I need to focus on building a new life."

Emily gave me a hug and said she would keep in touch.

I walked through the house less than an hour after getting the keys. It was all mine now, but I wished my family were there to fill the empty rooms with laughter. I could picture my daughter sliding down the banister. It was a house made for the holidays.

But I would be celebrating them alone.

After making a list of supplies I'd need for the monumental task of transforming the drafty old house into a warm comfortable home, I headed back to the boat.

Now, I needed to make a decision about the *Lovely Lady*. I made the turn into the marina and parked in front of the office.

The man with the beard was at the counter wearing a bright red plaid shirt. He looked up, smiling as I walked in. "Well, hello there, pretty lady. Made a decision?"

I smiled back at him, waving my new packet of checks. "Well, let's get this over with before I change my mind."

Gus and I had just returned to the office from looking at the dock. It was at the end of the pier and easy to get in and out of. We had completed the paperwork when the door opened and Travis walked in. He was dirty and greasy, and his hair looked as if he'd been running fingers through it all day. But his blue eyes had a magical twinkle and his smile prompted two dimples to appear. "I thought that was your car in the lot. Not many big black Mercedes around here."

"I took your advice and . . ."

Gus looked up me. "Excuse me, Mrs. Bentley, but you forgot to fill out your husband's name and information."

I hesitated for just a moment before answering. "There isn't a *Mr*. Bentley."

Travis cocked his head and raised one eyebrow in a quizzical look.

Glancing down at the ring on my finger, I continued. "He passed away recently."

Gus pushed the contract aside. "I'm real sorry for your loss, Mrs. Bentley, but you'll be fine here. Don't you worry none, we'll take real good care of you."

The moment was uncomfortable. I wasn't used to strangers wanting to help me—first Emily, then the bank manager, and now Gus.

"Hey, Travis, have you heard . . . some fool just bought the old Captain's house?" asked Gus with a chuckle.

"No! Really? That's gonna piss off someone!"

Clearing my throat, I interrupted. "Excuse me gentlemen, I would like to introduce myself." I shook each of their hands. "I'm Ms. Fool, nice to meet you!"

They both looked dumbfounded as they stared.

"It's true, I'm the new owner!"

Travis laughed. "First, the *Lovely Lady*. Now, the Captain's house. You certainly have a need to save relics of the past. You know, I've got an old cantankerous uncle you might be interested in!"

"No thanks. I think I've got about all I can handle at the moment."

Travis took a couple steps toward the door. "Well, I was just on my way in for dinner . . . care to join me?"

I was beginning to feel comfortable around these two easy-going guys, and Travis's smile won me over.

The hostess knew Travis and took us to a table by the window.

I remembered his earlier comment as I studied the menu. "What did you mean before, when you said that I was going to piss someone off?"

"There's a developer in Toledo, who's been putting up houses and condos around here as fast as he can get the land. That piece is prime, and he's been doing everything he can to get the sisters to sell—including some nasty, underhanded schemes."

"I've noticed the condos along the lake."

"What he can't get around is the love this town has for those two old ladies. We all watch over and protect them. He's been waiting for one or both to die, so he can get the land without any restrictions. But you have changed all that, and I can't see you dying anytime in the near future. Yep, I'd give anything to see his face when he finds out. You saved the day, Olivia . . . you're one of us now!"

We both ordered prime rib, and Travis chose a fine bottle of Cabernet Sauvignon.

"I'm glad I could save the house for future generations. I fell in love with it when I was fifteen, about the same time I fell in love with the *Lovely Lady*, while sitting on the rocks with my grandparents at the base of the lighthouse."

The meal was excellent, and I was pleased to learn that the restaurant was open for breakfast. With the boat being just steps away, and the house being down the road, it would be very convenient. While we ate, Travis looked at the list of supplies I had made earlier. He said the hardware store in Port Clinton would have everything

I needed, and he would bring over a ladder and tools. We finished our meal, and the waitress gave Travis a sly wink as she removed our plates.

It could have been the effects from the bottle of wine we had consumed over dinner. But warm feelings rushed to parts of my body that I thought died months before every time Travis looked into my eyes and smiled.

Travis leaned forward. "Would you like dessert? Or perhaps a sherry or cognac?"

I was surprised Travis even knew what cognac was, let alone ask if I would like one. We both ordered a cognac.

"I really am sorry about your husband. He was a man who loved life and got along with everyone."

I was surprised at his words, and my face must have shown it. "You're a very beautiful woman, with a face I could never forget. You and your husband made a striking couple."

"I don't understand. It sounds like you knew Brian."

"I was having dinner with my parents at the Island House last year when you and your husband walked in with two other couples. I just happened to be facing you and Brian. He was very charismatic."

"I'm flattered you remembered me. Brian is the one who got all the attention. And you're correct, Brian did get along with everyone and was always the life of the party." My fingers twisted the wedding band as I gazed out the window, not really seeing the boats resting quietly in the marina. The waitress brought our cognacs, and I took a warming sip.

"His death must have been sudden. From what I could tell he seemed to be in excellent health."

Travis's voice was soft and encouraging. I told him how Brian died and how everything else went wrong after that. And how I was determined to start again here in Marblehead.

"You're a brave and courageous woman, Olivia Bentley. And I admire you for not wallowing in self-pity."

My eyes went to the wedding band sparkling on my finger. "I don't know how brave I am. I'm still wearing Brian's ring. I'm not sure if it's out of love and respect for him, or a shield against everyone else."

"You'll know when it's time to take it off."

His comment about my ring made me uneasy. I needed to change the subject, and said that I would like to move the boat next week. "The sooner I leave the club, and all those viper-tongued bitches, the better!"

Travis laughed with his whole body. "Olivia, you're gonna fit in here just fine!"

Travis paid the bill, and said he would let Gus know I was ready to move and get some dock lines ready. It was Friday night, and the weekenders were arriving to their cottages, boats and trailers. The ferryboats were all lit up as they took passengers to the islands, for a weekend of fun, sun, eating and drinking.

Weekend festivities were already well underway in the clubhouse, and I hurried along the dock before someone saw me and wanted to stop and *talk*. The *Lovely Lady* gave a slight bow when I stepped aboard. The moonlight danced around the cabin, as I thought about the vast differences between Brian and Travis. Brian had been so worldly and polished. With the looks of a movie star, he had gotten attention wherever he went. Travis, on the other hand, was somewhat rough around the edges, but good-looking in a boyish sort of way. Yet, he had excellent manners and was far more knowledgeable than one would expect from a mechanic in a small town. He made me feel good about myself. I wished I were in the market for a relationship . . . but I wasn't.

CHAPTER 31

The morning sun streamed in through the Venetian blinds. Travis crept into my thoughts, and I found myself looking forward to seeing him again. The warm rays were already heating the cabin, as I put on jeans and an old shirt. Thinking I might want to change later in the afternoon, I grabbed a pair of shorts, a tank top and a pair of white sandals, and shoved them into a tote bag. I wanted to be on my way before the Saturday morning activities began with the other boaters. So after a quick breakfast, I was off to the hardware store with my list.

After helping load what seemed like every inch of the car, the clerk laughed and said he hoped I had a band of merry men to help me with my project.

The SOLD sign greeted me as I drove through the gates, and it was with an overwhelming sense of pride that I climbed the three steps to the side door with my fist full of keys. The rather ornate brass key slid easily into the equally ornate lock of the large Oak door. I remembered to lift as I turned the carved knob. The air inside was damp and musty. It wasn't long before I had all the first floor windows opened to breathe some fresh new life back into this tired old house.

I had just gone back outside to begin unloading when a white Chevy Blazer pulled into the drive. Travis got out with a smile. "Good morning, Olivia."

"Ah, at last! My band of merry men has arrived!"

He turned and looked down the drive, then back at me, bewildered. "What do you . . . ?"

"Never mind. I sure am glad to see you!"

We emptied my car, and he brought in a ladder and toolbox from his. After Travis determined the vintage refrigerator and stove were both in working order, I began cleaning them. He went to the basement to check out the hot water tank and boiler. By the time the kitchen was usable, Travis came up from the basement and declared I would have heat when it was needed. He also told me the wiring and plumbing needed to be checked out by a professional. He could have a cousin of his stop by next week if I wanted. I did.

In early afternoon, we walked through the door of the diner. Travis waved to his Aunt Mavis, who owned the quaint old establishment. She came over to greet us with menus and a big smile. Before she could speak, Travis began enthusiastically. "You're not gonna believe this, but Olivia here just bought the . . ."

Mavis smiled and winked at me. "Captain's house. I know, the deal was written right here in this very booth."

Travis lifted his hand to his forehead in a rolling motion, like he was conjuring up a genie. "Mavis The Magnificent! She sees all and knows all! Anything you want to know about this town or anyone in it . . . just ask Aunt Mavis!" She lovingly hit him on the shoulder with the menus, as we both ordered tuna melts and fries.

"You've taken on a huge project all by yourself. Or, perhaps there's some wealthy man waiting in the wings to marry you and fill the house with kids?"

I laughed at the thought. I'd been married to two wealthy men and look where that got me. And neither one of them would live in a run-down old house in Marblehead. Then I remembered David Morgan. He would have liked the house, especially being so close to the lighthouse, and we would have filled it with many beautiful children. "No, there's no man in my life. Although, once-upon-a-time, I met someone who was staying at *Stone Cottage* for the summer. We fell in love, and talked of getting married when we finished school. But anger and jealousy spoiled our dreams, and kept us apart."

"Ah, yes, first love. You sound like you still care about him."

Memories of David filled my head. I thought about our lives and the paths we had taken. I couldn't ask a famous surgeon to move to a small town, and I couldn't go back to the medical community that I had just left with a tattered reputation. Letting out a long sigh, I looked into Travis's blue-green eyes. "No, that was twenty years ago. We met by accident at a fundraiser a couple of years ago. He's a prominent surgeon in Cleveland and is married with three children. The life we would have had together is only a childhood dream. We've both gone our separate ways."

Our sandwiches were placed in front of us.

His tone had become lighter. "Saving the house is a very noble deed, but I guess I still see that old mansion swallowing you up. Will you choose one bedroom for yourself? Or will you sleep in a different one each day of the week?"

I finished the first bite and decided it was my time to be serious. "Actually, the manager of the bank suggested that I consider opening a Bed and Breakfast. He's collecting some information for me. Emily Elfin thinks it would be a good investment and an asset to the area."

Travis frowned nodding his head. He seemed to ponder the idea as he continued to eat. "It's a grand old place. Until today I didn't realize how beautiful it was inside, and it certainly is large enough for a B & B. The winter months will be slow, but there are always local families looking for somewhere to put up holiday guests. Yes, it could work."

After finishing lunch, Travis mentioned he was going to visit his cousin, Michael, in Cleveland for a few days. However, he would be back on Wednesday and would be available to help me move the *Lovely Lady* to her new dock. We said goodbye in the parking lot, each going our separate ways. I was a little disappointed that he wouldn't be joining me for my first day in the house.

The afternoon was warm and sunny, and I was glad I had thought to bring a change of clothes. On my way back to the house, I decided it was the perfect day to improve the appearance of the yard. I changed into the shorts and top I'd brought and went outside. A black kitten came by to play with the rake and chase leaves, and I laughed at her antics. She disappeared just as quickly as she had appeared, and I missed her company. Finally at dusk, I gave in to sore muscles and stood back with rake in hand, admiring a yard that was clear of debris. A neighbor stopped by to say he was glad someone finally bought the old place. He promised to come by on Sunday with a riding mower and cut the grass. I realized I hadn't considered mowing in the total scheme of things. I'd better start a To Do List, and a Check Out List . . . plus a Budget!

I closed the windows and locked the side door before walking down to the water's edge. The evening was quiet and calm. The weekend boaters had all gone back to their docks. The air was still warm and I listened to the lapping of the water on the rocks. From far away I thought I heard a meow and began walking toward the old stone walls that lined the inlet. The walls were all that remained of the old boathouse. Over the years, sand had built up at the entrance making the water quite shallow, but the far end, which would have been near the back wall of the boathouse, had the dark green color of deep water. Tree roots and vines covered the back corner, obscuring the last several feet from view. I wondered if the black kitten could be in amongst the thicket. I began walking toward the rubble calling, "Here kitty, kitty." when a horn sounded in the drive. Maybe, Travis had changed his mind and come back. I began walking toward the house and was about halfway across the yard, when I turned and looked back. The soft evening glow of the sun's last rays filtered through the brambles, causing them to glow with an eerie light from within. It was as if death hovered, sending chills racing through my body.

A voice calling my name broke the spell. I turned back toward the house to see Emily Elfin waving. Her bright cheery smile chased away the demons. She enveloped me in her soft comforting arms before stepping back. She took my hand and pulled me over to the side porch to see two flats of bright pink geraniums. "I saw you working in the yard when I drove by earlier, and decided what this dreary old place needed was color!" Her high-pitched, singsong voice made me grin. "I love pink. Don't you? It's such a happy color, and feminine, and that's just what you need."

I loved her jubilance. I couldn't get my earlier vision of her as Mrs. Claus, out of my mind. "Yes, Emily, I love pink. And I can't thank you enough for thinking of me." Putting my arm around her as we walked to our cars, I had the feeling we had been friends forever. "I'm on my way to the Marina DelRay for dinner. I would love to have you join me, if you don't have other plans."

She tilted her head and grinned, as if she had some inner secret. "I'd love to spend the evening with you. I have the feeling we have a lot to talk about. I'll meet you there."

The restaurant was crowded, and we were seated at a corner table in the back of the room. It was a good place to people-watch as we both sat with our glass of wine. I noticed families with children of all ages, as well as older couples.

"We're the only locals here at the moment. These are all *Summer People*. They're here for the day, or the week, or maybe a month or two, or perhaps they have just taken the ferry from Kelleys Island. They all eventually go back to wherever they've come from, and life slows down for the rest of us until the next season." Emily tilted her head in that quirky sort of way. "I don't know what you're running from, what would cause a beautiful, smart, and obviously successful woman, to want to live in such a quiet little town, but I'm awfully glad you're here."

Emily's kind brown eyes evoked my trust and I took a deep breath. "I'm not running from anything worse than heartache, but I feel as though I've come home." She only smiled and nodded as I continued. "I started coming here when I was a young girl. My grandparents rented a cottage . . ." By the time I finished my story, the other customers had all left, except for a young couple who appeared very much in love and were not paying any attention to anyone but themselves. I felt as though I had just come out of a trance. I didn't even remember what I'd eaten, only the kind eyes of Emily and the occasional squeeze of her hand. I felt cleansed and relieved that I had finally told my story. Yet I also felt vulnerable.

Emily seemed to sense my thoughts and she took my hand. "Don't worry, Olivia. What you've told me will go no further. I have a gift . . . sometimes it's a curse. Call it ESP or intuition, but sometimes I just know things about people or feel what they feel. I've had many different emotions and messages from you since I first shook your hand in front of the house." I must have had a doubtful look on my face because she explained. "When I shook your hand, I felt unhappiness and tragedy. Yet your smile was warm and sincere. As we walked through the house, I saw you there happy with children, yet you said your husband had just died. Later, in the diner as I told you about myself, I could feel strong emotions of happiness, along with gut-wrenching heartache." Tears filled my eyes, as the realization came over me that what she was saying was true. "Let the tears come, Olivia. They cleanse the soul and let it begin to heal."

We sat in silence until we noticed the staff was shutting down for the night. Emily patted my hand. "It's time to go, Olivia, but the healing will continue. You've come home."

CHAPTER 32

I lay in my bunk thinking about all that Emily had told me. I didn't believe in ESP, tarot cards, palm readers, or fortunetellers. Playing with the cards that life dealt was hard enough without knowing in advance what was coming next. I had to admit, though, that whatever one called Emily's gift, it was not scary or frightening, but warm and comforting.

The morning sun cast shadows on the cabin walls, while the reflection of the water danced on the ceiling. I felt renewed both mentally and physically. It was a new day and a new beginning, and I was ready. I packed some clothes in a tote bag before heading to the upper deck with toast and a mug of strong coffee. I loved being on the water ... the sound of waves slapping against the many hulls, wind whistling through the masts and rigging of the sailboats, the smell of fresh air mingled with the slight odor of fish, seaweed, and engine fumes. Life slowed down here. I looked forward to moving the boat to Marina DelRay, a place where I wouldn't feel the need to hide every time I saw someone walking my way, or feel the obligation to participate in activities and events that would only lead to wounded emotions.

As I walked along the dock toward the car, my thoughts were completely absorbed in the stops I wanted to make before going to the house. My list contained items for the kitchen that needed to be purchased at the hardware store. Emily had given me directions to a nursery where I could obtain more flowers and plants for the yard, and I also wanted to stop at Mutach's Market.

It wasn't until I had nearly reached the car that the footsteps caught my attention. I looked up to see several of my former so-called friends hurrying to meet me. They were too close for me to just wave and jump into the car . . . I had no choice but to wait for their arrival. The emotional attack was swift and deadly. After their retreat, I found myself sitting behind the wheel shaking with tears running down my cheeks. As my friends, they had felt the need to warn me of the latest gossip. Word of the hospital scandal was running rampant through the club, and apparently, an affair with a doctor was thrown in for good measure. Some also believed Brian took his own life because he couldn't face the shame of my actions.

Emily had said the healing would begin, but there was only loneliness and Brian's ghost. It took several minutes before I could bring myself to start the engine. I decided to accept Emily's offer of help to move the boat because I couldn't wait for Travis to return.

That evening, as the sun began to set, I sat on the window seat in front of the big picture window on the landing. My knees were tucked up under my chin as I rested tired muscles and sipped a mug of chamomile tea reflecting over the day's activities.

The hardware store had been my first stop of the day. I purchased everything I needed for the kitchen, including a teakettle. At the nursery, I chose plants in various shades of pink and white for the front and side yards. Ivy and geraniums in a deep fuchsia would fill the two huge stone urns flanking the front steps. Everything would be delivered on Tuesday, including a truckload of compost I'd use to enrich the tired old soil. Mutach's Market hadn't changed much in twenty years. The wooden floors still creaked beneath my feet. I managed to find time to stop by Emily's office and make arrangements to move the boat the next morning at eight o'clock. She had an appointment in the afternoon to show some properties, but her morning was free.

The orange rays cast a shimmering glow across the water, and I began to relax under the calming effects of the tea. There were no ghosts here, only the promise of a new beginning.

I awoke early with the energy of one embarking upon a new adventure. After finishing breakfast I took my last mug of coffee to the upper deck and stood at the rail. Already the sun had begun warming the day. The sky was deep blue with only the occasional puffy cloud drifting by. Fish jumped, and seagulls called. The horn of the ferry to Put-in-Bay announced its departure. Yes, this was going to be a great day.

By the time Emily arrived, I had all the dock lines and fenders on board and the engines warmed up. We were ready to go. There was little traffic on the Portage River that morning. Emily stowed the lines as I guided us into open water.

She had just finished and climbed up to join me on the flying bridge, as the *Lovely Lady* dipped her bow into the large waves made by the crossing ferry traffic, then settled back for the smooth ride to her new home. I took a northeast course toward South Bass Island with Perry's Monument glistening white in the morning sun. Just off Mouse Island, I made the turn to the east and headed into the South Passage, which we would follow until reaching the entrance into East Harbor. The gentle surges vibrated beneath our feet as the old boat cut through the waves, and the sun kept us warm against the cool breeze. I took in a deep breath and looked over at Emily. Our eyes met, and we smiled. No words needed to be spoken as we were both in tune with nature, and our senses drank in our surroundings.

We were halfway between South Bass and Kelleys when I saw the ferry to Kelleys Island crossing in the distance. I nodded toward the ferry. "It was twenty years ago I stood at the rail of that ferry with my friend Patsy Paterson and declared that I wanted to live here. She didn't think I would like it in the winter when everything was frozen, but that only made me more determined."

"Patsy Paterson! Not the fruit farm Paterson's?"

"Yes, they had a farm toward the Sandusky Bay side. I haven't seen or heard from her since."

"Well, she must not think the winters are all that bad because she never left. She's a nurse at Magruder Hospital and married to a pediatrician. They have several kids. Her name is Romanov now. You should give her a call. I'm sure she would like to see you. She and Travis are . . ."

"I think I'll wait awhile. I need time to get my life in order before I bring old friends back into it. I guess you could say I'm still trying to get my sea legs." Emily nodded as she watched the ferry. I went on, "Maybe it's too soon for me to be saying this, but this is where I want to spend the rest of my life. I feel so alive when I'm on the water. Just watching its many moods is both invigorating and soothing. I love the house, and I have never been this happy and sure of what I'm doing."

"Yes, Olivia, I see that the healing has begun. I'm glad you're letting me be a part of it."

It was a perfect day for a cruise. We listened to the drone of the engines and the waves breaking off the bow. Gulls shrieked and swooped over and around the fishing boats. Suddenly, Emily gasped and put both hands to her throat. I pulled back on the throttles and slowed the boat. Turning toward her, I looked into terror-stricken eyes. "Emily, what is it? Are you ill? Should I call the Coast Guard?"

She shook her head from side to side as she shifted her gaze from Kelleys Island to me. Her voice was low and raspy, a haunted look in her eyes. She dropped her hands to the arms of the chair. "I'm all right. How do your gauges look?"

Everything looked normal, but still my heart thumped erratically in my chest. "Fine. Why? What's wrong?"

"Nothing. Take her slow and head for the channel markers. I'm going below for a couple of minutes."

Emily gave me a weak smile before starting down the steps to the cabin below. "Don't look so concerned. I'm fine . . . really."

Maybe she was fine, but I wasn't. She'd scared the shit out of me, but I did as I was told and headed slowly toward the channel markers that would lead us into East Harbor. Glancing to my left at Kelleys Island, I saw the old concrete and steel ore docks. They gave me the same creepy feeling they had twenty years ago, sending a shiver up my spine. The bow was just making the turn into the channel when I saw Emily coming up the stairs.

"Everything looks fine below. I checked the engine room, and nothing seems out of order. The bilge pump is working fine, but I think you should have Travis overhaul the engines and check the wiring."

"What did you expect to find?"

"I don't know. I just had a feeling. I get them sometimes . . . it's usually nothing. Let me take the helm. This channel is pretty narrow, and it gets shallow fast."

After Emily took over, she pointed out several landmarks along the way. I could see the bright blue roof of the marina office and restaurant off in the distance. She seemed back to normal, like nothing had happened. But I was still shaking and was glad she had the wheel. I was impressed at how well she handled the boat, as it had been many years since she'd been aboard.

She returned control back to me as we approached the entrance to the marina. I saw Gus standing on the dock waving. It was an easy dock to get into. After a few unnecessary directions from Gus, I eased the bow slowly toward the center, put the throttles in reverse, and gently kissed the dock. The *Lovely Lady* sat quietly as Emily tossed the bowline to Gus while I wrapped the stern line around the dock cleat. Gus came around the side to help position the fenders while I shut down the engines.

"You handled that like a pro, little lady. I'm impressed! Wait till some of the guys who take five or six tries with their wives hanging off the bow see you! I want a front row seat!"

"Thanks for the compliment, Gus. I have to admit that the *Lovely Lady* and I get a lot of attention."

Emily got her things from below and jumped onto the dock. "Come on, Olivia. I need to get you back to your car in time for me to make my afternoon appointment. Gus, Travis needs to check out the engines and wiring so Olivia has a safe boating season. We don't want anything to happen to our newest resident."

"Sure, I'll mention it to him when he gets back."

The day was still picture perfect, but something had definitely cooled within Emily. I promised to call her with my new number as soon as the phone was installed later in the week.

Arriving back at Marina DelRay, everything was quiet. The rows of boats nestled against their docks with canvas buttoned tightly awaiting the coming weekend. Hours later, a blanket of a million stars covered the night sky while I lounged on the bridge sipping the last glass of a very expensive bottle of Bordeaux. I celebrated the *Lovely Lady's* new home. I just knew we were going to be happy here.

CHAPTER 33

A strong wind blew the boat against the dock. Several times, I got out of bed and retied the lines, but the boat still rubbed against the fenders. The screeching of wood against rubber wasn't helping a headache that was probably the outcome of too much good wine, and it was well into the night when I finally fell asleep. Dawn came all too quickly. I felt as groggy and gray as the day.

Emily's behavior the day before still bothered me. Although I didn't consider myself to be superstitious, I hoped it wasn't an omen of things to come. Between the after-effects of the bottle of Bordeaux and my lack of sleep, I didn't feel like doing much. Walking the short distance to the restaurant for breakfast was about all I could manage.

But after a heaping plate of eggs, bacon, fresh warm muffins, and several cups of strong coffee, I felt ready to take the boxes of personal items that were stored in the forward cabin over to the house. Gus must have seen me struggling with the first box because he came to help with the rest. We soon had both the trunk and back seat full.

Gray was definitely the color of the day. The gray sky had turned the water a darker shade of gray, while the stone of the house appeared even darker against its background. Even the gravel of the driveway matched the day's color scheme. The pink geraniums were the only color in an otherwise gray landscape.

When I carried a box up the steps to the porch, the black kitten I'd seen earlier ran out from the shrubs to greet me. "Good morning, little one." It purred as I bent down and picked it up. "Well, at least you're in a happy mood. I'd love to play, but I have work to do." I brought a few more boxes from the back seat and stacked them on the porch. Struggling with the heavy door, I turned the key in the lock. The kitten purred and rubbed against my legs. I finally got the door open and reached down to move my little friend away. "Sorry kitty, but you need to stay outside."

The inside of the house was just as dreary as the outside. I went around the house turning on the ceiling lights and wall sconces. With years of dust and grime built up, the lights cast a dim glow at best. Each room seemed more depressing than the last. Bringing in the boxes while trying to keep the kitten out was quite an ordeal, but by noon I had all the boxes safely stored in the old coatroom off the side hall.

While walking through the downstairs rooms, it became obvious that the first order of business was to get the ceiling fixtures washed. The old lights, although beautiful, didn't give off much light and just added to the depression closing in on me.

By early afternoon the fixtures in the kitchen were finished. I moved the ladder to the front parlor and positioned it under the ornate fixture that had been converted years ago from gas to electricity. The room's high ceilings required me to stand on the top step in order to reach the chandelier's three globes. The first one came off easily, but the second refused to budge. Stretching even further to get a better grip, I tried once more to turn the tiny screw that would release the delicate globe. Just then, a flash of black leaped in front of me. I jerked my body in response sending the ladder tipping sideways. I screamed while me and the ladder crashed to the floor.

A rough tongue, not unlike damp sandpaper, licked my face. My whole body hurt as I looked into the black, furry face of my new friend. The kitten moved off to a safe distance while I used my right arm to push the ladder aside. "You nearly scared me to death! How did you get in here?" She came over to bat the ladder with her paw as if we were both on the floor for her amusement. My left arm didn't want to support my weight as I tried to get to my knees. My left leg buckled from the pain when I tried to stand. Sitting in the middle of the floor, watching the kitten walk along the side of the ladder, I wondered what to do next. "You are one spooky cat! Now, how am I going to get out of this mess?"

I was on my own, without a phone or anyone who would look in on me. Screaming wouldn't help since there wasn't anyone close enough to hear. Although my shoulder hurt, it seemed to be okay, but my left ankle throbbed. I feared it might be broken. I needed to get to the hospital, and I would have to go alone. I crawled to the side hall with kitty at my side. I used the built-in bench to pull myself to a standing position. Exhausted by the exertion, I rested on the bench until my throbbing ankle said it was time to move on. My purse was in the kitchen, which now seemed miles away, but I could feel keys in my pocket. Now, if only I could get to my car parked in front of the side steps.

I scooted down the steps, pulled myself up then hopped to the car. The leather seat of the Mercedes cradled me as I sat behind the wheel, exhausted, short of breath and in a great deal of pain. I hadn't bothered to close the heavy oak door, and now the kitten sat behind the screen door watching me. Fortunately, I didn't need to use my left foot to drive. Putting the car in gear, I headed toward Port Clinton.

Feeling silly and helpless after having a series of x-rays taken of my shoulder and ankle, I was wheeled back to the emergency department. It appeared that a shift change had occurred while I was in radiology, and a different staff was at the desk. A dark haired nurse followed me back to my bed and bent down to flip-up the foot pedals on my wheelchair. "I'll help you back into bed, Ms. Bentley, and make you as comfortable as possible until the doctor arrives."

She wore her hair pulled back in a short ponytail, and her voice was soft and cheerful. She smiled as she straightened and reached out to help me stand. I could only stare in disbelief. That face, I remembered it so well, only younger. "Patsy Paterson?"

She looked at me with a confused expression, then her eyes widened. "Olivia! I can't believe it's you! What are you doing here?" Helping me into bed, she chuckled. "That was stupid of me. I read your chart. I know why you're here. Now, let's see if we can't make you more comfortable."

Patsy propped up my foot and arranged pillows behind my head.

"I live here now. Well, sort of. Right now, I'm living on my boat, while I try to make the house I bought habitable."

Patsy just stood there looking at me with an amazed expression. I remembered Mom saying that Patsy was like a butterfly, and she would one day turn into a beauty. Mom had been right. Patsy's complexion was flawless. Her bright green eyes, framed by thick black lashes, had a slightly exotic look. The mischievous twinkle I remembered was still there.

Just then the doctor walked in, his head bent over my chart, x-rays hugged under his arm. A tall man with a head full of thick curly brown hair, he looked up at me with soft brown eyes and a generous smile. I thought he was probably in his mid fifties and extremely handsome. "Good afternoon, Ms. Bentley. I'm Dr. Madison. Please tell me what happened that brought you to our lovely establishment."

Well, at least he had a sense of humor. While he examined my foot and shoulder, I recounted the events that lead to my being there. He and Patsy both laughed at the picture I painted of the scene on the ladder with the black kitten leaping in front of me.

"The good news, Ms. Bentley, is that Kitty isn't responsible for any broken bones. However, you do have a sprained ankle that will probably feel worse than if you had broken it. You're going to have some nasty bruising on your shoulder and arm, too. I'll prescribe something for the pain, but you are going to need to stay off the foot for a few days. I hope there is someone at home, other than Kitty, to take care of you. Do you have crutches?"

"No, I don't have any, and right now I'm living on a boat . . . alone."

He nodded. "Patsy, will you take care of ordering crutches and show Mrs. Bentley how to use them. We don't want her falling off the dock."

"Yes, Doctor. Actually, Olivia and I are old friends. I'd be happy to keep an eye on her and make sure our patient stays out of trouble."

"Sounds like you will have your hands full. But in that case, she doesn't need to come back for a checkup unless you feel it's necessary. Goodbye, Mrs. Bentley, I hope I don't see you again—unless it's under more pleasant circumstances."

Patsy called Emily and arranged for her to drive me home. My biggest concern, as Emily drove toward Marblehead, was getting the cat out of the house before locking the door, since it would be a few days before I could get back there. The gravel crunched beneath the tires as we pulled up to the side door. "Is that your mysterious black cat lurking in the bushes?"

My eyes followed her pointing finger over toward the corner of the house. Sure enough, there the kitten sat as if just waiting for some unsuspecting bird or chipmunk to cross its path. "How did it get out? That is one spooky cat!"

"She probably pushed the screen door open. I'll make sure the lights are turned off and lock the door for you."

Emily was only gone a short time before she returned with my purse. "Everything is fine. I put the ladder in the kitchen. Now, let's see if we can get you to the boat without one of us falling off the dock."

CHAPTER 34

I felt the boat rock. It had to be Gus. I'd given the telephone company the number for the marina office as a contact. Yesterday, Gus had taken the message that the installer would be at the house between noon and four. He'd promised to drive me. Gus noticed the folded lounge chair on the rear deck, along with a small round table neatly collapsed alongside. It was your typical boater's must-have accessory with nautical knots along the edge and a compass in the center. He carried both items along with my crutches to his truck then returned for me.

Gus had just settled me on the front seat when Liz came running over waving a brown paper bag. "Here's your lunch. A club sandwich, bag of chips, an iced tea, and a piece of apple pie for dessert." Liz was the manager of the marina restaurant, and had made sure while I was laid-up that I had three meals a day, usually carrying them out to the boat herself. She turned to leave then stopped. "Oh . . . the special tonight is a lightly breaded grouper with a lovely lime sauce. Have a nice afternoon. I'll see you later."

Storm clouds were building to the north as Gus helped me into the house. He set up the lounge chair with the table next to it in the kitchen. "Where's this black cat that's caused all this trouble?"

The kitten had been my first thought as we pulled in the drive, but there didn't seem to be any sign of the little fur-ball. "I don't know. Maybe she's found a dry place to wait out the storm."

The air was musty and the rooms gloomy. Gus sniffed as he looked around the kitchen. "You're a brave woman for taking on this old hulk. I sure couldn't do it. If this were a boat, they'd take her out in the middle of the lake and pull the plug! Call when you need a ride home."

I found it interesting that he called my boat home, but not my house. I watched him walk over to the kitchen table and open the large windows. "Thanks for everything, Gus. You've been like a big brother to me, and I really appreciate it, but don't worry about picking me up. I'll call Emily once the phone is installed, maybe she can give me a lift."

I prayed the rickety old chair at the kitchen table would hold my weight. I opened the paper bag and removed my lunch.

By the time I finished lunch, my ankle was throbbing and the rain had started. Not the gentle showers we had been having off and on for the past two days, but a downpour that had followed a show of thunder and lightning against a black sky. Briefly, I thought about the kitten, hoping she'd found some place dry and safe.

Tucking my crutches under my arms, I made it to the lounge chair without incident. It was comfortable enough, while I waited for Ma Bell to show up to install the phone. The pain pill I had taken with lunch was beginning to take effect. I set the romance novel I'd brought in my lap. I wasn't ready to open it just yet. The wide porch protected this side of the house from the storm, but a cool damp breeze blew in through the open windows. I watched dust-bunnies tumble across the floor. My thoughts drifted back over the last two days. Patsy had come by each morning, splashing down the dock in the rain to check my ankle and rewrap it. Emily faithfully stopped by on her way home from the office each evening, bringing me a magazine or flowers. Liz, whom I hardly knew, never forgot a meal, regardless of how busy she was or what the weather. I was beginning to understand the true meaning of friendship. I no longer felt alone in the world. I had friends to lean on, to help fight my battles and walk beside me into the unknown. Not because they had to, but because they honestly cared about me.

It was nearly twenty years since that horrible day in August when I lost my family . . . the family that I'd been trying to replace ever since. Now, I was making my own family, one I hoped would grow with the coming years.

I closed my eyes. Thoughts of Travis pushed everything else aside. He had called Gus on Monday to say he would be back later than expected but would be available to help me move the *Lovely Lady* on the weekend. Gus explained how Emily and I had already moved her and that Travis didn't need to rush back. He had said he was visiting his cousin, Michael, but was there a woman in Cleveland, too? Although I didn't want a romantic relationship—that would only bring pain and heartache—I was honest enough with myself to admit I missed him. I missed gazing into those strange blue-green eyes. I missed his sensuous mouth that always seemed ready to burst into a dimpled smile. I missed his thick sandy-colored hair that begged to be touched. With those thoughts, I drifted off to sleep.

The sound of someone banging on the screen door woke me. It took me a minute before I realized where I was and that the noise came from the telephone installer. Struggling to get up from the flimsy aluminum lounge chair, it slipped out from under me. My scream brought the man running with tools and things swinging from a belt slung around his hips. "I didn't mean to barge in like this, but are you okay, lady? I was knockin' on the side door for a long time when I heard a scream and thought you were hurt." He looked down at the crutches lying on the floor next to the overturned lounge and then back to me with a questioning expression.

"I had a slight accident with a ladder a few days ago and sprained my ankle. Today's my first day up and about, and I'm still a little unsteady. I really am okay, and the phone niche is around the corner in the hall."

He set the lounge chair back up and helped me to my feet before handing me the crutches. I followed him into the hall.

"Wow! I never seen a phone this old. Well, except in the movies... you should keep this, it might be worth somethin'. Maybe it still works if you wanna use it." He moved around the hall, peeking into several rooms. "That old phone sorta fits the house. You just buy this place? It's like the Addams family's house. I hope your husband is real handy."

Here was one more person who assumed only a married woman with a handy husband would take on this place. What a joke! Win wouldn't have entered this house, let alone buy it, and Brian never even changed light bulbs.

My leg throbbed, and I lost what little patience I had left. "No, I want a standard pushbutton, something I can hook-up to an answering machine," I snapped. "I would also like jacks installed in the kitchen and the other rooms."

After helping me back to the lounge chair, he checked out the bedrooms upstairs, then went down to the basement. Only about ten minutes had gone by when I heard him clanking up the steps and back into the kitchen. "I ain't never seen nothin' like this. It looks like Mr. Bell, himself, installed this system!" I was ready to scream. I couldn't even get a phone installed without trouble. He must have sensed my distress. "Now, don't you worry lady. I can get you set up with a new phone right quick now. But those other jacks ain't gonna be so easy. I'm gonna need help. You need to call the office for another work-order, and tell them it'll be an all-day job."

I picked up the novel that had been sitting on the floor next to the lounge. I'd never had much interest in reading fiction. Looking back over my life, it had been run by the clock. And time was too valuable to be spent reading for pleasure. Emily had brought me books to help pass the hours spent sitting with my leg up. It was nice to bury myself in someone else's world and forget about mine—at least for the moment. I opened the cover and began to read. But whether it was his constant babbling and singing or just my mood, I couldn't seem to get past the first page. Perhaps I had made a terrible mistake in thinking I could save this place. Perhaps this was just one more failed attempt at saving something of my childhood. This house had intrigued me as far back as I could remember, but childhood dreams and fantasies die with adulthood. Perhaps I should have let this one die as well. I had worked myself into a corner of depression by the time the installer was finished.

"I'm done. You have a phone now. You know, it really wasn't safe for you to be out here alone, in this big house without a phone and bein' on crutches and all."

Taking a deep breath, I looked at my injured foot. "I know."

"If it's okay with you, I'll take that old phone and rewire it for you. You could use it in one of the bedrooms. Or you could put it back on that little shelf in the hallway when we get the wall phone installed in the kitchen."

"Okay, sure. Whatever you want to do with it is fine."

He picked up the old phone and started for the side door. "By the way, that sure is a cute kitten you have. It was playing with my tools and scraps of wire."

The back of my neck prickled, and a chill ran through me. I hadn't let the kitten in. I tried to stand. "Kitten?"

He saw me struggling and came to my side, helping me to stand. "Yeah, the little kitten you have in the basement . . . just as black as a piece of coal. Good choice for this house!"

Before leaving, he moved one of the kitchen chairs over to the new phone he'd installed in the old niche in the foyer so I could sit while making calls. I dialed Vanessa's number at East Side General. I had promised to call once I got settled. Joann answered the phone, and said Vanessa had left that morning for a two-week vacation in Hawaii with her boyfriend. He was attending a conference in Maui and invited her along. We chatted about the continued budget problems before I told her that I'd call back in a few weeks. I then called Vanessa's home and left a message on her answering machine, with my address and phone number, and told her to call when she got back in town.

The kitten voiced her displeasure at being locked in the basement. I would let her out when I finished my last call. After thinking about it, I realized that she must have followed the phone man in during one of his many trips to his truck.

My next call was to CeCe, and we talked for an hour. I gave her my phone number and address and filled her in on everything that had happened. She provided me updates on the latest Cedar Hill gossip. When I told her that I had bought a house on the water, she went on about how nice it must be to have a small cottage like my grandparents had. Knowing a lecture would follow an accurate description of my new residence, I chose to leave her to her assumptions. I'd let her be surprised when she viewed it for the first time. I promised to invite her for an extended visit as soon as the house was presentable and mentioned how lucky Vanessa was to be staying in

Hawaii for two weeks. Perhaps, if Vanessa's schedule permitted, they could both come together. It would be like old times.

The rain finally started to let up. I was about to call Emily to pick me up when the side door opened and heavy footsteps sounded in the hall. Panic drove me to grab my crutch, the only means of defense at hand. Too many people were telling me I should be afraid of being in this creepy old house alone. Now, I was faced with an intruder and a crutch for a weapon. But instead of fear, my heart did a flip-flop of joy as I heard Travis calling my name.

He entered the foyer with a big, warm smile. But, it suddenly turned to concern as he took in the scene of me sitting on a rickety old chair ready to swing a crutch in his direction. "Are you really planning to hit me with that?"

With a long sigh of relief, I lowered the crutch to the floor.

He got down on his knees in front of my chair and looked at my wrapped ankle. "Olivia, what's happened? Why didn't someone call me?"

I warmed at his obvious concern.

Travis went to the kitchen and brought two glasses of iced tea, and sat down on the floor in front of me and waited, as I tried to figure out where to start. I finished my story as we finished our drinks, and he helped me to stand then handed me the crutches. I went through the kitchen to the basement stairs and opened the door. No coal black kitten waited on the top step. I called "kitty-kitty" several times with no results. Finally Travis went down to get her.

Minutes went by. My leg was throbbing again by the time I heard footsteps coming up the stairs.

Travis appeared, empty-handed. "I couldn't find it, but I'm sure it will be fine until you return."

CHAPTER 35

I reached up to pull the cord closing the Venetian Blinds. There was too much sunlight flooding the cabin and I wasn't ready to get up yet.

An hour later, as I was struggling into shorts and a tee shirt, I heard Patsy's voice on the dock. "Knock, knock . . . Olivia, are you up?" The boat dipped slightly to port as she came aboard, and we both reached the main saloon at the same time. "I'm sorry to be so early," she said. "But I start the night shift, and there's a million things for me to do today. Now, let's see how my patient is doing." After Patsy un-wrapped my ankle, I stood and tried to walk. The pain wasn't as bad as I expected, and she seemed satisfied. "You'll probably need to continue the wrap for a few more days, but I think you can begin walking on it. Using one crutch may help in the beginning, but you're definitely on the mend." As I practiced walking up and down the cabin, she said, "You're doing fine. I won't be coming back unless you need me."

Liz arrived, with my breakfast tray, just as Patsy stepped onto the dock. She removed the stainless steel covers and placed a plate of blueberry pancakes and sausage on the table followed by a pitcher of warm maple syrup.

"You'll be happy to know that my own personal nurse just left proclaiming me fit-as-a-fiddle and ready to walk."

Liz looked at me with a mock frown. "Gee whiz, Olivia. Now what am I going to do for my daily exercise? Besides, it got me out of the kitchen." She set the empty tray on the counter as I slid onto the seat. "Seriously, Olivia, I really haven't minded, and I would like to stop by the house from time-to-time to see how you're progressing. I would offer to help, but this is our busy season. These trips down the dock were my only break."

The weekend families had started arriving. I cocked my head to children's laughter and the sound of boat engines starting for their day on the water or perhaps a trip to the islands. Their wakes gently rocked the *Lovely Lady* as they went by. I would miss the calming motion once I moved into the house and no longer had a keel beneath my feet.

My breakfast finished, I struggled up the short flight of steps to the flying bridge with my last mug of coffee. The boat made a sudden dip to starboard. That movement wasn't made by a wake, and I poked my head up to see Travis walking along the deck. "Ahoy, there, Olivia! Mind if I come aboard?"

His blue eyes had the same sparkle as the morning sun reflecting off the water. I reminded myself that I needed to be wary of his magnetic charm. I wasn't looking for another relationship. "It appears that you're *already* on board, Mr. Tanner!"

His gray-and-white striped shirt was tucked neatly into white cotton shorts with a crisp crease running the length of each leg. Surely he hadn't taken the time to iron shorts? Or had he sent them to a dry cleaner? He climbed up to the bridge and sat down in the chair next to mine, gazing out over the marina. His long tan legs, covered in a veil of sandy colored hair, stretched out in front of him. I felt the urge to run my fingers along his muscular thighs and mentally slapped myself for such dangerous thoughts.

"You look very nice today . . . I take it you won't be crawling around in a machine shop working on boat motors." I was angry with myself for seeing him in this sexual manner and perhaps lashed out with sarcasm I didn't mean.

"No, I took the day off, hoping to spend it with you. I was even foolish enough to think you might take a day off from working on the house and play. But I see that fun and play aren't in your vocabulary, so I guess I should change into the work clothes that are in my truck."

"I'm sorry, Travis. I didn't mean it to sound like it did. I guess I'm just tired of sitting around being waited on while my list of things to-do keeps getting longer. I would love to spend the day playing, but I'm truly not mentally or physically up to it yet. Would it be alright if I take a rain-check?"

He smiled and nodded. "Deal! Now, what's at the top of your list?" After working out a plan for the day, we closed up the boat and drove to the house.

Travis did most of the work and I spent much of my time sitting in the lounge chair with my foot propped on a rolled-up shirt. Later, we sat at my favorite table in front of the large windows overlooking the marina. Most of the weekenders had already gone home. On a Sunday evening, only a few tables were occupied in the Marina DelRay restaurant. We both ordered Shrimp Alfredo, then chose a bottle of Chardonnay to go with it. I was exhausted and too tired for conversation. I let my mind wander back over the last couple days.

I felt good about my decision to turn the house into a Bed and Breakfast. My business degree and management experience were a plus. Not to mention the rigorous instruction on how to be the perfect hostess my former mother-in-law had given me.

Based on the plan of turning the house into a B & B, Travis agreed with my supply list and we stopped at the hardware store before going to the house. We left with wallpaper stripper, scrapers, paint in a soft yellow, as well as delft blue to match the blue, yellow and red speckled linoleum in the kitchen. Travis agreed with my suggestion that since the sisters lived comfortably on the first floor, I could as well, leaving the renovation of the second and third floors to the professionals.

We pulled into the drive with all our supplies. As Travis helped me out of the Blazer, the kitten came bounding across the yard.

I couldn't believe my eyes. "That is one spooky kitten! How do you suppose it got out of the basement?"

"There's probably a broken window somewhere. I'll take a look once I get this stuff unloaded. Are you going to keep it?"

Gazing down at that darling little face with golden eyes, I couldn't bring myself to say no. "It doesn't appear like I have a choice."

Travis helped me up the steps to the side porch. "What are you gonna name it?"

"Spooky!"

Travis couldn't find a broken window and we decided to leave further searching for another day. He climbed the ladder and removed all the light fixtures, while I stood at the kitchen sink and washed the beautiful globes. Afterward we stored them in the library to be brought back after the rooms were painted.

After a quick lunch at the diner, we stopped at Mutach's Market for cat food, then went back to the house and began stripping the dingy old wallpaper. Travis climbed the ladder getting the high areas, while I stayed on my feet or sat on the floor and got everything within easy reach.

After locking up the house, we headed to the Marina DelRay for dinner. By the time our waitress arrived with our meals, every muscle in my body hurt, and my ankle throbbed. I wanted nothing more than to hurry through dinner, get back to the boat, and get my feet up. Travis was tired too. He said he was going to have a busy week and could help me in the evenings. The meal was excellent, but neither of us felt like conversation. We left the restaurant as soon as we finished eating.

Travis helped me down the dock and onto the boat. Once I'd made my way to the aft cabin, he propped up several pillows on my bunk. When I was settled on the bed, he gently took off my shoes. His hand brushed against my ankle sending tingles through sensitive skin. I admired his broad shoulders as he reached to turn on the TV. The pain pill I'd taken at dinner was beginning to take effect. My foot was no longer throbbing. I thanked Travis for taking such good care of me. He bent down and kissed my cheek. "See you tomorrow." He walked out without another word, turning out the main cabin lights and closing the door behind him. There was something so comforting and intimate in his actions. I knew we were no longer just friends.

CHAPTER 36

Spooky lay curled in my lap for one of her short naps. I sat with my legs stretched before me on the window seat in the bedroom that still had hopes of once again becoming a dining room. The oriental patterned wallpaper had once been a bold Chinese red, but over the years had faded to salmon. The large trees, birds, bridges and pagodas had also faded, but overall it was still pleasing for this east facing room.

The past two days had been rainy, but I didn't mind working inside. Travis had come by in the evenings to help, and we had finished painting the kitchen and parlor. The house was beginning to feel like home. I was getting anxious to move in.

Spooky heard the footsteps before I did and ran off to investigate. Travis entered the room carrying the kitten and put her down on the bed.

I swung my legs down to the floor. "This is a surprise! You're here in the middle of the day with clean clothes on. What's up?"

"The rain has stopped. It's too nice a day to be inside working, so I decided to play hooky . . . wanna come?"

"Well, I was just sitting here thinking that this wallpaper is beginning to grow on me. Maybe this room can stay just the way it is until the upstairs is finished."

"And that means?"

"Yes, I would love to play hooky with you! What do you have in mind?"

"The lake's flat. I thought it might be a good day for me to check out the *Lovely Lady*. Emily seemed to think there might be a problem with the engines or wiring."

"Nonsense, she's running like a Swiss watch, but a cruise around the islands sounds like a wonderful idea."

An hour later we were heading west in the South Passage toward South Bass Island. Kelleys Island, to our starboard side, looked lush and green against the azure sky. Off the bow, Perry's Monument glistened in the hot afternoon sun. Travis nodded toward the three-hundred-and-fifty-two foot Doric column. "The memorial commemorates Commodore Oliver Hazard Perry's defeat of the British in the Battle of Lake Erie on September 10, 1813. On a clear day like this, from up top you can see the shores of Michigan and Ontario. It really is a beautiful view, and I would love to show it to you."

I didn't have the heart to spoil this experience by telling him that the beach at the base of the monument had been a favorite place of mine to anchor my grandfather's small boat when I came looking for a fun day on the island.

"I'd love to see it with you." The day was hot, and I was getting hungry. "If you'll take the helm, I'll go below and fix lunch." While Travis took over, I went down and fixed tuna salad sandwiches, potato chips, and a bowl of fresh grapes and strawberries. Before taking the tray up to the bridge, I changed into a pair of white cotton short shorts and a blue and white halter-top, then brushed out my ponytail until my hair fell in waves around my shoulders.

Travis whistled as I came up the ladder. "Wow! You did more than fix lunch! You look good enough for dessert! Maybe we should hang a right here and head up to North Bass Island for the afternoon. I know a great little secluded cove."

"I don't think so! Sightseeing sounds like a much better idea."

The Dock Master greeted us as we approached an open dock. "Hello, Travis. It's good to see you again, and it's nice to have the *Lovely Lady* back with us." After docking at The Crew's Nest, Travis signed out one of the golf carts the club kept for use by members and guests.

We drove down Bay View Avenue, past DeRivera Park, to the monument. After parking the golf cart, we climbed the stone steps to the impressive rotunda. The remains of the three American and three British officers who were killed during the Battle of Lake Erie are buried beneath the floor. The names of Perry's ships, along with the names of the American sailors who were killed or wounded in the battle, are carved into the walls. It was the first time I had really noticed, or cared, about what the Memorial stood for, and I was in awe of its magnificence. The elevator took us up to the observation deck where we walked over to its massive stone ledge. Peering down on the small harbor of Put-in-Bay, we could see the many boats looking like little toys bobbing in the water. We found the *Lovely Lady*, just a speck in the distance.

"It's hard to believe that a major naval battle was fought right here," I said. The area hardly seems big enough with all these little islands scattered around."

Travis looked off in the distance. "Perry's own flagship, the *Lawrence*, flew a banner that read 'Don't give up the ship'. His ship was battered so badly he transferred his command to the U.S. Brig *Niagara*. And aboard that ship, he was able to break the British battle line. 'We have met the enemy and they are ours' is the famous message he sent to General William Henry Harrison."

As we circled the platform Travis casually put his arm protectively around my waist. I felt as if the enchanting vistas surrounding us promised a new and adventurous life to come.

We took the elevator back down to the waiting golf cart and headed toward the tiny town. We parked on Delaware Avenue in front of the Crescent Tavern then strolled through DeRivera Park. Travis pushed me on the swings. After climbing onto the cannons like a couple of kids, we sat on the rim of the large stone fountain that was the centerpiece of the park. We watched boats coming and going from the city dock, as well as the ferry from Port Clinton. Weekdays were my favorite times, when the island was more refined and quiet. Not like the rowdiness of the weekend when every dock was taken and the rafting-off of one boat to another was not uncommon. Lonz Winery was just a short ferry ride away, and the returning revelers would stumble off the ferry and into the park. It was not unheard of to see someone in the fountain, and The Round House Bar would be full until the wee hours.

After browsing through several shops bordering the park, we found our way to a small restaurant for dinner. "I've never been here before," I said. "Brian and I always came to the island with friends. If we bothered with large meals, it was usually at The Crew's Nest. The rest of the time was spent drinking and eating pizza or burgers, and we could be rowdy right along with the best of them."

"I can't imagine you being rowdy. You're so calm and reserved, very proper and controlled. I can't see you drunk and falling into the fountain."

I gazed out over the park. "My family was killed in an automobile accident while on their way to pick me up from the cottage when I was fifteen. At sixteen, I brought my friends Vanessa and CeCe here for the first time. It was easy to blend in with the many college kids who flocked here every weekend. I was quite rebellious back then.

My grandmother was rather strict and wanted to keep me a little girl, but my grandfather understood my need for freedom. The summer after the accident, he bought a Lyman that we used for fishing and water skiing. He would tell Gran we were going fishing, but we would come here. He would have a few beers, and I would hang out at the beach."

Travis covered my hand with his. "I can't imagine losing my family. It must have been devastating to someone so young and vulnerable."

"I felt life had cheated me. My whole world was turned upside-down. My grandmother said it was God's will, but I couldn't accept that. It sounded like a cop-out. So I took control of my life." Travis gently squeezed my hand as if telling me he understood my pain. I continued, "In the early 70s when I was in college, I was pretty self-absorbed and wild. Sex, drugs, and rock-and-roll was my motto. I got married in Las Vegas during Spring break in my senior year at Ohio State. Win and I were both rebelling and trying to prove we were in control of our lives, but my mother-in-law soon took the wind out of my sails."

Our waitress walked toward us with our meals. I gently disengaged my hand from his. Travis changed the subject, talking about his childhood and what it was like to grow up with the islands as his playground. That explained why so many people seemed to know him as we walked through town.

We left the harbor at Put-In-Bay then rounded Gibraltar Island and headed north past Middle Bass Island and Ballast Island into open water. The sun was low on the horizon. Travis pulled back on the throttles and turned off the engines, letting us drift with the gentle waves. I went below to get a bottle of Chardonnay from the refrigerator. Travis took the bottle and headed forward to the bow, and I followed with the glasses. We climbed onto the cabin roof where we would have a front-row seat for the sunset. Travis poured the chilled wine into the glasses. Smiling, I gazed into eyes that were the same color as the water. I felt so comfortable being with him.

He swirled the wine in his glass then calmly asked "Were you in love with your first husband? Were you happy?"

His question deserved an answer even though it meant I would have to resurrect the pain and deception I'd suffered. I told Travis about Win and I being childhood friends, about marrying to spite our families. Then, I told him about life with the Montgomerys, the death of my unborn child, and finally the death of my marriage.

Travis raised his glass in a toast. "To the bravest and most beautiful woman I've ever met."

It felt good to share my story with Travis, yet I now felt vulnerable. My track record with men had been disastrous and I didn't want to set myself up for another failed relationship. But my body was screaming for his touch, and all I could do was smile and look away toward the setting sun. Travis took my hand and guided me to the bow rail. Before us, the sky exploded in brilliant reds and yellows as the giant orange globe dipped toward the horizon. Travis put his arm around my shoulder and drew me against him as we watched the glowing ball slowly descend and disappear into the water.

His expression was serious as he looked down at my mouth. "I'm so glad you're in my life, Olivia." His voice was soft and sensuous. He bent down and kissed me, gently at first. The passion I'd been holding in check exploded as the sun dropped below the water. The sky was a blanket of vibrant streaks of reds and pinks against the blue background. He lifted his head. "Oh, Olivia, I've wanted to do that for so long. I've been afraid to tell you how I feel, for fear it would scare you away."

Just as I was trying to find the right words, the wake from a passing speedboat caught the bow. The deck rolled beneath our feet.

I caught the rail for balance, laughing. "I think that's our cue to head back to the dock."

It was dark when we arrived. Travis handled the lines as I took the *Lovely Lady* slowly into the dock. After everything was tied-off and secured, we stood on the dock beneath a canopy of a million stars. A soft warm breeze blew in off the lake. It was a romantic moment and my body wanted to continue where we'd left off under the sunset. But that nagging little voice of caution told me to slow down. Travis seemed to sense my uncertainty. He took me in his arms and looked down. "It's late and time for me to leave. As much as I would like to stay, it's too soon. The move to the next level will be yours. Hard as it may be, I'm willing to wait until you're ready. You've had to deal with too much heartache in your life. I don't want to be the cause of any more." His kiss was soft and gentle. "Good night, Olivia Bentley, I'll call you tomorrow."

Standing at the rail on the upper deck, I gazed up and found the Big and Little Dippers. A shooting star streaked across the sky, reminding me of how much I used to love to stretch out on the cool grass at the cottage and wish upon the stars. They were the wishes of a young girl full of love for her beau. Now that I was older and wiser, I knew about the constellations. I also knew there was no magic granting of wishes. But that same warm, giddy feeling was washing over me tonight, and I knew from experience I was heading into dangerous waters.

CHAPTER 37

The next morning, I woke early with the energy of a young girl. After a quick breakfast, I left the marina and headed for the house. Spooky greeted me as I opened the door. She rubbed against my legs, which I had learned meant 'feed me.' Perhaps it was the cheerful yellow walls, or the clean smell of the kitchen, or Spooky greeting me at the door, but this was home and I was happy. After opening the windows on the first floor to let in the fresh, cool morning air, I decided to call the storage company and have my things delivered . . . I was ready to begin my new life.

Travis stopped by in the afternoon and offered to take me shopping in Sandusky. We went to Sears, where I purchased a mattress set for the Captain's old bed, and a washer and dryer, which would be delivered on Tuesday. Next came new bedding in a soft gold satin, and sheets and towels in a creamy white, along with white rugs for the bath. JC Penney proved to be the place for curtains and rugs and small appliances. Travis had been patient as I took my time choosing each item, and he carried all the bags, so I wouldn't put any more pressure on my ankle than was necessary.

Brian would not have been as generous with his time. I realized since taking off my rose colored glasses, that I had begun to see Brian in a new light. I had easily slid into his life, but he seldom spent time in mine.

With the Bronco full, we headed back to Marblehead. While still in Sandusky, we passed several posters announcing an Antique and Classic Car Show to be held at the fairgrounds in three weeks. Travis pointed to the sign. "Owning a classic car is something I've always wanted to do, but I've never had the time to actually look for the right car, and then get it into pristine condition for a show."

"What kind of car do you want?"

He thought for a minute or two. "Oh, maybe a '57 Chevy convertible. Or maybe a Corvette, if it were old enough."

"I was always partial to the '64 Mustang convertible."

"That would work, too."

The wheels were turning in my head, but I didn't say anything. Perhaps, I could give Travis a surprise that would make his dream come true.

We stopped at the diner for a late dinner. Mavis greeted us then we saw Emily in the back corner booth. She waved at us to join her. Her smile turned to a frown of concern as she saw me limping.

"I stopped by the house this evening, but although your car was there, you weren't. You shouldn't push it, Olivia. Travis, have you checked out the engines yet?"

Travis and I slid into the booth across from Emily. This overly solicitous attitude was new to me, and I bristled. "Emily, whatever it was that you think you felt that day had nothing to do with the boat. The only accident has been me falling off the ladder. And that was Spooky's fault."

"Spooky?"

"The kitten. Since I can't seem to keep her out of the house, I decided to adopt her. She's much happier now."

Emily looked at Travis with a frown. "Well, have you checked out the boat? It's important. You can't put this off."

"Yes, Emily, as a matter of fact we took the *Lovely Lady* over to Put-in-Bay yesterday afternoon, and she's never run better." He glared at Emily in a way I hadn't seen him do before. "I would never have sold . . . ah . . . ah . . . sold . . . Olivia on the idea of going so far if I didn't believe the engines were sound. But as soon as my workload settles down in September, I'll give the boat an overhaul."

Travis studied the menu with clenched teeth. I picked up on uncomfortable vibes from someone who should know the menu by heart and decided I'd better change the subject. "Travis drove me into Sandusky to buy a washer and dryer. I can't quite get the knack of working that old wringer washer in the basement. It keeps eating my socks. The things I've had in storage will be delivered next Tuesday. I think I'll be able to officially move in by the end of next week."

"I'm glad to hear that. I just know you're going to be happy there." Emily finished her meal with little conversation, and after Mavis brought her check she excused herself and left.

Travis and I finished our meal in silence, then he drove me home and unloaded my purchases. After putting food down for Spooky, we locked the door behind us. Travis helped me down the steps and walked me to my car.

I thought back over the evening and realized Travis hadn't spoken during most of it. He'd seemed distracted, almost like he wasn't there. I couldn't let him go without finding out what was going on. "Travis, is anything wrong? Was it something Emily said? Are you upset with me about something?"

Bending down, he gave me a quick kiss. "I'm just tired, Olivia, I'll see you tomorrow."

Friday came and went and I didn't see him. In fact it would be almost a week before I would see him again. He was in Cleveland

and called at least once a day. It seemed odd that he left town immediately after our dinner with Emily. He said he had a lot on his mind and it had nothing to do with me. That left Emily, but I couldn't understand why her odd behavior and comments should affect him so. I put it out of my mind.

CHAPTER 38

By late Wednesday afternoon, I was exhausted and sat with my feet resting on the ottoman in the parlor sipping a cup of tea. The morning before, Sears had delivered the washer, dryer, and mattress set. The storage company's truck arrived in the afternoon. Most of the boxes were still stacked in the entrance hall, and the music room was crammed with my grandparents' bedroom furniture. The beautiful rice poster bed and tall chest-on-chest looked stately, even propped against one wall. The grandfather clock held a prominent position in the parlor, along with a Sheraton sofa and a delicate wingback chair with a down-filled cushion. Between them was a small cherry piecrust table, and to one side of the fireplace sat Gramps's leather club chair and ottoman. His smoking cabinet and brass floor lamp were next to the chair and the smell of his favorite tobacco still clung to its surface. I felt safe and secure as I nestled into the cushions, as if Gramps himself was holding me.

The sturdy round oak pedestal table and chairs that had been in my grandparent's dining room, had been passed down to my grandmother from her mother. I still found pleasure in the heavily carved lion paw feet. The table was perfect in the morning room, along with its matching sideboard. Together they looked as if they had always sat in this room.

Gran's blue and white Chinese-patterned china now resided safely in the cabinet in the butler's pantry. I had taken my time washing and drying each piece, reflecting back over the many times I had eaten from them and washed them afterwards. Gran hadn't believed in dishwashers even though I offered to buy her one on several occasions. She wasn't the easiest person to live with, but they were still good times . . . I just didn't realize it until now.

My colorful LeCreuset cookware, which I'd had to fight to keep as the auction company stripped the house after Brian's death, was carefully unpacked. I had grown to love Brian's house, and it had hurt when it was wrenched away from me. I vowed to myself that no one would ever take my home away from me again.

I had saved this rundown old house and made it my home. Now I was ready to spend my first night within its walls. Only one thing could have made it better, to have my family here with me, sharing the joy of my accomplishment. My throat tightened as I imagined Mom flitting around with her apron on, arranging everything in the kitchen. Andy and Bud would be twenty-eight. In my mind, I could see them moving furniture and boxes.

Travis found me sitting in Gramps's leather chair . . . crying. I looked up at him through a blur of tears to see his arms filled with a huge bouquet of colorful flowers. "I did knock, but there was no answer and . . ." Before he could finish his sentence he was kneeling at my feet. "Olivia, what's wrong? Has something happened?"

I couldn't stop crying and tried to speak, "I . . . miss . . . my . . . family."

He took a handkerchief from his pocket and wiped my eyes and laid the flowers in my lap. "Here, will these help?"

Nodding, I tried to smile, and without thinking, I put my arms around his neck. Tears still blurred my vision but I saw his concern. He gently kissed my lips, before kissing away my tears. His lips found mine again sending a flood of warmth through me. My hands reached for his head, my fingers felt their way into his soft thick waves. The kiss that had started out so gentle and comforting released a passion in me that I'd thought long dead.

"Oh, Livy, I want you so much."

His whispered words stopped me.

"What's the matter?" "What did I do?"

I had let no one but my family and David Morgan call me Livy, not even Brian. But I liked the way it rolled off Travis's tongue so casually, almost sensuously. Pulling him closer, I let go of my caution and kissed him with abandonment. When his hand found my breast, a quiver of excitement raced all the way to my toes. My breath caught. My fingers fumbled to unbutton his shirt. I stroked the soft hairs on his chest. He pulled my tee-shirt over my head. I shivered as his lips moved to my neck. Those little betraying moans told him everything that I couldn't. His mouth found its way to my waiting nipple, and my body screamed for more. Travis stopped and stood looking down at me with a question.

I reached out my hand to his and he pulled me to my feet. We walked hand-in-hand down the hall.

The bedroom was awash in a rosy pink glow. Contentment filled me. I moved my head off of Travis's shoulder, rolling to the other side of the bed. Fluffing the pillow, I pulled the sheet to my chest and curled up on my side to watch him sleep. He looked like a little boy, with his hair mussed and a slight smile. He snored softly. But it was no little boy who had made love to me just a couple of hours before. The memory of our love making only left me hungry for more.

As if he sensed me watching him, he began to stir and opened his eyes.

"I was having the most wonderful dream. I dreamt that I made love to you all night." He gave me a devilish grin. "Maybe it wasn't a dream."

It had been a long time since I felt so alive. I wasn't ready to let that feeling end. "It's only a little after midnight. You only made love to me once."

He rolled toward me pulling the sheet down and tossing it toward the end of the bed. "Well, then, in that case, I have some catching up to do." His mouth took control of mine. His hands explored and caressed my breasts. My senses exploded in rapture.

The morning sun filled the room, and Spooky's purring was the only sound. I reached over for Travis. But there was only a kitten to share my bed. My mind reflected back over the night, but my nose smelled the welcome aroma of coffee and bacon. I sat up, noticing my wedding band on the nightstand. I didn't remember taking it off. Travis had once said I would know when I was ready to let go of Brian.

I slipped into a turquoise silk robe before going to the kitchen. Travis was dishing out scrambled eggs and bacon. Two slices of toast popped out of the toaster. Setting the plates on Gran's old yellow and chrome kitchen table in front of the window, he came over and took me in his arms. His hair was damp. I breathed in the fresh clean smell of soap. His kiss was easy, as if he started each day this way.

"Good morning, Livy. I hope you don't mind that I took over your house this morning, but I really needed a shower. And I figured you'd be hungry after all that vigorous exercise last night. I was going to serve you breakfast in bed, but all I could find were cookie sheets."

"I don't mind at all. But I am hungry . . . and sore."

He took my hand and walked me over to the table, holding onto the chair as I sat down. "At your service, my lady." After bringing the toast and pouring two mugs of coffee, he sat down across from me. It felt so natural to be sharing breakfast with him.

A crystal pitcher sat at the end of the table attempting to hold the flowers, and I laughed at the sight. Overall, they were pretty wilted. Some of them were terribly bent over with broken stems. Others were missing petals. Shredded leaves littered the table at its base.

"I found them on the parlor floor. I think Spooky believed we'd left them for her enjoyment. They were strewn all over the room. I saved the good ones."

We rested our elbows on the table, savoring the last of the coffee and gazing into each other's eyes. Back in the far reaches of my mind, I remembered words of love being spoken last night. This time had been different. Our lovemaking had been exciting and abandoned, and giving and pleasing. Not the lust I had experienced in the past. This was the feeling Mom had tried to explain so many years ago. I felt both happy—and terrified of what might follow. Life was rushing at me so fast. I only hoped that I could keep up.

"My, but you're deep in thought . . . care to tell me what's causing that pretty little frown? Does it have anything to do with the fact that you're not wearing your wedding ring?"

My wedding ring still rested on the nightstand. I was falling in love with Travis and that scared the hell out of me. But it was too soon to talk about my fears to this man who had caused all the turmoil. I needed to get back on safer ground.

"How would you like to take a drive with me next Sunday?" I said. "It's approaching the twentieth anniversary of the accident, and I have a need to go back to Cedar Hill."

He took my hand and gave it a squeeze. "I would love to spend the day seeing your hometown and getting a better understanding of what made you the wonderful, kind, generous, and exciting woman you are. I'll be all yours for the whole day."

His hand rested gently on mine. It was a hand that was strong, yet could be gentle and loving. It was a hand that could be greasy and dirty after a day of working on boats and engines, and yet the next minute be as clean and manicured as any executive's. What a picture of contradictions this man was. I looked forward to the challenge of putting the pieces of this puzzle together.

CHAPTER 39

Sunday was one of those perfect August days with an intense blue sky and puffy clouds drifting by as the morning sun sparkled on the ripples of the lake. The temperature was already close to eighty as I turned south onto Route 250 toward Cedar Hill. But nagging feelings of apprehension invaded my earlier excitement.

Last Monday morning, I had called Martin's Garage and talked to Vanessa's father, telling him that I would be picking up my Mustang on Sunday. It felt good talking to him after so many years, and it was as if I had never left. He was one of those who had taken me under his wing and added me to his already large family. He had stored the Mustang at the time of my divorce, as part of our original agreement when I sold him Dad's Pontiac convertible. He promised to give it a tune-up and put on four new tires. I told him to expect me around two o'clock.

The conversation with CeCe didn't go as well. I told her I was coming back for the Mustang and would be bringing someone with me that I wanted her to meet. She oozed with excitement to know the details. I told her how I met Travis and how much he had helped me adjust to life without Brian. Somewhere in my story her enthusiasm changed to concern.

"Don't tell me you're falling in love with this guy? Olivia, what's happened to your good sense?"

"Does it matter? I'm happy!"

"Olivia, this guy is a nobody! Your first husband was a member of one of the wealthiest families in the state. They practically own this town! Your second husband carried you off to his Shaker Heights mansion, bought you diamonds and furs, and took you to Paris for Christmas every year! Now you fall in love with a mechanic? Really, Olivia, think about it!"

CeCe and I had been friends since we were toddlers, and she suddenly had me doubting myself. "Who said anything about marriage? We're talking about great sex and me being happy! Period! Can't you just accept this?"

CeCe sighed and sounded exasperated as she continued. "Look, I really don't care what you do with your life. It's none of my business, but you do have me curious about this guy. Be here for brunch."

She never called back with the details. Since I didn't want to get into another conversation over how unsuitable Travis was for me, I just assumed brunch meant somewhere around eleven o'clock.

The flat farmland become hillier as the miles flew by. By the time I turned onto the county road that would take us into Cedar Hill, feelings of apprehension overwhelmed me. "This is the first time that I've been back since my grandparent's house was sold. I have to admit there's a part of me that wants to turn around and return to safety."

We reached the edge of town, and I slowed as the scene spread before us. Cedar Hill looked like a typical turn-of-the-century town, with the church steeples rising above the treetops. Farmland bordered it to the west and north, and wooded hills to the east and south.

"It's beautiful . . . like a painting. What a perfect place to grow-up."

I could feel my eyes narrow as I looked at the place that only reminded me of the pain and betrayal Win had caused me. "More like Peyton Place."

Driving down the hill, we passed the housing developments that had sprung up over the years, being the last 'crop' of the farmer's fields. Reaching the oldest part of town, I turned down Maple Lane and stopped before the large white colonial. It still had the black shutters and shiny black front door, with the large lion head doorknocker that had always fascinated me as a child. "This is it ... the house that I called home from the time I was fifteen until I graduated from college. There was a beautiful rose garden in the back. It was the one thing my grandmother really took pride in ... and loved."

Travis frowned. I suspected he had questions for me, but he only asked how they had died.

"I had booked a surprise trip for Brian and me to a secluded Caribbean Island. It was very romantic, with a cottage on the ocean and our own patio complete with pool. Being part of the resort, the meals would be prepared by the chef each day and served in our cottage. My surprise backfired when Brian announced he would be in London that week on business. My grandparents hadn't traveled abroad. After much cajoling, they agreed to use my tickets, and I drove them to the airport in Cleveland. It was wonderful watching the two of them walking hand-in-hand as they approached the gate. I can see them as they turned to wave after the attendant took their tickets. I was so happy I could give them something special. That was the last time I ever saw them. The small commuter plane crashed in the ocean after taking off on their return trip."

Travis reached over and put an arm around me. "I'm so sorry, Olivia."

"It was my fault. If it wasn't for me they'd still be alive and living in the house they loved."

"Livy, don't do this to yourself. It was an accident."

Shaking my head, as if that would erase the memories, I started the car and drove on through town toward the eastern hills. We passed the Montgomery Drug Store, then the Montgomery Savings and Loan, and as I continued down Main Street, we passed Montgomery Hospital. Travis chuckled as he exclaimed rather sarcastically. "I'm surprised the town isn't named Montgomeryville."

"It probably would have been if they'd arrived earlier."

We were passing the Cedar Hill Country Club when Travis said, his voice thick with sarcasm, "At least they don't own the country club!"

"Well, actually they do. They own the land and built the clubhouse."

Just beyond the golf course, we passed the rustic sign announcing that we were entering Cedar Ridge Estates. We drove up the hill past trendy brick and stone ranch-style houses of the early '60s that perched along the ridge. The street ended in a cul-de-sac, and I pulled into the furthest drive. The house hadn't changed. Even the tangerine lacquered double doors with the brass Chinese style plates surrounding the knobs, was the same. "This is where I grew up until the accident." Turning off the engine, I opened my door, "I guess we can't put this off any longer. Let's go in."

Travis looked confused. "I thought we were going to CeCe's house?"

"We're here."

CeCe had greeted us at the door, whispering in my ear about what a "gorgeous hunk" Travis was, and then held out both arms toward him and kissed him on the cheek. It appeared all was going to be fine, and that my fears had been unwarranted.

Danny was on the patio watching the kids as they splashed each other in the pool. He greeted us with a grin and a pitcher of mimosas.

"You're early! But this is good, it will give us time alone before the crowd descends upon us!"

Before I could comment, CeCe brought out enough silverware and napkins for a wedding reception, and put them on a large buffet table. The mimosa was cold and delicious. I found myself relaxing as Travis and Danny hit it off right from the start, discussing sports and their golf games. CeCe insisted that I take Travis on a tour of the house, then excused herself and went to the kitchen to continue preparations.

Shrugging my shoulders, I stood. "I don't know what that was about, but I guess I'd better take Travis on a tour. You two can pick up on the world of sports when we get back."

My childhood came flooding back to me with wonderful memories of Mom beautifully dressed, presiding over lavish cocktail parties. I realized for the first time what a glamorous house I'd lived in. As we ended our tour, we followed the aroma of muffins baking. But the kitchen was empty. I noticed the large skillet and griddle on the stove, and several large casserole and chafing dishes on the counter. All were empty. It seemed odd that the food still wasn't started, and large serving dishes were ready and waiting. Surely this wasn't catered?

Danny refreshed our drinks after we returned to the patio. We sat down at one of several tables, set with colorful tablecloths, and flowers floating in festive bowls. I looked around and asked CeCe if she was expecting someone else.

"I tried to invite Vanessa, but Joann said she took a six week leave-of-absence to go to Italy with her boyfriend. I just don't know how the two of you do it! You both have men falling all over you and dragging you off to exotic places, while I'm trapped in this one-horse town with Danny and three kids!"

Where was this coming from? She sounded jealous. "There's nothing wrong with your life, CeCe! You have a wonderful loving family, which neither Vanessa or I have." I waved my arm in the direction of all the decorated empty tables and asked again, "Who is supposed to fill these empty chairs and eat all this food?"

Danny suddenly frowned at CeCe, "What have you done, Celeste? Doesn't Olivia know about this?"

A sick feeling settled in the pit of my stomach. A chill ran down my neck. With a sense of impending doom, I asked, "Know about what? Travis and I were just going to stop by to say hello, and you mentioned brunch. You failed to give me any details. Those chafing dishes in the kitchen can hold a lot more food than the four of us and three kids can eat. What's up?"

Danny's face grew red and he raised his voice. "It appears Celeste has organized a lavish party in your honor and forgot to tell you about it. She's invited nearly the whole town to see you again after all these years. And, of course, to inspect the new man in your life."

Why had she done this? She knows how I feel about this town and everyone in it. Had she invited the Montgomerys? I felt hurt and betrayed, but I remained calm. "I'm sorry, CeCe, but we're on a tight schedule. We need to get to the cemetery, stop by Martin's Garage, and be back home for a dinner engagement. I hate to spoil your plans, but we must run."

Travis backed me up on our need to leave. Danny said that he hoped we could get together again soon.

Travis waited until we were in the car heading down the hill before he spoke. "We could have stayed, Livy. We're not on a schedule. I really like Danny. I thought it was a generous act of kindness for CeCe to invite all your old friends."

I took a deep breath. "The party wasn't out of kindness . . . she wanted to humiliate me. Don't you see? I don't have any friends here. I turned my back on the Montgomery's power and walked away with my head held high. CeCe is the last friend I have here . . . or did have."

We drove to the cemetery in silence. Travis stayed at the car as I carried armloads of flowers to the family plot and placed them with care. I felt responsible for six of these graves. After a few minutes, I returned to Travis with a heavy heart, and tears of sorrow for all the lost years and the happy times that could have been.

Neither of us spoke until I turned into Martin's Garage. "Mr. Martin is my friend, as well as Vanessa's father. He has something I want you to see." The red Mustang caught my eye as soon as I pulled into the lot and came to a stop next to it. Travis took no time getting out of the car, and was running his hand along the hood when Mr. Martin walked out and gave me a hug. "It's been too long, Olivia, but I'm glad to see you now."

I introduced Travis and said that he loved to work on vintage boats.

"This is one beautiful car, Mr. Martin." Travis took his hand from the hood long enough to shake the man's hand. "I've always wanted something like this, but just never seemed to get around to looking for one."

"I've taken real good care of her over the years. Kept it in the back of the shop under a tarp. Drove it once in a while during the summers . . . just to blow the dust out. She's running like a top now. Just finished the tune-up this morning."

I watched with pride as Travis walked around the Mustang caressing its curves as if he were caressing a beautiful woman.

"Wanna sell her?"

In the process of handing me the keys, Mr. Martin turned to Travis with a puzzled frown. "Well now son, I guess you'd have to ask . . ."

Travis came full circle around the car to stop beside me, looking like a little boy in a candy store. I held the keys out to him. "No, the car isn't for sale, but maybe you might like to drive it home."

He beamed from ear-to-ear as he took the keys and opened the door. "I don't understand, but I'd love to drive her."

"My father gave this to me for my sixteenth birthday," I told him. "I think it would make Dad happy if I started enjoying it again."

Travis put the key in the ignition. "I'll take good care of her, Mr. Martin. Both of them."

CHAPTER 40

Travis took the Mustang to the boat yard and washed and polished until every inch of it glistened. He entered it in the classic car show. We won for the best classic in its original condition. The show was a new experience for both of us, and we had fun together and grew closer while preparing for the competition.

The following weeks flew by in a blur of activity as August turned into September, and the weekenders and cottage people put off their pilgrimages for another year. We cruised the now quiet islands, and spent many hours on the *Lovely Lady* making love and exploring each other and our new feelings. Travis's occasional comments about filling the house with kids scared me, but I couldn't imagine not being with him. I wanted children more than anything, but that meant marriage. I didn't have good luck with marriage.

CeCe called and apologized for the brunch and blamed her behavior on jealousy and hormones—she was pregnant again. She liked Travis and said she'd never seen me looking happier. I could never stay mad at CeCe or Vanessa for long. But there was still a part of me that wondered if CeCe's original comparison to Win and Brian held some truth. Would his occupation become an issue? Why would it? After all, I was giving up my high-profile life to become an innkeeper.

Travis took the *Lovely Lady* to his father's boat yard and gave her a complete overhaul including the wiring, and pronounced her in tip-top shape.

Patsy called to say she was organizing a party for her daughter's sixteenth birthday on Kelleys Island and would I like to come. The whole Paterson clan would be there. Since it was going to be a real beach party complete with bonfire, Patsy suggested that I bring the *Lovely Lady* and anchor in the bay near the beach. It sounded like a lot of fun. I asked Travis to come, only to find out that Patsy was his cousin. He already knew about the party and was going to ask me if I would go with him. He said he couldn't wait to give the kids rides in the dinghy. We both got caught up in the festivities.

We took a few lengths of colorful flags and decorated the antennas and bow rail. We decided to tie Helium-filled balloons to the stern rail and the dinghy. I planned to put a *Happy Birthday* banner on the transom. The decorations were our major topic of conversation for a week. But our plans changed when Mavis called early that morning to say her cooler had suddenly stopped working. Travis said he'd stop by to look at it. Seeing as the cooler might be an all-day project, he insisted I take the *Lovely Lady* and go to the party without him. The weather forecast predicted a warm clear day and a night with light winds. Since I knew the waters around the islands so well, Travis said it shouldn't be a problem for me to return after dark. I expected to be back around ten. Travis promised to meet me at the marina.

After feeding Spooky, I grabbed the carefully wrapped gift and my purse off the kitchen counter and left through the side door. Although it was a clear day, it was still chilly and the jeans and sweatshirt felt good. There were plenty of clothes still on the boat. I could change into shorts later if it got warmer.

The usual, overwhelming sense of pride filled me as I looked toward the last dock and saw the *Lovely Lady* waiting for me. Her brass glistened in the morning sun, and the beautiful mahogany sides were warm and welcoming next to the harsh white fiberglass hulls of her neighbors. She didn't seem to smell as bad as she did at the beginning of summer, or maybe I was getting used to it. I climbed into the helm seat and started the powerful engines. There was no mistaking the deep throaty rumble of an old Chris-Craft. Every nerve in my body responded to its vibration.

Leaving the marina, I pushed the throttles forward and eased out into traffic. Quite a few boats were coming and going, but the smaller ones usually gave way to a boat this large, especially when they realized a woman was at the helm.

I missed Travis and silently cursed the cooler that was keeping him from the festivities. We had planned to spend the night in the protected bay, and I was looking forward to making love under a blanket of stars. But I understood better than anyone the importance of family and was happy that he could help his Aunt Mavis.

Turning the bow, I jockeyed into position with the rest of the boats heading down the channel and into Lake Erie. After clearing the entrance to the harbor, I eased forward on the throttles and felt the surge as she effortlessly cut through the waves. I then headed toward the north side of Kelleys Island. The sky was dotted with wispy white clouds, and the warm breeze caressed my face. "Come on old girl, we're going to a party!"

It was about noon when I slowed and put the engines in neutral, so I could go below and bring out the balloons to tie to the rails and attach the banner to the transom. A short time later I was ready to proceed around the point and enter the bay, where the party would be in full swing. As I got closer and saw everyone waving, I took the microphone for the loud speaker and began singing *Happy Birthday*. Later, after setting the anchor and letting down the dinghy from the davits, I rowed to shore. My beautiful boat looked like a circus clown with all those flags and balloons fluttering in the gentle breeze!

The afternoon passed far too quickly. The Paterson clan accepted me as one of their own, and Patsy's mom treated me like another daughter. With enough food to feed half the islanders, the grills were fired up all afternoon and well into the night. We played badminton, volleyball, horseshoes and croquet, and the kids made sand castles. The older kids rowed the younger ones around the bay in the dinghy, and took some of the grown-ups out to the boat for tours of the *Lovely Lady*.

As early evening clouds began to build, the gentle breeze grew stronger. I began feeling uneasy about the weather and thought about leaving, but reminded myself the forecast had predicted no rain or storms until tomorrow morning. Besides, the Paterson's were the large happy family of my dreams. I was having too good of a time to leave. The kids had been untying the balloons from the rail and bringing a few back to the beach with each trip. I asked them to bring my sweatshirt, which I had left laying on my bunk.

With the temperature dropping, my sweatshirt felt good. Everyone huddled around the fire and sang songs and roasted marshmallows. It was almost nine when I looked at my watch and decided I had better leave and get back to the dock before Travis began to worry. Saying goodbye was hard, but I promised that I would take everyone on a cruise around the islands to look at the fall colors. One of the last adults to take the boat tour had turned on the cabin lights. The *Lovely Lady* sat out in the bay welcoming me home with a soft glow.

The wind was now out of the north and getting stronger, making it hard to row against the white caps. My arms ached by the time I reached the swim platform. Just as I climbed out of the dinghy, a bright flash off in the distance caught my eye. Once I reached the upper helm station, I turned on the blower. After flipping on the console lights I started the engines, giving them time to come up to temperature while I raised the dinghy and anchor. I was heading down the ladder when I heard Travis on the ship-to-shore radio. "*Lovely Lady*, come in *Lovely Lady*." I heard urgency in his voice that didn't sound good.

I quickly grabbed the mike from its holder. "*Lovely Lady*, over."

"Where are you? I've been trying to reach you for an hour!" He sounded angry.

"I just got back on board and have the engines warming up. I should be pulling out in about fifteen minutes."

"You waited too long, Livy. There's a storm blowing across the lake from the north with a lot of lightning. It looks like it could be bad. I think you should stay put for the night and come back in the morning."

Travis didn't know how terrified of storms I was, so he didn't have to tell me twice. A storm killed my family. Ever since, thunder and lightning meant potential death. I had brought enough leftovers from the party to last me for days, and there were enough clothes and toiletries on board to last even longer. I didn't need to go anywhere . . . not in this weather.

"Sounds like a good idea. The *Lovely Lady* will keep me warm, dry and safe tonight. I'll see how it looks in the morning." I clicked off.

After shutting down the engines, I turned on the generator and the anchor light. Then, I got on the loud speaker. I told everyone on shore that a storm was moving in, and I would spend the night here.

They waved in return, and I saw they immediately began putting out the fire and packing up to leave.

The outside spotlight allowed me to see enough to check the anchor line, and I felt confident that it would hold through the storm. Then I returned to the aft deck and got out the smaller anchor. The bow pointed into the wind, so I tossed the anchor out as far as I could. Once it was set, I tied it off and climbed down onto the swim platform. With the wind now trying to push the dinghy away from the boat, I needed to attach the lines to the small boat and lift it out of the water with the davits. But I couldn't get the davits to work, and my arms were so tired that lifting the dinghy myself was out of the question. Pulling it against the swim platform was all I could manage and I secured it to the transom for the night. The kids had tucked the two life jackets under the seat of the dinghy, and I decided to leave them where they were. I paused for a minute and noticed the lightning getting closer. Thunder rumbled, I looked toward shore and saw car headlights leaving the area just as the first cold raindrops began hitting my face.

I snapped the canvas curtains in place and checked that everything was secure. Then grabbed the bag of food I'd left sitting on the stern seat and headed down to the galley. Just as I finished making one last check of the windows and hatches, the rain started coming down with a vengeance. Glad that I'd finished preparing the boat before the worst of the storm hit, I put the kettle on the stove for hot chocolate.

After changing into a pair of warm sweats, I slid into the dinette and wrapped my cold hands around the warm mug and nibbled at a chocolate brownie. Lightning lit every corner of the cabin. Thunder rattled the windows and shook the old boat to its very core. I felt the *Lovely Lady* pulling on the anchor line. If it didn't hold, we would be smashed against the rocks before reaching the sandy bottom of the beach. Storms, meant death, I thought about the watery grave that faced me. Tears filled my eyes, spilling onto my cheeks. With each clap of thunder I cursed all the somebodies and some things responsible for me having to deal with this alone. I cursed Win for his lying and cheating and making me leave Cedar Hill. I cursed Hilda for taking my job away from me and destroying my reputation. I cursed Brian for taking the coward's way out when life got tough. I cursed Mavis's cooler most of all. Why did it have to break down *now*?

Another loud clap of thunder brought me out of my morbid thoughts. My eyes sought the old brass clock on the wall. It was after midnight. Well, I couldn't sit trembling all night. Turning out all but one light, I went down to the aft cabin and turned down the bed. Then I went to the head to brush my teeth and take two aspirin to ease my aching muscles. Back in the cabin, I pulled the blanket over my head to block out the lightning and tried to relax as I listened to the drone of the generator. But other sounds intruded. The boat creaked and groaned with the wind, the anchor line chafed against the cleat, and the waves slapped against the hull. I began to relax, when the sounds melded together in a calming lullaby. My gentle old *Lady* held me in her arms and rocked me to sleep.

CHAPTER 41

The call of the seagulls woke me in the morning. I opened my eyes realizing that the only other sound was the generator. Peeking through the blinds next to the bunk, I could tell we were in the same spot. The storm had moved off, leaving a gray sky behind. I felt amazingly refreshed. I put on a pot of coffee and went up to the bridge to look for any damage. Everything seemed to be in order. I rolled up the side-curtains, and then went back down and turned off the generator before pouring coffee into a mug. Balancing a plate of fried chicken and potato salad, along with a piece of homemade apple pie, I made my way to the bridge and curled up on the big settee to enjoy my breakfast. The small bay was quiet and calm, and I was thankful that I'd made it through the frightening night. This grand old lady had taken care of me once again. Looking out over her long expanse of roof and decks, I thought back to this past spring when having lost my husband, my home and my job, I arrived at her dock with little more than my clothes. She welcomed me and provided a safe and comfortable shelter for the four long months until I moved into the house. I vowed that, in return, I would take care of her for the rest of her years.

I noticed the sky was beginning to clear in the west. It was time to move out. The engines were hard to start, but after a little coaxing they both turned over with that soft throaty rumble. Pulling up the anchors was next, and after seeing that the dinghy was still safely secured, I then went to the bow to start the windlass that would raise the large Danforth anchor. Free of her restraints, the *Lovely Lady* began to move gently with the waves. I went back up to the bridge to take the controls and ease her out into deeper water. The gray clouds gave way to patches of blue and the promise of a beautiful day. "Come on old girl, we're going home!"

There were no boats in sight as I rounded the point and headed for the harbor. Usually the waters were dotted with fishing boats, but perhaps the storm and the rough water was keeping them on shore. The *Lovely Lady* cut through the waves with ease. I gave her more speed as we cruised along the Kelleys Island shoreline. We were just off the old quarry docks when the starboard engine began to sputter then stopped. But I had often limped home on one engine, so I wasn't concerned. After all, Travis had checked them out the week before.

Since it would take a lot longer to reach the dock with only one engine, I thought about calling Travis. Suddenly I smelled something like hot wires. The port engine gauges still read normal, but the smell was pretty intense. I turned off the engine and went below. Smoke poured from the engine room. I grabbed the fire extinguisher before lifting the heavy engine room door. Smoke was everywhere but I couldn't see flames, so I sprayed until the smoke stopped. After opening a few windows and the side door, I went back up to the bridge. With a shaking hand, I took the mike and called in a mayday to the Coast Guard.

The officer asked what the problem was.

"I think it's an electrical fire." I took a breath. "I put it out, but I'm going to need a tow. I'm just off Kelleys ore docks."

I heard a loud whoosh and felt the boat shake. Then there was more smoke. "Oh, my God!"

"*Lovely Lady*, what happened?"

"There's more smoke. Lot's of smoke!"

"We're on our way. You need to get off the boat."

I raced down the steps to the lower deck and grabbed my purse, slipping the strap over my head then climbed over the rail onto the swim platform. My fingers fumbled to untie the dinghy. For a minute I wondered if my sense of urgency was an over-reaction. But, as I looked up at the boat, thick black smoke billowed out from the upper helm station. Stepping into the dinghy, I gave a hard push off the platform, put the oars in the chocks and began rowing away from the boat as fast as I could.

Quickly, the black smoke turned to flames. Orange fingers sprang from the open windows and door, licking the colored flags still attached to the mast and bow rail. I frantically rowed away from her, watching in horror while my beloved boat died before my eyes. Just then, BOOM. What was left of the boat flew in all directions. Debris landed all around me, and I panicked as the small boat was nearly swamped by a sudden wave. I looked up to see the concrete ore docks, the rust oozing down the sides like blood.

The shrill sound of a siren brought me back to reality. My body began to shake, first just a tremor and then uncontrollable spasms. I grabbed onto the sides of the dinghy, watching as the Coast Guard pulled alongside. When they lifted me to safety, I heard a loud keening. "I killed her! She was dying, and I couldn't help her!"

"Miss, was there someone else onboard?"

"Everyone in my life dies."

"Miss, we're trying to help. You must pull yourself together! Who was with you? Who died?"

The next thing I remembered was looking into the soft brown eyes of a fatherly sort of man in a uniform. He stretched out his hand and helped me off the rescue boat.

One of the officer's stepped forward. "She seems to be in shock, Commander. She said her family died, but we circled the site and didn't see anyone in the water. She keeps saying the name 'Travis' over and over."

"It's okay. He's already here, and you don't need to go back out," the man said. She was alone. Travis Tanner called just after you left the dock. He'd been trying to reach her on the radio and called to ask if we knew anything about a boat in trouble off Kelleys. Olivia, let's get this off you, so you'll be more comfortable."

I watched numbly as he untied the life jacket I couldn't remember putting on. Then he guided me into the office of the Marblehead Coast Guard Station.

Travis was waiting in the Commander's office and took me in his arms. "Thank God, you're all right."

I seemed to be looking at the world through a fog of flames, with voices far off in the distance.

"Miss Bentley, you'll need to sit down while I fill out a report of the incident." The Commander guided me to a chair, but all I felt was numbness and the sensation of floating. "Can you tell me what happened?" he asked at he sat down behind his desk.

"She died . . . like the rest of them . . . everyone I loved." My reply seemed to come from somewhere outside myself.

There was urgency in the Commander's voice. "Please, Miss Bentley, who died? The crew searched the area there was no sign that anyone else was onboard."

I stared out the window at the gray sky. But in my mind I could only see bizarre images of flames and flags.

Travis took the chair next to me and spoke softly. "She seems to be in shock, Gill. She loved that old boat like a member of the family. She moved it to the Marina DelRay and lived on it until she was able to move into the old Captain's House. That boat's been a part of her life for twenty years, I understand why she feels as though it died."

"I take it she was returning to her dock. Where was she last night?"

"The Patersons had a birthday party on the north side of Kelleys yesterday. Olivia went over for the day and was to return last night around ten. But that storm blew in so fast she decided to spend the night in the protection of the bay."

The fog was beginning to lift in my head, and an irrational anger set in. I'd barely escaped certain death—while Travis was never in danger. Had the cooler really broken down? "You worked on the engines last week! *You* were supposed to come with me. And then Mavis's cooler conveniently broke down yesterday morning! *You* convinced me to go alone! *You* expected me to come back late last night. I could have died out there in the dark with no way to see through all that smoke! And the explosion . . . it came so fast!"

"Do you really think I caused this? Why? What possible reason could I have? I love you, Olivia, and I can only imagine how you're feeling right now. But I will not sit here and have you accuse me of such a heinous crime!"

Travis slowly got up from the chair. He just looked at me, shaking his head.

The Commander waited until Travis walked out the door. "I, too, grew up watching the *Lovely Lady*. In fact, I thought I would buy her one day. But when that day came, I realized it would take a lot more money than I had to give her the attention she needed. It broke my heart when I heard your distress call. The loss of the *Lovely Lady* is the end of an era. I remember a time when life was slower. On any given day you could still look out over the water and see a fine wooden boat with her bright-work glistening. Now, it's cold hard plastic that roars through the water." He stared out the window at the still rough water with Kelleys Island just beyond. When he finally turned his attention back to me, he said "Look, I know this has been traumatic for you. Since you live in the area, we can finish adding the details to this report when you're up to it." He stood and picked up my life jacket from the chair next to me. "Come on, I'll drive you home."

As he opened the door for me, I was struck again by his calm, fatherly manner. "I've known Travis since he was a kid. You'd have to search far and wide before you'd find someone as kind and generous as he is. He does have a stubborn streak—and more than his share of pride. I suspect your words hurt him."

He opened the door to an official looking vehicle, and I slid onto the front seat. He walked around to the driver's side and got in, but didn't turn the key. Instead, he turned and looked at me. "I haven't seen Travis so upset over someone since his best friend died in a boating accident many years ago. They were kids, out racing around one of the smaller islands. His buddy's boat hit a submerged log. This morning, Travis was beside himself with worry, thinking something might have happened to you. And then we heard the explosion." He turned back to face the front and started the vehicle, backing out of the parking space. Turning left onto West Main Street, he continued, "Give him some time to cool off. He'll realize you were frightened and spoke the first thing that came into your head."

"Travis was the only one who knew my plans."

"Travis knows boat engines as well as anyone around here. If he worked on it, the *Lovely Lady's* engines were all right. Besides, you're forgetting that it was an old boat. Electrical problems are impossible to predict."

He pulled into my drive, stones crunching under the tires. He helped me out of the car and walked me to the side of the house.

"There used to be a boathouse out there. I think it was built in the 1920s and sat in line with this addition. It was old and rickety when I was a kid. A big storm finally took it down." He put his arm around my shoulders in a protective sort of way. "This house sits on one of the roughest spots on Lake Erie, and a nor'easter can be brutal. Living out here isn't going to be easy, and you're going to need all the friends you can get. Always remember that you're one of us now. We don't mind helping each other."

"Thanks, Commander. I'll be fine now. I just need some rest. I promise to stop by later in the week to finish the report."

"The name's Gill, and I'm only five minutes away." He said, handing me his card. We shook hands, then he turned toward his car. "And don't be too hard on Travis."

Walking up the steps to the porch, I fumbled in my purse for the keys, thankful I had grabbed it on the way to the dinghy. Although it probably wasn't the smartest thing to do . . . wrapping it around my neck while trying to save myself.

CHAPTER 42

An hour later, my hands clutched a large mug of chamomile tea as I huddled in the corner of the window seat in the bedroom. Clouds had swept off to the east, leaving a clear blue sky. Gentle waves lapped at the rocks, the sound rhythmic and soothing. After several sips of the hot, fragrant tea, I began to relax. The house held me in its big strong stone arms. I pushed my terror-filled morning to the back of my mind.

My bed looked too inviting to ignore. Slipping beneath the covers, I realized this was the first time since I'd lost the baby that I indulged myself in an afternoon nap.

I awoke from a sound sleep to the sound of the phone ringing. At first I wasn't sure where I was. Then in a split second, I remembered the horrors of the day and ran for the phone. "Hello, Travis?"

"No, Olivia, it's Gill. I'm getting ready to leave for the day and wondered how you're doing?"

"I'm okay, and really appreciate your help today. I'll stop by tomorrow to finish the paperwork."

"Don't rush it, Olivia, I'm not going anywhere."

"I think I need to finish my statement while everything is fresh in my mind. I've had time to think about what you said about Travis. Maybe, I did jump to conclusions based solely on my fear. I needed someone to blame."

"I'm glad to hear that, Olivia. See you tomorrow."

It was four o'clock and my stomach growled, reminding me I hadn't eaten since breakfast—if you could call it that. Within an hour, I sat down at the kitchen table to a salad, steak and baked potato, and my second glass of cabernet. The setting sun cast the lighthouse in shadows, but the sky was ablaze with shades of reds and oranges and streaks of pink across a baby blue background. It reminded me of the burning of Atlanta in the movie *Gone With The Wind* . . . how appropriate! My mind went back to the morning as it watched my *Lovely Lady* burning against a cloud-streaked sky.

The next morning, I awoke to a magnificent sunrise and watched the colors intensify as they filtered through the clouds. The placement of the bed in the center of the room allowed me to look out on an uninterrupted view of the ever-changing Lake Erie. The water was the first thing I saw each morning. Sometimes at night, I would see lights from a passing freighter or pleasure boats. Considering my ordeal of the day before, I felt surprisingly refreshed and ready to begin my day.

The doorbell interrupted my preparation of a rather large omelet. I opened the door to find Patsy standing with her hands outstretched.

"Nurse Patsy, here to administer to the wounded, or just to give a friendly hug, whichever is needed."

I appreciated seeing a friendly face. "A hug will do." I was suddenly enveloped in caring arms and soon felt that familiar lump in my throat. Then the sobs let loose.

"Its okay, Olivia. You're safe. That's all that matters. Travis called me yesterday and told me what happened, but he said I should give you some time before calling." She pushed me away as she sniffed. "Is that breakfast I smell? I'm starving!"

"An omelet, and it just so happens that I made more than I can eat." I put a couple of pieces of bread in the toaster and finished the omelet while Patsy poured herself a cup of coffee. As we sat down at the kitchen table, my attention was drawn toward the lighthouse. Its surface glowed bright in the morning sun. Dark slate-blue water shimmered at its feet, and the backdrop of trees wore brilliant fall colors. "Have you ever seen a more beautiful picture? I wish I was an artist and could capture these wonderful scenes on canvas."

"Why don't you try? What else do you have to do out here, except fix up this old run-down relic of a house?"

"Actually, I've been thinking about turning it into a Bed and Breakfast."

"Really? That sounds ambitious. I see you like our jam and apple butter. Did you know that our family makes this and sells it at the Cheesehaven and various local stores?"

"What doesn't your family do?"

"Hmm, I'll have to think about that." Patsy paused to look around the room. "When I was a kid, we used to think this house was haunted."

"I have to admit, sometimes I think it *is* haunted! During high winds, I hear moaning and howling sounds, and there's the smell of dead fish."

Patsy paused before taking another bite of her omelet. "That sounds creepy."

"Emily Elfin told me the house was built in 1867 by a wealthy Captain who owned several steam ships that carried both passengers and freight."

"I know all about it. His ships traveled to the local islands and Sandusky and Port Clinton, as well as, Detroit, Cleveland, and Erie. His first wife died while giving birth to their eighth child, and he built this house for his new young bride. I guess he figured he'd need a big house if his new wife produced as many kids as the first one. You know she ended up giving him six more!"

I shook my head. "What's with you people and big families? It must be something in the water!"

"Well, we know he didn't spend *all* his time on the boats! By the way, this is a great omelet," Patsy said before taking another bite.

"Thanks. I was beginning to think at least a few of the fourteen kids were still hanging around. In fact, I said as much to Travis shortly after I met him. That's when he said I should talk to his Aunt Mavis. By the way, is she your aunt, too?"

"No, she isn't."

"Well, it turns out that Mavis was this sexy little flapper during the 1920s and knows all about what went on around here during prohibition. She said they blasted out the stone for a boathouse after several severe storms kept washing out the dock. During the blasting they found a cave that came almost to the house."

"Yeah, I think I remember something about that."

"Well, after building the boathouse, they forgot about the cave until prohibition, when liquor was coming across the lake from Canada. The garage-and-storage addition was added to the back of the house and part of it was built over the cave. The cargo of illegal liquor would be unloaded in the boathouse, and the cases stored in the cave. Vehicles pulled into the garage, and the cases would be brought up through a trapdoor."

"That's really funny. Eliott Ness and President Hayes used to come to Lakeside, just down the road because of its Christian philosophy, which didn't allow liquor!"

"Well, after hearing all Mavis had to say, Travis and I came back and searched the floor in the garage. We found a trapdoor and a ladder that leads down into the cave. About an inch or two of water covered the cave floor, but it did lead out toward where the old boathouse was located. Just like Mavis said."

"Wow, Olivia. Weren't you scared that some creepy thing would be living down there?"

"Not with Travis next to me. We squeezed between a few large rocks and came out in the middle of the thicket down near the beach. Travis vaguely remembers the boathouse from when he was a kid, but it was all but falling down then. Gill said one of the major storms in the 1950s finally took it down. The boulders were put in as fill, a break against waves and storm surges. We figured that, during storms, especially from the east, the wind enters the cave producing the howling sounds. And dead fish float in with the waves and rising water level, causing my mysterious fish smell."

We finished breakfast and put the dishes in the sink. Patsy looked around again, "You really do need a dishwasher, but I love that old stove. Can I see the rest of the house?"

Patsy wasn't very impressed with the condition of the house until we got to the top floor.

"I call this the Captain's Room. I was told that his wife used to watch for his return through a telescope. With windows on all sides, it was the perfect place to sew and read to the children."

Patsy slowly walked around the room, looking out each of the windows at the view beyond. "You can see the old quarry from here."

"Yeah, I noticed it when I was up here one day. It took a while until I found an easy way in. The quarry's a magical place. I often take a book with me when I need quiet time and the lake is too rough to go to the lighthouse."

"Be careful, Olivia, it's not safe to be in the quarry alone."

"I just sit on the rocks, nothing dangerous. I did find a little cave with a passage down to the quarry floor." I felt the need to change the subject. I nodded toward town. "That's an interesting church steeple over there."

Patsy squinted. "That's the Russian Orthodox Church. I believe the Captain's second wife was a Russian girl, so you have a connection. You should stop by and take a look inside."

"I don't do well with churches. I'd rather admire it from here."

Patsy shrugged and moved to the opposite wall. "I can see you in this charming room reading to four or five of your own kids. Remember, you're drinking the water, too!"

"I think I should have a husband first, and I don't see that happening!"

Patsy grinned the same silly grin that I remembered from when we were kids. "I know someone who would like to be the first in line."

"I know, and Travis is a wonderful guy. I don't mind that he's just a boat mechanic, but . . ."

"Sometime back in June or July, he told me about this fabulous woman he'd met. He said she was beautiful and smart and had a great personality. But he also said she'd suffered more than her fair share of heartache and tragedy and wasn't very trusting of relationships. I figured he must have met her in Port Clinton or Cleveland. I even began calling her his mystery woman. He talked about her all summer, but he never mentioned her name. Why did you call him a boat mechanic?"

"Are you serious, Patsy? He actually talked about me?"

She nodded. "Yeah, and when I invited him to the party on Kelleys Island, he asked if he could bring Libby. At least that's what I thought he said. I didn't think anything else about it. Since I had already asked you to come, I didn't connect Libby and Livy until last night when he called me. The only person besides your family who I ever heard call you Livy was David Morgan."

That little piece of information made me happy. Travis was referring to me as Livy to his family. My insides smiled.

"You know, that sure was a mean thing that Meg did to you, but..."

"That's ancient history. I really don't want to talk about..."

"She's back, you know. There was some kind of scandal where she worked and her husband kicked her out. He has the kids, and she moved into the cottage. She called me to see if I could get her a job somewhere. She blames you for ruining her life. Says she wouldn't have become pregnant at fifteen if she weren't trying to prove she was as popular as you were. I wonder if she knows you live here?"

I didn't like the thought of Meg living so close, and I wondered what the scandal was about. A creepy feeling pushed me to end this visit.

"We'd better go back downstairs, I have to stop by the Coast Guard Station to fill out a report."

We walked down the large staircase in silence, the clomping of our shoes and creaking of the stairs echoing through the house. I was feeling weary and wanted to rest before going out, so I guided Patsy back through the house to the side door.

"The church is on the way to the Coast Guard Station. I know you said you don't want to go in, but think of it as just one of our most prized historical sites."

We walked out onto the side porch and down the steps to her car. She leaned against the door and looked up at the house. "This is going to make a great Bed and Breakfast... even if it is haunted!"

Just then a black cat jumped on the hood of her car and Patsy screamed.

"Her name is Spooky." I said as I picked up the kitten.

"How appropriate!"

CHAPTER 43

After Patsy had gone, the sun reflected off the lighthouse and the bold colors of the leaves drew me for a closer look. I grabbed my parka and headed out the side door with Spooky darting between my feet. She ran ahead in the direction of the lighthouse with her tail held straight up, stopping every so often to bat at a leaf or acorn. The air had turned crisp and cool, and had that wonderful scent which only happens in the fall. I felt energized and renewed after the long hot summer. Leaves crackled beneath my feet. A faint smell of wood smoke wafted in from some distance. Autumn was my favorite time of year, a time for sweaters and fluffy socks, the smell of well-worn leather jackets and bonfires.

Spooky and I crossed in front of St. Mary Byzantine Church and walked down the drive to the lighthouse. St. Mary's wasn't here when I'd first started coming to this spot years ago to eat ice cream cones with my grandparents on warm summer evenings. I thought they would be happy I found my way back to this place. Skirting the large boulders along the shore, I walked across a smooth flat ledge of stone and headed for the rocks at the base of the lighthouse. I sat down. The afternoon sun had warmed the stone. I took a long deep breath and began to relax. My house was bathed in sunlight. Its tall windows sparkled, and the Captain's Room reminded me of a big ornate crown. The place looked happy now, not like the dark foreboding house I had saved from the wrecking ball.

Fate must have brought me back here, along with the need to put life back into perspective. I thought about Meg and what Patsy had said. An overwhelming sense of sadness that I could have caused her so much pain washed over me. So much so, that Meg still seemed to carry it with her. I had avoided Meg at East Side General. Was she the one who had altered my budget reports? Was that the mysterious scandal that caused her to lose her job? I needed to put her out of my mind.

Trouble, tragedy, and turmoil seemed to follow me through life. Was that the real reason I kept Travis from getting too close? Perhaps subconsciously I was afraid that he too would become one of my casualties. He'd become everything I wanted in a friend and lover, my soul mate, my rock to lean on. So why had I immediately accused him of trying to kill me? I'd been out-of-my-mind with fear and the exhaustion of rowing away from the burning boat.

Suddenly a sense of wellbeing came over me. Travis once said that perhaps this is where I find God. I get His energy from the motion of the waves, and gain strength from the very stone I sit on. And although I didn't trust His house of worship or the messengers of His word, I could accept His pure love here, in His world. Spooky broke my concentration as she darted from one fluttering leaf to another. My special moment had passed. It was time to go home.

After changing into a pair of black wool slacks and a black cashmere turtleneck, I pulled my hair back in a chignon and finished off the look with Mom's large gold hoop earrings. After all these years, they were still my favorite. When I wore them, it was as if Mom was at my side.

I walked into the Coast Guard Station and gave the person at the desk my name. Gill must have heard me and came out of his office. "Wow, Olivia. It's a good thing you didn't look like this yesterday, or my men would have been falling all over themselves trying to rescue you. Then we would have been fishing *them* out of the water!"

I heard the desk clerk chuckle as Gill guided me to his office. I gave him the details as accurately as I could remember. I told him old wiring must have caused the fire.

"You know, Olivia, there are still a few old classic boats in the area. I bet that, between Travis and me, we could find you another boat."

"Thanks for the offer, Gill, but that's a closed chapter in my life. I loved the experience, but it's time to move on. Besides, it was the *Lovely Lady* that was my dream. Anything else would just be an old boat."

He nodded as if he understood. "Have you heard from Travis?"

"No, and I don't expect to. That's just the way my life is."

"I'm sure he just needs time to lick his wounds. You're too good a catch to let get away."

"That's the problem. I don't think I want to be caught."

After completing the report, Gill promised to keep in touch and walked me to my car. I turned left onto Main Street and headed toward the tiny town. Without thinking, I pulled into the parking lot of the Holy Assumption Orthodox Church. "What the heck, it's only a building," I said out loud as I opened the car door.

My car was the only one in the lot. Perhaps no one was inside. The door might be locked, and I could just go home. But to my chagrin, I found the front door to be unlocked. I took a deep breath and convinced myself that I was just exploring one of Marblehead's historic landmarks. I felt as though I was trespassing, but I walked in and quietly found my way to the last pew and sat down. The small church had a sort of old-world charm and beautiful stained glass windows. I found the smell of many years of dampness, incense, dust, and wood, soothing. This was a church of old traditions that held within its walls the joys and sorrows of its flock.

I could feel the pain and suffering which had been bottled up inside me for twenty years, along with the hate toward God for cheating me out of my family. Then an overwhelming feeling of peace and love filled me with the absolute knowledge that God loved me, as if a warm cloak was draped over me. I tried to swallow the lump in my throat. I could no longer contain the tears. The room glowed with a light that came through the windows, filling the space with glorious colors that shimmered and danced through my tears.

A soft voice and a hand on my shoulder brought me back to the present. "I don't mean to startle you, my child, but are you all right?"

An old man, with the aura of someone at peace with himself and the world, looked down at me wearing a black robe. "I . . . I . . . yes, I'm all right. I'm sorry, but I'm not a member of this church."

"I know. We're a small flock, and I can safely say I know everyone very well."

I started to get up, but he put his hand back onto my shoulder. "It doesn't matter. Everyone is welcome, and you look as if you need to be here. Has something happened that you want to talk about?"

"A lot has happened in my life that I could talk about, but I think God just helped me."

He nodded his head and smiled with a knowing look that made his eyes sparkle.

"My life hasn't been easy." I inhaled deeply, letting it out slowly. "Then yesterday, the boat that I've loved since I was fifteen blew-up off Kelleys Island."

"Ah, you must be Olivia Bentley, the young lady who bought the Captain's old house. Yes, I heard all about the boat. Such a tragedy. Well, you are one of us now."

I turned toward him. "People keep telling me that, and I'm not sure if it's good or bad."

"With only about a thousand full-time residents in Marblehead, we're a small town and we take care of our own—although you wouldn't know it during the summer when the number swells to *many* thousand. It seems we are all either family or friends or somewhere in between."

"I've noticed. I have to admit, I kind of like it—since a family is something that I've wanted for a long time." His questioning look compelled me to tell my story. I told him of my connection to Marblehead growing up, and the death of my family. I told him how years later, I came back to recuperate after the death of my unborn child. I told him of Brian finding the *Lovely Lady* and restoring it for me. Then how I came back here after his death. "It was on impulse that I bought the house."

"You *have* had a great deal of tragedy in your life. But it sounds to me that God has guided you back here for a reason. The Captain's second wife—I believe her name was Natalya—was Russian, and he donated quite a lot of money for the building of this church. So you see, you already have a connection here, and you are always welcome."

Tears filled my eyes as I stood to leave. He reached out to take my hands in his. "Are you sure you're all right?"

"This is the first time I've been in a church in twenty years." He merely squeezed my hands as he nodded his head, but the love in his eyes told me everything I needed to hear. I walked to the door and turned around to see him still watching me.

"Please come back . . . anytime."

I felt reborn, spiritual. Somehow spiritual was a word I'd never applied to myself before, but it felt right. I was ready to begin my new life once again, but I needed to stop by the marina office and officially end the old one first.

Everything looked the same as it had the last time I pulled into the parking lot, except that the *Lovely Lady* wasn't floating majestically at the end of the dock.

"Olivia!" Gus came forward to greet me. "What a terrible thing to happen, and you being alone! You don't look any the worse for wear, so I guess you're okay. At least that's what I've heard."

Shaking my head, I chuckled. "I must say this town has the healthiest grapevine I've ever seen! I must find a way to use it to my advantage!"

"I've already taken you off the haul-out list, but I'll save the dock for you for next year."

Why did everyone think I was already planning for my next boat? I remembered the brass plaque on the wall of the *Lovely Lady's* main cabin that read, *A boat is a hole in the water surrounded by wood into which you throw money.* That was one hole that would see no more of my money.

"No thanks, I'm officially giving up the dock. I'll be in the restaurant."

I sat at my favorite table next to the large windows overlooking the marina. I gazed around the room, remembering my first time here just six months before. The first time I met Travis was in this very room. It seemed like a lifetime ago.

Liz handed me a menu. "Hello, Olivia, will Travis be joining you? I'm so sorry about your boat, but at least you're okay."

"No, I'm alone today, and I don't need to look at the menu." I knew it by heart and gave her my order, including a glass of merlot. The grapevine wasn't as well-oiled as I thought, or Liz would know that Travis wasn't speaking to me. I enjoyed my glass of merlot and reminisced until my food arrived. The meal was excellent, but my eyes glanced to the hostess station every time I heard the door open. Travis wasn't among the few diners to arrive. My thoughts wandered to what I had experienced in the church. I had turned another corner in my life, and I was looking forward to the journey with all my new friends. After all, I was one of them now. And, I wanted Travis in my life.

CHAPTER 44

My mind had been so focused on Travis that I failed to notice the clouds building just beyond the tree line, until I walked to my car. A strong wind whipped leaves across the parking lot and the sky had become dark and menacing. While I was in the restaurant the temperature had dropped, too. I hadn't brought a warm jacket to slip on. I shivered as I turned the key in the ignition.

It took less than ten minutes to drive home, but already the wind off the lake had gotten stronger and bitterly cold. I was chilled to the bone by the time I had the car tucked away and put the key in the lock of my side door. I made another mental note to replace the door between the breezeway and the garage. The one that was there was falling off its rusted hinges. I could have used a shorter route into the house tonight.

The house was dark and cold. What a difference from the warm sunny afternoon that I'd left behind just a few hours before. Luckily Travis had checked out the boiler when I first moved in. After turning up the thermostat, I grabbed a pair of sweats and headed for the bathroom for a hot shower. It helped, and I felt warm again as I hung up my slacks on the makeshift rack and put my sweater in the drawer. That's when I noticed that the bedspread was wrinkled. I frowned because I distinctly remembered smoothing it that morning, but then the answer came to me. Spooky must have been napping there while I was away.

The clanking of the radiator brought me back to the needs of the present. I walked through the downstairs rooms turning on lights to keep the gloom at bay. I glanced at the phone, hoping to see a blinking light on the answering machine, but there were no messages. I wanted to talk to Travis. I wanted to let him know that I didn't blame him. I had spoken with fear, not my heart. But my stubborn pride wouldn't let me call him.

I could hear the wind howling through the cave. I went over to the sink to put away the breakfast dishes. It seemed more like days rather than hours since Patsy and I had sat here in this kitchen eating breakfast. She'd been right. I felt like a different person since taking her advice and stopping by the church. I paused when I noticed only one mug on the drain-board. That was odd. There should have been two. I glanced back at the table. That's when I saw the other one . . . on the floor, just a pile of broken pieces. A sudden chill ran through me. Had someone been in my house? But the door had been locked, I reasoned. To settle my nerves I checked the front door and all the windows on the first floor. Everything was locked, just as it should be. Spooky must have gone on a rampage while I was gone. I made a mental note to get her some toys.

The house was cozy and warm by the time I propped up several pillows and climbed into bed to read. Wind still howled and the windows rattled. The radiator hissed, and I felt comfortable and safe in the big bed. An hour or so later I put the book on the bedside table, turned out the light, and snuggled down under the covers. Through the window, I watched the reflection of the lighthouse beacon through the dense clouds. It circled rhythmically, warning any boats or ships that had the misfortune to be out in the storm.

A banging on the front door woke me an hour later. Putting on slippers and robe, I went to see who could be looking for me at this hour. Perhaps it was a stranded motorist. The banging continued even though there was no one on the front porch. I finally traced the offending sound to the steam pipe in the old music room. I made another mental note to have this checked out soon . . . the list was certainly getting longer.

The sounds of waves crashing and the rain beating against the windows woke me earlier than usual. With the pipes banging throughout the night, a good night's sleep hadn't been possible. A hot shower helped bring me back to life, and I put on jeans and a blue cable knit sweater. While making the bed, I remembered the wrinkled bedspread. It had seemed more than one small kitten could make. I felt a chill . . . a chill that had nothing to do with the drafty old windows.

I sat down to breakfast remembering that I needed to pick up a jar of the Paterson's raspberry preserves the next time I drove by the Cheesehaven. The sun was coming up as I put the dirty dishes in the sink and looked out the window.

Waves crashed on the huge rocks, sending a spray of water ten or more feet into the air. The wind from the east caused the lake to rise. The water was beyond the rocks, and beginning to creep into the yard. This side of the house was taking the brunt of the storm. The windows rattled, and the winds continued howling through the cave. It was definitely a day to stay in. I remembered how good it felt to bake cookies with Gran on bad weather days. Yes, that's what I would do today. Bake cookies.

I was just taking the third tray of cookies out of the oven when there was a knock on the side porch window. Through the window, Gill motioned for me to let him in. I set the tray aside to cool, then went to struggle with the heavy door.

"Hmmm, smells good. Nothing like homemade cookies."

"Chocolate chip. It's my therapy to combat raging storms and the moans and groans of the house."

"That bad, is it?"

"Well, let's just say that my home has a personality all its own!"

He laughed. Then a frown creased his brow. "Hey, why didn't you return my phone call yesterday? I tried to warn you about this storm moving in. The weather report showed it moving fast and furious, straight down the lake. You were going to be the first thing it hit!"

"Gill, I didn't have any messages. And I checked, hoping that Travis had called."

"It was your voice on the recording." Gill said as he followed me to the kitchen.

"That's strange, but then a lot of strange things happened yesterday. Maybe I just need a new machine."

"What kind of things?"

"Nothing to worry about. I think Spooky was just having a bad day and took it out on the house. She messed up the bed, and jumped on the sink and knocked a mug on the floor and broke it. It was just an accident. The answering machine is old and probably needs to be replaced."

"Are you sure you're okay here alone?"

"I'm fine, Gill. Storms just make me nervous."

"Well, I have to go. It's a busy day for us, and it's only going to get worse."

I had put the cookies into a plastic container as we talked. Now I handed it to him.

"Thanks. My guys put their lives on the line in weather like this. Rarely does anyone do anything for them. This will mean a lot."

After putting another tray into the oven, I sat down with a fresh cup of coffee. How nice of Gill to stop by to make sure I was all right even though he had his hands full at the station. I would make sure his men would get the tasty results of my next baking binge. I thought about his call. He must have dialed the wrong number and got someone who sounded like me.

The last of the cookies done and the dishes washed and put away, I began to think about Patsy's enthusiasm for my idea of turning this house into a Bed and Breakfast. Sitting down at the kitchen table with a legal pad in front of me, I began making notes on what I'd have to do when the phone rang.

"Olivia, are you okay?" Patsy sounded upset.

"I'm fine. I'm more than fine. By the way, thanks for suggesting I visit the church. I . . ."

"Why didn't you call Travis back yesterday? Now he's sure you don't care about him! And I don't like you calling him, 'just a boat mechanic', when he owns . . ."

"What are you talking about? Travis *didn't* call me!"

"Yes, he *did*. He told me he left a long message on your machine asking you to forgive him!"

I was beginning to get a sick, sinking feeling in my stomach.

"What's with you, Olivia? What kind of game are you playing? Travis is my cousin, and I don't want you treating him like you treated David Morgan. I don't wanna see him hurt!"

"Patsy, I swear, there were no messages when I got home. There must be something wrong with my phone. Gill stopped by this morning because he, too, left a message—which I didn't get. I thought he called the wrong number, but Travis wouldn't have made that mistake. It must be my machine."

"Whatever . . . I have to go. I'll tell Travis what you said, or better yet . . . *you* call him!"

The afghan was wrapped tightly around my shivering body, but it couldn't protect me from the storm that raged within me. The waves crashed beyond as I sat huddled in the corner of the window seat. Patsy's words hurt. I realized, too late, that I should have listened to my gut feelings and called David Morgan, if only to yell and scream and tell him how much he'd hurt me. I'd let my stubborn pride stop me. I'd been a child then, but that was no longer the case. I hoped that I'd learned along the way, and could swallow my pride and act as an adult. Maybe it was time to take a hard look at myself and decide what I really wanted. That might be the hardest part of all, because right now I didn't have the answers.

I needed to talk to Travis. There was still the mystery of how two messages got lost on the answering machine. I went to check the cord and then the tape, but everything looked okay. When Gill didn't hear back from me, he stopped by to check on me. When Travis didn't get a return call, he called Patsy. That continued to gnaw at me.

I made another stab at my list of home repairs and suppliers over dinner. After the dishes were out of the way, I decided to test the fireplace in the parlor. After the Chimney Sweep people had pronounced them all in good order, Travis had brought over a truckload of wood, and stacked it in the breezeway.

The chimney had a good draw, and the flickering flames in the fireplace quickly enveloped the room in a warm glow. I grabbed my book and a glass of wine and curled up in Gramp's chair, resting my feet on the ottoman in front of the fire. Being on the southwest corner of the house, the wind wasn't as loud in this room. I wondered if I was getting used to the clanking and hissing and all the other house noises.

Perhaps it was the wine and the fire that made me suddenly feel warm and grateful that I could be sitting here in this wonderful old house, near the place I had loved for so long. If only my parents and brothers could be here with me. I chuckled, thinking about how Gran would disapprove of a house this big, and only me living in it . . . such an extravagance. But only Gramps would have understood my need to save this old place. If there were a way, he would be right here in this room enjoying it with me.

Later, feeling content and relaxed, knowing that my big sturdy house would protect me, I snuggled into the down-filled comforter in my big bed and fell asleep to the now familiar sounds. But whether it was the relentless roar of the storm raging outside, or my anxiety over Patsy's phone call, the dream came again. This time the crashing of the waves on the rocks below the cliff seemed more real. The person in black was so close. I could see the hand of a woman before I fell to the rocks below. I woke, my heart racing. I put on slippers and robe, then went to the parlor and sat on the ottoman to watch the last of the dying embers. They crackled and glowed with a soft orange mass that seemed to beat with a heart of its own, mesmerizing and drawing me into its very center. I remembered the last time the dream invaded my sleep . . . the night before Brian's death. The dream always came before a tragedy. The first time just before the accident that killed my family, then just before the night Win drove his car over the bridge nearly killing me. I wondered what would come next. The glowing coals worked their hypnotic magic, and I once again began to relax and found my way back to bed.

CHAPTER 45

The sun was beginning to rise when I opened my eyes to the continuing assault of rain and wind. I'd been told about the fierceness of a three-day nor'easter, and this one was beginning to get on my nerves. It was relentless . . . the pounding of the waves, the rattle of the windows, the howling of the wind. I wondered how many more days I could take of this fury. The sky was gray, the lake was gray, and my mood was gray as I watched the lake rising, creeping closer to the garage. I still felt safe within my stone fortress, but decided I should keep busy.

I remembered I still had some boxes in the breezeway. Now seemed as good a time as any to go through them. The smell of fish assailed me as I opened the kitchen door and went down the few steps. I stopped abruptly. The door to the garage was ajar. I never used that door. Its hinges were either badly rusted or broken off, causing the door to be wedged in its frame. Creepy, prickly sensations ran through me. I slowly moved toward the open door and poked my head inside. There were only two small windows set high up near the roof, but I could see the Mercedes, and beyond it the Mustang. Nothing seemed to be out of place or disturbed.

I'd had an electric garage door opener installed shortly after buying the place. The side where I kept the Mustang still had the old swing-out doors, but I kept those padlocked. Maybe the garage had shifted or settled in this battering wind and popped the door out of place. It wasn't likely someone could have gotten in from the outside. I quickly retreated to the safety of the kitchen. Still, I felt uneasy and nearly jumped out of my skin, when there was a knock on the window. The face of the strange man on the other side didn't allay my nerves.

"I'm Nick Tanner. Travis is my cousin." he called in through the window. I opened the door. "Travis told me a few weeks ago that you were thinking about turning this place into a Bed and Breakfast and that I should stop around. With this storm not letting up the way it is, I thought I'd better swing by and make sure you're okay." Nick was a big guy. With his heavy jacket and plaid shirt, baggy jeans and work boots, an image of Paul Bunyan came to my mind. His hair was a sandy blond with a touch of gray. His face showed the signs of many years spent out of doors, and he had a large full beard and mustache. His warm, brown eyes glistened under bushy eyebrows. The many laugh lines at their corner suggested a man who enjoyed life.

"Yes, I remember Travis talking about you. In fact, I've been making some notes."

"Could you show me around and tell me what you have in mind?"

We started at the top in the Captain's Room and worked our way down, discussing the addition of several new bathrooms and closets, along with new plumbing and wiring. He told me the floors were in good shape and just needed refinishing. The kitchen needed updating, but he liked the stove and thought it should stay . . . so did I. As we opened the back door to the breezeway, the smell of fish was waiting for us. I explained about the dead fish in the cave. He chuckled.

"Yeah, I know all about it. We used to sneak in there when we were kids. You know, this door has to be replaced."

"Yeah, the strange thing is, when I first moved in I couldn't budge it. Now, there's enough space for someone to squeeze through. Do you think an intruder got in?"

He knocked the door to the garage off its hinges and set it off to the side. "Why would anyone want to break in? There's never been a problem with vandalism. I think it shifted with the storm. Just a fluky accident of Mother Nature." He flipped a switch. One I'd never noticed, and flooded the room with light. "Nice Mustang. Travis told me about it. But I was real sorry to hear about the *Lovely Lady*. At least you're okay. It could have been a lot worse."

He was a gentle giant, and I was beginning to hope that he was someone I could lean on. "You know, Miss Olivia, this garage isn't all that sound anymore. My guess right now is that it should come down. While we're at it, we'll fill in the cave. It's not safe and could be a liability. Besides, filling it in would take care of the fishy smell, which your guests may find offending. We could put up a four-or-five-car garage opposite the porch. It would look like an old carriage house, and you'd still have plenty of room for guest parking."

"Just as long as you don't block the view of the lighthouse from the kitchen window."

"You know, part of the problem here could have been the nor'easter of '74. That storm came in the spring and drove huge chunks of ice clear up to the back wall of this building. It did a lot of damage in the area. Do you know that you're living on the roughest point in Lake Erie? She's the shallowest of the Great Lakes, so it doesn't take much to get her kickin' up." The pipes began banging to their own tune as we went back into the kitchen.

I cocked my head toward the sound. "That's another thing on my list! Guests might come because of the charm of this place, but they sure won't spend a second night if the heat is on!"

"I'll bleed the lines now. Then we can work on a cushion that will prevent them from banging on the floors and ceilings. But, you have to remember that old steam heat is noisy heat, and there's no way around it! Hopefully, your guests will think its part of the charm."

After two hours, Nick was back in the kitchen. "You've got a lot of spunk living here all alone, and you've survived your first nor'easter. You're one of us now!"

"I don't know about that. The storm sounds like it still has a firm grip on us."

"It's beginning to weaken. I predict that by tomorrow at this time the winds will change direction and blow this nasty gal back where she came from."

Nick said he could do the inside work this winter while business was slow and he would stop by in a week or two with a proposal. He gave me his card saying that I could call him at any time if I needed help. I had a warm, confident feeling as I watched him drive away with the rest of the cookies sitting on the seat of his truck. My renovation project no longer seemed so overwhelming. I knew I could count on Nick Tanner.

That night, I built another fire in the fireplace and enjoyed a glass of wine while reading. The sound of the pipes no longer banged and echoed throughout the house, and the hissing of the radiator had become soft and soothing. The only thing that would make my evening perfect would be if Travis were here sharing it with me. He hadn't called, and I hadn't called him. What could I say? How should I begin? I was sorry for saying the first things that came into my head while I was hysterical. I was sorry that I might have accused him of sabotaging my boat. But, he *was* the last person who worked on it. I loved Travis even though he was a bit of a puzzle. He'd been the perfect gentleman, and seemed to be genuinely caring and considerate.

But I was still a little afraid of commitment. Perhaps not of him as much as myself . . . I'd never been very lucky at the game of love.

Something startled me out of a sound sleep, and I awoke still sitting in the chair. The fire, just a soft glow, was nearly out. The hissing of the radiator and the ticking of Gran's Grandfather clock were the only sounds, but I had the distinct feeling that I was being watched. Spooky didn't seem concerned about anything as she lay curled in a ball on the hearth. The tall windows looked shiny and black against the night sky. I walked over to the side window, pressing my forehead against the cool glass. I didn't see anyone outside, but just to make sure, I turned on the porch light. One of the large pots of geraniums was on its side . . . another accident of Mother Nature. It was just my over-active imagination. I decided it was time to put up curtains, or at least replace the torn shades that Travis had taken down. The clock chimed midnight. I checked all the window locks then turned out the lights and headed for the big old bed with its warm comforter.

CHAPTER 46

I awoke to the familiar sound of rain hitting the window. The howling of the wind during the night had subsided. I wondered what it would be like in the winter, when a nor'easter would carry the additional punch of snow and ice and frigid temperatures. I remembered standing on the deck of the ferry from Kelleys Island twenty years ago with Patsy telling me how lonely life is here during the winter months.

After breakfast, I decided I could not remain here a day longer as a prisoner of this storm. I would escape and run to the mall in Sandusky. Driving in storms had always terrified me, and I avoided it whenever possible. But there was every indication that the winds had shifted. Memories of my last shopping trip with Travis crept into my thoughts, and I wished that he were coming with me. I dialed his number, but before he answered, I hung up . . . I wasn't ready yet. With a new mission and remembering the creepy feeling the night before of someone watching me, I got out the stepladder and measuring tape and began measuring the windows.

By noon, I was pulling into a fast-food place near the mall. Marblehead didn't have fast food, and probably never would, unless you counted Netty's Chili Dogs. I spent the afternoon going from one store to the next, never thinking about the storm. When I finally walked out of the fifth store, knowing I couldn't carry another bag, the rain had let up.

I crossed the Bay Bridge just as the sun was setting. The clouds had broken up, and the show of colors streaking through the sky was magnificent. I thought about Travis and how much I missed him as I pulled in the parking lot of the Marina DelRay. The waitress took my dinner order. As I sat back to relax with a glass of Merlot, Liz came over to the table and sat down. She told me she hadn't seen Travis since the last time he and I were there together and she promised to stop by my house later. Remembering the time Travis stopped by the restaurant, just because he saw my car in the lot, I looked up every time the door opened, but each time I was disappointed.

With no reason to linger, I paid the bill and headed for the parking lot. It still felt strange not to see the *Lovely Lady* resting at her dock.

Reaching the end of East Main Street, I saw my house ahead, looking big and strong. It was the fortress that had kept me safe through my first battle with Mother Nature.

The wind shifted and was now out of the west, just as Nick had predicted, and the rain had stopped. As I looked toward the lake, I could see that the water was already receding from the back yard. The light on the answering machine was blinking. I eagerly pressed the button. "Olivia, it's Travis. We need to talk. Call me when you get in."

My heart skipped a beat. I quickly dialed his number, groaning with frustration when I got his machine. "Travis, it's Olivia. I just got in and am returning your call. I guess something happened to my machine the other day, but it seems to be working now. Call me." I disconnected, but, just on a whim, I dialed the number for the diner. "Hello, is this Mavis?"

"No, it's Vicky, can I help you?"

"This is Olivia Bentley. Is Travis there by any chance?"

"No, he isn't. In fact, I don't believe he's been in for several days. I'll tell him you're looking for him, if I see him."

I didn't remember a Vicky working there, but her voice sounded familiar.

My marathon-shopping trip had left me tired. I decided to climb into bed with the book that was now half-finished. I was happy that Travis had called, but a little wary, too. His tone had sounded very business-like.

It was nice not hearing the howling wind or driving rain against the window and, thanks to Nick, no more banging pipes. It wasn't long before my eyes could no longer focus and my brain no longer wanted to think. I turned out the light and soon fell into a deep sleep.

The dream came again. But this time is was different. I was running along the cliff, as always, and looked back to see the person in a black cloak running after me, arm out-stretched to push me over the edge. I turned just as a woman's hand reached out, then grabbed me and pulled me back to safety. She wasn't trying to push me over the edge, but save me from falling! The dream was so vivid. I wondered who the woman could be, and if I'd made her up, why did I make her so old?

Friday, I awoke feeling groggy and noticed that it was later than usual. I was relieved to see clouds outside the window instead of the solid mass of gray of the last few days. The lake was nearly back to its normal level. I thought about the dream. It had come two nights in a row. Did this mean that something terrible was going to happen today? Spending the day in bed with a good book sounded safe. Then, I remembered all the bags waiting for me in the parlor. Grabbing a pair of sweats, I headed for the shower. The hot water washed away the demons, and I felt ready to tackle the day.

My hair was still a little damp when I passed the phone on the way to the parlor and noticed the flashing light on the answering machine. I pushed the button and heard, "Olivia, I'm sorry I missed you again. I'll be at the diner."

Travis had called again! Suddenly the world was looking brighter. I dialed the number for the diner.

"Good morning, Mavis' Diner."

"Hello, this is, Olivia Bentley, is Travis still there?"

"No, he just left. Said something about having to drive to Cleveland for the day." Even though her voice sounded muffled, I could tell it was Vicky.

"Thanks, tell him I called if he comes back, and that I'll be home this evening."

At least Travis and I were trying to communicate. That was a step in the right direction. I pushed thoughts of the call away while I opened packages and got all the necessary tools lined up to install the drapes.

I stood back to view the first window I'd completed, pleased with the effect—both of the drapes and the view out the glass. A warm front had moved in from the southwest, pushing the storm back to the east. The water was still receding, leaving the large rocks and sand visible. The sky was an oil painting of contrasts. The once angry, gray-and-eggplant sky was now dotted with puffy white clouds. Patches of blue were trying to push their way through.

Every day offered a new vista, I thought. I could sit for a few minutes on the window seat at the landing on my way to or from the shower, taking in the view or watching a passing boat. The cupola would be the perfect place to watch a thunderstorm or the majesty of a rising sun. Yes, despite the hardships, I was going to like living here.

I installed the second set of drapes. I was adjusting the folds, when I noticed that the paneled side of the window casing seemed loose. My fingers just fit into the opening. When I pulled, it opened back on rusty hinges. It was a built-in shutter! I was to discover that most of the windows had them, but the hinges had become rusty and they would no longer close. They were the perfect way to keep out drafts. I was sure that Nick could get them back in working order. I wondered how many other treasures the house would give forth during the coming renovation.

It took the rest of the afternoon to finish the first floor rooms. It was early evening, I went outside to get the mail and look at my handywork from the street. Yes, the old girl was definitely looking like home. I wished that Travis were here to share in this happy moment.

When I went back inside, the wonderful aroma of the pot-roast that I'd put in the big oven that morning wafted through the house, reminding me that it was time to eat.

After finishing the few dishes, I headed for the parlor. I put a jazz tape into the stereo and stood back to admire the new look of the room. Warm and homey, it invited you to sit down, put your feet up, and relax. The only things missing were my cherished pictures of family and friends, the touch that always made a house become my home. I searched and found the box of framed photos that CeCe had hastily packed from the Shaker Heights house back in April. I pulled out the ones of Mom, Dad, Bud and Andy taken at the cottage, and one of Gran and Gramps in the Rose Garden, and a lovely photo of Mom and Dad taken just after they were married. I arranged them all on the mantle, saving room in the center for my two favorites. The picture of CeCe and I standing on either side of Vanessa, which was taken after CeCe and I graduated from high school, and the other picture was of the three of us taken the day I married Brian. The graceful marble mantle now held the images of my life.

CHAPTER 47

The music soothed my senses. My life was good, and I would do whatever it took to get Travis back.

"Isn't this *homey*!"

Turning around, I couldn't believe my eyes. "Vanessa, what are you doing here? I mean . . . it's nice to see you! CeCe said you were in Italy with your boyfriend. You must have gotten the messages I left you. I wanted you to know where I was and to have my new address."

"Yes, I did." She looked around the room. "It's looking much better, Olivia. The drapes are a nice touch, and I especially like that big old Victorian bed. What a waste to be in it alone."

A shiver ran through me. The wrinkled bed, she's been in here before.

"You look puzzled. Yes, I was here to see you. But you weren't home, and then I had to leave. Sorry I broke your cup, it was an accident."

"Vanessa, are you saying you broke into my house?"

She chuckled. "Did I? I think you'll find all the doors and windows still locked."

My heart raced. I swallowed hard. "I don't understand. You and CeCe are my best friends. You're always welcome. But you should have . . ."

She pursed her lips and tilted her head, as she waved her left arm in a circle toward the fireplace.

"How do you do it, Olivia? How do you always manage to land on your feet, and be better than before your tragedies? Why don't you ever have to suffer . . . as I have?"

"I *have* suffered ever since I was fifteen, or have you forgotten? And now that we're counting, how have *you* suffered?"

"Through *you*, Olivia! You ruin everyone's life that you touch."

"Me? What have I ever done to you, or anyone else? I put you through secretarial school. Every time you lose a job, I get you a new one. You wouldn't be at East Side General if it wasn't for me."

"*Was*! I got canned because of you!"

Vanessa's face was getting red. That only happened when she got really angry. "What are you talking about?" I didn't know what this was all about or where she was going with these accusations. "Look, I think we should just sit down and you can tell me what happened."

"You really don't see it! And now you've got your claws into poor Travis!"

I was beginning to feel her energy. It radiated from her with a force I could touch, and it was evil. "How do you know . . ."

"I won't let you destroy him, like you've destroyed all the other men in your life. He's good and kind. And he sees through you! He's in love with *me* now!"

"Look, I don't know what you're . . ."

"*You* are the cause of all my problems. I must get rid of you, so I can go on with my life. I can't let you ruin my future with Travis! I made sure that he knew Gill was here the other day. Poor Gill, I think he's falling for you . . . his wife is dying, you know."

"Gill? How do you know Gill?"

"What is it about you that makes all the men fall in love with you? I can't believe Travis left that mushy message on your answering machine, when he knows what you're really like! And now Nick is infatuated with you! He told Travis what a great place this will be when its finished, and how it will be a gold mine for you."

"You're crazy! You're not making any sense!"

She raised her right hand, which she'd kept behind her, and pointed a gun at my chest, then began waving it around. "This lovely old ruin of a house is not going to be your gold mine. It's going to your *tomb*."

This was no game, and I had to remain calm and think of a way out. There were times in my life that I would have welcomed a way to end my misery, but now I had made peace with God, and had a new direction and path to follow.

"No one will ever find your body. I'm going to put you in the cave with just enough dynamite to seal it. I heard Nick say it's very unsafe down there. They'll think that three days of pressure from the pounding water shifted things and caused a cave-in."

I wasn't sure if she really intended to use the gun or just scare me. I had to keep her talking. "How do you know about the cave?"

"I overheard Mavis talking to Travis about it. Since I'm the new kid on the block, she told me all the history of the cave and how to find it."

"Vicky! I knew your voice sounded familiar. How come I've never seen you there?"

"I just started working part-time. You haven't come in since your little tiff with Travis. Sitting at the counter is a great way to keep up on all the gossip, and start a little of my own."

Vanessa lowered the gun to her side.

"I've been here for weeks, planning this . . . watching you. We would have met sooner, but that tiresome storm flooded the entrance to the cave. I tore my sweater trying to get through that stupid door in the garage." she chuckled. "You don't lock the kitchen door. Every evening you check all the windows and doors to make sure they're locked. But you forgot about that one. See? You're not perfect after all."

Somehow, I had to get out of the house. "You'll never get away with this, I have friends here."

"They won't do anything. After all, what do they really know about you? I've let Travis know that I've seen you with his old friend Gill. Besides, he loves me now. He thinks you went to Cleveland today to be with your old lover, Dr. David Morgan!"

"Come on, Vanessa. This isn't funny."

She took a deep breath. "You're right. The game's over."

She was sick, demented. I had to think and watch for the right moment to get to the side door. Once the door closed, it would take her awhile to figure out how to open it. That big old heavy door might just buy me enough time to get away. Somehow, I had to get to the door. *Please God, help me. Give me a sign!*

Vanessa raised the gun, aiming it at my chest. "This is the night you die."

CHAPTER 48

Just then, Spooky leaped off the top step of the ladder where she'd been napping. With a loud fierce meow, the kitten landed on the floor with a thud. Vanessa screamed. Spooky dashed for the door just as the ladder came crashing in Vanessa's direction. She raised her arm to protect her head from the falling ladder. The gun went off, the blast sent it flying out of Vanessa's hand. That was my cue to run—and I did. I lifted the side door in one quick motion, set the deadbolt, and closed it behind me. Then I took off down the drive as fast as I could go.

But before I could take a deep breath, my inner voice screamed, *Run! Run!* To my left, the lighthouse was silhouetted as the full moon peeked out from behind huge, billowing black clouds. Turning, I ran toward that beacon in the night sky. The Marblehead Lighthouse was to me what Tara was to Scarlett O'Hara. It had always been a safe haven, the place that called to me when I needed to put my problems in perspective or gain the strength to go on after the tragedies that plagued my life. But just as I had my course plotted, that voice in my head was back. *No! The rocks are too slippery, there's no place to hide!* Without thinking of the consequences or danger, I veered toward the old stone quarry.

Crossing the deserted road, I could hear her laughter behind me. "Run, Olivia!"

Feelings of terror pushed me faster than I had ever run before. The road stretched before me, the asphalt disappearing in the distance without the welcoming sight of headlights. Just a hundred feet or more and I would get to the path that would lead me through the field to the edge of the quarry. Being petite has its share of disadvantages, and having short legs was definitely the problem of the moment. I was already winded, and the path still wasn't in sight. My thirty-five-year-old body was miserably out of shape.

"Olivia, I could shoot you right now. But I want to see you suffer first."

The path was almost hidden from view by the tall weeds growing alongside the road. I plowed through the tall growth that threatened to grab my ankles. She was getting closer, each step echoing on the pavement, her long legs quickly shortening the distance between us.

The path offered a glimmer of hope. It wasn't very wide, with half-buried rocks along the way. The outline of boulders lining the quarry's rim loomed before me. The terrain would be treacherous from here on, and one wrong turn, one missed step in the dark, could mean a terrifying fall of two hundred feet or more.

The path followed the rim to the south and the tiny opening that would lead me to safety.

Behind me, the gravel crunched beneath her feet. She'd made it down the path . . . and she was close. Just then, her horrible, high-pitched shrieking pierced the cool night air. "Olivia, you can't hide!"

Part of me wanted to stop and confront her. *Don't stop. Remember the cave. Get to the rocks on the far side of the ledge.* Without a glance back, I took another deep breath and moved on. No running here. Even though I was out in the open, it wasn't safe. I prayed that the clouds would continue to cover the moon and slow her progress.

"Give up. You can't escape me. I've been planning this for too long to fail now. You're going to die tonight, bitch." There was a gasp of exhaustion before she continued. "You ruined my life, and now you're going to pay."

I still didn't know what I had done, but my survival instinct focused on the ledge, just a few steps away. One side of the large flat stone extended out over the edge of the quarry. I needed to concentrate and stay calm. This was no place to get careless. Once safely across I took a deep breath and focused on the shapes ahead as they began to shine in the darkness. The pile of boulders, my safety, glistened, showing me the way. But that meant the moon was out once again!

I glanced behind me, she stood tall and proud against the dark indigo sky. Bathed in moonlight, her long hair shimmered like gold, cascading down around her shoulders. She would have been beautiful had it not been for the grotesque, almost demonic look on her face. The gun held casually at her side. She wasn't ready to kill me just yet.

Turning back to the rocks ahead of me, I heard her laughter. "Poor Olivia, poor little Olivia."

She was playing with me, like a cat plays with a mouse before it pounces for the kill. Just a few more feet and I would be out of her sight and safe behind the rocks. Then I could slide down through the hole and into the cave. The crevasse inside would lead me to the floor below.

She was so close! Instinct told me to scream, but my inner voice said run. The way was clear in the bright moonlight. I ran, my heart pounding, my lungs about to burst, and the muscles in my legs quivering from the unusual strain. A sudden sharp pain in my right thigh brought me to my knees. In the seconds it took me to fall to my knees, I remembered seeing the jagged edge of rock. Behind me, her laughter echoed in the still night. Damn, my only way out was so agonizingly close. Exhaustion prevented me from going on, and the pain was too great to even try. The sensation of something wet running down my leg sent a new fear through me. I was bleeding. Shifting my weight, I eased into a sitting position. My body shook as I leaned against the rock for support.

She took a deep breath before shouting victoriously. "You lose!" She stopped just short of the ledge. Her voice was now soft and slightly breathless, as our eyes met. "Surprised that I made it? I had to. I've been waiting a long time for this moment. You look so pathetic sitting there, all dirty, with your pants torn. My, my, that's a lot of blood running down your leg." She shook her head as if pondering a problem. "You're probably going to bleed to death. I can't let you cheat me out of my greatest pleasure."

"Why?" A stab of pain shot through my leg. "Why are you doing this?"

Her calm façade changed to one of agitation, her face growing red. "I tried to destroy your perfect life, to ruin your spotless reputation, like you ruined mine. Did you think I'd already been arrested?"

A droplet of sweat burned my eye while my mind tried to make sense out of this nightmare. Why would she have been arrested? Fighting the dizziness that was threatening to take control, I looked up into the eyes of a woman gone mad. "You're wrong."

"Shut up! I have the brains, but you got all the glory! I struggled everyday just to keep my lifestyle, while you couldn't do anything wrong. No matter how far down life pushed you, you always sprang right back up to the top. But it was *me* that made you who you are! *I* molded you into the woman that Brian wanted. Dear Brian. He really loved you, you know. He loved you so much that he chose death over watching the hurt and betrayal on your face. He couldn't bear the thought of you leaving him, and you would have . . . I made sure he understood that."

My heart ached, but not from fatigue. "Please, I don't understand."

"My plan was perfect. You were supposed to have died on that precious boat of yours, out in deep water, at night, and all alone. You've lived a charmed life, Olivia. Until now . . . now you're going to die!" The steel barrel glistened in the moonlight.

I closed my eyes, waiting for the blast. Would the first bullet kill me or would she want to watch me die slowly? I heard her shoe scrape the stone ledge. "*Shit! Noooo!*" Then shuffling sounds.

Curiosity overcame my fear as I opened my eyes. She was before me, her arms waving frantically as she tried to regain her balance. She screamed as the gun went off. The distinctive sound of metal hitting stone was followed by a long blood-curdling scream that seemed to go on forever.

Then all was quiet.

CHAPTER 49

The sounds of familiar voices and the smell of fresh coffee brought me back from troubled dreams of the past twenty years—and Vanessa. It took a minute for my eyes to adjust to the morning sun streaming in through an unfamiliar window.

"Good morning, sleepy head, you had a pretty rough night."

"Travis, you're here." My whole body hurt. "Where am I?"

"You're in the hospital."

"I . . . I dreamed . . . everything. It was like I died and lived the last twenty years of my life over."

Travis bent down and kissed my forehead. "You're okay. You're safe now."

A soft, gentle hand took mine, and I looked over into big, soft brown eyes. "CeCe, you came."

"Of course I came. I almost lost my best friend, you know. I'll be here for as long as you need me. I hope you don't mind, but I intend to stay at the house with you, if there's room. It's pretty obvious that you need someone to take care of you."

"CeCe, she tried to kill me . . . Vanessa tried to kill me."

"I know. Travis called me. He's the one who found you unconscious at the quarry."

"My dream was so real. But I still don't understand. How did I cause so much anger and hate to be bottled-up inside her? All I have ever done was try to help. I loved her like a sister."

"I don't believe Vanessa ever really wanted your help. She wanted to *be* you. She was jealous of everything you had. She was always saying that she hated you, because you had everything, and she had nothing. I thought she was joking. I *never* thought she was actually serious."

"But I don't have anything. My family, my baby, my marriages, my jobs, everything important has been taken away from me. Why would *anybody* want to be me?"

Just then Patsy entered the room. "I'm sorry to interrupt, but I need you both to leave the room for awhile." She came over to the bed and looked down with a smile. "I'm glad to see you awake. You had us scared." Her smile turned to a frown. "The police are here. They need to talk to you about what happened."

Travis and CeCe left the room and two officers entered. I didn't recognize either of them, but I heard Travis exchange greetings as he passed them in the hall. I told them the entire story from the time Vanessa appeared in my house until I blacked out. To me, the story sounded sketchy at best. I hadn't heard her come in—because she snuck in through the cave and a door that didn't open. She waved a gun, accusing me of ruining her life—yet, it was my life which always seemed to be in shambles. One of the officers asked if it was self-defense. Did I push her over the edge? "No—she tripped." He asked if she screamed and the gun went off—or did the gun go off and she screamed? "I don't remember." He asked what her motive was. What had I done to Vanessa? "I don't know." He stated that this was premeditated. She was my best friend. Didn't I realize that she hated me? "No."

A machine behind my bed started beeping. Patsy came in and turned it off. "I have to ask the two of you to leave. Olivia needs to rest." She removed the stethoscope from around her neck. "You know where Olivia lives. Any further questions can wait until she gets home."

I awoke to see Travis and CeCe sitting at my side. "I must have fallen asleep. What time is it?"

CeCe chuckled and shook her head. "I know you've always run your life by the clock, but for once time doesn't matter."

I sighed, and turned toward Travis. "I thought you were mad at me. How did you find me?"

"I'd been told that you went to Cleveland for a few days. You and Dr. Morgan were having an affair. But when I drove by your house last night I saw that the lights were on. I pulled in the drive, hoping you would talk to me. The side door was wide open, and I could hear your stereo. After calling your name and getting no response, I was afraid you might have fallen or been hurt, so I went inside. I saw the ladder on its side in the parlor, and then I noticed the pictures on the mantle." He paused and glanced at CeCe, then back to me. "It was when I saw the two pictures of the three of you that I began to think something was very wrong. Vicky, I mean, Vanessa, had never mentioned that she knew you. But from the pictures I could see she'd known you since you were kids. I made sure you weren't in the house, then I went outside to check the backyard. That's when I heard angry voices coming from the direction of the quarry . . . then the gunshot."

"I can't believe you found me. It was so dark."

Travis took my hand. "The gunshot echoed. I'm sure the whole town heard it. I focused on the direction of the voices and ran toward the quarry. I really don't know how I found you. It was as if some inner voice directed me." His eyes filled with tears. "Oh, my God, Livy. I thought you were dead."

He pulled a handkerchief from his pant's pocket and wiped his eyes. "After they brought you to your room here at the hospital and you were settled, I remembered that CeCe was in the pictures as well. I thought she should know what happened, so I called information and got her phone number."

"I couldn't believe what Travis told me." CeCe leaned forward and took up the story. "I told him that I was on my way. And here I am!"

When a nurse walked in with my chart to take my vitals, Travis stood and moved out of her way. "Livy, I've got several things to attend to and will be gone for a couple hours, but I'll be back later."

CeCe stood, too. "And I'm gonna take my things to your house, if I can have a key and directions. Is there anything I should do, besides get the mail?"

"Feed Spooky. Her food is in the pantry."

"Spooky?"

"My kitten. She'll be lurking around . . . don't let her startle you, or you could end up in the next bed!"

After getting the keys and directions from Travis, they both walked toward the door.

"Oh, one more thing, CeCe," I said. "Would you please bring Brian's suicide note back with you? You'll find the envelope in the center drawer of the desk in the library. It has his name on the front."

"Library? You have room in a cottage for a library?"

"Never mind. Just bring the note."

"I don't think that's a good idea. Wait until you're stronger."

"CeCe, I need it! It's important, and I want you here with me when I read it. I've remembered something."

Travis frowned and shook his head as the nurse asked them to leave, and pulled the curtain for privacy. "This doesn't sound good.

I thought she was over that. But it must be important, so call me at my office if you can't find it. Here's my card."

Why, I wondered, do people talk as if you can't hear them when there's just a thin piece of fabric between you. And what office was he talking about? Travis didn't have an office. But, at least he was calling me Livy again.

CHAPTER 50

My lunch was waiting for me as Patsy wheeled me back into the room, after spending the past hour in the radiology department. She had asked to be assigned to me when she came on her shift. Patsy had just gotten me settled in bed, and my tray table in place, when CeCe came charging through the door with my answering machine tucked under her arm.

"Wow, lunch looks good. I was in such a rush to get back here that I forgot to stop at one of those fast-food places."

Patsy offered to bring CeCe the tray of a patient in the room next door who had been discharged earlier. CeCe lifted the lids and inspected the contents on the tray, declaring them edible. She settled into the chair next to me and began cutting into her open-faced roast beef sandwich. "You could have told me about the trick door. Travis clued me in on the way to the parking lot about the size of your *cottage*. And you certainly gave that cat an appropriate name. She nearly scared the crap out of me! I saw her running across the back yard when I pulled in, then she greets me in the kitchen. How did she get into the house before me?"

"How Spooky gets in and out of the house is a long story. I'll show you when we get home. As for the door, it probably saved my life. It would have taken Vanessa a few minutes to figure out that you have to lift the door as you turn the knob. Otherwise, Travis would have found me lying dead in the driveway."

"You certainly have an interesting living arrangement. With probably ten bedrooms in that place, you're sleeping in the dining room. And that stove of yours is right out of the Addams Family!"

"Nick, my contractor, wants to start at the top of the house and work down, so it works fine the way it is. And, I'll have you know, I love that stove."

"I'm just teasing you! I like the house. It's a little *bigger* than I expected, but it has great potential. The living room is already warm and cozy. You've always had the knack for making everyplace that you hang your hat a very special home." CeCe cut another piece of roast beef.

"Thanks, you've always been there for me . . . I thought Vanessa was too."

"That reminds me, listen to this!" CeCe plugged in the answering machine and hit the PLAY button.

"Olivia, its Joann. I must talk to you. It was Vanessa who was embezzling the money. I wanted to tell you, but she was blackmailing me and threatened to kill my son. There's a warrant out for her arrest, but the police can't find her. Her landlord said that he hasn't seen her for several weeks, and her boyfriend stopped paying the rent back in April. It's like she dropped off the edge of the earth or something. The worst part is that she left, threatening to kill you. She thinks it was you that figured everything out and turned her in, but it was Meg. I'm sorry it's taken so long to call, but we didn't know where you were. I finally found your number in Vanessa's desk. Please be careful, Olivia. Vanessa's a sick and evil woman. Call me."

CeCe went back to her lunch. "This is serious shit, Olivia. I can't believe that she didn't tell you before this! You could have died!"

I thought about Joann's odd behavior on my last day. "I think she did want to tell me. She was scared, and she had her son to think about. But she did search for my number and call. I really don't blame her . . . her timing was just off a bit."

"I've had some long talks with Travis, and he's been sick with worry. Wow, Olivia, he loves you and wants to get married, and fill that huge old house with kids! What's the problem? I'd marry him in a heartbeat!" CeCe said while pushing the tray table to the side.

"Really! That's not what you said when I first told you about him. If I remember correctly . . . you said I was crazy!"

CeCe hesitated. "Yeah, well, now I know him."

"I'm scared, CeCe. I love Travis with all my heart and soul. He's good and kind and a wonderful lover. He's the man I've been looking for all my life, and I'm scared to death of losing him. Everyone in my life who means anything to me either leaves me or dies. Losing my family all at once changed my life forever. I was just beginning to let go of that . . . with the help of Travis. Win was a mistake right from the beginning. I should have known he would never change. My Grandparents tried to warn me, but my need for an instant family and the prestige that came with the name blinded me. I was so naive. Then there was Brian, which brings us to the letter. Did you find it?"

Patsy's appearance just outside the door caught my attention. I wondered how long she'd been there and how much she'd heard.

Her words didn't give anything away. "Do you need anything, Olivia? If not, I'll stop back after my rounds?"

"Yes, as a matter of fact I do! I need answers! I overheard Travis mention his office to CeCe. Why does a boat mechanic need an office?"

"Well, Olivia, I really don't know what to say, since Travis seems to have started this ruse."

"How about the truth!"

"Well, Travis likes to work on old boats, always did. His dad lets him know when ever one comes in. Actually, Travis owns the Port Clinton Yacht Sales, the one that sold the *Lovely Lady* to Brian. He also owns Cleveland Yacht Sales, some lakefront condos, and some property on Kelleys and South Bass Islands. Other than that, my cousin's a pretty ordinary guy."

I glanced over at CeCe. Her mouth was hanging open. "Close your mouth, CeCe. So I take it, he doesn't live with his parents?"

"Travis stays there sometimes when he doesn't want to drive back home, or if he's helping them with something around the house or the shop. But he lives in one of the beautiful new condos he built in Port Clinton, overlooking the lake and with its own boathouse." Patsy's pager went off. "I really need to leave right now, there are other patients."

CeCe and I watched her leave in silence, and I realized that my whole life seemed to be made up of lies. "Well, that certainly explains a lot. Like why he spends so much time in Cleveland, and why he got all tongue-tied when he talked to Emily about the condition of the boat. It also explains how he seemed to know so much about Brian. He's the Mr. T that Brian talked about when he and Gramps first found the *Lovely Lady*."

"I have Brian's note. But, Olivia, if you love Travis, and he certainly appears to be the best catch around, why don't you forget about this? Why would you want to relive Brian's death? The police were certain that he killed himself. That's a fact, and it didn't have anything to do with Vanessa. You found his body, and the police and coroner's reports were very clear that it was suicide."

"It's the *why* that I'm not so sure about. She made some comments about Brian before she fell. She talked about wanting to be like me, to have my life, and to have my husband. What if she did?"

"What are you talking about, Brian worshipped you. He treated you like a princess. No one has a marriage like you had. It was a fairy-tale come true."

I took the letter out of the envelope and gently unfolded it. "Brian was meticulous about everything, especially what he wrote. He always said 'you cannot take back what is written.' Now, in the first paragraph he talked about his gambling problem and how it was out of control. But I knew about that, it was not as if he'd been hiding some big secret. He went on to say that he knew I could bail him out."

CeCe appeared totally confused. "I didn't know you had that much money of your own?"

"I could have used the money from my trust fund to pay the debts. So gambling wasn't reason enough to kill himself. But look at this second paragraph. Remember, Brian wouldn't begin a new paragraph unless he was finished with the first! He talks about how much he loves me, and how he couldn't bear the thought of watching my love die and turn to hate before his eyes, and he mentions being weak. That has nothing to do with gambling. What if it has something to do with Vanessa?"

"What . . . you think Vanessa made him shoot himself? Please, Olivia, now you're going way out on a limb!"

"It's like what she said to me." I thought for a moment getting her words right. "Her exact words were, 'Dear Brian. He really loved you, you know. He loved you so much that he chose death over watching the hurt and betrayal on your face. He couldn't bear the thought of you leaving him, and you would have . . . I made sure he understood that'. Don't you see the connection?"

"Okay, I see that. But . . . "

"But think about the times you were at the house or at our parties. Did anything seem odd? Either Vanessa's behavior or Brian's?"

CeCe laughed. "You have to be kidding! When was Vanessa's behavior not odd?"

"I'm serious, CeCe . . . think!"

"Well, now that you mention it, there was the time I stayed at your house, when Consuelo was on vacation. I had come downstairs the next morning for coffee, and was still in my pajamas when Vanessa came through the back door. I was opening cabinet doors looking for a mug when she walked over to one, opened the door and pulled out two mugs. Later she offered to make us breakfast and seemed to know where everything was. At the time, I thought she must spend a lot of time with you, so I never mentioned it."

That sick feeling was back in my stomach, but I needed to hear more.

"We had just finished breakfast when you called to invite me to attend the fundraiser, but I didn't have a formal gown with me. You told me I could wear anything of yours, except the dress hanging on the dressing room door. I mentioned to you that Vanessa was there, but all you said was, 'how nice,' so I didn't question you."

"Yeah, I do remember that. I thought it odd . . . she'd called in sick that day."

"Well, Vanessa came upstairs and helped me pick out the black dress I wore. She made the comment several times that 'this could all be mine'. I just laughed and made sarcastic remarks, you know how she was. She was always looking for a man wealthy enough to give her what you had. But, I also thought it odd, the way she seemed to make herself at home."

"That *is* odd, since she really didn't come over that much. During the summer she would use the pool, but I think she usually changed in the pool house and enjoyed the bar. Then she met that rich boyfriend, and I only saw her at work. He moved her into that townhouse and paid the rent each month. After that she only came to the house for parties."

CeCe poured herself a glass of water. "I never saw the townhouse, did you?"

"Once, when she first moved in. I think she wanted to impress me."

"What was he like? Was he handsome? Although, I guess it doesn't matter if he had enough money to keep her happy!"

"CeCe, money isn't everything, and I don't know if he was good-looking or not, because I never met him." I hesitated for a moment. "Now, *that* seems odd, since she was always parading her new lovers in front of our noses like trophies. I remember she was always hanging all over Brian, but that was Vanessa. She needed the attention of men . . . all men. We'd seen this behavior since we were in high school. It wasn't a big deal."

"Olivia, I know I'm not as smart as you, but I don't see where you're going with this. What does this have to do with Brian killing himself?"

"What if Brian's *weakness* was an affair with Vanessa? What if it was just a weak moment, a one-time fling and she wanted more? What if she was demanding more? She told me that she wanted my life . . . she wanted Brian. She told him that I would never forgive him."

"She always was jealous of you, and wanted every man who was ever interested in you. She was so angry when Win dumped her and married you."

"Win was never serious about her. She was just one of the many women he lost interest in. Their relationship was over long before we got married."

CeCe's face went pale.

"What is it? What are you thinking?"

"There are things I never told you because you were both my friends, and I felt loyal to you *and* Vanessa. I guess it doesn't matter anymore." CeCe got up and walked over to the window. "I suspected that Vanessa was having an affair with Win. It began shortly after she started working at the hospital. I confronted her, but she only laughed at me. She was convinced that he was gonna divorce you and marry her, and she could step right into your shoes. She was furious when it turned out that he was cheating on both of you, and already had a son, and a baby on the way! I think it was Vanessa that sent the anonymous note to Winston that started the whole fiasco at the country club, ending in the accident."

The old pain of betrayal came back in a flood of feelings. "I never knew, or even suspected."

"I think it was Winston that fired her from the hospital."

"Vanessa assured me she was let go because of something having to do with a doctor. She promised me it wasn't her fault. She was my friend. I always believed her."

"I'm sorry for not telling you, but you were both like my sisters and I felt caught in the middle. It was easier just to keep quiet."

"You're right, CeCe, you should have told me." I folded the note and put it back into the envelope. "I'll look at Brian's check book and bank records when I get home, maybe the answer is there."

CHAPTER 51

Travis walked in just as I handed the envelope back to CeCe. He was now clean-shaven and wearing tan trousers with a white shirt and tan cashmere sweater. Instead of the usual tennis shoes, he wore what looked like very expensive brown Italian loafers.

I turned to get a better look. "Wow, I like this new Travis! Going somewhere special?"

"Just came by to see my two favorite ladies!"

"Three favorite ladies!" Patsy walked in and stood next to Travis.

"Oh, hello Patsy! Yes, I stand corrected, my *three* favorite ladies. I'm sorry that I was away so long. Did I miss much or was this all girl-talk?"

"Girl-talk? Shit, no! Travis, you have to listen to this message from Olivia's secretary!" CeCe walked over to the answering machine and played the tape for them.

Travis began to frown and shook his head. "I can't believe she's talking about Vicky . . . I mean Vanessa."

My heart sank. Maybe he really did care about her. "Travis, why don't you tell us what you know about her?"

"Well, she arrived in town about a month ago and told Mavis she was staying at the Surf Motel and was looking for a job. She was very friendly and seemed to care about everyone. She had a great personality and people opened up to her. Mavis took her under her wing, and a week later moved her into one of the cottages she owns down by my dad's repair shop and the marina."

Patsy took my vitals and noted them on my chart before saying, "It's funny that Vanessa was living at the motel just down the street from you, Olivia, and you never saw her. That must be how she found out so much about you so fast."

The pieces were beginning to fall into place. "Living near the repair shop gave her access to the tools necessary to sabotage the *Lovely Lady*."

Travis chuckled and shook his head, "Now, that sounds pretty far-fetched! It would take a really good mechanic to know what to do in order for the fire to start on your way back from the island and not before! I don't think she would have been able to figure that out."

"Like hell she couldn't! Vanessa was the best mechanic in Cedar Hill! Her father owns the local service garage. Why, she was taking apart carburetors before she could walk! And why are you defending her?" CeCe was nearly yelling.

"I'm not defending her, but this whole scenario sounds like the plot in a bad movie."

"We know from the tape that she came here to kill Olivia. She befriended Mavis, and not only got a job, but was privy to everything Olivia did and everyone she saw. She found out about the cave from Mavis."

I could feel my blood pressure rising, and the whole situation was getting out of control, and I didn't like what Travis was saying. "Look, this is what I know for sure. Vanessa watched and learned my habits, using Mavis and all the regulars at the diner to gain information. I know the day after the accident, while I was out, that she was in my house. She told me she planned to come back the next day and kill me. But the storm prevented her from getting into the cave. The cave was how she and Spooky entered the house. She told me, while she was in the house, she listened to the message from Gill, asking how I was, and the mushy one from you, Travis, and then she erased them."

Travis had been frowning, but now it was as if a light in his head had come on. "Aunt Mavis was never a good bookkeeper, and she was elated when Vanessa developed a new system that she could easily follow. By the end of her first week, Aunt Mavis was treating her like another daughter and moved Vanessa into the cottage."

It all made sense to me. "Yes, that sounds like Vanessa. Everyone instantly took a liking to her. And she was smart when it came to anything administrative, especially accounting."

Travis nodded. "She started coming on to me about a week after she started at the diner, and was always interested in any conversation about you. I just ignored her. It was Vanessa who told Mavis about the cooler not working, and insisted that I be the one to fix it. That day she hung around long after her shift was over, and talked about all the places in the area that she wanted me to show her. I suggested she talk to Nick." Travis was quiet for a moment. "Now that I think back. It was as though she was deliberately keeping me there."

"Didn't that seem strange?" I asked. "Didn't you worry about me? Was the cooler really broken?"

"Yes, it did seem strange at the time, because the problem was loose parts, not bad or broken ones. Each time I puzzled about how all those parts could get loose she had a logical answer. I did express my frustration over not being with you, but she stated, very emphatically, that any woman who could buy the old Captain's house and live in it alone, could take care of herself. It made sense at the time."

Shaking my head that he could be that gullible, I let him continue.

"Over the next few days, she told me several times that she'd seen you with Gill, and that his car had been in your driveway. I didn't know what to think. Yesterday morning, she told Mavis that if Nick came in, to tell him that you had gone to Cleveland for a few days. Then later, she told me that she'd heard you had a boyfriend in Cleveland, and that he was some famous doctor."

Travis took my hand in his and kissed my fingers. "I'm so sorry. But when I ran into Gill and asked him if he'd seen you, he said that he had. You'd even given him a box of cookies you'd just made. I was angry and jumped to all the wrong conclusions. I see now that it was all a deception."

The dirt and grime may have been washed away, but he still had some explaining to do. "Speaking of deceptions, is there something you want to tell me?"

Before he could speak, a nurse from the desk came in. "Is there a Celeste here? I have a call at the desk, from Montgomery Hospital." CeCe got up and hurried out, her heels clicking down the hall.

Travis got up from his chair and sat on the side of my bed. "I'm sorry, Olivia, I should have told you. But when you first met me at the marina restaurant, I had just come from my dad's shop, and you assumed that I was some dumb mechanic. I figured I'd never see you again, so what did it matter? Then I got to know you and quickly fell in love with you. I wanted to win your respect . . . and your love for who I am, not for my money or my connections. It just sort of snow-balled, and I didn't know how to stop it." He leaned over and kissed me.

A cough at the door brought us back to the present. CeCe walked over to the foot of the bed. "Sorry to interrupt this lovely scene, but that was bad news. It seems that Danny Jr. disobeyed my orders and was out with a group of older kids that I don't approve of and got into a wreck. He's gonna be fine, but they said he'll need to be in the hospital for a day or two."

Travis and I both agreed that she should leave at once, and told her that, after collecting her bags, to leave the house key under the mat. Travis promised I would be well taken care of, and CeCe promised to call with news of Danny Jr. CeCe bent down and we hugged as if we were afraid to let go of each other. Neither of us tried to speak, we just held on. I remembered that horrible day twenty years ago, sitting on my bed after the funeral when CeCe and Vanessa promised to be my family forever. Now our little family was no more, and our lives would never be the same. It was with tear-filled eyes that we finally said goodbye.

Travis sat on the side of the bed. He leaned over and held me in those wonderful strong arms. The cashmere of his sweater was soft against my cheek, and his cologne did erotic things to my senses.

That's how Patsy found us. "I'm officially off duty, but it doesn't look like you need me."

The moment was broken. Travis sat down in the chair with a thud, and I grabbed a tissue from the box on my tray-table to wipe away my tears. A doctor walked in behind Patsy, flipping through my chart and mumbling. "Hello, Ms. Bentley, I'm Dr. Hertzeller. You're quite the talk of the hospital, you know." He looked up from the chart over small glasses that rested on the tip of his nose. "Your tests all look good, nothing to worry about, although you do have a nasty gash in that leg. You're lucky, there are no signs of permanent damage." He seemed to notice Patsy and Travis for the first time. "Oh, hello, Travis, old boy. Nice to see you again. So you know this young lady who has caused such a ruckus around town?" The two spent several minutes talking about their golf games and catching up on the news of mutual friends. I picked-up a bit of a German accent in the doctor's voice. "Well now, Ms. Bentley, I don't see much need to keep you here any longer, when there is a whole town just down the road that wants you back. That dressing will need to be changed once a day. Patsy, do you think you can make a few house calls?"

Patsy had a big grin and laughed. "Yes, doctor, I'm getting rather used to it!"

"You need to stay off that leg for several days. Use crutches, and I don't want to hear about you running through the neighborhood anymore!"

"No, Doctor, I promise." I said with a chuckle.

"Okay, I want to see you in my office in a week. And Travis, can I assume that you are also going to take an active role in Ms. Bentley's care?"

"Yes, Doctor, you can."

Travis helped me change into the clothes that CeCe had brought back with her from the house. I brushed my hair and let it fall loose around my shoulders. Travis wrapped his arms around me, then buried his head in my hair and kissed my neck. Tingles sent a shiver of desire through me.

Just then, Patsy came back into the room. "Oh, excuse me." She giggled then handed me a bag containing the clothes that I was wearing when I arrived. "Do you want these?"

I pulled away from Travis. "No. They're a part of my past, and God's given me a new future."

Patsy held the bag above a trash bin for a few seconds, as if it were my old life, and let it go. Then she helped me into a wheel chair, and pushed me down the hall while Travis went on ahead and pulled the car around to the front entrance.

Patsy stopped just short of the entrance doors and walked around to stand in front of me. "You know, Olivia, Travis loves you. And I know that you love him. I sure would like to call you cousin."

Patsy was right about me loving Travis. And I was sure that he loved me. Our love had just survived a well-calculated war of lies, deceit, and traitorous acts. My heart was too full to answer, so I just sat silently and nodded.

She pushed me through the front doors. Travis stood waiting next to the car with a huge smile. "Thanks, Patsy, for everything you've done for me."

Travis helped me into the Mercedes. After sliding in behind the wheel, he turned toward me, resting his arm on the back of my seat.

"So what's this about God?" he asked softly.

"I guess you've been away too long. I feel like a new person. Like the weight of the world has been lifted off my shoulders." His sensuous blue-green eyes pulled me in to his very soul, and my heart jump with joy. I'd finally found Mom's kind of love. She'd had complete faith and trust in that love, and never looked back . . . and I wouldn't either. I smiled back at him as he turned the key in the ignition. The engine roared to life.

"Let's go home."

Pamela Ann Cleverly is a novelist and member of Romance Writers of America and Sisters in Crime who lives and writes in northeastern Ohio. She is in the finishing stages of a second book, *A Beacon in the Dark*, and encountering some fascinating research for her third, *It Started with Besse*.

Cleverly is executive director for CANTER Ohio—a nonprofit organization dedicated to providing thoroughbred ex-racehorses the opportunity for a new life, home, and career through rehabilitation, retraining, and rehoming.

Made in the USA
Middletown, DE
22 January 2023